OXFORD WORLD'S CLASSICS

THE PRIVATE MEMOIRS AND CONFESSIONS OF A JUSTIFIED SINNER

JAMES HOGG was born at Ettrick Farm, Ettrickhall, in 1770. He was the second son of Robert Hogg, ex-shepherd and tenant farmer. In 1788 he was hired as a shepherd, and in 1793 he started writing poetry. His poetical gift was discovered by Scott, for whom he collected ballads for the *Border Minstrelsy*. In 1807 his own early ballads were published under the title of *The Mountain Bard*. In 1810 he went to Edinburgh, where he met Wordsworth, Southey, and De Quincey. He achieved fame in 1813 with *The Queen's Wake*, and in 1815 *The Pilgrims of the Sun* was published. In the same year, the Duke of Buccleuch granted him the farm of Altrive in Yarrow, where he resided mainly for the rest of his life. His prose works include *The Three Perils of Man* (1822), *The Confessions of a Justified Sinner* (1824), and *The Domestic Manners and Private Life of Sir Walter Scott* (1834). He died in 1835.

IAN DUNCAN is Professor of English at the University of California, Berkeley. Among his editions for Oxford World's Classics are Doyle's *The Lost World*, Scott's *Ivanhoe* and *Rob Roy*, and *Travel Writing 1700–1830* (with Elizabeth Bohls). His books include *Scott's Shadow: The Novel in Romantic Edinburgh* (2007), and the forthcoming *Edinburgh Companion to James Hogg* (with Douglas S. Mack).

T0058856

OXFORD WORLD'S CLASSICS

*For over 100 years Oxford World's Classics have brought
readers closer to the world's great literature. Now with over 700
titles—from the 4,000-year-old myths of Mesopotamia to the
twentieth century's greatest novels—the series makes available
lesser-known as well as celebrated writing.*

*The pocket-sized hardbacks of the early years contained
introductions by Virginia Woolf, T. S. Eliot, Graham Greene,
and other literary figures which enriched the experience of reading.
Today the series is recognized for its fine scholarship and
reliability in texts that span world literature, drama and poetry,
religion, philosophy, and politics. Each edition includes perceptive
commentary and essential background information to meet the
changing needs of readers.*

OXFORD WORLD'S CLASSICS

JAMES HOGG

The Private Memoirs and Confessions of a Justified Sinner

Edited with an Introduction and Notes by
IAN DUNCAN

OXFORD
UNIVERSITY PRESS

OXFORD

UNIVERSITY PRESS

Great Clarendon Street, Oxford OX2 6DP

Oxford University Press is a department of the University of Oxford.
It furthers the University's objective of excellence in research, scholarship,
and education by publishing worldwide in

Oxford New York

Auckland Cape Town Dar es Salaam Hong Kong Karachi
Kuala Lumpur Madrid Melbourne Mexico City Nairobi
New Delhi Shanghai Taipei Toronto

With offices in

Argentina Austria Brazil Chile Czech Republic France Greece
Guatemala Hungary Italy Japan Poland Portugal Singapore
South Korea Switzerland Thailand Turkey Ukraine Vietnam

Oxford is a registered trade mark of Oxford University Press
in the UK and in certain other countries

Published in the United States
by Oxford University Press Inc., New York

Introduction, Note on the Text, Select Bibliography, Chronology, Explanatory Notes © Ian
Duncan 2010

Glossary © Graham Tulloch 1990, Graham Tulloch and Ian Duncan 2010

British Library Cataloguing in Publication Data

Data available

Library of Congress Cataloging-in-Publication Data

Data available

Typeset by GLYPH International Ltd., Bangalore, India
Printed in Great Britain by
Clays Ltd., Elcograf S.p.A.

ISBN 978–0–19–921795–3

17

ACKNOWLEDGEMENTS

My thanks must first go to Judith Luna for giving me the opportunity to edit *The Private Memoirs and Confessions of a Justified Sinner*. Her patience is exceeded only by the acuteness of her editorial eye. I am profoundly grateful to Nick Nace, whose collaboration has once again been indispensable. Matt Seidel, Janice Crooks, Katrin Haegele, and Deanna Yanagisako assisted in the late stages of preparation, and Monica Soare with proofs. Support for my work on the edition has come from the Committee on Research of the Academic Senate at the University of California, Berkeley. I have benefited, more than may be apparent in these pages, from the generosity and expertise of the community of scholars of James Hogg, especially Peter Garside, to whose edition of *Confessions* all scholars and readers are in debt, and Gillian Hughes and Douglas Mack, who carefully read and commented upon a draft of the explanatory notes. I thank Ian Alexander, Val Bold, Hans de Groot, Meiko O'Halloran, Claire Lamont, Neil Richardson, and George Starr for their helpful—in some cases painstaking—responses to my queries, Penny Fielding and Enrica Villari for sharing their insights into this novel, Graham Tulloch for granting me permission to use his glossary to the previous World's Classics edition, and Ayşe Agiş for all-round encouragement and support. Lastly, I wish to acknowledge my debt to John Carey's edition of *The Private Memoirs and Confessions of a Justified Sinner*, the distinguished predecessor of this Oxford World's Classics edition and the version in which I, like many readers of my generation, first encountered Hogg's masterpiece.

CONTENTS

CONTENTS

INTRODUCTION

AFTER a century of neglect following its first appearance in 1824, *The Private Memoirs and Confessions of a Justified Sinner* is more alive today than it has ever been. James Hogg's novel of religious fanaticism and serial murder enjoys a rare reputation as a cult book and a classic, a work of startling originality, sophistication, and sardonic verve. A strong force in the novel's resurgence has been its influence on contemporary fiction, especially in Scotland, where it was written. Muriel Spark, Alasdair Gray, James Kelman, Alice Munro, A. L. Kennedy, Emma Tennant, Irvine Welsh, Ian Rankin, James Robertson, and Louise Welsh (the list could go on) have acknowledged, or critics have pointed out, its impress on their work.[1] *Confessions of a Justified Sinner* has displaced the novels of Walter Scott, which for so long cast Hogg's in their shade, to become the world's favourite nineteenth-century Scottish novel. Now, it seems, we prefer our classics not to be altogether respectable. A farm labourer and shepherd before he became a professional author, Hogg never gained a secure foothold in polite literary circles, and in *Confessions of a Justified Sinner* he wrote the definitive tale of the outcast, at once terrifying, pitiful, and funny.

With its local settings in and around Glasgow, Edinburgh, and the Scottish Borders, its precise attention to Presbyterian church history and theology, and its vivid representations of popular speech and folk belief, Hogg's is an intensely Scottish work of the imagination. However its Scottishness buoys up rather than detracts from the status of *Confessions of a Justified Sinner* as a 'world's classic', one which keeps company with the great nineteenth-century fables of the crisis of the modern self: tales of the doppelgänger, by Hoffmann, Poe, Gogol, Dostoevsky, and Stevenson; the pact with the Devil, in Goethe's *Faust*; the poor youth who commits murder in the belief that he transcends the moral law, in Dostoevsky's *Crime and Punishment*. Like much modern Scottish writing, Hogg's masterpiece has more in

---

[1] For Hogg's novel and contemporary Scottish writing see Douglas S. Mack, *Scottish Fiction and the British Empire* (Edinburgh, 2006), 227–9, and Gillian Hughes, 'Afterlives of the Justified Sinner', in Ian Duncan and Douglas S. Mack (eds.), *The Edinburgh Companion to James Hogg* (2011).

common with works of German, Russian, or North American fiction than with anything produced in England—perhaps because radical experiments are more likely to be made in the provincial capitals of the 'world republic of letters' than at its metropolitan core. The divided and doubled self haunts nineteenth-century Edinburgh, Berlin, Philadelphia, or St Petersburg more than Paris or London.

The Private Memoirs and Confessions of a Justified Sinner presents itself as an authentic document, the early eighteenth-century spiritual and criminal autobiography of one Robert Wringhim, prepared for publication by a modern editor. The long introductory 'Editor's Narrative' purports to give an objective account of Wringhim's career, compiled from historical sources and local tradition. We read of his birth in a divided household, his conflict with his elder brother George, George's mysterious death, and the discovery of Robert's complicity in George's murder. In the 'Private Memoirs and Confessions of a Sinner' that follows, Robert tells his own story. An 'outcast in the world', adopted by a heretical Calvinist minister, Robert is brought up to believe that he is one of the elect, predestined for salvation and thus above the moral law. Under the influence of an uncanny shape-shifting stranger who calls himself Gil-Martin, he wages a war of extermination against God's enemies. Wringhim ends up a hunted vagrant and suicide, upon whose name and memory even his editor heaps 'everlasting detestation'.

The editor's narrative and the sinner's memoir are clenched in a struggle that tears the book in two. The editor is a graduate of Glasgow University, one of the centres of the Scottish Enlightenment, and he dismisses Wringhim's account of his own life as the delusions of 'a religious maniac'. Far from explaining the memoir, however, his narrative intensifies its more baffling and bizarre aspects. 'In this day, and with the present generation', he insists, 'it will not go down, that a man should be daily tempted by the devil, in the semblance of a fellow-creature' (p. 189). Yet the editor's admission of eyewitness reports of Gil-Martin's existence countermines the reader's suspicion, encouraged by psychotic episodes of dissociation and fugue in the memoir, that Wringhim's familiar may be a figment of his disturbed imagination. Narrative and memoir are at odds not just in matters of interpretation but in the record of events and circumstances. They do not so much tell different versions of the same story as tell different stories, opening up irreconcilable, rival realities.

At the level of form, this division of the book replicates the virulent divisions and doublings—within the family, within national religious and political life, within the psyche—that riddle the justified sinner's story.

Divisions and doublings split wide open in the book's conclusion, in which the editor recounts his discovery of the sinner's memoir. His interest is piqued by the publication of an 'authentic letter', signed 'James Hogg', in the August 1823 issue of *Blackwood's Edinburgh Magazine*, which describes the exhumation of the hundred-year-old corpse of a suicide in the Scottish Borders. *Blackwood's* was the most popular and influential magazine of the Romantic era; Hogg, one of its leading contributors, enjoyed international fame as the 'Ettrick Shepherd', the author of ballads, songs, and tales from Scottish rural life. The editor and a college friend go looking for Hogg, who turns out actually to be a shepherd, trading livestock at a country fair. Hogg refuses to show them the grave: 'I hae muir ado than I can manage the day,' he growls, 'foreby ganging to houk up hunder-year-auld banes' (p. 183). The gentlemen hire another guide, dig up the grave, and bring back souvenirs, including a 'damp, rotten, and yellow' roll of paper—the memoir we have been reading.

Hogg's novel concludes with a grisly parody of the late Enlightenment project of antiquarian and literary 'revival'—the attempt by scholars and poets to recover the remains of national traditions, buried in a primitive countryside, and reanimate them for the modern imagination.[2] This all too literal raising of the dead brings nothing back to life, not even the meaning of the sinner's words, which the editor complains he cannot understand. Lost too in the suicide's grave is the identity of the author of *Private Memoirs and Confessions of a Justified Sinner*: since the appearance of 'James Hogg' in its pages as a real Ettrick shepherd, refusing in rugged dialect to have anything to do with the literary quest, must mean that he cannot be the person who wrote this book. *Confessions of a Justified Sinner* was published anonymously, and Hogg took considerable pains to guard his incognito, dedicating the novel to the Lord Provost of Glasgow and asking his friends at *Blackwood's* to spread the word that

---

[2] See Margaret Russett, *Fictions and Fakes: Forging Romantic Authenticity, 1760–1845* (Cambridge, 2006), 184–91; Ian Duncan, *Scott's Shadow: The Novel in Romantic Edinburgh* (Princeton, 2007), 272–86.

it was by someone from that city.[3] In this, as in other respects, *Confessions of a Justified Sinner* is anomalous. Hogg had been publishing under his own name since his breakthrough success with *The Queen's Wake* in 1813. Settled in a happy marriage, he found himself at the height of his creative powers in the early 1820s; *Confessions of a Justified Sinner* crowned a prolific and varied run of books that included a collection of Jacobite song, his own collected poems, a new epic poem, and three novel-length works of fiction.[4] These track Hogg's attempt to rise beyond the rustic persona of the 'Ettrick Shepherd' and make his name as an author of the metropolitan genres of the long narrative poem and novel, for which Scott, the most successful author of the day, had gained unprecedented profits as well as fame and critical prestige. With the growth of his ambitions, however, Hogg met stiffening resistance from the Edinburgh literary circles that had once encouraged him. The higher he reached, the more they pushed him back into the role of Ettrick Shepherd—even if that meant reinventing the Shepherd as a creature separate from the struggling individual, James Hogg.

The Author and His Work

The son of a tenant farmer in the valley of Ettrick, near Selkirk in the Scottish Borders, Hogg had worked as a shepherd for over two decades before he turned to a professional literary career at the age of 40. His family had been too poor to keep him in school, so he spent the greater part of his childhood and youth doing hired work for local farmers, and largely taught himself to read and write. He had won a local reputation for his poems and songs when he met another aspiring poet, the well-connected Edinburgh lawyer and county magistrate Walter Scott, in 1802. Hogg helped Scott complete his collection of traditional ballads, *Minstrelsy of the Scottish Border* (1802–3), and in turn Scott helped Hogg publish his own book of ballads and songs, *The Mountain Bard* (1807). Scott remained Hogg's patron as well as friend in the early years of his literary career, and psychologically the relationship persisted, vexing Hogg's later attempts to establish his work on its own terms. Scott dominated

---

[3] James Hogg, *Collected Letters*, vol. ii, ed. Gillian Hughes (Edinburgh, 2006), 202.
[4] See Gillian Hughes, *James Hogg: A Life* (Edinburgh, 2007), 191–2.

Edinburgh literary life in an era when the city came to pose a serious challenge to London as a national literary capital. From 1802 through the 1830s Scottish periodicals, poetry, and fiction won an international reading public and defined what would be the major genres of nineteenth-century literature in English. Hogg began to claim a distinctive place for himself with his romantic ballad miscellany *The Queen's Wake* (1813) and two sets of prose fiction, *The Brownie of Bodsbeck* (1818) and *Winter Evening Tales* (1820), works that make their own accommodation between modern literary techniques and the poetic and narrative traditions of the Scottish Borders.

By 1817 Hogg was part of the rising literary circle associated with the publisher William Blackwood, whose new *Blackwood's Edinburgh Magazine* became the most influential Scottish publication after Scott's Waverley novels and the rival *Edinburgh Review*. Arch-Tory in its politics, notorious for its attacks on Romantic radicals such as Leigh Hunt, Keats, and Hazlitt, *Blackwood's* provided the chief forum for experiment and innovation in British prose writing throughout the 1820s. It seemed, at least for a few years, as though Hogg must flourish there. Hogg ran into trouble with Blackwood, however, when he attempted to extend his literary range. After *The Brownie of Bodsbeck* Blackwood declined to publish Hogg's book-length works of prose fiction, although his poems and tales would continue to appear in *Blackwood's Magazine*. *The Three Perils of Man* (1822), *The Three Perils of Woman* (1823), and *The Private Memoirs and Confessions of a Justified Sinner*, all published by the London bookseller Longman & Co., make up a series of increasingly audacious reckonings with the novel-length forms of Scottish Romantic fiction: historical romance, national domestic tale, and fictional autobiography. They were received with growing coolness, in some cases outright hostility, by critics and the public, and *Confessions of a Justified Sinner* would be the last of Hogg's experiments in the novel.

In the early 1820s Hogg found himself at odds with the other leading contributors to *Blackwood's Magazine*, his friends John Wilson and John Gibson Lockhart. Sons of gentlemen, educated at Glasgow, Oxford, and the Scottish Bar, Wilson and Lockhart (who was also Scott's son-in-law) liked to typecast Hogg as a gifted, lovable, but uncouth rustic who might excel in songs and sketches of the Scottish peasantry but who blundered grotesquely when he attempted more elevated literary forms. Wilson published outlandish attacks on

Hogg's literary character in *Blackwood's* in 1821 and 1823, and he
and Lockhart (in the general spirit of mischief that prevailed at the
magazine) began signing Hogg's name to contributions that were not
by him. They were the main authors of the 'Noctes Ambrosianae', a
series of festive dialogues satirizing Edinburgh literary and political
life, which began running in *Blackwood's* in 1822; the dialogues fea-
tured real as well as fictitious characters, including the 'Shepherd', a
carnivalesque exaggeration of Hogg as rural genius. Rowdy, lyrical,
and outrageous, the Shepherd proved to be the most popular character in the series, which ran into the 1830s. As Wilson took over sole
authorship of the 'Noctes', the Shepherd became his most brilliant
literary invention—an apotheosis of the Romantic peasant-poet as
visionary clown. Hogg at first claimed to be amused by the portrait,
but grew increasingly offended, especially as he began to feel the
ways in which the 'boozing buffoon' of the 'Noctes' was taking over
his public identity. Critics have not failed to discern a foundation for
the plight of Robert Wringhim—his agency usurped by a double
—in Hogg's relations with his peers at *Blackwood's*, citing
exasperated references in his correspondence to Wilson and Lockhart
as 'two devils' and to his feelings for Wilson as 'a mixture of terror
admiration and jealousy just such a sentiment as one deil might be
supposed to have of another'.[5]

The closing episode of *Confessions of a Justified Sinner* casts itself
as a set piece of *Blackwood's* literary game-playing, like the 'Noctes
Ambrosianae', bristling with in-jokes and allusions to real people.
Hogg's 'authentic letter' can indeed be found in the August 1823
number of *Blackwood's Magazine*, and it may describe an exhumation
that actually took place; the college friend whom the editor consults,
wary of Blackwoodian hoaxes, is quite transparently Lockhart. 'God
knows! Hogg has imposed as ingenious lies on the public ere now',
L——t remarks (p. 183), but by this time Hogg was more often the
butt of *Blackwood's* 'lies' than the perpetrator of them, and his own
'Memoir of the Author's Life' comments on Lockhart's addiction to
fibbing.[6] Hogg's appearance as a real Ettrick Shepherd, who snubs

[5] See Hogg, *Letters*, i. 365; ii. 60. On Hogg's dealings with Wilson, Lockhart, and
Blackwood's see Thomas C. Richardson's introduction to his edition of Hogg's
Contributions to Blackwood's Edinburgh Magazine, i. *1817–1828* (Edinburgh, 2008),
pp. xviii–lxx.

[6] See Hogg, *Altrive Tales*, ed. Gillian Hughes (Edinburgh, 2003), 74.

the literary gentlemen in order to mind his farming business, reclaims the folk-identity with which he had begun his career: seizing it back from the *Blackwood's* wits. (The episode also, implicitly, reclaims the native and virginal meaning of Hogg's name—'a young sheep from the time when it is weaned until it is shorn of its first fleece'[7]—from the obnoxious English association with which Lockhart and Wilson liked to bait him.) At the same time, the gesture invites us to consider its cost. This shepherd, with his admirably organic truculence, cannot be the anonymous, alienated author of the *Private Memoirs and Confessions of a Justified Sinner*. He cannot be that other—the genuine?—James Hogg. The joke turns against Hogg himself at this hard stage of his career.

Hogg's refusal to take part in the literary expedition, from compounding a Blackwoodian hoax, gains depth and poignancy when we recognize that it is spoken upon the intimate terrain of his own countryside. The final pages of the memoir record Robert Wringhim's flight from Edinburgh, where he has tried to publish his story, to the Scottish Borders, where he goes to ground in the 'garb of a common shepherd' (p. 176). The last stage of the sinner's career sketches, in short, an uncanny reversal of his author's. Wringhim spends his last days on a farm adjoining Hogg's own cottage at Altrive Lake. Fall Law, where his body is buried, is one of the wild hills midway between Hogg's birthplace at Ettrickhall and Altrive Lake, where he would die just over a decade later. Hogg's letter and the concluding narrative allude to local names, known to Hogg personally or through tradition, but not otherwise a part of the historical record, in an implicit rebuke to the decorum of the historical novel and *Blackwood's* gossip column alike.[8] At the same time, Hogg's refusal sets off a quiet obliteration of his own name and presence from the landscape: which falls instead under the shadow of his old friend and patron, Scott. The editor understands the quest for the suicide's grave as taking him into what even then had become famous as the 'Scott country'; Lockhart borrows a pony from his father-in-law and procures the services of his estate manager, William Laidlaw, who was also an old friend of Hogg's (he had introduced Scott to Hogg) and a relative on

[7] *Scottish National Dictionary*, 'Hog', n. 1.
[8] See Peter Garside, 'Hogg, Eltrive, and *Confessions*', *Studies in Hogg and His World*, 11 (2000), 1–24.

his mother's side. Finally, the sinner's grave is found not at the junction of three estates, as Hogg's letter had advertised, but on land owned by Scott's 'clan chief', the Duke of Buccleuch. Nameless, accursed, now desecrated, the suicide's grave lies squarely in the domain of the Scotts.

This obliteration forecasts, with eerie aptness, the fate of Hogg's masterpiece over the next hundred years. Few copies were sold, so that after two years the author's profits amounted to 'only two pounds'.[9] The novel was noticed in the press (although not in *Blackwood's*), with reviewers preferring to wrangle over its theological content than to attend to its artistic achievement, which most of them condemned in any case as confused and unpleasant.[10] Although there is evidence of a planned reissue in 1828, *Confessions of a Justified Sinner* remained one of the more obscure titles in the oeuvre of an otherwise well-known minor author throughout the nineteenth century. An extensively revised version of the novel, given a new title, *The Private Memoirs and Confessions of a Fanatic*, was included in a posthumous edition of Hogg's fiction published in 1837. The revisions, which are almost certainly not by Hogg, erase or blur the original's theological arguments, remove all hints of impropriety, and undo some of its technical experiments, including the closing cameo of James Hogg. 'The doctrinal and psychological hinges of the work', in John Carey's summary, are 'patiently unscrewed'.[11] This was the version of the novel that remained current until a new edition reprinted the original text in 1895.

The 1895 reissue marked a modest revival of interest in *The Private Memoirs and Confessions of a Justified Sinner* in the Victorian *fin de siècle*, when it was noticed by influential critics George Saintsbury and Andrew Lang (who both thought, however, that

---

[9] Hughes, *James Hogg*, 193.

[10] On the novel's contemporary reception see Garside's introduction to his edition of *Confessions of a Justified Sinner* (Edinburgh, 2001), pp. lxvii–lxx. There is evidence that the novel fared better outside Scotland. A letter from James Emerson, dated 19 August [1824], printed in the May 1836 issue of *The Zodiac* (vol. ii, p. 164), reports that Hogg's new novel 'is very much liked in London, though in Edinburgh it was rather reprobated. Here it is looked on as an original and strikingly clever production, and proves clearly, that Hogg can do something yet, though when I spoke of him to Wordsworth, he muttered something about "exhausted genius," written out, and a few other phrases.' I thank Gillian Hughes and Peter Jackson for this reference.

[11] Carey, 'Note on the Text', *Private Memoirs and Confessions of a Justified Sinner* (Oxford, 1969), p. xxv. For a full account of the 1837 revisions see Garside's introduction, *Confessions*, pp. lxxiv–lxxix.

Hogg could not have written it all by himself). Hogg's masterpiece returned to currency as an underground classic or *roman maudit*, admired by the likes of Robert Louis Stevenson, who drew on it for *Dr Jekyll and Mr Hyde* and *The Master of Ballantrae*, and André Gide, who read it in the 1920s. Gide's discovery of Hogg would echo Baudelaire's discovery of that other literary outcast, Poe, one hundred years earlier. His enthusiastic introduction to the 1947 Cresset Press edition of *Confessions of a Justified Sinner*, emphasizing the work's psychological power, at last secured the attention of a wider public. The benediction of Gide, champion of Wilde and Dostoevsky, effected the canonization of an accursed book, too savage and perverse for Victorian taste but coming into its own, at last, after the aesthetic revolutions of modernism. 'I take it just as it is, without question', wrote Gide: 'marvelling, terror-stricken, in presence of this monstrous fruit of the Tree of Knowledge'.[12]

John Carey's 1969 edition for Oxford English Novels gave us the first properly edited text of *Confessions of a Justified Sinner*. It stimulated reassessments of Hogg's larger achievement, by scholars such as Douglas Gifford, Douglas Mack, and David Groves, and a surge of criticism of the novel itself, which brought to bear psychoanalytic, sexual, textual, theological, and (more recently) national-historical interests. The emergence of a scholarly edition of Hogg's collected works, beginning in 1995 and now more than two-thirds complete, has massively enlarged our understanding of this author and his career. Peter Garside's Stirling/South Carolina edition of *The Private Memoirs and Confessions of a Justified Sinner* (2001) provides, at last, an authoritative reckoning not just with Hogg's text but with its production, reception, and cultural contexts. The present World's Classics edition (like all subsequent scholarship on Hogg's novel) is indebted to it. While most people would probably still agree that *The Private Memoirs and Confessions of a Justified Sinner* is Hogg's masterpiece, it no longer looks like the inexplicable sport of an eccentric talent.

Hogg's Novel in Romantic Fiction

'What can this work be?' the editor asks at the close of the sinner's memoir. It is a question he fails to answer: 'I cannot tell . . . I do not understand it' (pp. 178, 188). Hogg himself called *The Private*

---

[12] Hogg, *Confessions of a Justified Sinner* (London, 1947), 'Introduction', p. x.

Memoirs and Confessions of a Justified Sinner 'a story replete with horror', so much so that 'after I had written it I durst not venture to put my name to it'.[13] Modern criticism has tended to classify it as a 'Gothic novel', meaning (in the loose sense of the term) a period novel of terror and the supernatural. But the label does not fit very well. Hogg's detailed, intimate, imaginatively intense rendition of Scottish Presbyterian experience so completely reworks the Continental Roman Catholic settings of late eighteenth-century English Gothic fiction as to make for a different kind of story.

Certainly *Confessions of a Justified Sinner* has affinities with the English strain of 'terrorist' Gothic that derived from German Romanticism, the most notable example of which is Matthew Lewis's *The Monk* (1796), a tale of the fall into debauchery and crime of a would-be saint who pledges himself to the Devil. Scholars have discussed the detailed resemblances between *Confessions of a Justified Sinner* and a more recent German novel influenced by *The Monk*, E. T. A. Hoffmann's *Die Elixiere des Teufels* (1816), which features not only a pact with the Devil but religious mania, psychosis, and a sinister double (Doppelgänger). Hogg is likely to have known about Hoffmann's novel through his friend R. P. Gillies, who was translating it into English (as *The Devil's Elixir*) at the same time that Hogg was writing *Confessions of a Justified Sinner*. (Both books were published in the same month, June 1824.)[14] The resemblances, while striking in themselves, are local rather than general, and scarcely detract from the originality of Hogg's more coherent and subtle achievement.

Johann Wolfgang von Goethe had made the pact with the Devil one of the core fables of European Romanticism in his *Faust* (Part 1, 1808), several incomplete English versions of which were published in the early 1820s, including one possibly by Coleridge. It is likely that Hogg read the substantial extracts translated by John Anster that were printed in *Blackwood's Magazine* in June 1820. As well as spurring imitations by Byron (*Manfred*; *The Deformed Transformed*) and other Romantic authors, Goethe's masterpiece revived British critical interest in Christopher Marlowe's *Tragical History of Dr Faustus*,

---

[13] Hogg, *Altrive Tales*, 51.
[14] See Reinhard Heinritz and Silvia Mergenthal, 'Hogg, Hoffmann, and Their Diabolical Elixir', *Studies in Hogg and His World*, 7 (1996), 47–58.

excerpts from which (including the whole of the last scene) were also printed in *Blackwood's*, in an 1817 article by John Wilson. Hogg's devil, Gil-Martin, has some affinities with Marlowe's and Goethe's, such as deadpan wit and dialectical skill. Scholars have detected verbal echoes of *Dr Faustus* in the novel,[15] and there is at least one striking resonance of *Faust*. Assured by Gil-Martin that he has committed a series of atrocious crimes, Wringhim reflects: 'I have two souls, which take possession of my bodily frame by turns, the one being all unconscious of what the other performs' (pp. 143–4). His words give a pathological twist to Faust's famous outcry, 'Zwei Seelen wohnen, ach! in meiner Brust' (in the Anster translation, 'In my breast | Alas two souls have taken their abode, | And each is struggling there for mastery').[16] The pact with the Devil also features in Charles Maturin's astounding modern Gothic novel *Melmoth the Wanderer* (1820), which anticipates Hogg in adapting the theme to a national historical subject, in this case the decadence of the Anglo-Irish ascendancy.[17]

Arguably, however, the main literary current that flows from the turbulent 1790s into *Confessions of a Justified Sinner* has its source in William Godwin's *Things as They Are, or, The Adventures of Caleb Williams* (1794), one of the key works of North Atlantic Romanticism. Godwin pioneered a Calvinist fiction of doubling, flight, and pursuit that was quickly taken up by American and Scottish writers, as Susan Manning has shown.[18] *Caleb Williams* traces, in an anguished first-person narrative, the perversion of an obsessional bond between men (here, master and servant) from fascination and admiration to paranoia, persecution, and terror. Caleb's opening outcry, 'My life has for several years been a theatre of calamity. I have been a mark for the vigilance of tyranny, and I could not escape. My fairest prospects have been blasted,'[19] finds a clear echo in Robert Wringhim's more

---

[15] David Groves, 'Allusions to *Dr. Faustus* in James Hogg's *A Justified Sinner*', *Studies in Scottish Literature*, 18 (1983), 157–65.

[16] Goethe, *Faust*, pt. 1 (1114–17); 'Horae Germanicae, No. V: The Faustus of Goethe', *Blackwood's*, 7 (June 1820), 235–58 (245).

[17] See Murray Pittock's linking of Maturin and Hogg as authors of national Gothic, *Scottish and Irish Romanticism* (Oxford, 2008), 211–34, and Ian Campbell, 'Hogg's *Confessions* and the *Heart of Darkness*', *Studies in Scottish Literature*, 15 (1980), 187–201.

[18] Susan Manning, 'The Pursuit of the Double', in *The Puritan-Provincial Vision* (Cambridge, 1990), 70–84.

[19] William Godwin, *Caleb Williams*, ed. Pamela Clemit (Oxford, 2009), 3.

menacing exordium: 'My life has been a life of trouble and turmoil; of change and vicissitude; of anger and exultation; of sorrow and of vengeance. My sorrows have all been for a slighted gospel, and my vengeance has been wreaked on its adversaries' (p. 75). Drawing on themes of feudal oppression and injustice developed contemporaneously in the Gothic, Godwin uses the persecution plot to criticize an entire political, legal, and social order, making *Caleb Williams* a touchstone of the so-called 'Jacobin novel' that flourished in the 1790s. Godwin's last novel *Mandeville* (1817), another outcast's tale, anticipates *Confessions of a Justified Sinner* in its historical setting (the seventeenth-century civil wars), its first-person narrative of a doctrinally specific Calvinist delirium, and the fatal antipathy that grips the melancholy Presbyterian protagonist and the glamorous cavalier, Clifford. (The school episodes of the first volume look forward to Wringhim's youthful run-ins with M'Gill and the young George Colwan, which are also inflected by Henry Fielding's treatment of the young Jones and Blifil in *Tom Jones*.) Influenced by Godwin and influencing, in turn, *Mandeville*, the American Charles Brockden Brown's novel *Wieland, or the Transformation* (1798) features a hapless protagonist who commits suicide after a supernatural-seeming trickster has convinced him to do God's will by murdering his family—making *Wieland*, a quarter-century before *Confessions of a Justified Sinner*, the first religious-fanatic serial-killer novel in English.

Novels in English had been calling themselves 'memoirs' ever since the 'private memoirs' and 'secret histories' of the early eighteenth century (the period at which *Private Memoirs and Confessions of a Justified Sinner* is set).[20] More recently there had been a run of Rousseau-inspired 'confessions', of which Thomas De Quincey's *Confessions of an English Opium Eater* (1821), with its lavish evocations of hallucinatory delirium, was by far the most consequential, spawning imitations and parodies, and no doubt providing Hogg (in Garside's phrase) with a 'creative trigger'.[21] (De Quincey also wrote

---

[20] See Ina Ferris, 'Scholarly Revivals: Gothic Fiction, Secret History, and Hogg's *Private Memoirs and Confessions of a Justified Sinner*', in J. Heydt-Stevenson and C. Sussman (eds.), *Recognizing the Romantic Novel: New Histories of British Fiction, 1780–1830* (Liverpool, 2008), 267–84.

[21] Garside, 'Introduction', *Confessions of a Justified Sinner*, p. xlvii; Garside also notes a vogue for criminal 'confessions', e.g. the 1818 republication of *The Confession of Nichol Muschet of Boghall* (1721) and the contemporary *Life of David Haggart* (1821), pp. xxi, li. On the larger topic see Susan Levin, *The Romantic Art of Confession* (Columbia, SC, 1998).

for *Blackwood's*, and Hogg knew him.) While Hogg's novel may have capitalized on the Romantic vogue for confessions, the Godwinian first-person narrative of social isolation, persecution, and derangement informs *Confessions of a Justified Sinner* at a profounder level: as, indeed, it informed a flurry of one-volume novels of Calvinist obsession and fatality produced in Scotland in the mid-1820s alongside Hogg's masterpiece, including examples by Lockhart (*Matthew Wald*, 1824) and John Galt (*The Omen*, 1825).[22]

Hogg's novel takes its place in the front rank of British Romantic fiction as the last (and arguably best) of a spectacular trio of Godwinian terror novels published after the Napoleonic Wars, the others being *Frankenstein* (1818), by Godwin's daughter Mary Shelley, and *Melmoth the Wanderer* (influenced by *Mandeville*), which has already been mentioned. (Both *Frankenstein* and *Melmoth* were reviewed favourably in *Blackwood's*.) *Frankenstein* shares with *Confessions of a Justified Sinner* a 'dystopian plot of violent doubling and fraternal or filial pursuit' adapted from Godwin;[23] Shelley's novel also installs a formal technique, variously developed by Hogg and Maturin, of nesting the accursed protagonist's monologue within a narrative frame in such a way as to amplify rather than mut fle its alarming power. The monster's story and the sinner's memoir, enclosed in the envelope of an enlightened narration, subvert the impartiality and reliability of the enlightened narrator and call into question his deeper motives. The challenge also strikes at our relation to the story we are reading: daring us to sympathize with the monstrous antihero, forcing us to question the limits of sympathy as a medium of moral intelligence.

Hogg's device of an editor presenting the story in the form of a historical document, originating in the 'found manuscript' set-up of eighteenth-century Gothic, derives more proximately from Irish and Scottish national and historical novels, which restored seriousness and complexity to what had become an empty convention. Maria Edgeworth's *Castle Rackrent* (1800) pitches an Irish servant's memoir of the extinction of a landed family in an ironical stand-off with the

---

[22] For these see Peter Garside, 'Hogg and the Blackwoodian Novel', *Studies in Hogg and His World*, 15 (2004), 5–20.

[23] Jill Heydt Stevenson and Charlotte Sussman, 'The Ethical Experiments of the Romantic Novel', in *Recognizing the Romantic Novel*, 22. See also Nicola Watson, *Revolution and the Form of the British Novel* (Oxford, 1994), 147–76.

commentary of an enlightened editor. However the all but over-powering treatment of the convention came in the historical novels of Scott, which reshaped the terrain of British fiction in the decade after the publication of *Waverley* in 1814. *The Private Memoirs and Confessions of a Justified Sinner* is also a Scottish historical novel, set with deceptive precision in the years 1687–1712, and much of its scandalous force comes from its fusion of the rival—ostensibly incompatible—genres of Godwinian terror-tale and Scottish histor-ical romance. Incompatible, because Scott's novels set out at once to recognize and to defuse the dangerous psychic and political energies given play by Godwin. Scott's novels dramatize a violent crisis in the national past in order to lay it to rest, its clashing extremes absorbed into a modern liberal dispensation built on moderation and com-promise. In *Old Mortality* (1816), Scott's great novel of Presbyterian insurgency, the elaborate (and blatantly fictitious) editorial frame-work marks the historical distance that quarantines us, citizens of a pacified present, from the bitter conflict narrated in its pages, with its escalations of murderous fanaticism.

There is no room for moderation and compromise in *Confessions of a Justified Sinner*. The sinner's doomed utterance remains inassimilable: the modern editor cannot understand it, just as the earth itself has refused to digest Robert Wringhim's remains. (*Old Mortality* opens with a vision of once-furious militants quietly decomposing in their graves.) The force of this intractability comes from Hogg's decision to let his protagonist (like Caleb Williams, like Frankenstein's monster) present his own case in full, in a first-person account, unlike the characters in Scott's novels, embedded within an impersonal historical narrative. Here Hogg draws on another strain of Scottish Romantic fiction that had developed (out of *Castle Rackrent*) in reaction to Scott, the fictitious local-historical memoir, given virtuoso treatment by John Galt in his *Annals of the Parish* and *The Provost* (both 1821). More explosively than Galt, Hogg activates the subversive potential of having the historical specimen tell his story in his own words. He radicalizes the local memoir by reconnect-ing it with its modern roots in the Godwinian romance of the outcast, whose story bears witness to a disturbing failure of integration into a larger national destiny.

Linguistic difference marks another technique, absent from Godwinian first-person narration (rendered in an often turgid standard English), with which Hogg tests the bounds of historical fiction. Scott's *Waverley* and its successors opened British fiction to a vastly expanded range of regional and social languages, including representations of spoken Scots, while retaining the authority of English as their dominant narrative medium. In his earlier tales Hogg had developed the narration of prose fiction in Scots, affirming the truth of local structures of experience, above all rural working-class experience. In *Confessions of a Justified Sinner* both the editor and Robert Wringhim write in English: the Editor in the polite dialect of literary Edinburgh, Wringhim in an idiom dense with scriptural echoes and allusions, especially to the Pauline sources of the doctrine of election, the more vengeful verses of the Old Testament, and the Book of Revelation. (His usage reflects the adoption of the King James Bible and an English metrical translation of the Psalms by the Presbyterian Church.) Drawing on his mastery of the literary vernacular, Hogg admits other voices into *The Private Memoirs and Confessions of a Justified Sinner* besides the sinner's and editor's narratives. These are, more literally, voices, the demotic utterances of Scottish labourers and servants, whose speech performs a shrewd resistance to authority in the form of a resistance of Scots to English. The servant lass Bessie Gillies outwits Edinburgh lawyers, John Barnet defies the Reverend Wringhim, and James Hogg himself issues a gruff dismissal to gentlemen and scholars. In the novel's deepest immersion in popular idiom, Robert Wringhim's servant Samuel Scrape tells an oral tale in Scots (relayed by Scrape from the old wives of the village, relayed to us in turn through Wringhim and the editor), the upshot of which is that traditional sources of wisdom can deliver us from evil. Wringhim, like the editor, like the villagers in the tale, has cut himself off from those sources (split, intriguingly, between orthodox Christian ethics—the 'gouden rule'—and an occult elemental lore—knowledge of the speech of hellish ravens). Scrape's tale looks forward to the end of the story, when the Border peasants know as if by instinct that Wringhim is the Devil's own. *Confessions of a Justified Sinner* casts Scots as the language of 'organic' popular life, a traditional moral ecology, which makes for a utopian alternative to the deadly duality staked out by sinner and editor.[24]

---

[24] See Gary Kelly, *English Fiction in the Romantic Period* (London, 1989), 261–73; Mack, *Scottish Fiction and the British Empire*, 159–66.

Hogg does not give in to pastoral nostalgia, however. The organic world rejects Wringhim and rebuffs the editor, and we ourselves, modern novel-readers, are also by a remorseless formal logic set outside it—together with its anonymous author.

The most elaborate development of an 'alternative perspective'[25] in the 'Editor's Narrative' comes towards its end, structurally balancing Scrape's tale and the scenes among the peasantry towards the end of the sinner's memoir, in the episode of Bell Calvert and Mrs Logan. Opening onto an urban underworld of thieves and prostitutes (a professional criminal society, in contrast to the 'ideological' and pathological criminality of the justified sinner), the episode spawns yet more doubles in this text rife with doubling. Like Robert Wringhim, Bell Calvert is a persecuted outcast, tempted and betrayed by a 'lordly fiend' (p. 47). But this sinner's career offers a redemptive counterpart to Robert's. A female work of sympathy forges a bond between Calvert and Mrs Logan, overcoming their initial hostility, in a reversal of the book's compulsive antagonism between men. The bond proves ethically formidable as the women turn detective and track down young George's killer. This glimpse of a moral regime of feminine cooperation is closed, however, with the onset of Robert's memoir.

History, Religion, and Fanaticism

Among other things, then, *The Private Memoirs and Confessions of a Justified Sinner* is a Scottish historical novel, and consequently it is worth attending to the history it invokes. The story opens with the marriage of the elder George Colwan in 1687, following his succession to the Dalcastle estate. A second son, christened Robert Wringhim, is born one year after the first, George Colwan junior, thus no earlier than in the autumn of 1688. This chronology is at odds with Robert's memoir, which records his first meeting with Gil-Martin on 'the 25th day of March 1704, when I had just entered the eighteenth year of my age' (p. 91). The last entry in Robert's journal, written just before his death, is dated 18 September 1712. His lifetime coincides with a series of major turning points in national history, notably the 'Glorious Revolution' of 1688–9, which dislodged the last of the

---

[25] Mack, *Scottish Fiction and the British Empire*, 160.

Stuarts, James II and VII, from the British throne in favour of William III, and the Treaty of Union of 1707, which dissolved the Scottish Parliament for a joint English and Scottish assembly in Westminster. Officially, these events brought an end to the civil wars that had torn the country apart for much of the seventeenth century. The ensuing constitutional settlement would prevail until the reconvening of the Scottish Parliament in 1999. Anticipating the main conceit of Salman Rushdie's *Midnight's Children*, Hogg's novel synchronizes its protagonist's story with the foundation of the modern state—meaning, in this case, not the birth but the demise of an independent nation.

The philosophers of the eighteenth-century Scottish Enlightenment, and Scott's novels after them, narrated this modern history as a progress from chaos to order, a resolution of bloody rival fanaticisms into a peaceful, prosperous, ideologically temperate civil society. Others deplored the loss of an authentic Scotland, even as they held incompatible views of what that Scotland might be like. The new Whig order was committed to a constitutional balance between Crown and Parliament, an economy based on international trade and credit, and a moderate Presbyterianism as the national form of religion in Scotland. Excluded from the new order were the adherents of the exiled Stuarts, called Tories or 'Jacobites' after the exiled James and his son, who endorsed the absolute authority of the Crown over the Church (via the appointment of bishops) as well as State. Also excluded were radical Whigs, the heirs of militant Presbyterian resistance to the Stuart regime, who despised the new settlement for its doctrinal and political compromises.

Early in *Confessions of a Justified Sinner*, the principal characters visit Edinburgh during the parliamentary session of 1703. (Once again, the division of the narratives confounds the apparent precision of historical reference: Wringhim's memoir dates the session in 1704, although the circumstances described point to 1703.) This episode, the novel's only excursion onto the stage of national politics, burlesques the 'epic' rendering of the relation between private motives and public events in Scott's historical fiction. Hogg represents the contest between parties—the revolution-settlement Whigs versus the Tories or 'cavaliers'—as blindly irrational and chaotic, breaking out in a riot in which the combatants attack each other with kitchen utensils without even knowing who is on which side, let alone why they are fighting. Collective action, driven by mass hysteria, subsides into bathos. The narrative withholds any explanation of the historical significance of the 1703 parliamentary session, a critical stage in the negotiations that issued four years later in the Treaty of Union. Indeed the Union, the major public event in Wringhim's lifetime, is never once mentioned in *Confessions of a Justified Sinner*. Politically, as at other levels, 'union' remains an impossible condition in Hogg's text.

In Scotland the seventeenth-century civil wars took the form of a ferocious struggle over the national religion. Lowland religious and political leaders had reaffirmed their commitment to the Presbyterian forms of worship and Church government, against the encroachments of Charles I and his bishops, in two great public declarations, the National Covenant (1638) and the Solemn League and Covenant (1643). Ministers and congregations who kept faith with those principles after the Stuart restoration in 1660 became known as 'Covenanters'. The reintroduction of an Episcopal Church of Scotland by Charles II and his successor James II and VII ignited a bloody cycle of Covenanter resistance and government repression which culminated in an armed uprising in the south-west of Scotland (1679), followed by a state terror, the so-called 'killing time' (1680–5). This regional civil war makes up the immediate prehistory of *Confessions of a Justified Sinner*. George Colwan senior, we learn, has been a moderate Tory laird who secretly sympathized with the Covenanters and refrained from persecuting them during the 'killing time'. However his wife's sectarian extremism chills that sympathy and drives him to a wholehearted embrace of the Royalist cause. The editor, himself biased towards the Tory side, stages their factional difference as a (somewhat conventional) clash of custom and temperament: the old laird cleaves to a pre-Reformation culture of merrymaking and 'promiscuous dancing', while his Puritan wife disdains the pleasures of the flesh. The country's political, religious, and cultural schisms materialize in a partition of the house ('a miniature x-ray of a nation split in two'[26]), followed by a genealogical doubling of fathers and sons.

'Hers were not the tenets of the great reformers,' the editor says of Lady Dalcastle, 'but theirs mightily overstrained and deformed' (p. 6);

---

[26] Enrica Villari's phrase, 'una piccolo radiografia di un paese spaccato in due', from her introduction to the Italian translation of Hogg's novel, *Confessioni di un peccatore eletto* (Turin, 1995), p. xii.

while her spiritual adviser, the Reverend Wringhim, stands accused of 'splitting the doctrines of Calvin into thousands of undistinguishable films' (p. 15). Jean Calvin's *Institutes of the Christian Religion*, one of the great documents of the European Reformation, supplied the theological core of Scottish Presbyterianism. Its principles were codified by John Knox and other leading Reformers in 1560–2, and again in the Westminster Confession of Faith in 1646, which became the official doctrinal statement of the Church of Scotland when Presbyterianism was re-established in 1690.[27] The key tenet of Calvinism at stake in Hogg's novel is that of unconditional election, with its corollaries, predestination and justification by faith. The doctrine of election, which has its scriptural basis in the epistles of St Paul, holds that all human beings are sinners, born under sentence of damnation, except for the few, the 'elect', whom God has chosen to save before time began. Salvation is not earned according to a sinner's individual merit, as though it is a wage God is obliged to pay, but is the unconditional gift of God's sovereign grace. The Reverend and Robert Wringhim press this logic to the conviction, called antinomianism, that the elect are exempt from the moral law, meaning not just man-made legal systems but the Ten Commandments given by God to Moses, since salvation is guaranteed without reference to their earthly conduct. 'How delightful to think that a justified person can do no wrong!' sighs Lady Dalcastle. The principles of 'the infallibility of the elect, and the pre-ordination of all things that come to pass' (p. 96) rationalize her son's bloody career. 'I was now a justified person, adopted among the number of God's children—my name written in the Lamb's book of life', Robert muses: 'no bypast transgression, nor any future act of my own, or of other men, could be instrumental in altering the decree' (p. 88). The justified sinner's syllogism is the reverse of Ivan Karamazov's (in Dostoevsky's *The Brothers Karamazov*): God exists, therefore everything is permitted.

Antinomianism was condemned as heretical by Protestant establishments, including the Church of Scotland. Calvin himself denounced as a 'calumny' the charge 'that men are invited to sin' by the doctrine of unconditional election. Far from believing themselves released from the moral law, he argued, those who accept justification

---

[27] J. H. S. Burleigh characterizes the *Westminster Confession* as 'a carefully balanced formulation of Calvinism in its later scholastic phase': *A Church History of Scotland* (Oxford, 1960), 287.

by faith must 'conceive a greater horror of sin than if it were said to be wiped off by a sprinkling of good works'.[28] The principle is reiterated in the Westminster Confession: 'The moral law doth forever bind all, as well justified persons as others, to the obedience thereof' (ch. 29: v); 'although [the elect] can never fall from the state of justification, yet they may by their sins fall under God's Fatherly displeasure, and not have the light of his countenance restored unto them, until they humble themselves, confess their sins, beg pardon, and renew their faith and repentance' (ch. 21: v). Repentance, the inner working of God's grace, remains possible for the justified sinner, so that those who are hardened against it cannot by definition be among the elect. The Wringhims' religion, in short, is a perversion of orthodox Calvinism, as their misapplications of Scripture reveal. Nevertheless antinomianism represents an exaggeration of the logic of election—forcing it to an ethical impasse—rather than a contradiction of it. The argument that the elect will be moved to obey the moral law, even though such obedience is not a condition of their salvation, is a circular one, as is the argument that any lapse into sin must be temporary, since the justified sinner is sure to repent. Gil-Martin, who tempts Wringhim by reasoning with him rather than by inflaming his passions, mixes perfectly orthodox pronouncements (since the Devil too is bound by revelation) with such logical snakes and ladders.[29]

Scholars have identified the 'Marrow controversy', a heresy case that broke out in the Scottish Borders in 1718–23, as a possible historical context for *Confessions of a Justified Sinner*. The General Assembly of the Church of Scotland reprimanded Thomas Boston, minister of Ettrick, James Hog of Carnock (no relation of our author, although he must have been struck by the shared name), and several other persons for reprinting a Calvinist tract of 1645, *The Marrow of Modern Divinity*, on the grounds that it fomented antinomianism. Boston's piety, intelligence, and pastoral zeal kept his memory warm

---

[28] Jean Calvin, *Institutes of the Christian Religion*, trans. Henry Beveridge (Edinburgh, 1845), bk. III, ch. 16, iv (vol. ii, p. 39). The Westminster Confession of Faith is cited from http://www.reformed.org/documents.

[29] For a detailed account of the novel's theology see Crawford Gribben, 'James Hogg, Scottish Calvinism and Literary Theory', *Scottish Studies Review*, 5/2 (2004), 9–26. On the Wringhims' use of Scripture see Ian Campbell, 'James Hogg and the Bible', in D. F. Wright (ed.), *The Bible and Scottish Literature* (Edinburgh, 1988), 94–109.

in Ettrick for the next hundred years, and Hogg, who admired him, would probably have known about the controversy. Neither Boston and his associates nor *The Marrow* can plausibly be characterized as antinomian, and antinomianism seems to have been a bugbear invoked in internecine doctrinal disputes more than it was a position actually professed by anyone in eighteenth-century or early nineteenth-century Scotland. Church historians see the Marrow controversy as 'the first sign of the rise of an evangelical party' in the Church of Scotland following the 1690 settlement:[30] a century-long resurgence that came to a head in the decades after the Napoleonic Wars, part of a general reaction against moderatism and Enlightenment values. Heresy cases erupted in the later 1820s and 1830s, shortly after publication of *Confessions of a Justified Sinner*, forecasting the 'Great Disruption' of 1843.

Attuned to the evangelical revival, *Blackwood's Magazine* was in many respects sympathetic to it. Hogg's own position was complex. He tended to profess moderate theological views, along the lines of those he gives to the minister Blanchard in *Confessions of a Justified Sinner*, even as he revered the popular Presbyterianism of his countryside. His distrust of 'enthusiasm' did not prevent him from holding the Covenanters in high esteem as 'intrepid sufferers in the cause of civil and religious liberty'.[31] In an 1817 *Blackwood's* article reviewing Charles Kirkpatrick Sharpe's edition of James Kirkton's *The Secret and True History of the Church of Scotland* (a key document of the Covenanting era), Hogg upbraids the gentleman Tory editor for using his scholarly apparatus to undermine 'the manly narrative of honest Kirkton' with partisan sneers and innuendo. Peter Garside and Ina Ferris have detected a source here for the antagonism between the editor's and sinner's narratives in *Confessions of a Justified Sinner* (although no one would claim that Wringhim is a heroic witness in the manner of Kirkton).[32]

[30] Andrew L. Drummond and James Bulloch, *The Scottish Church 1688–1843: The Age of the Moderates* (Edinburgh, 1973), 37; for a general account of the Marrow affair, see pp. 33–44, and Burleigh, *A Church History of Scotland*, 288–90.

[31] Hogg, *Contributions to Blackwood's Magazine*, 49.

[32] 'A Letter to Charles Kirkpatrick Sharpe, Esq., On his Original Mode of Editing Church History', *Blackwood's*, 2 (Dec. 1817), 305–9; repr. in Hogg, *Contributions to Blackwood's Magazine*, 47–54; Garside, 'Introduction', *Confessions*, p. xxxvi; Ferris, 'Scholarly Revivals', 277–82.

Hogg's *Blackwood's* article spoke to a larger debate around the legacy of the Covenanters, which had become a contemporary flashpoint for political radicalism as well as the evangelical revival. When the editor says of Wringhim's memoir, 'We have heard much of the rage of fanaticism in former days, but nothing to this' (p. 71), he is probably referring to the controversy stirred up in 1817 by Scott's novel of the 1679 rising, *Old Mortality*. Reviewers in the evangelical press attacked Scott for caricaturing the Covenanters as wild fanatics, the prototypes of Jacobin revolutionary terrorists. Hogg's own novella of the killing time, *The Brownie of Bodsbeck* (1818; taken to be a rejoinder to *Old Mortality*, although it was probably written earlier), includes a sympathetic depiction of persecuted Covenanters hiding out among the Ettrick peasantry. More recently, Galt's 1823 novel *Ringan Gilhaize, or The Covenanters* posed an explicit challenge to Scott's account of the legacy of the Reformation in modern Scottish history. War crimes committed by government troops drive Ringan, a descendant of heroes of the Reformation, to become an avenging assassin in the name of the Lord. Douglas Mack has suggested that Galt's novel provided an impetus for *Confessions of a Justified Sinner* (hinted at, perhaps, in Bessy Gillies's reference to the Wringhims as 'the Ringans', p. 52).[33] Hogg's editor insinuates a set of historical connections between Covenanter extremism and the Wringhims' antinomian sect in the early pages of his narrative; but in such matters he is hardly to be trusted. Once Robert tells his story, 'fanaticism' fixes itself as a more intractable and enigmatic phenomenon—one less easily resolved into a particular historical cause—than it is in either Galt's novel or Scott's.

The 'rage of fanaticism' frightens the editor because of the threat it poses to the liberal norms of civil society: norms shared by the editor, a citizen of the Scottish Enlightenment republic of letters, and by ourselves, fellow citizens (whatever our local origins or beliefs) by virtue of our being readers of Hogg's trickily sophisticated work of fiction. *Confessions of a Justified Sinner* directs critical energy not only at Calvinism and its offshoots but at the ideology of modern civil

---

[33] Mack, '"The Rage of Fanaticism in Former Days": James Hogg's *Confessions of a Justified Sinner* and the Controversy over *Old Mortality*', in Ian Campbell (ed.), *Nineteenth-Century Scottish Fiction* (Manchester, 1979), 37–50; see also Ina Ferris, *The Achievement of Literary Authority: Gender, History, and the Waverley Novels* (Ithaca, NY, 1991), 137–94; Duncan, *Scott's Shadow*, 40–1, 247–58.

society forged in Scottish Enlightenment moral philosophy and taken over in Scott's historical novels. Hogg's novel represents fanaticism as a modern phenomenon, a radical alienation from traditional forms of belief, rather than as some primitive psychic force or historical leftover. Gary Kelly has pointed out the editor's frequent references to the Wringhims as 'incendiaries', a term in the early nineteenth-century anti-Jacobin vocabulary roughly equivalent to today's 'terrorist'.[34] The division of the narratives maps the opposition by which civil society and fanaticism, according to political theorist Dominique Colas, 'have mutually defined each other since the beginning of the sixteenth century', forming a conceptual antithesis which is one of the foundations of our modern political imagination.[35] It seems that we need the fanatic, our implacable, inscrutable other, in order to know ourselves. What happens—Hogg's novel asks—when he tells his own story? *Confessions of a Justified Sinner* rebukes the bad faith of those more recent fictions that cast the fanatic as the enemy of the liberal imagination and at the same time claim to understand him in its terms.[36]

The architects of the Protestant Reformation, including Calvin, applied the term 'fanatic' to those who rejected the authority of Scripture for private revelation, and who sought to abolish civil society so as to found the Kingdom of God on earth.[37] The Reverend Wringhim characterizes his experience of private revelation as a wrestling match with God (pp. 76, 88): a violent antagonism that perpetuates itself theoretically, 'splitting the doctrines of Calvin into thousands of undistinguishable films', splitting civil society into warring sects, splitting the pathologically lonely Robert[38] and driving him on his mission as 'the sword of the Lord' (p. 103). Splitting generates a compensatory, excessive, abominable fantasy of unity. 'I am wedded to you so closely, that I feel as if I were the same person',

---

[34] Kelly, *English Fiction of the Romantic Period*, 264–5.

[35] Dominique Colas, *Civil Society and Fanaticism: Conjoined Histories*, trans. Amy Jacobs (Stanford, Calif., 1997), p. xvi.

[36] e.g. Ian McEwan, *Enduring Love* (London, 1997); John Updike, *Terrorist* (New York, 2006).

[37] See Calvin, *Institutes*, vol. i: bk. 1, ch. 9.

[38] Hogg owned an 1808 edition of J. G. Zimmerman's treatise *On Solitude*, which may inform Wringhim's psychology: see Gillian Hughes, 'Robert Wringhim's Solitude', in S. Alker and H. F. Nelson (eds.), *James Hogg and the Literary Marketplace* (Farnham, 2009).

gloats Gil-Martin: 'Our essences are one, our bodies and spirits . . . united' (p. 170).

'I am indeed your brother, not according to the flesh, but in my belief of the same truths', Gil-Martin had introduced himself to Robert at their first meeting (p. 89). The idea of a fraternity forged through ideological uniformity, rather than kinship or customary association, overrides the liberal conception of a civil society based on differences among individuals formulated by the Scottish Enlightenment philosophers. Lord Kames argued that evangelical conversion, the promotion of 'belief of the same truths', destroys the 'necessary variety in sentiment and opinion' that provides an essential principle of social cohesion:

Different countenances in the human race, not only distinguish one person from another, but promote society, by aiding us to chuse a friend, an associate, a partner for life. Differences in opinion and sentiment have still more beneficial effects: they arouse the attention, give exercise to the understanding, and sharpen the reasoning faculty. With respect to religion in particular, perfect uniformity, which furnisheth no subject for thinking nor for reasoning, would produce languor in divine worship, and make us sink into cold indifference. How foolish then is the rage of making proselytes? Let every man enjoy his native liberty, of thinking as well as acting.[39]

But Robert's new friend appears to be exactly 'the same being as myself', in dress, form, and features (p. 89). Gil-Martin's 'cameleon art of changing [his] appearance' enacts a systematic cancellation of other people's difference, beginning with difference of countenance:

If I contemplate a man's features seriously, mine own gradually assume the very same appearance and character. And what is more, by contemplating a face minutely, I not only attain the same likeness, but, with the likeness, I attain the very same ideas as well as the same mode of arranging them, so that, you see, by looking at a person attentively, I by degrees assume his likeness, and by assuming his likeness I attain to the possession of his most secret thoughts. (p. 95)

Hogg's devil parodies the most famous of the Scottish Enlightenment treatises on socialization, Adam Smith's *The Theory of Moral*

---

[39] Henry Home, Lord Kames, *Sketches of the History of Man*, 2nd edn. (4 vols., Edinburgh, 1788), ii. 438–9.

Sentiments (1759). Smith promotes *sympathy* as the psychological operation by which the inhabitants of civil society, estranged from customary bonds, form relationships with one another. 'By the imagination we place ourselves in [the other's] situation', Smith proposes: 'we enter as it were into his body, and become in some measure the same person with him, and thence form some idea of his sensations'.[40] Sympathy is a moral technique which regulates the boundaries of self and other in order to maintain individual 'propriety' as the ethical basis of civil society.

Still more closely than it recalls *The Theory of Moral Sentiments*, however, Gil-Martin's talent for infiltrating other people's 'secret thoughts' echoes an anecdote related by Edmund Burke about the 'celebrated physiognomist' (and heretical Renaissance philosopher) Tommaso Campanella:

This man, it seems, had not only made very accurate observations on human faces, but was very expert in mimicking such as were any way remarkable. When he had a mind to penetrate into the inclinations of those he had to deal with, he composed his face, his gestures, and his whole body, as nearly as he could into the exact similitude of the person he intended to examine; and thus carefully observed what turn of mind he seemed to acquire by this change. So that, says my author, he was able to enter into the dispositions and thoughts of people as effectually as if he had been changed into the very men.[41]

Gil-Martin's 'cameleon art' hijacks the Scottish Enlightenment ethos of sympathy with the techniques of physiognomy, the 'science' (popularized in Great Britain in the 1790s) of discovering people's inward character by interpreting their facial forms and expressions. Colonizing the supposedly inalienable private self, dissolving its internal integrity, Gil-Martin's art collapses the system of individual differences that sympathy, in Smith's account, was meant to secure. Hogg may have come across Burke's anecdote in Dugald Stewart's *Elements of Philosophy of the Human Mind* (based on his influential Edinburgh University lectures), where it is quoted in a discussion of 'sympathetic imitation', a phenomenon that Stewart—writing by now

---

[40] Adam Smith, *The Theory of Moral Sentiments*, ed. D. D. Raphael and A. L. Macfie (Oxford, 1976), 9.

[41] Burke, *A Philosophical Enquiry into the Origin of Our Ideas of the Sublime and the Beautiful*, ed. Adam Phillips (Oxford, 1990), 120.

in the wake of the French Revolution—views as politically dangerous. Sympathetic imitation (our instinctive susceptibility to one another's expressions and feelings) betrays the vulnerability of the individual imagination to 'the contagious nature of convulsions, of hysteric disorders, of panics, and of all the different kinds of enthusiasm'— above all, 'the infectious tendency of religious enthusiasm'.[42] Promising fraternity, sympathy brings terror.

Hogg's story of a 'fanatical' disintegration of the individual subject, Robert Wringhim, grapples with Enlightenment theories of sympathy that provided a template for the act of novel-reading as well as for civic morality in the early nineteenth century. The Devil harnesses the sympathetic imagination to a totalitarian command of other people's 'inmost thoughts'—in other words, he reads people as though they are no more than literary characters. Not for nothing does Wringhim mistake him for 'the Czar Peter of Russia' (p. 99), that monstrous prototype of the Enlightened Despot. Meanwhile the justified sinner, consigned to 'everlasting detestation', tells his story from beyond the pale of sympathetic exchange. Hogg's novel poses its challenge to the liberal reader. What relationship does our act of reading forge with the wretched author of these confessions, if not one of sympathy? What can this work be?

---

[42] Dugald Stewart, *Elements of Philosophy of the Human Mind*, ii (Edinburgh, 1814), 195–6, 203.

NOTE ON THE TEXT

The Private Memoirs and Confessions of a Justified Sinner was published by Longman & Co. of London in June 1824 in an edition of 1,000 copies. This was the only edition of the novel to be published in Hogg's lifetime. (A plan to reissue remaindered copies of the original in 1828 with a new title page, *The Suicide's Grave; or, Memoirs and Confessions of a Sinner*, does not seem to have come to fruition.) There is no persuasive evidence that Hogg had a hand in the extensive revisions made to the posthumous version of the novel published by Blackie & Son in volume v of *Tales and Sketches by the Ettrick Shepherd* (Glasgow, 1837) under the title 'The Private Memoirs and Confessions of a Fanatic', despite the publishers' claims that not only Hogg himself but Sir Walter Scott had overseen the venture. No modern editor has accepted these claims, and 1824 remains the sole authoritative text of *The Private Memoirs and Confessions of a Justified Sinner*.

The whereabouts of the manuscript of *Confessions of a Justified Sinner*, if it has survived, are unknown. It was last heard of in 1895, when Hogg's daughter, Mary Garden, responded to speculation that Hogg was not the sole author of the novel by announcing that she had the manuscript in her possession, written neatly throughout in her father's hand. *Confessions of a Justified Sinner* was printed in Edinburgh by James Clarke & Co., whose services, Peter Garside has shown, Hogg took considerable pains to secure, circumventing the wishes of his publishers.[1] Hogg evidently trusted Clarke to print his manuscript accurately and without interference—conditions that experience had taught him not to take for granted. Garside makes a convincing case that the published text is exceptionally faithful to Hogg's intentions, even in the absence of evidence of the manuscript. Garside's edition of *Private Memoirs and Confessions of a Justified Sinner* (Edinburgh, 2001) contains a detailed account of the work's textual state and publication history, and anyone with a serious interest in the novel will need to consult it. Other modern editions I have consulted include David Groves's for Canongate Classics

---

[1] Garside, 'Printing *Confessions*', *Studies in Hogg and his World*, 9 (1998), 16–31.

(Edinburgh, 1991), Adrian Hunter's for the Broadview Press (Peterborough, Ontario, 2001) and Karl Miller's for Penguin Classics (London, 2006).

The present edition of *The Private Memoirs and Confessions of a Justified Sinner* is based on the 1824 text, copies of which have been consulted at the National Library of Scotland, the University of South Carolina, and the Houghton Library at Harvard University. Like other recent editors I have adopted a conservative editorial policy, emending 1824 only in cases of typographical error. The 1824 text's (few) errors were corrected in the 1837 Blackie edition (along with its more egregious alterations); most of those corrections were accepted by John Carey in his 1969 edition for Oxford English Novels, the precursor to the present Oxford World's Classics edition. I have made three additional emendations to Carey's (pp. 28, 123, and 182). Following Groves and Garside, I have restored two of Carey's emendations back to the 1824 original, 'understanding' for 'undertaking' (p. 119) and 'effect' for 'effort' (p. 161), on the grounds that, although arguably improvements, those cannot convincingly be said to be corrections. I have however retained three of the emendations Carey accepted from 1837 which are rejected by Garside: the elimination of the first 'with' from 'with which she had to deal with' (p. 50), the emendation of the adjectival form 'trust' to 'trusty' (p. 135), and the regularization of 'round an' round' to 'round and round' (p. 154). The first case seems to me ungrammatical as well as clumsy; in the second case I have not found 'trust' recorded as an adjective after the fifteenth century, making it unlikely, in my view, that Hogg would have used it in an otherwise accurate pastiche of late seventeenth-century charter style; in the third, Wringhim writes in English, never in Scots, except where he is quoting others' direct speech. Like Carey I have retained the idiosyncratic spelling 'acquiline' on p. 133. This edition reproduces the facsimile frontispiece, dedication, and running titles from the first edition.

Emendation List

The 1824 edition reading is printed in the left-hand column and the emendation in the right. All emendations are editorial and in agreement with the 1837 Blackie edition of *Private Memoirs and Confessions of a Fanatic*.

p. 28, l. 39: the the blighting	the blighting
p. 50, l. 4: with which she had to deal with	which she had to deal with
p. 86, l. 34: lest worthy	least worthy
p. 104, l. 31: their had	there had
p. 115, l. 25: dost not not know	dost not know
p. 123, ll. 1–2: completly	completely
p. 135, l. 11: right trust	right trusty
p. 154, l. 30: round an' round	round and round
p. 182, l. 38: His answer was.	His answer was,

SELECT BIBLIOGRAPHY

Bibliography and Biography

A definitive scholarly edition of Hogg's complete writings, the Stirling/ South Carolina Research Edition of the Collected Works of James Hogg, is in progress, under the general editorship of Douglas S. Mack and Gillian Hughes (Edinburgh, 1995–). Peter Garside's edition of *The Private Memoirs and Confessions of a Justified Sinner* (2001) is volume ix in the edition.

Edith C. Batho, *The Ettrick Shepherd* (Cambridge, 1927), includes a general bibliography that remains useful, together with the same author's 'Notes on the Bibliography of James Hogg, the Ettrick Shepherd', in *The Library*, 16 (1935–6), 309–26. More recent bibliographies are by Gillian K. Hughes, *Hogg's Verse and Drama: A Chronological Listing* (Stirling, 1990), and Douglas S. Mack, *Hogg's Prose: An Annotated Listing* (Stirling, 1985).

Hogg wrote four versions of his autobiography: 'Further particulars in the life of James Hogg', *Scots Magazine* (July and Nov. 1805), 501–3, 820–3; 'Memoir of the Life of James Hogg' in *The Mountain Bard* (1807); 'A Memoir of the Author's Life' in the third edition of *The Mountain Bard* (1821); and 'Memoir of the Author's Life' in *Altrive Tales* (1832). Both the 1807 and 1821 versions of *The Mountain Bard* (ed. Suzanne Gilbert, 2007) and *Altrive Tales* (ed. Gillian Hughes, 2003) are available in the Stirling/ South Carolina Edition. Gillian Hughes's *The Collected Letters of James Hogg*, also part of the Stirling/South Carolina Edition (3 vols.; Edinburgh, 2005, 2006, 2008), and her *James Hogg: A Life* (Edinburgh, 2007) are authoritative, superseding earlier lives and letters. Karl Miller's *Electric Shepherd: A Likeness of James Hogg* (London, 2003) is part biographical evocation, part critical meditation.

Criticism

Book-Length Studies of Hogg

Alker, Sharon, and Nelson, Holly Faith (eds.), *James Hogg and the Literary Marketplace* (Farnham, 2009).
Bold, Valentina, *James Hogg: A Bard of Nature's Making* (Oxford, 2007).
Duncan, Ian, and Mack, Douglas S. (eds.), *The Edinburgh Companion to James Hogg* (Edinburgh, 2011).
Gifford, Douglas, *James Hogg* (Edinburgh, 1976).
Groves, David, *James Hogg: The Growth of a Writer* (Edinburgh, 1988).

Mergenthal, Silvia, *James Hogg: Selbstbild und Bild* (Frankfurt am Main, 1990).

Simpson, Louis A. M., *James Hogg: A Critical Study* (New York, 1962).

Books including Significant Critical Discussion of Confessions of a Justified Sinner

Craig, Cairns, *Out of History: Narrative Paradigms in Scottish and English Culture* (Edinburgh, 1996).

Craig, David, *Scottish Literature and the Scottish People, 1680–1833* (London, 1961).

Daffron, Benjamin Eric, *Romantic Doubles: Sex and Sympathy in British Gothic Literature, 1790–1830* (New York, 2002).

Duncan, Ian, *Scott's Shadow: The Novel in Romantic Edinburgh* (Princeton, 2007).

Kelly, Gary, *English Fiction of the Romantic Period, 1789–1830* (London, 1989).

Kiely, Robert, *The Romantic Novel in England* (Cambridge, Mass., 1973).

Levin, Susan M., *The Romantic Art of Confession: De Quincey, Musset, Sand, Lamb, Hogg, Frémy, Soulié, Janin* (Columbia, SC, 1998).

Mack, Douglas S., *Scottish Fiction and the British Empire* (Edinburgh, 2006).

Manning, Susan, *The Puritan-Provincial Vision: Scottish and American Literature in the Nineteenth Century* (Cambridge, 1990).

Miller, Karl, *Doubles: Studies in Literary History* (Oxford, 1985).

Pittock, Murray, *Scottish and Irish Romanticism* (Oxford, 2008).

Robertson, Fiona, *Legitimate Histories: Scott, Gothic and the Authorities of Fiction* (Oxford, 1994).

Russett, Margaret, *Fictions and Fakes: Forging Romantic Authenticity, 1760–1845* (Cambridge, 2006).

Segwick, Eve Kosofsky, *Between Men: English Literature and Male Homosocial Desire* (New York, 1985).

Watson, Nicola, *Revolution and the Form of the British Novel, 1790–1805: Intercepted Letters, Interrupted Seductions* (Oxford, 1994).

Articles and Chapters

Barrell, John, 'Putting Down the Rising', in Leith Davis, Ian Duncan, and Janet Sorensen (eds.), *Scotland and the Borders of Romanticism* (Cambridge, 2004), 130–8.

Beveridge, Allan, 'James Hogg and Abnormal Psychology: Some Background Notes', *Studies in Hogg and His World*, 2 (1991), 91–4.

Bligh, John, 'The Doctrinal Premises of Hogg's *Confessions of a Justified Sinner*', *Studies in Scottish Literature*, 19 (1984), 148–64.

Bloedé, Barbara, 'James Hogg's *Private Memoirs and Confessions of a Justified Sinner*: The Genesis of the Double', *Études anglaises*, 26/2 (1973), 174–86.

Brewster, Scott, 'Borderline Experience: Madness, Mimicry and Scottish Gothic', *Gothic Studies*, 7/1 (2005), 79–86.

Campbell, Ian, 'Hogg's *Confessions* and the *Heart of Darkness*', *Studies in Scottish Literature*, 15 (1980), 187–201.

—— 'James Hogg and the Bible', in David F. Wright (ed.), *The Bible and Scottish Literature* (Edinburgh, 1988), 94–109.

—— 'Afterword: Literary Criticism and *Confessions of a Justified Sinner*', in James Hogg, *Private Memoirs and Confessions of a Justified Sinner*, ed. P. D. Garside (Edinburgh, 2001), 177–94.

Crawford, Thomas, 'James Hogg: The Play of Region and Nation', in Douglas Gifford (ed.), *The History of Scottish Literature, 3. Nineteenth Century* (Aberdeen, 1988), 89–105.

Duncan, Ian, 'The Upright Corpse: Hogg, National Literature, and the Uncanny', *Studies in Hogg and His World*, 5 (1994), 29–54.

—— 'Sympathy, Physiognomy, and Scottish Romantic Fiction', in Jillian Heydt-Stevenson and Charlotte Sussman (eds.), *Recognizing the Romantic Novel: New Histories of British Fiction, 1780–1830* (Liverpool, 2008), 249–69.

—— 'Fanaticism and Enlightenment in *Confessions of a Justified Sinner*', in Alker and Nelson (eds.), *James Hogg and the Literary Marketplace*, 57–69.

Evans, Meredith, 'Persons Fall Apart: James Hogg's Transcendent Sinner', *Novel: A Forum on Fiction*, 36/2 (2003), 198–218.

Fang, Karen, 'A Printing Devil, a Scottish Mummy, and an Edinburgh Book of the Dead: James Hogg's Napoleonic Complex', *Studies in Romanticism*, 43/2 (2004), 161–86.

Ferris, Ina, 'Scholarly Revivals: Gothic Fiction, Secret History, and Hogg's *Private Memoirs and Confessions of a Justified Sinner*', in Jillian Heydt-Stevenson and Charlotte Sussman (eds.), *Recognizing the Romantic Novel: New Histories of British Fiction, 1780–1830* (Liverpool, 2008), 267–84.

Fox, Warren, 'Violence and the Victimization of Women: Engendering Sympathy for Hogg's Justified Sinner', *Studies in Scottish Literature*, 32 (2001), 164–79.

Garside, Peter, 'Hogg and the Blackwoodian Novel', *Studies in Hogg and His World*, 15 (2004), 5–20.

—— 'Hogg, Eltrive, and *Confessions*', *Studies in Hogg and His World*, 11 (2000), 1–24.

—— 'Hogg's *Confessions* and Scotland', *Studies in Hogg and His World*, 12 (2001), 118–38.

—— 'Printing *Confessions*', *Studies in Hogg and His World*, 9 (1998), 16–31.

Gribben, Crawford, 'James Hogg, Scottish Calvinism and Literary Theory', *Scottish Studies Review*, 5/2 (2004), 9–26.

Groves, David, 'Allusions to *Dr. Faustus* in James Hogg's *A Justified Sinner*', *Studies in Scottish Literature*, 18 (1983), 157–65.

—— 'James Hogg's *Confessions* and *The Three Perils of Woman* and the Edinburgh Prostitution Scandal of 1823', *Wordsworth Circle*, 18 (1987), 127–31.

—— 'Parallel Narratives in Hogg's *Justified Sinner*', *Scottish Literary Journal*, 9/2 (1982), 37–44.

Heinritz, Reinhard, and Mergenthal, Silvia, 'Hogg, Hoffmann, and Their Diabolical Elixir', *Studies in Hogg and His World*, 7 (1996), 47–58.

Hughes, Gillian, 'The Critical Reception of *The Confessions of a Justified Sinner*', *Newsletter of the James Hogg Society*, 1 (1982), 11–14.

—— 'Robert Wringhim's Solitude', in Alker and Nelson (eds.), *James Hogg and the Literary Marketplace*, 71–80.

Hutton, Clark, 'Kierkegaard, Antinomianism, and James Hogg's *Private Memoirs and Confessions of a Justified Sinner*', *Scottish Literary Journal*, 20/1 (1993), 37–48.

Jones, Douglas, 'Double Jeopardy and the Chameleon Art in James Hogg's *Justified Sinner*', *Studies in Scottish Literature*, 23 (1988), 164–85.

Lang, Andrew, 'Confessions of a Justified Sinner', *Illustrated London News*, 105, suppl. (24 Nov. 1894), 12.

Letley, Emma, 'Some Literary Uses of Scots in Hogg's *Confessions of a Justified Sinner* and *The Brownie of Bodsbeck*', in Gillian Hughes (ed.), *Papers Given at the First Conference of the James Hogg Society* (Stirling, 1983), 29–39.

Mack, Douglas S., ' "The Rage of Fanaticism in Former Days": James Hogg's *Confessions of a Justified Sinner* and the Controversy over *Old Mortality*', in Ian Campbell (ed.), *Nineteenth-Century Scottish Fiction: Critical Essays* (Manchester, 1979), 37–50.

—— 'The Suicide's Grave in *The Confessions of a Justified Sinner*', *Newsletter of the James Hogg Society*, 1 (1982), 8–11.

—— 'The Body in the Opened Grave: Robert Burns and Robert Wringhim', *Studies in Hogg and His World*, 7 (1996), 70–9.

—— 'Revisiting *The Private Memoirs and Confessions of a Justified Sinner*', *Studies in Hogg and His World*, 10 (1999), 1–26.

MacKenzie, Scott, 'Confessions of a Gentrified Sinner: Secrets in Scott and Hogg', *Studies in Romanticism*, 41/1 (2002), 3–32.

MacLachlan, Christopher, 'The Name "Gil-Martin"', *Newsletter of the James Hogg Society*, 4 (1985), 32.

Manning, Susan, 'That Exhumation Scene Again: Transatlantic Hogg', *Studies in Hogg and His World*, 16 (2005), 86–111.

Mason, Michael York, 'The Three Burials in Hogg's *Justified Sinner*', *Studies in Scottish Literature*, 13 (1978), 15–32.

Monnickendam, Andrew, 'The Paradigm of Borders in *The Private Memoirs and Confessions of a Justified Sinner*', *Studies in Hogg and His World*, 5 (1994), 55–69.

Petrie, David, 'The Sinner Versus the Scholar: Two Exemplary Models of Mis-Remembering and Mis-Taking Signs in Relation to Hogg's Justified Sinner', *Studies in Hogg and His World*, 3 (1992), 57–67.

Pittock, Murray G. H., 'Hogg's Gothic and the Transformation of Genre: Towards a Scottish Romanticism', *Studies in Hogg and His World*, 15 (2004), 67–75.

Redekop, Magdalene, 'Beyond Closure: Buried Alive with Hogg's *Justified Sinner*', *English Literary History*, 52/1 (1985), 159–84.

Rubenstein, Jill, 'Confession, Damnation and the Dissolution of Identity in Novels by James Hogg and Harold Frederic', *Studies in Hogg and His World*, 1 (1990), 103–13.

Saintsbury, George, *Essays in English Literature, 1780–1860* (London, 1890), 33–66.

Smith, Iain Crichton, 'A Work of Genius: James Hogg's Justified Sinner', *Studies in Scottish Literature*, 28 (1993), 1–11.

Starr, G. A., 'The Bump Above Robert Wringhim's Ear: Phrenology in Hogg's *Confessions of a Justified Sinner*', *Studies in Hogg and His World*, 19 (2009), 81–9.

Steig, Michael, 'Unearthing Buried Affects and Associations in Reading: The Case of the *Justified Sinner*', in Daniel Rancour-Laferriere (ed.), *Self-Analysis in Literary Study: Exploring Hidden Agendas* (New York, 1994), 190–208.

Tulloch, Graham, 'Hogg in the 1890s', *Studies in Hogg and His World*, 17 (2006), 19–35.

Velasco, Ismael, 'Paradoxical Readings: Reason, Religion and Tradition in *James Hogg's Private Memoirs and Confessions of a Justified Sinner*', *Scottish Studies Review*, 7/1 (2006), 38–52.

Further Reading in Oxford World's Classics

De Quincey, Thomas, *Confessions of an English Opium-Eater and Other Writings*, ed. Grevel Lindop.

Godwin, William, *Caleb Williams*, ed. Pamela Clemit.
Goethe, Johann Wolfgang von, *Faust, Part One*, trans. David Luke.
Maturin, Charles, *Melmoth the Wanderer*, ed. Douglas Grant and Chris Baldick.
Shelley, Mary, *Frankenstein*, ed. Marilyn Butler.
Scott, Walter, *Old Mortality*, ed. Jane Stevenson and Peter Davidson.
—— *Waverley*, ed. Claire Lamont.

A CHRONOLOGY OF JAMES HOGG

1770 (Nov.?) Born at Ettrickhall farm, Ettrick (baptized 9 Dec.), second of four sons of Robert Hogg, ex-shepherd and tenant farmer, and Margaret (née Laidlaw), distant cousin of William Laidlaw, later Scott's amanuensis.

1776 Bankruptcy of father brings J.H.'s formal schooling to an end. American colonists sign Declaration of Independence.

1783 Peace of Versailles concludes American War of Independence.

1785 J.H. has worked, by this date, for 'a dozen masters' as cow-herd and labourer. 'All this while I neither read nor wrote; nor had I access to any book save the Bible.'

1786 Robert Burns, *Poems, Chiefly in the Scottish Dialect*, published in Kilmarnock.

1788 J.H. hired as a shepherd in Ettrick, first at Willenslee farm, and then (1790) at Blackhouse farm, by James Laidlaw, who lends him books.

1789 French Revolution begins; storming of the Bastille in Paris. Edmund Burke, *Reflections on the Revolution in France* (1790).

1793 Great Britain at war with Revolutionary France; execution of Louis XVI.

1794 (Oct.) J.H.'s first poem published, 'Mistakes of a Night', in the *Scots Magazine*. William Godwin, *Caleb Williams*.

1798 William Wordsworth and Samuel Taylor Coleridge, *Lyrical Ballads*. United Irishmen rising.

1799 France: Napoleon Bonaparte establishes dictatorship.

1800 J.H. starts managing Ettrickhouse farm for his father. Maria Edgeworth, *Castle Rackrent*.

1801 (Jan.) Publishes slim volume of *Scottish Pastorals*. Makes popular hit with recruiting song 'Donald MacDonald'. Act of Union with Ireland.

1802 First two volumes of Walter Scott's *Minstrelsy of the Scottish Border* published. William Laidlaw seeks J.H.'s assistance collecting ballads for the third volume. (Summer) J.H. meets Scott. Visits the Highlands and contributes an account of his tour to the *Scots Magazine*. Treaty of Amiens: peace between Britain and France. *Edinburgh Review* founded.

1803 J.H. buys lease of a sheep-farm on Harris; loses savings (£150) the following year over a legal technicality. War breaks out again with Napoleonic France.

1805 J.H. works as a shepherd in Dumfriesshire.

1807 (Feb.) Constable publishes *The Mountain Bard* (original ballads) and (June) *The Shepherd's Guide* (a treatise on the care of sheep). J.H. invests proceeds in Locherben farm, Dumfriesshire (1808), where he leads a reckless life. British Parliament votes to abolish the slave trade.

1808 J. W. von Goethe, *Faust*, Part 1 (Tübingen).

1809 J.H. ruined and returns to Ettrick, but cannot find employment.

1810 (Feb.) Decamps to Edinburgh. (Aug.) Constable publishes *The Forest Minstrel* (songs). (Sept.) J.H. starts literary weekly, *The Spy*, writing most of each number himself. It runs for one year, losing subscribers with a risqué story in numbers iii and iv.

1811 The Regency: George, Prince of Wales, assumes duties of George III.

1812 George Gordon, Lord Byron, *Childe Harold's Pilgrimage* (Cantos I and II).

1813 (Jan.) *The Queen's Wake* (ballad miscellany with national-historical frame), declined by Constable, published by Goldie; fame at last. Goldie bankrupt after the third edition (1814); Blackwood buys up the remainder. J.H. befriends John Wilson.

1814 (Aug.) Meets Wordsworth in Edinburgh; (Sept.–Oct.) visits the Lake District and meets De Quincey and Southey. Becomes croupier of 'Right or Wrong Club'; drinks heavily, is seriously ill. (Dec.) Blackwood publishes *The Pilgrims of the Sun* ('wild and visionary' poem about a virgin's trip to heaven). Walter Scott, *Waverley*.

1815 Duke of Buccleuch leases J.H. Eltrive Moss farm and house (Altrive Lake), effectively rent-free for life. Decisive defeat of Napoleon at the battle of Waterloo.

1816 (Apr.) Blackwood publishes *Mador of the Moor* (narrative-descriptive poem in five cantos, written in 1814). (Oct.) Longmans publish *The Poetic Mirror* (volume of parodies); first edition sells out in six weeks. Jane Austen, *Emma*; Scott, *Old Mortality*.

1817 (Apr.) Blackwood begins *Edinburgh Monthly Magazine*, edited by Pringle and Cleghorn; sales are weak and (Sept.) the editors defect to Constable. (Oct.) The first number of the revamped *Blackwood's Edinburgh Magazine* contains the 'Chaldee Manuscript' (a parody of the prophet Daniel, satirizing Constable, Pringle, Cleghorn, and associates, originally by J.H. but enlarged by Wilson and Lockhart); outcry ensues; *Blackwood's* readership leaps to 10,000.

1818 (Mar.) Blackwood publishes *The Brownie of Bodsbeck; and Other Tales* (novel of Ettrick during the 'killing time'). Mary Shelley, *Frankenstein*.

1819 (Dec.) Blackwood publishes *Jacobite Relics of Scotland*, first series. Political unrest in England and Scotland. 'Peterloo massacre' in Manchester: troops attack a crowd demonstrating for political reform, killing 11, wounding 400.

1820 (Apr.) J.H. marries Margaret Phillips (age 31). Oliver & Boyd publish *Winter Evening Tales* (collection of tales, poems and sketches), J.H.'s most successful work of fiction; it goes into a second edition the following year. Death of George III, succession of George IV. Charles James Maturin, *Melmoth the Wanderer*.

1821 (Feb.) Blackwood publishes second series of *Jacobite Relics*. (Mar.) Oliver & Boyd publish third (revised) edition of *The Mountain Bard*, including updated 'Memoir of the Author's Life'; (Aug.) reviewed savagely by Wilson in *Blackwood's*, leading to temporary breach with Blackwood. J.H. declines Scott's invitation to accompany him to the coronation of George IV on the grounds that he has to attend to farming business. Thomas De Quincey, *Confessions of an English Opium-Eater*.

1822 (Mar.) 'Noctes Ambrosianae' series begins in *Blackwood's*. (June) Constable publishes J.H.'s *Poetical Works* (four volumes). Longmans publishes *The Three Perils of Man* (three-volume magical-realist 'Border romance'). George IV's visit to Edinburgh, stage-managed by Scott.

1823 Longmans publishes *The Three Perils of Woman* ('a series of domestic Scottish tales' in three volumes); (Oct.) sneering review by Wilson in *Blackwood's*.

1824 (June) Longmans publish *The Private Memoirs and Confessions of a Justified Sinner*. (Dec.) Longmans and Blackwood publish *Queen Hynde* (epic poem set in ancient Caledonia); altered and bowdlerized in press, a failure.

1829 (Spring) Blackwood publishes *The Shepherd's Calendar* (tales of Ettrick life, first published in *Blackwood's*). Catholic Emancipation bill passed.

1830 Financial difficulties come to a head; J.H. loses lease of Mount Benger, returns to Altrive.

1831 (Jan.) Blackwood publishes *Songs, by the Ettrick Shepherd* ('a selection of my best'). (Dec.) J.H. embarks on the 'Edinburgh Castle' for London.

1832 (Jan.–Mar.) Lionized in London. (Apr.) Cochrane, young London publisher, brings out first volume of *Altrive Tales* (intended as a complete edition of J.H.'s fiction), then goes bankrupt. Blackwood publishes *A Queer Book* (ballads), but is offended by the introductory memoir of *Altrive Tales*. (Sept.) Death of Scott. Reform bill passed, extending the franchise and restructuring the electoral map.

1834 (Apr.) *Familiar Anecdotes of Sir Walter Scott* published in New York and (June, a pirate edition) in England as *The Domestic Manners and Private Life of Sir Walter Scott*. Lockhart, at work on the official biography, outraged.

1835 (Mar.) Cochrane, in business again, publishes *Tales of the Wars of Montrose* (historical fiction), bankrupt within a few months. (21 Nov.) J.H. dies, buried in Ettrick kirkyard. Wordsworth writes 'An Extempore Effusion upon the Death of James Hogg'.

September 8.— My first night of trial in this place is over past! Would that it were the last—that I should ever be in this detestable world! Of the horrors of hell are equal to those I have suffered, eternity will be of short duration here, for no created energy can support them for one single Month, or week. I have been buffeted as never living creature was. My vitals have all been torn and every faculty and feeling of my soul racked, and tormented into callous infayfibility. I was even dying by the looks over a yawning chasm to which I could perceive no bottom, and then — not till then, did I repeat the tremendous prayer! — I was instantly at liberty; and what I now am, the Almighty knows! Amen.

Facsimile frontispiece, 1824

THE PRIVATE MEMOIRS

AND CONFESSIONS

OF A JUSTIFIED SINNER:

WRITTEN BY HIMSELF:

WITH A DETAIL OF CURIOUS TRADITIONARY FACTS, AND
OTHER EVIDENCE, BY THE EDITOR

TO

THE HON. WILLIAM SMITH,

LORD PROVOST OF GLASGOW,
&c. &c. &c.

THIS WORK IS RESPECTFULLY INSCRIBED,

AS A SMALL MARK OF

THE EDITOR'S

ESTEEM FOR HIM AS A MAN,

AND RESPECT FOR HIM AS A MAGISTRATE.

THE EDITOR'S NARRATIVE

IT appears from tradition, as well as some parish registers still extant, that the lands of Dalcastle (or Dalchastel,* as it is often spelled) were possessed by a family of the name of Colwan, about one hundred and fifty years ago, and for at least a century previous to that period. That family was supposed to have been a branch of the ancient family of Colquhoun, and it is certain that from it spring the Cowans* that spread towards the Border. I find, that in the year 1687,* George Colwan succeeded his uncle of the same name, in the lands of Dalchastel and Balgrennan; and this being all I can gather of the family from history, to tradition I must appeal for the remainder of the motley adventures of that house. But of the matter furnished by the latter of these powerful monitors, I have no reason to complain: It has been handed down to the world in unlimited abundance; and I am certain, that in recording the hideous events which follow, I am only relating to the greater part of the inhabitants of at least four counties of Scotland, matters of which they were before perfectly well informed.

This George was a rich man, or supposed to be so, and was married, when considerably advanced in life, to the sole heiress and reputed daughter of a Baillie Orde, of Glasgow. This proved a conjunction any thing but agreeable to the parties contracting. It is well known, that the Reformation principles* had long before that time taken a powerful hold of the hearts and affections of the people of Scotland, although the feeling was by no means general, or in equal degrees; and it so happened that this married couple felt completely at variance on the subject. Granting it to have been so, one would have thought that the laird, owing to his retired situation, would have been the one that inclined to the stern doctrines of the reformers; and that the young and gay dame from the city would have adhered to the free principles cherished by the court party,* and indulged in rather to extremity, in opposition to their severe and carping contemporaries.

The contrary, however, happened to be the case. The laird was what his country neighbours called 'a droll, careless chap,' with a very limited proportion of the fear of God in his heart, and very nearly as little of the fear of man. The laird had not intentionally wronged or

offended either of the parties, and perceived not the necessity of deprecating their vengeance. He had hitherto believed that he was living
in most cordial terms with the greater part of the inhabitants of the
earth, and with the powers above in particular: but woe be unto him
if he was not soon convinced of the fallacy of such damning security!
for his lady was the most severe and gloomy of all bigots to the principles of the Reformation. Hers were not the tenets of the great
reformers, but theirs mightily overstrained and deformed. Theirs was
an unguent hard to be swallowed; but hers was that unguent embit-
tered and overheated until nature could not longer bear it. She had
imbibed her ideas from the doctrines of one flaming predestinarian
divine alone; and these were so rigid, that they became a stumbling-
block* to many of his brethren, and a mighty handle for the enemies
of his party to turn the machine of the state against them.

The wedding festivities at Dalcastle partook of all the gaiety, not of
that stern age, but of one previous to it. There was feasting, dancing,
piping, and singing: the liquors were handed around in great fulness,
the ale in large wooden bickers, and the brandy in capacious horns of
oxen. The laird gave full scope to his homely glee. He danced,—he
snapped his fingers to the music,—clapped his hands and shouted at
the turn of the tune. He saluted every girl in the hall whose appearance was any thing tolerable, and requested of their sweethearts to
take the same freedom with his bride, by way of retaliation. But there
she sat at the head of the hall in still and blooming beauty, absolutely
refusing to tread a single measure with any gentleman there. The only
enjoyment in which she appeared to partake, was in now and then
stealing a word of sweet conversation with her favourite pastor about
divine things; for he had accompanied her home after marrying her to
her husband, to see her fairly settled in her new dwelling. He addressed
her several times by her new name, Mrs. Colwan; but she turned
away her head disgusted, and looked with pity and contempt towards
the old inadvertent sinner, capering away in the height of his unregenerated mirth. The minister perceived the workings of her pious
mind, and thenceforward addressed her by the courteous title of Lady
Dalcastle, which sounded somewhat better, as not coupling her name
with one of the wicked: and there is too great reason to believe, that
for all the solemn vows she had come under, and these were of no
ordinary binding, particularly on the laird's part, she at that time
despised, if not abhorred him, in her heart.*

The good parson* again blessed her, and went away. She took leave of him with tears in her eyes, entreating him often to visit her in that heathen land of the Amorite, the Hittite, and the Girgashite:* to which he assented, on many solemn and qualifying conditions,—and then the comely bride retired to her chamber to pray.

It was customary, in those days, for the bride's-man and maiden, and a few select friends, to visit the new married couple after they had retired to rest, and drink a cup to their healths, their happiness, and a numerous posterity. But the laird delighted not in this: he wished to have his jewel to himself; and, slipping away quietly from his jovial party, he retired to his chamber to his beloved, and bolted the door. He found her engaged with the writings of the Evangelists, and terribly demure. The laird went up to caress her; but she turned away her head, and spoke of the follies of aged men, and something of the broad way that leadeth to destruction.* The laird did not thoroughly comprehend this allusion; but being considerably flustered by drinking, and disposed to take all in good part, he only remarked, as he took off his shoes and stockings, 'that whether the way was broad or narrow, it was time that they were in their bed.'

'Sure, Mr. Colwan, you won't go to bed to-night, at such an important period of your life, without first saying prayers for yourself and me.'

When she said this, the laird had his head down almost to the ground, loosing his shoe-buckle; but when he heard of *prayers*, on such a night, he raised his face suddenly up, which was all over as flushed and red as a rose, and answered,—

'Prayers, Mistress! Lord help your crazed head, is this a night for prayers?'

He had better have held his peace. There was such a torrent of profound divinity poured out upon him, that the laird became ashamed, both of himself and his new-made spouse, and wist not what to say: but the brandy helped him out.

'It strikes me, my dear, that religious devotion would be somewhat out of place to-night,' said he. 'Allowing that it is ever so beautiful, and ever so beneficial, were we to ride on the rigging of it at all times, would we not be constantly making a farce of it: It would be like reading the Bible and the jest-book, verse about, and would render the life of man a medley of absurdity and confusion.'

But against the cant of the bigot or the hypocrite, no reasoning can aught avail. If you would argue until the end of life, the infallible creature must alone be right. So it proved with the laird. One Scripture text followed another, not in the least connected, and one sentence of the profound Mr. Wringhim's sermons after another, proving the duty of family worship, till the laird lost patience, and, tossing himself into bed, said, carelessly, that he would leave that duty upon her shoulders for one night.

The meek mind of Lady Dalcastle was somewhat disarranged by this sudden evolution. She felt that she was left rather in an awkward situation. However, to show her unconscionable spouse that she was resolved to hold fast her integrity, she kneeled down and prayed in terms so potent, that she deemed she was sure of making an impression on him. She did so; for in a short time the laird began to utter a response so fervent, that she was utterly astounded, and fairly driven from the chain of her orisons. He began, in truth, to sound a nasal bugle of no ordinary calibre,—the notes being little inferior to those of a military trumpet. The lady tried to proceed, but every returning note from the bed burst on her ear with a louder twang, and a longer peal, till the concord of sweet sounds* became so truly pathetic, that the meek spirit of the dame was quite overcome; and after shedding a flood of tears, she arose from her knees, and retired to the chimney-corner with her Bible in her lap, there to spend the hours in holy meditation till such time as the inebriated trumpeter should awaken to a sense of propriety.

The laird did not awake in any reasonable time; for, he being overcome with fatigue and wassail, his sleep became sounder, and his Morphean* measures more intense. These varied a little in their structure; but the general run of the bars sounded something in this way,—'Hic-hoc-wheew!' It was most profoundly ludicrous; and could not have missed exciting risibility in any one, save a pious, a disappointed, and humbled bride.

The good dame wept bitterly. She could not for her life go and awaken the monster, and request him to make room for her: but she retired somewhere; for the laird, on awaking next morning, found that he was still lying alone. His sleep had been of the deepest and most genuine sort; and all the time that it lasted, he had never once thought of either wives, children, or sweethearts, save in the way of dreaming about them; but as his spirit began again by slow degrees to verge towards the boundaries of reason, it became lighter and more buoyant from the effects of deep repose, and his dreams partook of that buoyancy, yea, to a degree hardly expressible. He dreamed of the reel, the jig, the strathspey, and the corant; and the elasticity of his frame was such, that he was bounding over the heads of the maidens, and making his feet skimmer against the ceiling, enjoying, the while, the most extatic emotions. These grew too fervent for the shackles of the drowsy god to restrain. The nasal bugle ceased its prolonged sounds in one moment, and a sort of hectic laugh took its place. 'Keep it going,—play up, you devils!' cried the laird, without changing his position on the pillow. But this exertion to hold the fiddlers at their work, fairly awakened the delighted dreamer; and though he could not refrain from continuing his laugh, he at length, by tracing out a regular chain of facts, came to be sensible of his real situation. 'Rabina, where are you? What's become of you, my dear?' cried the laird. But there was no voice, nor any one that answered or regarded. He flung open the curtains, thinking to find her still on her knees, as he had seen her; but she was not there, either sleeping or waking. 'Rabina! Mrs. Colwan!' shouted he, as loud as he could call, and then added, in the same breath, 'God save the king,—I have lost my wife!'

He sprung up and opened the casement: the day-light was beginning to streak the east, for it was spring, and the nights were short, and the mornings very long. The laird half dressed himself in an instant, and strode through every room in the house, opening the windows as he went, and scrutinizing every bed and every corner. He came into the hall where the wedding festival had held;* and, as he opened the various window-boards, loving couples flew off like hares surprised too late in the morning among the early braird. 'Hoo-boo! Fie, be frightened!' cried the laird. 'Fie, rin like fools, as if ye were caught in an ill turn!'—His bride was not among them; so he was obliged to betake himself to farther search. 'She will be praying in some corner, poor woman,' said he to himself. 'It is an unlucky thing this praying. But, for my part, I fear I have behaved very ill; and I must endeavour to make amends.'

The laird continued his search, and at length found his beloved in the same bed with her Glasgow cousin, who had acted as bride's-maid. 'You sly and malevolent imp,' said the laird; 'you have played me such a trick when I was fast asleep! I have not known a frolic so clever, and, at the same time, so severe. Come along, you baggage you!'

'Sir, I will let you know, that I detest your principles and your person alike,' said she. 'It shall never be said, Sir, that my person was at the controul of a heathenish man of Belial,—a dangler among the daughters of women,—a promiscuous dancer,*—and a player at unlawful games. Forego your rudeness, Sir, I say, and depart away from my presence and that of my kinswoman.'

'Come along, I say, my charming Rab. If you were the pink of all puritans, and the saint of all saints, you are my wife, and must do as I command you.'

'Sir, I will sooner lay down my life than be subjected to your godless will; therefore, I say, desist, and begone with you.'

But the laird regarded none of these testy sayings: he rolled her in a blanket, and bore her triumphantly away to his chamber, taking care to keep a fold or two of the blanket always rather near to her mouth, in case of any outrageous forthcoming of noise.

The next day at breakfast the bride was long in making her appearance. Her maid asked to see her; but George did not choose that any body should see her but himself: he paid her several visits, and always turned the key as he came out. At length breakfast was served; and during the time of refreshment the laird tried to break several jokes; but it was remarked, that they wanted their accustomed brilliancy, and that his nose was particularly red at the top.

Matters, without all doubt, had been very bad between the new-married couple; for in the course of the day the lady deserted her quarters, and returned to her father's house in Glasgow, after having been a night on the road; stage-coaches and steam-boats having then no existence in that quarter.* Though Baillie Orde had acquiesced in his wife's asseveration regarding the likeness of their only daughter to her father, he never loved or admired her greatly; therefore this behaviour nothing astounded him. He questioned her strictly as to the grievous offence committed against her; and could discover nothing that warranted a procedure so fraught with disagreeable consequences. So, after mature deliberation, the baillie addressed her as follows:—

'Ay, ay, Raby! An' sae I find that Dalcastle has actually refused to say prayers with you when you ordered him; an' has guidit you in a rude indelicate manner, outstepping the respect due to my daughter,—as my daughter. But wi' regard to what is due to his own wife, of that he's a better judge nor me. However, since he has behaved in that manner to *my daughter*, I shall be revenged on him for aince; for I shall return the obligation to ane nearer to him: that is, I shall take pennyworths of his wife,—an' let him lick at that.'

'What do you mean, Sir?' said the astonished damsel.

'I mean to be revenged on that villain Dalcastle,' said he, 'for what he has done to my daughter. Come hither, Mrs. Colwan, you shall pay for this.'

So saying, the baillie began to inflict corporal punishment on the runaway wife. His strokes were not indeed very deadly, but he made a mighty flourish in the infliction, pretending to be in a great rage only at the Laird of Dalcastle. 'Villain that he is!' exclaimed he, 'I shall teach him to behave in such a manner to a child of mine, be she as she may; since I cannot get at himself, I shall lounder her that is nearest to him in life. Take you that, and that, Mrs. Colwan, for your husband's impertinence!'

The poor afflicted woman wept and prayed, but the baillie would not abate aught of his severity. After fuming, and beating her with many stripes, far drawn, and lightly laid down, he took her up to her chamber, five stories high, locked her in, and there he fed her on bread and water, all to be revenged on the presumptuous Laird of Dalcastle; but ever and anon, as the baillie came down the stair from carrying his daughter's meal, he said to himself, 'I shall make the sight of the laird the blithest she ever saw in her life.'

Lady Dalcastle got plenty of time to read, and pray, and meditate; but she was at a great loss for one to dispute with about religious tenets; for she found, that without this advantage, about which there was a perfect rage at that time, her reading, and learning of Scripture texts, and sentences of intricate doctrine, availed her nought; so she was often driven to sit at her casement and look out for the approach of the heathenish Laird of Dalcastle.

That hero, after a considerable lapse of time, at length made his appearance. Matters were not hard to adjust; for his lady found that there was no refuge for her in her father's house; and so, after some sighs and tears, she accompanied her husband home. For all that had passed, things went on no better. She *would* convert the laird in spite of his teeth: The laird would not be converted. She *would* have the laird to say family prayers, both morning and evening: The laird would neither pray morning nor evening. He would not even sing psalms, and kneel beside her, while she performed the exercise; neither would he converse at all times, and in all places, about the sacred mysteries of religion, although his lady took occasion to contradict flatly every assertion that he made, in order that she might spiritualize him by drawing him into argument.

The laird kept his temper a long while, but at length his patience wore out; he cut her short in all her futile attempts at spiritualization, and mocked at her wire-drawn degrees of faith, hope, and repentance. He also dared to doubt of the great standard doctrine of absolute pre-destination,* which put the crown on the lady's christian resentment. She declared her helpmate to be a limb of Antichrist,* and one with whom no regenerated* person could associate. She therefore bespoke a separate establishment, and before the expiry of the first six months, the arrangements of the separation were amicably adjusted. The upper, or third story of the old mansion-house, was awarded to the lady for her residence. She had a separate door, a separate stair, a separate garden, and walks that in no instance intersected the laird's; so that one would have thought the separation complete. They had each their own parties, selected from their own sort of people; and though the laird never once chafed himself about the lady's companies, it was not long before she began to intermeddle about some of his.

'Who is that fat bouncing dame that visits the laird so often, and always by herself?' said she to her maid Martha one day.

'O dear, mem, how can I ken? We're banished frae our acquaint-ances here, as weel as frae the sweet gospel ordinances.'

'Find me out who that jolly dame is, Martha. You, who hold com-munion with the household of this ungodly man, can be at no loss to attain this information. I observe that she always casts her eye up toward our windows, both in coming and going; and I suspect that she seldom departs from the house empty-handed.'

That same evening Martha came with the information, that this august visitor was a Miss Logan, an old and intimate acquaintance of the laird's, and a very worthy respectable lady, of good connections, whose parents had lost their patrimony in the civil wars.*

'Ha! very well!' said the lady; 'very well, Martha! But, nevertheless, go thou and watch this respectable lady's motions and behaviour the next time she comes to visit the laird,—and the next after that. You will not, I see, lack opportunities.'

Martha's information turned out of that nature, that prayers were said in the uppermost story of Dalcastle-house against the Canaanitish woman,* every night and every morning; and great dis-content prevailed there, even to anathemas and tears. Letter after letter was dispatched to Glasgow; and at length, to the lady's great consolation, the Rev. Mr. Wringhim arrived safely and devoutly in her elevated sanctuary. Marvellous was the conversation between these gifted people. Wringhim had held in his doctrines that there were eight different kinds of FAITH, all perfectly distinct in their operations and effects. But the lady, in her secluded state, had discovered other five,—making twelve in all:* the adjusting of the existence or fallacy of these five faiths served for a most enlightened discussion of nearly seventeen hours; in the course of which the two got warm in their arguments, always in proportion as they receded from nature, utility, and common sense.* Wringhim at length got into unwonted fervour about some disputed point between one of these faiths and TRUST; when the lady, fearing that zeal was getting beyond its wonted barrier, broke in on his vehement asseverations with the following abrupt discomfiture:—'But, Sir, as long as I remember, what is to be done with this case of open and avowed iniquity?'

The minister was struck dumb. He leaned him back on his chair, stroked his beard, hemmed—considered, and hemmed again; and then said, in an altered and softened tone,—'Why, that is a secondary consideration; you mean the case between your husband and Miss Logan?'

'The same, Sir. I am scandalised at such intimacies going on under my nose. The sufferance of it is a great and crying evil.'

'Evil, madam, may be either operative, or passive. To them it is an evil, but to us none. We have no more to do with the sins of the wicked and unconverted here, than with those of an infidel Turk; for all earthly bonds and fellowships are absorbed and swallowed up in the holy community of the Reformed Church. However, if it is your wish, I shall take him to task, and reprimand and humble him in such a manner, that *he* shall be ashamed of his doings, and renounce such deeds for ever, out of mere self-respect, though all unsanctified the heart, as well as the deed, may be. To the wicked, all things are wicked; but to the just, all things are just and right.'*

'Ah, that is a sweet and comfortable saying, Mr. Wringhim! How delightful to think that a justified person can do no wrong! Who would not envy the liberty wherewith we are made free?* Go to my husband, that poor unfortunate, blindfolded person, and open his eyes to his degenerate and sinful state; for well are you fitted to the task.'

'Yea, I will go in unto him, and confound him. I will lay the strong holds of sin and Satan as flat before my face, as the dung that is spread out to fatten the land.'*

'Master, there's a gentleman at the fore-door wants a private word o' ye.'

'Tell him I'm engaged: I can't see any gentleman to-night. But I shall attend on him to-morrow as soon as he pleases.'

'He's coming straight in, Sir.——Stop a wee bit, Sir, my master is engaged. He cannot see you at present, Sir.'

'Stand aside, thou Moabite! my mission admits of no delay. I come to save him from the jaws of destruction!'

'An that be the case, Sir, it maks a wide difference; an', as the danger may threaten us a', I fancy I may as weel let ye gang by as fight wi' ye, sin' ye seem sae intent on't.——The man says he's comin' to save ye, an' canna stop, Sir.—Here he is.'

The laird was going to break out into a volley of wrath against Waters, his servant; but before he got a word pronounced, the Rev. Mr. Wringhim had stepped inside the room, and Waters had retired, shutting the door behind him.

No introduction could be more *mal-a-propos*: it is impossible; for at that very moment the laird and Arabella Logan were both sitting on one seat, and both looking on one book, when the door opened. 'What is it, Sir?' said the laird fiercely.

'A message of the greatest importance, Sir,' said the divine, striding unceremoniously up to the chimney,—turning his back to the fire, and his face to the culprits.—'I think you should know me, Sir?' continued he, looking displeasedly at the laird, with his face half turned round.

'I think I should,' returned the laird. 'You are a Mr. How's-tey-ca'-him, of Glasgow, who did me the worst turn ever I got done to me in my life. You gentry are always ready to do a man such a turn. Pray, Sir, did you ever do a good job for any one to counterbalance that? for, if you have not, you ought to be ——.'

'Hold, Sir, I say! None of your profanity before me. If I do evil to any one on such occasions, it is because he will have it so; therefore, the evil is not of my doing. I ask you, Sir,—before God and this witness, I ask you, have you kept solemnly and inviolate the vows which I laid upon you that day? Answer me?'

'Has the partner whom you bound me to, kept hers inviolate? Answer me that, Sir? None can better do so than you, Mr. How's-tey-ca'-you.'

'So, then, you confess your backslidings,* and avow the profligacy of your life. And this person here, is, I suppose, the partner of your iniquity,—she whose beauty hath caused you to err! Stand up, both of you, till I rebuke you, and show you what you are in the eyes of God and man.'

'In the first place, stand you still there, till I tell you what *you* are in the eyes of God and man: You are, Sir, a presumptuous, self-conceited pedagogue, a stirrer up of strife and commotion in church, in state, in families, and communities. You are one, Sir, whose righteousness consists in splitting the doctrines of Calvin into thousands of undistinguishable films, and in setting up a system of justifying-grace against all breaches of all laws, moral or divine. In short, Sir, you are a mildew,—a canker-worm* in the bosom of the Reformed Church, generating a disease of which she will never be purged, but by the shedding of blood. Go thou in peace, and do these abominations no more;* but humble thyself, lest a worse reproof come upon thee.'

Wringhim heard all this without flinching. He now and then twisted his mouth in disdain, treasuring up, mean time, his vengeance against the two aggressors; for he felt that he had them on the hip,* and resolved to pour out his vengeance and indignation upon them. Sorry am I, that the shackles of modern decorum restrain me from penning that famous rebuke; fragments of which have been attributed to every divine of old notoriety throughout Scotland. But I have it by heart; and a glorious morsel it is to put into the hands of certain incendiaries. The metaphors were so strong, and so appalling, that Miss Logan could only stand them a very short time: she was obliged to withdraw in confusion. The laird stood his ground with much ado, though his face was often crimsoned over with the hues of shame and anger. Several times he was on the point of turning the officious sycophant to the door; but good manners, and an inherent respect that he entertained for the clergy, as the immediate servants of the Supreme Being,* restrained him.

Wringhim, perceiving these symptoms of resentment, took them for marks of shame and contrition, and pushed his reproaches farther than ever divine ventured to do in a similar case. When he had finished, to prevent further discussion, he walked slowly and majestically out of the apartment, making his robes to swing behind him in a most magisterial manner; he being, without doubt, elated with his high conquest. He went to the upper story, and related to his metaphysical associate his wonderful success; how he had driven the dame from the house in tears and deep confusion, and left the backsliding laird in such a quandary of shame and repentance, that he could neither articulate a word, nor lift up his countenance. The dame thanked him most cordially, lauding his friendly zeal and powerful eloquence; and then the two again set keenly to the splitting of hairs, and making distinctions in religion where none existed.

They being both children of adoption,* and secured from falling into snares, or any way under the power of the wicked one, it was their custom, on each visit, to sit up a night in the same apartment, for the sake of sweet spiritual converse;* but that time, in the course of the night, they differed so materially on a small point, somewhere between justification and final election,* that the minister, in the heat of his zeal, sprung from his seat, paced the floor, and maintained his point with such ardour, that Martha was alarmed, and, thinking they were going to fight, and that the minister would be a hard match for her mistress, she put on some clothes, and twice left her bed and stood listening at the back of the door, ready to burst in should need require it. Should any one think this picture over-strained, I can assure him that it is taken from nature and from truth; but I will not likewise aver, that the theologist was neither crazed nor inebriated. If the listener's words were to be relied on, there was no love, no accommodating principle manifested between the two, but a fiery burning zeal, relating to points of such minor importance, that a true Christian would blush to hear them mentioned, and the infidel and profane make a handle of them to turn our religion to scorn.

Great was the dame's exultation at the triumph of her beloved pastor over her sinful neighbours in the lower parts of the house; and she boasted of it to Martha in high-sounding terms. But it was of short duration; for, in five weeks after that, Arabella Logan came to reside with the laird as his house-keeper, sitting at his table, and carrying the keys as mistress-substitute of the mansion. The lady's grief and indignation were now raised to a higher pitch than ever; and she set every agent to work, with whom she had any power, to effect a separation between these two suspected ones. Remonstrance was of no avail: George laughed at them who tried such a course, and retained his house-keeper, while the lady gave herself up to utter despair; for though she would not consort with her husband herself, she could not endure that any other should do so.

But, to countervail this grievous offence, our saintly and afflicted dame, in due time, was safely delivered of a fine boy, whom the laird acknowledged as his son and heir, and had him christened by his own name, and nursed in his own premises. He gave the nurse permission to take the boy to his mother's presence if ever she should desire to see him; but, strange as it may appear, she never once desired to see him from the day that he was born. The boy grew up, and was a healthful and happy child; and, in the course of another year, the lady presented him with a brother. A brother he certainly was, in the eye of the law, and it is more than probable that he was his brother in reality. But the laird thought otherwise; and, though he knew and acknowledged that he was obliged to support and provide for him, he refused to acknowledge him in other respects. He neither would countenance the banquet, nor take the baptismal vows on him in the child's name; of course, the poor boy had to live and remain an alien from the visible church* for a year and a day; at which time, Mr. Wringhim, out of pity and kindness, took the lady herself as sponsor for the boy, and baptized him by the name of Robert Wringhim,—that being the noted divine's own name.

George was brought up with his father, and educated partly at the parish-school, and partly at home, by a tutor hired for the purpose. He was a generous and kind-hearted youth; always ready to oblige, and hardly ever dissatisfied with any body. Robert was brought up with Mr. Wringhim, the laird paying a certain allowance for him yearly; and there the boy was early inured to all the sternness and severity of his pastor's arbitrary and unyielding creed. He was taught to pray twice every day, and seven times on Sabbath days; but he was only to pray for the elect, and, like David of old, doom all that were aliens from God to destruction.* He had never, in that family into which he had been as it were adopted, heard ought but evil spoken of his reputed father and brother; consequently he held them in utter abhorrence, and prayed against them every day, often 'that the old hoary sinner might be cut off in the full flush of his iniquity, and be carried quick into hell;* and that the young stem of the corrupt trunk might also be taken from a world that he disgraced, but that his sins might be pardoned, because he knew no better.'

Such were the tenets in which it would appear young Robert was bred. He was an acute boy, an excellent learner, had ardent and ungovernable passions, and withal, a sternness of demeanour from which other boys shrunk. He was the best grammarian, the best reader, writer, and accountant in the various classes that he attended, and was fond of writing essays on controverted points of theology, for which he got prizes, and great praise from his guardian and mother. George was much behind him in scholastic acquirements, but greatly his superior in personal prowess, form, feature, and all that constitutes gentility in deportment and appearance. The laird had often manifested to Miss Logan an earnest wish that the two young men should never meet, or at all events that they should be as little conversant as possible; and Miss Logan, who was as much attached to George as if he had been her own son, took every precaution, while he was a boy, that he should never meet with his brother; but as they advanced towards manhood, this became impracticable. The lady was removed from her apartments in her husband's house to Glasgow, to her great content; and all to prevent the young laird being tainted with the company of her and her second son; for the laird had felt the effects of the principles they professed, and dreaded them more than persecution, fire, and sword. During all the dreadful times that had overpast, though the laird had been a moderate man, he had still leaned to the side of the kingly prerogative, and had escaped confiscation and fines, without ever taking any active hand in suppressing the Covenanters.* But after experiencing a specimen of their tenets and manner in his wife, from a secret favourer of them and their doctrines, he grew alarmed at the prevalence of such stern and factious principles, now that there was no check nor restraint upon them; and from that time he began to set himself against them, joining with the cavalier party* of that day in all their proceedings.

It so happened, that, under the influence of the Earls of Seafield and Tullibardine,* he was returned for a Member of Parliament in the famous session that sat at Edinburgh, when the Duke of Queensberry was commissioner, and in which party spirit ran to such an extremity.* The young laird went with his father to the court, and remained in town all the time that the session lasted; and as all interested people of both factions flocked to the town at that period, so the important Mr. Wringhim was there among the rest, during the greater part of the time, blowing the coal of revolutionary principles* with all his might, in every society to which he could obtain admission. He was a great favourite with some of the west country gentlemen of that faction, by reason of his unbending impudence. No opposition could for a moment cause him either to blush, or retract one item that he had advanced. Therefore the Duke of Argyle* and his friends made such use of him as sportsmen often do of terriers, to start the game, and make a great yelping noise to let them know whither the chace is proceeding. They often did this out of sport, in order to teaze their opponent; for of all pesterers that ever fastened on man he was the most insufferable: knowing that his coat protected him from manual chastisement, he spared no acrimony, and delighted in the chagrin and anger of those with whom he contended. But he was sometimes likewise *of real use* to the heads of the presbyterian faction, and there-fore was admitted to their tables, and of course conceived himself a very great man.

His ward accompanied him; and very shortly after their arrival in Edinburgh, Robert, for the first time, met with the young laird his brother, in a match at tennis.* The prowess and agility of the young squire drew forth the loudest plaudits of approval from his associates, and his own exertion alone carried the game every time on the one side, and that so far as all along to count three for their one. The hero's name soon ran round the circle, and when his brother Robert, who was an onlooker, learned who it was that was gaining so much applause, he came and stood close beside him all the time that the game lasted, always now and then putting in a cutting remark by way of mockery.

George could not help perceiving him, not only on account of his impertinent remarks, but he, moreover, stood so near him that he several times impeded him in his rapid evolutions, and of course got himself shoved aside in no very ceremonious way. Instead of making him keep his distance, these rude shocks and pushes, accompanied sometimes with hasty curses, only made him cling the closer to this king of the game. He seemed determined to maintain his right to his place as an onlooker, as well as any of those engaged in the game, and if they had tried him at an argument, he would have carried his point: or perhaps he wished to quarrel with this spark of his jealousy and aversion, and draw the attention of the gay crowd to himself by these means; for, like his guardian, he knew no other pleasure but what consisted in opposition. George took him for some impertinent student of divinity, rather set upon a joke than any thing else. He perceived a lad with black clothes, and a methodistical face, whose countenance and eye he disliked exceedingly, several times in his way, and that was all the notice he took of him the first time they two met. But the next day, and every succeeding one, the same devilish-looking youth attended him as constantly as his shadow; was always in his way as with intention to impede him, and ever and anon his deep and malignant eye met those of his elder brother with a glance so fierce that it sometimes startled him.

The very next time that George was engaged at tennis, he had not struck the ball above twice till the same intrusive being was again in his way. The party played for considerable stakes that day, namely, a dinner and wine at the Black Bull tavern;* and George, as the hero and head of his party, was much interested in its honour; consequently, the sight of this moody and hellish-looking student affected him in no very pleasant manner. 'Pray, Sir, be so good as keep without the range of the ball,' said he.

'Is there any law or enactment that can compel me to do so?' said the other, biting his lip with scorn.

'If there is not, they are here that shall compel you,' returned George: 'so, friend, I rede you to be on your guard.'

As he said this, a flush of anger glowed in his handsome face, and flashed from his sparkling blue eye; but it was a stranger to both, and momently took its departure. The black-coated youth set up his cap before, brought his heavy brows over his deep dark eyes, put his hands in the pockets of his black plush breeches, and stepped a little farther into the semi-circle, immediately on his brother's right hand,* than he had ever ventured to do before. There he set himself firm on his legs, and, with a face as demure as death, seemed determined to keep his ground. He pretended to be following the ball with his eyes; but every moment they were glancing aside at George. One of the competitors chanced to say rashly, in the moment of exultation, 'That's a d——d fine blow, George!' On which the intruder took up the word, as characteristic of the competitors, and repeated it every stroke that was given, making such a ludicrous use of it, that several of the on-lookers were compelled to laugh immoderately; but the players were terribly nettled at it, as he really contrived, by dint of sliding in some canonical terms, to render the competitors and their game ridiculous.

But matters at length came to a crisis that put them beyond sport. George, in flying backward to gain the point at which the ball was going to light, came inadvertently so rudely in contact with this obstreperous interloper, that he not only overthrew him, but also got a grievous fall over his legs; and, as he arose, the other made a spurn at him with his foot, which, if it had hit to its aim, would undoubtedly have finished the course of the young laird of Dalcastle and Balgrennan. George, being irritated beyond measure, as may well be conceived, especially at the deadly stroke aimed at him, struck the assailant with his racket, rather slightly, but so that his mouth and nose gushed out blood; and, at the same time, he said, turning to his cronies,—'Does any of you know who the infernal puppy is?'

'Do you not know, Sir?' said one of the onlookers, a stranger: 'The gentleman is your own brother, Sir—Mr. Robert Wringhim Colwan!'

'No, not Colwan, Sir,' said Robert, putting his hands in his pockets, and setting himself still farther forward than before,—'not a Colwan, Sir; henceforth I disclaim the name.'

'No, certainly not,' repeated George: 'My mother's son you may be,—but *not a Colwan!* There you are right.' Then turning round to his informer, he said, 'Mercy be about us, Sir! is this the crazy minister's son from Glasgow?'

This question was put in the irritation of the moment; but it was too rude, and too far out of place, and no one deigned any answer to it. He felt the reproof, and felt it deeply; seeming anxious for some opportunity to make an acknowledgment, or some reparation.

In the meantime, young Wringhim was an object to all of the uttermost disgust. The blood flowing from his mouth and nose he took no pains to stem, neither did he so much as wipe it away; so that it spread over all his cheeks, and breast, even off at his toes. In that state did he take up his station in the middle of the competitors; and he did not now keep his place, but ran about, impeding every one who attempted to make at the ball. They loaded him with execrations, but it availed nothing; he seemed courting persecution and buffetings, keeping stedfastly to his old joke of damnation, and marring the game so completely, that, in spite of every effort on the part of the players, he forced them to stop their game, and give it up. He was such a rueful-looking object, covered with blood, that none of them had the heart to kick him, although it appeared the only thing he wanted; and as for George, he said not another word to him, either in anger or reproof.

When the game was fairly given up, and the party were washing their hands in the stone fount, some of them besought Robert Wringhim to wash himself; but he mocked at them, and said, he was much better as he was. George, at length, came forward abashedly toward him, and said,—'I have been greatly to blame, Robert, and am very sorry for what I have done. But, in the first instance, I erred through ignorance, not knowing you were my brother, which you certainly are; and, in the second, through a momentary irritation, for which I am ashamed. I pray you, therefore, to pardon me, and give me your hand.'

As he said this, he held out his hand toward his polluted brother; but the froward predestinarian took not his from his breeches pocket, but lifting his foot, he gave his brother's hand a kick. 'I'll give you what will suit such a hand better than mine,' said he, with a sneer. And then, turning lightly about, he added,—'Are there to be no more of these d——d fine blows, gentlemen? For shame, to give up such a profitable and edifying game!'

'This is too bad,' said George. 'But, since it is thus, I have the less to regret.' And, having made this general remark, he took no more note of the uncouth aggressor. But the persecution of the latter terminated not on the play-ground: he ranked up among them, bloody and disgusting as he was, and, keeping close by his brother's side, he marched along with the party all the way to the Black Bull. Before they got there, a great number of boys and idle people had surrounded them, hooting and incommoding them exceedingly, so that they were glad to get into the inn; and the unaccountable monster actually tried to get in alongst with them, to make one of the party at dinner. But the innkeeper and his men, getting the hint, by force prevented him from entering, although he attempted it again and again, both by telling lies and offering a bribe. Finding he could not prevail, he set to exciting the mob at the door to acts of violence; in which he had like to have succeeded. The landlord had no other shift, at last, but to send privately for two officers, and have him carried to the guard-house;* and the hilarity and joy of the party of young gentlemen, for the evening, was quite spoiled, by the inauspicious termination of their game.

The Rev. Robert Wringhim was now to send for, to release his beloved ward. The messenger found him at table, with a number of the leaders of the Whig faction, the Marquis of Annandale* being in the chair; and the prisoner's note being produced, Wringhim read it aloud, accompanying it with some explanatory remarks. The circumstances of the case being thus magnified and distorted, it excited the utmost abhorrence, both of the deed and the perpetrators, among the assembled faction. They declaimed against the act as an unnatural attempt on the character, and even the life, of an unfortunate brother, who had been expelled from his father's house. And, as party spirit was the order of the day, an attempt was made to lay the burden of it to that account. In short, the young culprit got some of the best blood of the land to enter as his securities, and was set at liberty. But when Wringhim perceived the plight that he was in, he took him, as he was, and presented him to his honourable patrons. This raised the indignation against the young laird and his associates a thousand fold, which actually roused the party to temporary madness. They were, perhaps, a little excited by the wine and spirits they had swallowed; else a casual quarrel between two young men, at tennis, could not have driven them to such extremes. But certain it is, that from one at first arising to address the party on the atrocity of the offence, both in a moral and political point of view, on a sudden there were six on their feet, at the same time, expatiating on it; and, in a very short time thereafter, every one in the room was up, talking with the utmost vociferation, all on the same subject, and all taking the same side in the debate.

In the midst of this confusion, some one or other issued from the house, which was at the back of the Canongate,* calling out,—'A plot, a plot! Treason, treason! Down with the bloody incendiaries at the Black Bull!'

The concourse of people that were assembled in Edinburgh at that time was prodigious; and as they were all actuated by political motives, they wanted only a ready-blown coal to set the mountain on fire.* The evening being fine, and the streets thronged, the cry ran from mouth to mouth through the whole city. More than that, the mob that had of late been gathered to the door of the Black Bull, had, by degrees, dispersed; but, they being young men, and idle vagrants, they had only spread themselves over the rest of the street to lounge in search of farther amusement: consequently, a word was sufficient to send them back to their late rendezvous, where they had previously witnessed something they did not much approve of.

The master of the tavern was astonished at seeing the mob again assembling; and that with such hurry and noise. But his inmates being all of the highest respectability, he judged himself sure of protection, or, at least, of indemnity. He had two large parties in his house at the time; the largest of which was of the Revolutionist faction. The other consisted of our young tennis-players, and their associates, who were all of the Jacobite order; or, at all events, leaned to the Episcopal side.* The largest party were in a front-room; and the attack of the mob fell first on their windows, though rather with fear and caution. Jingle went one pane; then a loud hurra; and that again was followed by a number of voices, endeavouring to restrain the indignation from venting itself in destroying the windows, and to turn it on the inmates. The Whigs, calling the landlord, inquired what the assault meant: he cunningly answered, that he suspected it was some of the youths of the Cavalier, or High-Church party, exciting the mob against them. The party consisted mostly of young gentlemen, by that time in a key to engage in any row; and, at all events, to suffer nothing from the other party, against whom their passions were mightily inflamed.

The landlord, therefore, had no sooner given them the spirit-rousing intelligence, than every one, as by instinct, swore his own natural oath, and grasped his own natural weapon. A few of those of the highest rank were armed with swords, which they boldly drew; those of the subordinate orders immediately flew to such weapons as the room, kitchen, and scullery afforded;—such as tongs, pokers, spits, racks, and shovels; and breathing vengeance on the prelatic party, the children of Antichrist and the heirs of d—n—t—n! the barterers of the liberties of their country, and betrayers of the most sacred trust,*—thus elevated, and thus armed, in the cause of right, justice, and liberty, our heroes rushed to the street, and attacked the mob with such violence, that they broke the mass in a moment, and dispersed their thousands like chaff before the wind. The other party of young Jacobites, who sat in a room farther from the front, and were those against whom the fury of the mob was meant to have been directed, knew nothing of this second uproar, till the noise of the sally made by the Whigs assailed their ears; being then informed that the mob had attacked the house on account of the treatment they themselves had given to a young gentleman of the adverse faction, and that another jovial party had issued from the house in their defence, and was now engaged in an unequal combat, the sparks likewise flew to the field to back their defenders with all their prowess, without troubling their heads about who they were.

A mob is like a spring-tide in an eastern storm, that retires only to return with more overwhelming fury. The crowd was taken by surprise, when such a strong and well-armed party issued from the house with so great fury, laying all prostrate that came in their way. Those who were next to the door, and were, of course, the first whom the imminent danger assailed, rushed backward among the crowd with their whole force. The Black Bull standing in a small square half way between the High Street and the Cowgate, and the entrance to it being by two closes, into these the pressure outward was simultaneous, and thousands were moved to an involuntary flight they knew not why.

But the High Street of Edinburgh, which they soon reached, is a dangerous place in which to make an open attack upon a mob. And it appears that the entrances to the tavern had been somewhere near to the Cross,* on the south side of the street; for the crowd fled with great expedition, both to the east and west, and the conquerors, separating themselves as chance directed, pursued impetuously, wounding and maiming as they flew. But, it so chanced, that before either of the wings had followed the flying squadrons of their enemies for the space of a hundred yards each way, the devil an enemy they had to pursue! the multitude had vanished like so many thousands of phantoms! What could our heroes do?—Why, they faced about to return toward their citadel, the Black Bull. But that feat was not so easily, nor so readily accomplished, as they divined. The unnumbered alleys on each side of the street had swallowed up the multitude in a few seconds; but from these they were busy reconnoitring; and, perceiving the deficiency in the number of their assailants, the rush from both sides of the street was as rapid, and as wonderful, as the disappearance of the crowd had been a few minutes before. Each close vomited out its levies, and these better armed with missiles than when they sought it for a temporary retreat. Woe then to our two columns of victorious Whigs! The mob actually closed around them as they would have swallowed them up; and, in the meanwhile, shower after shower of the most abominable weapons of offence* were rained in upon them. If the gentlemen were irritated before, this inflamed them still farther; but their danger was now so apparent, they could not shut their eyes on it, therefore, both parties, as if actuated by the same spirit, made a desperate effort to join, and the greater part effected it; but some were knocked down, and others were separated from their friends, and blithe to become silent members of the mob.

The battle now raged immediately in front of the closes leading to the Black Bull; the small body of Whig gentlemen was hardly bested, and it is likely would have been overcome and trampled down every man, had they not been then and there joined by the young Cavaliers; who, fresh to arms, broke from the wynd, opened the head of the passage, laid about them manfully, and thus kept up the spirits of the exasperated Whigs, who were the men in fact that wrought the most deray among the populace.

The town-guard* was now on the alert; and two companies of the Cameronian regiment, with the Hon. Captain Douglas,* rushed down from the Castle to the scene of action; but, for all the noise and hubbub that these caused in the street, the combat had become so close and inveterate, that numbers of both sides were taken prisoners fighting hand to hand, and could scarcely be separated when the guardsmen and soldiers had them by the necks.

Great was the alarm and confusion that night in Edinburgh; for every one concluded that it was a party scuffle, and, the two parties being so equal in power, the most serious consequences were anticipated. The agitation was so prevailing, that every party in the town, great and small, was broken up; and the lord-commissioner thought proper to go to the council-chamber himself, even at that late hour, accompanied by the sheriffs of Edinburgh and Linlithgow,* with sundry noblemen besides, in order to learn something of the origin of the affray.

For a long time the court was completely puzzled. Every gentleman brought in exclaimed against the treatment he had received, in most bitter terms, blaming a mob set on him and his friends by the adverse party, and matters looked extremely ill, until at length they began to perceive that they were examining gentlemen of both parties, and that they had been doing so from the beginning, almost alternately, so equally had the prisoners been taken from both parties. Finally, it turned out, that a few gentlemen, two-thirds of whom were strenuous Whigs themselves, had joined in mauling the whole Whig population of Edinburgh. The investigation disclosed nothing the effect of which was not ludicrous; and the Duke of Queensberry, whose aim was at that time to conciliate the two factions, tried all that he could to turn the whole *fracas* into a joke—an unlucky frolic, where no ill was meant on either side, and which yet had been productive of a great deal.

The greater part of the people went home satisfied; but not so the Rev. Robert Wringhim. He did all that he could to inflame both judges and populace against the young Cavaliers, especially against the young Laird of Dalcastle, whom he represented as an incendiary, set on by an unnatural parent to slander his mother, and make away with a hapless and only brother; and, in truth, that declaimer against all human merit had that sort of powerful, homely, and bitter eloquence, which seldom missed affecting his hearers: the consequence at that time was, that he made the unfortunate affair between the two brothers appear in extremely bad colours, and the populace retired to their homes impressed with no very favourable opinion of either the Laird of Dalcastle or his son George, neither of whom were there present to speak for themselves.

As for Wringhim himself, he went home to his lodgings, filled with gall and with spite against the young laird, whom he was made to believe the aggressor, and that intentionally. But most of all was he filled with indignation against the father, whom he held in abhorrence at all times, and blamed solely for this unmannerly attack made on his favourite ward, namesake, and adopted son; and for the public imputation of a crime to his own reverence, in calling the lad *his* son, and thus charging him with a sin against which he was well known to have levelled all the arrows of church censure with unsparing might.

But, filled as his heart was with some portion of these bad feelings, to which all flesh is subject, he kept, nevertheless, the fear of the Lord always before his eyes so far as never to omit any of the external duties of religion, and farther than that, man hath no power to pry. He lodged with the family of a Mr. Miller, whose lady was originally from Glasgow, and had been a hearer, and, of course, a great admirer of Mr. Wringhim. In that family he made public worship every evening; and that night, in his petitions at a throne of grace, he prayed for so many vials of wrath* to be poured on the head of some particular sinner, that the hearers trembled, and stopped their ears. But that he might not proceed with so violent a measure, amounting to excommunication, without due scripture warrant, he began the exercise of the evening by singing the following verses,* which it is a pity should ever have been admitted into a Christian psalmody, being so adverse to all its mild and benevolent principles:—

> Set thou the wicked over him,
> *And upon his right hand*
> *Give thou his greatest enemy,*
> *Even Satan, leave to stand.*

And when by thee he shall be judged,
    Let him remembered be;
And let his prayer be turned to sin,
    When he shall call on thee.
Few be his days; and in his room
    His charge another take;
His children let be fatherless;
    His wife a widow make:
Let God his father's wickedness
    Still to remembrance call;
And never let his mother's sin
    Be blotted out at all.
As he in cursing pleasure took,
    So let it to him fall;
As he delighted not to bless,
    So bless him not at all.
As cursing he like clothes put on,
    Into his bowels so,
Like water, and into his bones
    Like oil, down let it go.

Young Wringhim only knew the full purport of this spiritual song; and went to his bed better satisfied than ever, that his father and brother were cast-aways, reprobates, aliens from the church and the true faith, and cursed in time and eternity.

The next day George and his companions met as usual,—all who were not seriously wounded of them. But as they strolled about the city, the rancorous eye and the finger of scorn was pointed against them. None of them was at first aware of the reason; but it threw a damp over their spirits and enjoyments, which they could not master. They went to take a forenoon game at their old play of tennis, not on a match, but by way of improving themselves; but they had not well taken their places till young Wringhim appeared in his old station, at his brother's right hand, with looks more demure and determined than ever. His lips were primmed so close that his mouth was hardly discernible, and his dark deep eye flashed gleams of holy indignation on the godless set, but particularly on his brother. His presence acted as a mildew on all social intercourse or enjoyment; the game was marred, and ended ere ever it was well begun. There were whisperings apart—the party separated; and, in order to shake off the blighting influence of this dogged persecutor, they entered sundry houses of their acquaintances, with an understanding that they were to meet on the Links for a game at cricket.*

They did so; and, stripping off part of their clothes, they began that violent and spirited game. They had not played five minutes, till Wringhim was stalking in the midst of them, and totally impeding the play. A cry arose from all corners of 'O, this will never do. Kick him out of the play-ground! Knock down the scoundrel; or bind him, and let him lie in peace.'

'By no means,' cried George: 'it is evident he wants nothing else. Pray do not humour him so much as to touch him with either foot or finger.' Then turning to a friend, he said in a whisper, 'Speak to him, Gordon; he surely will not refuse to let us have the ground to ourselves, if you request it of him.'

Gordon went up to him, and requested of him, civilly, but ardently, 'to retire to a certain distance, else none of them could or would be answerable, however sore he might be hurt.'

He turned disdainfully on his heel, uttered a kind of pulpit hem! and then added, 'I will take my chance of that; hurt me, any of you, at your peril.'

The young gentlemen smiled, through spite and disdain of the dogged animal. Gordon followed him up, and tried to remonstrate with him; but he let him know that 'it was his pleasure to be there at that time; and, unless he could demonstrate to him what superior right he and his party had to that ground, in preference to him, and to the exclusion of all others, he was determined to assert his right, and the rights of his fellow-citizens, by keeping possession of whatsoever part of that common field he chose.'

'You are no gentleman, Sir,' said Gordon.

'Are you one, Sir?' said the other.

'Yes, Sir, I will let you know that I am, by G—!'

'Then, thanks be to Him whose name you have profaned, I am none. If *one* of the party be a gentleman, *I do hope in God I am not!*'

It was now apparent to them all that he was courting obloquy and manual chastisement from their hands, if by any means he could provoke them to the deed; and, apprehensive that he had some sinister and deep-laid design in hunting after such a singular favour, they wisely restrained one another from inflicting the punishment that each of them yearned to bestow, personally, and which he so well deserved.

But the unpopularity of the Younger George Colwan could no
longer be concealed from his associates. It was manifested wherever
the populace were assembled; and his young and intimate friend,
Adam Gordon,* was obliged to warn him of the circumstance, that he
might not be surprised at the gentlemen of their acquaintance withdrawing themselves from his society, as they could not be seen with
him without being insulted. George thanked him; and it was agreed
between them, that the former should keep himself retired during the
day-time while he remained in Edinburgh, and that at night they
should always meet together, along with such of their companions as
were disengaged.

George found it every day more and more necessary to adhere to
this system of seclusion; for it was not alone the hisses of the boys and
populace that pursued him,—a fiend of more malignant aspect was
ever at his elbow, in the form of his brother. To whatever place of
amusement he betook himself, and however well he concealed his
intentions of going there from all flesh living, there was his brother
Wringhim also, and always within a few yards of him, generally about
the same distance, and ever and anon darting looks at him that chilled
his very soul. They were looks that cannot be described; but they were
felt piercing to the bosom's deepest core. They affected even the on-
lookers in a very particular manner, for all whose eyes caught a glimpse
of these hideous glances followed them to the object toward which
they were darted: the gentlemanly and mild demeanour of that object
generally calmed their startled apprehensions; for no one ever yet
noted the glances of the young man's eye in the black coat, at the face
of his brother, who did not at first manifest strong symptoms of
alarm.

George became utterly confounded; not only at the import of this
persecution, but how in the world it came to pass that this unaccountable being knew all his motions, and every intention of his heart, as
it were intuitively. On consulting his own previous feelings and
resolutions, he found that the circumstances of his going to such and
such a place were often the most casual incidents in nature—the
caprice of a moment had carried him there, and yet he had never sat
or stood many minutes till there was the self-same being, always in the
same position with regard to himself, as regularly as the shadow is
cast from the substance, or the ray of light from the opposing denser
medium.

For instance, he remembered one day of setting out with the intention of going to attend divine worship in the High Church,* and when within a short space of its door, he was overtaken by young Kilpatrick of Closeburn, who was bound to the Grey-Friars* to see his sweetheart, as he said; 'and if you will go with me, Colwan,' said he, 'I will let you see her too, and then you will be just as far forward as I am.'

George assented at once, and went; and after taking his seat, he leaned his head forward on the pew to repeat over to himself a short ejaculatory prayer, as had always been his custom on entering the house of God. When he had done, he lifted his eyes naturally toward that point on his right hand where the fierce apparition of his brother had been wont to meet his view: there he was, in the same habit, form, demeanour, and precise point of distance, as usual! George again laid down his head, and his mind was so astounded, that he had nearly fallen into a swoon. He tried shortly after to muster up courage to look at the speaker, at the congregation, and at Captain Kilpatrick's sweetheart in particular; but the fiendish glances of the young man in the black clothes were too appalling to be withstood,—his eye caught them whether he was looking that way or not: at length his courage was fairly mastered, and he was obliged to look down during the remainder of the service.

By night or by day it was the same. In the gallery of the Parliament House, in the boxes of the play-house, in the church, in the assembly, in the streets, suburbs, and the fields; and every day, and every hour, from the first rencounter of the two, the attendance became more and more constant, more inexplicable, and altogether more alarming and insufferable, until at last George was fairly driven from society, and forced to spend his days in his own and his father's lodgings with closed doors. Even there, he was constantly harassed with the idea, that the next time he lifted his eyes, he would to a certainty see that face, the most repulsive to all his feelings of aught the earth contained. The attendance of that brother was now become like the attendance of a demon on some devoted* being that had sold himself to destruction; his approaches as undiscerned, and his looks as fraught with hideous malignity. It was seldom that he saw him either following him in the streets, or entering any house or church after him; he only appeared in his place, George wist not how, or whence; and, having sped so ill in his first friendly approaches, he had never spoken to his equivocal attendant a second time.

It came at length into George's head, as he was pondering, by himself, on the circumstances of this extraordinary attendance, that perhaps his brother had relented, and, though of so sullen and unaccommodating a temper that he would not acknowledge it, or beg a reconciliation, it might be for that very purpose that he followed his steps night and day in that extraordinary manner. 'I cannot for my life see for what other purpose it can be,' thought he. 'He never offers to attempt my life; nor dares he, if he had the inclination; therefore, although his manner is peculiarly repulsive to me, I shall not have my mind burdened with the reflection, that my own mother's son yearned for a reconciliation with me, and was repulsed by my haughty and insolent behaviour. The next time he comes to my hand, I am resolved that I will accost him as one brother ought to address another, whatever it may cost me; and, if I am still flouted with disdain, then shall the blame rest with him.'

After this generous resolution, it was a good while before his gratuitous attendant appeared at his side again; and George began to think that his visits were discontinued. The hope was a relief that could not be calculated; but still George had a feeling that it was too supreme to last. His enemy had been too pertinacious to abandon his design, whatever it was. He, however, began to indulge in a little more liberty, and for several days he enjoyed it with impunity.

George was, from infancy, of a stirring active disposition, and could not endure confinement; and, having been of late much restrained in his youthful exercises by this singular persecutor, he grew uneasy under such restraint, and, one morning, chancing to awaken very early, he arose to make an excursion to the top of Arthur's Seat,* to breathe the breeze of the dawning, and see the sun arise out of the eastern ocean. The morning was calm and serene; and as he walked down the south back of the Canongate, toward the Palace, the haze was so close around him that he could not see the houses on the opposite side of the way. As he passed the lord-commissioner's house,* the guards were in attendance, who cautioned him not to go by the Palace, as all the gates would be shut and guarded for an hour to come, on which he went by the back of St. Anthony's gardens, and found his way into that little romantic glade adjoining to the Saint's chapel and well. He was still involved in a blue haze, like a dense smoke,* but yet in the midst of it the respiration was the most refreshing and delicious. The grass and the flowers were loaden with dew; and, on taking off his hat to wipe his forehead, he perceived that the black glossy fur of which his chaperon was wrought, was all covered with a tissue of the most delicate silver—a fairy web, composed of little spheres, so minute that no eye could discern any one of them; yet there they were shining in lovely millions. Afraid of defacing so beautiful and so delicate a garnish, he replaced his hat with the greatest caution, and went on his way light of heart.

As he approached the swire at the head of the dell,—that little delightful verge from which in one moment the eastern limits and shores of Lothian arise on the view,—as he approached it, I say, and a little space from the height, he beheld, to his astonishment, a bright halo in the cloud of haze, that rose in a semi-circle over his head like a pale rainbow. He was struck motionless at the view of the lovely vision; for it so chanced that he had never seen the same appearance before, though common at early morn. But he soon perceived the cause of the phenomenon, and that it proceeded from the rays of the sun from a pure unclouded morning sky striking upon this dense vapour which refracted them. But the better all the works of nature are understood, the more they will be ever admired. That was a scene that would have entranced the man of science with delight, but which the uninitiated and sordid man would have regarded less than the mole rearing up his hill in silence and in darkness.

George did admire this halo of glory, which still grew wider, and less defined, as he approached the surface of the cloud. But, to his utter amazement and supreme delight, he found, on reaching the top of Arthur's Seat, that this sublunary rainbow, this terrestrial glory, was spread in its most vivid hues beneath his feet. Still he could not perceive the body of the sun, although the light behind him was dazzling; but the cloud of haze lying dense in that deep dell that separates the hill from the rocks of Salisbury, and the dull shadow of the hill mingling with that cloud, made the dell a pit of darkness. On that shadowy cloud was the lovely rainbow formed, spreading itself on a horizontal plain, and having a slight and brilliant shade of all the colours of the heavenly bow, but all of them paler and less defined. But this terrestrial phenomenon of the early morn cannot be better delineated than by the name given of it by the shepherd boys, 'The little wee ghost of the rainbow.'*

Such was the description of the morning, and the wild shades of the hill, that George gave to his father and Mr. Adam Gordon that same day on which he had witnessed them; and it is necessary that the reader should comprehend something of their nature, to understand what follows.

He seated himself on the pinnacle of the rocky precipice, a little within the top of the hill to the westward, and, with a light and buoyant heart, viewed the beauties of the morning, and inhaled its salubrious breeze. 'Here,' thought he, 'I can converse with nature without disturbance, and without being intruded on by any appalling or obnoxious visitor.' The idea of his brother's dark and malevolent looks coming at that moment across his mind, he turned his eyes instinctively to the right, to the point where that unwelcome guest was wont to make his appearance. Gracious Heaven! What an apparition was there presented to his view! He saw, delineated in the cloud, the shoulders, arms, and features of a human being of the most dreadful aspect. The face was the face of his brother, but dilated to twenty times the natural size. Its dark eyes gleamed on him through the mist, while every furrow of its hideous brow frowned deep as the ravines on the brow of the hill. George started, and his hair stood up in bristles as he gazed on this horrible monster. He saw every feature, and every line of the face, distinctly, as it gazed on him with an intensity that was hardly brookable. Its eyes were fixed on him, in the same manner as those of some carnivorous animal fixed on its prey; and yet there was fear and trembling,* in these unearthly features, as plainly depicted as murderous malice. The giant apparition seemed sometimes to be cowering down as in terror, so that nothing but its brow and eyes were seen; still these never turned one moment from their object—again it rose imperceptibly up, and began to approach with great caution; and as it neared, the dimensions of its form lessened, still continuing, however, far above the natural size.

George conceived it to be a spirit. He could conceive it to be nothing else; and he took it for some horrid demon by which he was haunted, that had assumed the features of his brother in every lineament, but in taking on itself the human form, had miscalculated dreadfully on the size, and presented itself thus to him in a blown-up, dilated frame of embodied air,* exhaled from the caverns of death or the regions of devouring fire. He was farther confirmed in the belief that it was a malignant spirit, on perceiving that it approached him across the front of a precipice, where there was not footing for thing of mortal frame. Still, what with terror and astonishment, he continued rivetted to the spot, till it approached, as he deemed, to within two yards of him; and then, perceiving that it was setting itself to make a violent spring on him, he started to his feet and fled distractedly in the opposite direction, keeping his eye cast behind him lest he had been seized in that dangerous place. But the very first bolt that he made in his flight he came in contact with a *real* body of flesh and blood, and that with such violence that both went down among some scragged rocks, and George rolled over the other. The being called out 'Murder;' and, rising, fled precipitately. George then perceived that it was his brother; and, being confounded between the shadow and the substance, he knew not what he was doing or what he had done; and there being only one natural way of retreat from the brink of the rock, he likewise arose and pursued the affrighted culprit with all his speed towards the top of the hill. Wringhim was braying out 'Murder! murder!' at which George being disgusted, and his spirits all in a ferment from some hurried idea of intended harm, the moment he came up with the craven he seized him rudely by the shoulder, and clapped his hand on his mouth. 'Murder, you beast!' said he; 'what do you mean by roaring out murder in that way? Who the devil is murdering you, or offering to murder you?'

Wringhim forced his mouth from under his brother's hand, and roared with redoubled energy, 'Eh! Egh! murder! murder!' &c. George had felt resolute to put down this shocking alarm, lest some one might hear it and fly to the spot, or draw inferences widely different from the truth; and, perceiving the terror of this elect youth to be so great that expostulation was vain, he seized him by the mouth and nose with his left hand, so strenuously, that he sunk his fingers into his cheeks. But the poltroon still attempting to bray out, George gave him such a stunning blow with his fist on the left temple, that he crumbled, as it were, to the ground, but more from the effects of terror than those of the blow. His nose, however, again gushed out blood, a system of defence which seemed as natural to him as that resorted to by the race of stinkards. He then raised himself on his knees and hams, and raising up his ghastly face, while the blood streamed over both ears, he besought his life of his brother, in the most abject whining manner, gaping and blubbering most piteously.

'Tell me then, Sir,' said George, resolved to make the most of the wretch's terror—'tell me for what purpose it is that you thus haunt my steps? Tell me plainly, and instantly, else I will throw you from the verge of that precipice.'

'Oh, I will never do it again! I will never do it again! Spare my life, dear, good brother! Spare my life! Sure I never did you any hurt?'

'Swear to me, then, by the God that made you, that you will never henceforth follow after me to torment me with your hellish threatening looks; swear that you will never again come into my presence without being invited. Will you take an oath to this effect?'

'O yes! I will, I will!'

'But this is not all: you must tell me for what purpose you sought me out here this morning?'

'Oh, brother! for nothing but your good. I had nothing at heart but your unspeakable profit, and great and endless good.'

'So then, you indeed knew that I was here?'

'I was told so by a friend, but I did not believe him; a—a—at least I did not know it was true till I saw you.'

'Tell me this one thing, then, Robert, and all shall be forgotten and forgiven,—Who was that friend?'

'You do not know him.'

'How then does he know me?'

'I cannot tell.'

'Was he here present with you to-day?'

'Yes; he was not far distant. He came to this hill with me.'

'Where then is he now?'

'I cannot tell.'

'Then, wretch, confess that the devil was that friend who told you I was here, and who came here with you? None else could possibly know of my being here.'

'Ah! how little you know of him! Would you argue that there is neither man nor spirit endowed with so much foresight as to deduce natural conclusions from previous actions and incidents but the devil? Alas, brother! But why should I wonder at such abandoned notions and principles? It was fore-ordained that you should cherish them, and that they should be the ruin of your soul and body, before the world was framed. Be assured of this, however, that I had no aim in seeking you *but your good!*'

'Well, Robert, I will believe it. I am disposed to be hasty and passionate: it is a fault in my nature; but I never meant, or wished you evil; and God is my witness that I would as soon stretch out my hand to my own life, or my father's, as to yours.'——At these words, Wringhim uttered a hollow exulting laugh, put his hands in his pockets, and withdrew a space to his accustomed distance. George continued: 'And now, once for all, I request that we may exchange forgiveness, and that we may part and remain friends.'

'Would such a thing be expedient, think you? Or consistent with the glory of God? I doubt it.'

'I can think of nothing that would be more so. Is it not consistent with every precept of the Gospel? Come, brother, say that our reconciliation is complete.'

'O yes, certainly! I tell you, brother, according to the flesh: it is just as complete as the lark's is with the adder; no more so, nor ever can. Reconciled, forsooth! To what would I be reconciled?'

As he said this, he strode indignantly away. From the moment that he heard his life was safe, he assumed his former insolence and revengeful looks—and never were they more dreadful than on parting with his brother that morning on the top of the hill. 'Well, go thy ways,' said George; 'some would despise, but I pity thee. If thou art not a limb of Satan, I never saw one.'

The sun had now dispelled the vapours; and the morning being lovely beyond description, George sat himself down on the top of the hill, and pondered deeply on the unaccountable incident that had befallen to him that morning. He could in nowise comprehend it; but, taking it with other previous circumstances, he could not get quit of a conviction that he was haunted by some evil genius in the shape of his brother, as well as by that dark and mysterious wretch himself. In no other way could he account for the apparition he saw that morning on the face of the rock, nor for several sudden appearances of the same being, in places where there was no possibility of any foreknowledge that he himself was to be there, and as little that the same being, if he were flesh and blood like other men, could always start up in the same position with regard to him. He determined, therefore, on reaching home, to relate all that had happened, from beginning to end, to his father, asking his counsel and his assistance, although he knew full well that his father was not the fittest man in the world to solve such a problem. He was now involved in party politics, over head and ears; and, moreover, he could never hear the names of either of the Wringhims mentioned without getting into a quandary of disgust and anger; and all that he would deign to say of them was, to call them by all the opprobrious names he could invent.

It turned out as the young man from the first suggested: old Dalcastle would listen to nothing concerning them with any patience. George complained that his brother harassed him with his presence at all times, and in all places. Old Dal asked why he did not kick the dog out of his presence, whenever he felt him disagreeable? George said, he seemed to have some demon for a familiar. Dal answered, that he did not wonder a bit at that, for the young spark was the third in a direct line who had all been children of adultery; and it was well known that all such were born half deils themselves, and nothing was more likely than that they should hold intercourse with their fellows. In the same style did he sympathise with all his son's late sufferings and perplexities.

In Mr. Adam Gordon, however, George found a friend who entered into all his feelings, and had seen and knew every thing about the matter. He tried to convince him, that at all events there could be nothing supernatural in the circumstances; and that the vision he had seen on the rock, among the thick mist, was the shadow of his brother approaching behind him. George could not swallow this, for he had seen his own shadow on the cloud, and, instead of approaching to aught like his own figure, he perceived nothing but a halo of glory round a point of the cloud, that was whiter and purer than the rest. Gordon said, if he would go with him to a mountain of his father's, which he named, in Aberdeenshire, he would show him a giant spirit of the same dimensions, any morning at the rising of the sun, provided he shone on that spot. This statement excited George's curiosity exceedingly; and, being disgusted with some things about Edinburgh, and glad to get out of the way, he consented to go with Gordon to the Highlands for a space. The day was accordingly set for their departure, the old laird's assent obtained; and the two young sparks parted in a state of great impatience for their excursion.

One of them found out another engagement, however, the instant after this last was determined on. Young Wringhim went off the hill that morning, and home to his upright guardian again, without washing the blood from his face and neck; and there he told a most woful story indeed: How he had gone out to take a morning's walk on the hill, where he had encountered with his reprobate brother among the mist, who had knocked him down and very near murdered him; threatening dreadfully, and with horrid oaths, to throw him from the top of the cliff.

The wrath of the great divine was kindled beyond measure. He cursed the aggressor in the name of the Most High; and bound himself, by an oath, to cause that wicked one's transgressions return upon his own head sevenfold.* But before he engaged farther in the business of vengeance, he kneeled with his adopted son, and committed the whole cause unto the Lord, whom he addressed as one coming breathing burning coals of juniper, and casting his lightnings before him, to destroy and root out all who had moved hand or tongue against the children of the promise.* Thus did he arise confirmed, and go forth to certain conquest.

We cannot enter into the detail of the events that now occurred, without forestalling a part of the narrative of one who knew all the circumstances—was deeply interested in them, and whose relation is of higher value than any thing that can be retailed out of the stores of tradition and old registers; but, his narrative being different from these, it was judged expedient to give the account as thus publicly handed down to us. Suffice it, that, before evening, George was apprehended, and lodged in jail, on a criminal charge of an assault and battery, to the shedding of blood, with the intent of committing fratricide. Then was the old laird in great consternation, and blamed himself for treating the thing so lightly, which seemed to have been gone about, from the beginning, so systematically, and with an intent which the villains were now going to realize, namely, to get the young laird disposed of, and then his brother, in spite of the old gentleman's teeth, would be laird himself.

Old Dal now set his whole interest to work among the noblemen and lawyers of his party. His son's case looked exceedingly ill, owing to the former assault before witnesses, and the unbecoming expressions made use of by him on that occasion, as well as from the present assault, which George did not deny, and for which no moving cause or motive could be made to appear.

On his first declaration before the sheriff, matters looked no better: but then the sheriff was a Whig. It is well known how differently the people of the present day, in Scotland, view the cases of their own party-men, and those of opposite political principles.* But this day is nothing to that in such matters, although, God knows, they are still sometimes barefaced enough. It appeared, from all the witnesses in the first case, that the complainant was the first aggressor—that he refused to stand out of the way, though apprised of his danger; and when his brother came against him inadvertently, he had aimed a blow at him with his foot, which, if it had taken effect, would have killed him. But as to the story of the apparition in fair day-light—the flying from the face of it—the running foul of his brother—pursuing him, and knocking him down, why the judge smiled at the relation; and saying, 'It was a very extraordinary story,' he remanded George to prison, leaving the matter to the High Court of Justiciary.*

When the case came before that court, matters took a different turn. The constant and sullen attendance of the one brother upon the other excited suspicions; and these were in some manner, confirmed, when the guards at Queensberry-house deponed, that the prisoner went by them on his way to the hill that morning, about twenty minutes before the complainant, and when the latter passed, he asked if such a young man had passed before him, describing the prisoner's appearance to them; and that, on being answered in the affirmative, he mended his pace and fell a-running.

The Lord Justice, on hearing this, asked the prisoner if he had any suspicions that his brother had a design on his life.

He answered, that all along, from the time of their first unfortunate meeting, his brother had dogged his steps so constantly, and so unaccountably, that he was convinced it was with some intent out of the ordinary course of events; and that if, as his lordship supposed, it was indeed his shadow that he had seen approaching him through the mist, then, from the cowering and cautious manner that it advanced, there was too little doubt that his brother's design had been to push him headlong from the cliff that morning.

A conversation then took place between the Judge and the Lord Advocate;* and, in the mean time, a bustle was seen in the hall; on which the doors were ordered to be guarded,—and, behold, the precious Mr. R. Wringhim was taken into custody, trying to make his escape out of court. Finally it turned out, that George was honourably acquitted, and young Wringhim bound over to keep the peace, with heavy penalties and securities.

That was a day of high exultation to George and his youthful associates, all of whom abhorred Wringhim; and the evening being spent in great glee, it was agreed between Mr. Adam Gordon and George, that their visit to the Highlands, though thus long delayed, was not to be abandoned; and though they had, through the machinations of an incendiary, lost the season of delight, they would still find plenty of sport in deer-shooting. Accordingly, the day was set a second time for their departure; and, on the day preceding that, all the party were invited by George to dine with him once more at the sign of the Black Bull of Norway. Every one promised to attend, anticipating nothing but festivity and joy. Alas, what short-sighted improvident creatures we are, all of us; and how often does the evening cup of joy lead to sorrow in the morning!*

The day arrived—the party of young noblemen and gentlemen met, and were as happy and jovial as men could be. George was never seen so brilliant, or so full of spirits; and exulting to see so many gallant young chiefs and gentlemen about him, who all gloried in the same principles of loyalty, (perhaps this word should have been written *disloyalty,*) he made speeches, gave toasts, and sung songs, all leaning slily to the same side, until a very late hour. By that time he had pushed the bottle so long and so freely, that its fumes had taken possession of every brain to such a degree, that they held Dame Reason rather at the staff's end, overbearing all her counsels and expostulations; and it was imprudently proposed by a wild inebriated spark, and carried by a majority of voices, that the whole party should adjourn to a bagnio for the remainder of the night.

They did so; and it appears from what follows, that the house to which they retired, must have been somewhere on the opposite side of the street to the Black Bull Inn, a little farther to the eastward. They had not been an hour in that house, till some altercation chanced to arise between George Colwan and a Mr. Drummond, the younger son of a nobleman of distinction.* It was perfectly casual, and no one thenceforward, to this day, could ever tell what it was about, if it was not about the misunderstanding of some word, or term, that the one had uttered. However it was, some high words passed between them; these were followed by threats; and in less than two minutes from the commencement of the quarrel, Drummond left the house in apparent displeasure, hinting to the other that they two should settle that in a more convenient place.

The company looked at one another, for all was over before any of them knew such a thing was begun. 'What the devil is the matter?' cried one. 'What ails Drummond?' cried another. 'Who has he quarrelled with?' asked a third.

'Don't know.'—'Can't tell, on my life.'—'He has quarrelled with his wine, I suppose, and is going to send it a challenge.'

Such were the questions, and such the answers that passed in the jovial party, and the matter was no more thought of.

But in the course of a very short space, about the length of which the ideas of the company were the next day at great variance, a sharp rap came to the door: It was opened by a female; but there being a chain inside, she only saw one side of the person at the door. He appeared to be a young gentleman, in appearance like him who had lately left the house, and asked, in a low whispering voice, 'if young Dalcastle was still in the house?' The woman did not know,—'If he is,' added he, 'pray tell him to speak with me for a few minutes.' The woman delivered the message before all the party, among whom there were then sundry courteous ladies of notable distinction, and George, on receiving it, instantly rose from the side of one of them, and said, in the hearing of them all, 'I will bet a hundred merks that is Drummond.'—'Don't go to quarrel with him, George,' said one.—'Bring him in with you,' said another. George stepped out; the door was again bolted, the chain drawn across, and the inadvertent party, left within, thought no more of the circumstance till the next morning, that the report had spread over the city, that a young gentleman had been slain, on a little washing-green at the side of the North Loch,* and at the very bottom of the close where this thoughtless party had been assembled.

Several of them, on first hearing the report, hasted to the deadroom in the old Guard-house,* where the corpse had been deposited, and soon discovered the body to be that of their friend and late entertainer, George Colwan. Great were the consternation and grief of all concerned, and, in particular, of his old father and Miss Logan; for George had always been the sole hope and darling of both, and the news of the event paralysed them so as to render them incapable of all thought or exertion. The spirit of the old laird was broken by the blow, and he descended at once from a jolly, good-natured, and active man, to a mere driveller, weeping over the body of his son, kissing his wound, his lips, and his cold brow alternately; denouncing vengeance on his murderers, and lamenting that he himself had not met the cruel doom, so that the hope of his race might have been preserved. In short, finding that all further motive of action and object of concern or of love, here below, were for ever removed from him, he abandoned himself to despair, and threatened to go down to the grave with his son.

But although he made no attempt to discover the murderers, the arm of justice was not idle; and it being evident to all, that the crime must infallibly be brought home to young Drummond, some of his friends sought him out, and compelled him, sorely against his will, to retire into concealment till the issue of the proof that should be led was made known. At the same time, he denied all knowledge of the incident with a resolution that astonished his intimate friends and relations, who to a man suspected him guilty. His father was not in Scotland, for I think it was said to me that this young man was second son to a John, Duke of Melfort, who lived abroad with the royal family of the Stuarts;* but this young gentleman lived with the relations of his mother, one of whom, an uncle, was a Lord of Session:* these having thoroughly effected his concealment, went away, and listened to the evidence; and the examination of every new witness convinced them that their noble young relative was the slayer of his friend.

All the young gentlemen of the party were examined, save Drummond, who, when sent for, could not be found, which circumstance sorely confirmed the suspicions against him in the minds of judges and jurors, friends and enemies; and there is little doubt, that the care of his relations in concealing him, injured his character, and his cause. The young gentlemen, of whom the party was composed, varied considerably, with respect to the quarrel between him and the deceased. Some of them had neither heard nor noted it; others had, but not one of them could tell how it began. Some of them had heard the threat uttered by Drummond on leaving the house, and one only had noted him lay his hand on his sword. Not one of them could swear that it was Drummond who came to the door, and desired to speak with the deceased, but the general impression on the minds of them all, was to that effect; and one of the women swore that she heard the voice distinctly at the door, and every word that voice pronounced; and at the same time heard the deceased say, that it was Drummond's.

On the other hand, there were some evidences on Drummond's part, which Lord Craigie, his uncle, had taken care to collect. He produced the sword which his nephew had worn that night, on which there was neither blood nor blemish; and above all, he insisted on the evidence of a number of surgeons, who declared that both the wounds which the deceased had received, had been given behind. One of these was below the left arm, and a slight one; the other was quite through the body, and both evidently inflicted with the same weapon, a two-edged sword, of the same dimensions as that worn by Drummond.

Upon the whole, there was a division in the court, but a majority decided it. Drummond was pronounced guilty of the murder; outlawed for not appearing, and a high reward offered for his apprehension. It was with the greatest difficulty that he escaped on board of a small trading vessel, which landed him in Holland, and from thence, flying into Germany, he entered into the service of the Emperor Charles VI.* Many regretted that he was not taken, and made to suffer the penalty due for such a crime, and the melancholy incident became a pulpit theme over a great part of Scotland, being held up as a proper warning to youth to beware of such haunts of vice and depravity, the nurses of all that is precipitate, immoral, and base, among mankind.

After the funeral of this promising and excellent young man, his father never more held up his head. Miss Logan, with all her art, could not get him to attend to any worldly thing, or to make any settlement whatsoever of his affairs, save making her over a present of what disposable funds he had about him. As to his estates, when they were mentioned to him, he wished them all in the bottom of the sea, and himself along with them. But whenever she mentioned the circumstance of Thomas Drummond having been the murderer of his son, he shook his head, and once made the remark, that 'It was all a mistake, a gross and fatal error; but that God, who had permitted such a flagrant deed, would bring it to light* in his own time and way.' In a few weeks he followed his son to the grave, and the notorious Robert Wringhim took possession of his estates as the lawful son of the late laird, born in wedlock, and under his father's roof. The investiture was celebrated by prayer, singing of psalms, and religious disputation. The late guardian and adopted father, and the mother of the new laird, presided on the grand occasion, making a conspicuous figure in all the work of the day; and though the youth himself indulged rather more freely in the bottle, than he had ever been seen to do before, it was agreed by all present, that there had never been a festivity so sanctified within the great hall of Dalcastle. Then, after due thanks returned, they parted rejoicing in spirit; which thanks, by the by, consisted wholly in telling the Almighty what he was; and informing him, with very particular precision, what *they* were who addressed him; for Wringhim's whole system of popular declamation consisted it seems in this,—to denounce all men and women to destruction, and then hold out hopes to his adherents that they were the chosen few, included in the promises, and who could never fall away. It would appear that this pharisaical doctrine is a very delicious one, and the most grateful of all others to the worst characters.

But the ways of heaven are altogether inscrutable, and soar as far above and beyond the works and the comprehensions of man, as the sun, flaming in majesty, is above the tiny boy's evening rocket. It is the controller of Nature* alone, that can bring light out of darkness, and order out of confusion. Who is he that causeth the mole, from his secret path of darkness, to throw up the gem, the gold, and the precious ore? The same, that from the mouths of babes and sucklings can extract the perfection of praise, and who can make the most abject of his creatures instrumental in bringing the most hidden truths to light.*

Miss Logan had never lost the thought of her late master's prediction, that Heaven would bring to light the truth concerning the untimely death of his son. She perceived that some strange conviction, too horrible for expression, preyed on his mind from the moment that the fatal news reached him, to the last of his existence; and in his last ravings, he uttered some incoherent words about justification by faith alone, and absolute and eternal predestination having been the ruin of his house. These, to be sure, were the words of superannuation, and of the last and severest kind of it; but for all that, they sunk deep into Miss Logan's soul, and at last she began to think with herself, 'Is it possible the Wringhims, and the sophisticating wretch who is in conjunction with them, the mother of my late beautiful and amiable young master, can have effected his destruction? if so, I will spend my days, and my little patrimony, in endeavours to rake up and expose the unnatural deed.'

In all her outgoings and incomings, Mrs. Logan (as she was now styled) never lost sight of this one object. Every new disappointment only whetted her desire to fish up some particulars concerning it; for she thought so long, and so ardently upon it, that by degrees it became settled in her mind as a sealed truth. And as woman is always most jealous of her own sex in such matters, her suspicions were fixed on her greatest enemy, Mrs. Colwan, now the Lady Dowager of Dalcastle. All was wrapt in a chaos of confusion and darkness; but at last by dint of a thousand sly and secret inquiries, Mrs. Logan found out where

Lady Dalcastle had been, on the night that the murder happened, and likewise what company she had kept, as well as some of the comers and goers; and she had hopes of having discovered a cue,* which, if she could keep hold of the thread, would lead her through darkness to the light of truth.

Returning very late one evening from a convocation of family servants, which she had drawn together in order to fish something out of them, her maid having been in attendance on her all the evening, they found on going home, that the house had been broken, and a number of valuable articles stolen therefrom. Mrs. Logan had grown quite heartless before this stroke, having been altogether unsuccessful in her inquiries, and now she began to entertain some resolutions of giving up the fruitless search.

In a few days thereafter, she received intelligence that her clothes and plate were mostly recovered, and that she for one was bound over to prosecute the depredator, provided the articles turned out to be hers, as libelled in the indictment,* and as a king's evidence had given out. She was likewise summoned, or requested, I know not which, being ignorant of these matters, to go as far as the town of Peebles on Tweedside, in order to survey these articles on such a day, and make affidavit to their identity before the Sheriff. She went accordingly; but on entering the town by the North Gate, she was accosted by a poor girl in tattered apparel, who with great earnestness inquired if her name was not Mrs. Logan? On being answered in the affirmative, she said that the unfortunate prisoner in the tolbooth requested her, as she valued all that was dear to her in life, to go and see her before she appeared in court, at the hour of cause, as she (the prisoner) had something of the greatest moment to impart to her. Mrs. Logan's curiosity was excited, and she followed the girl straight to the tolbooth, who by the way said to her, that she would find in the prisoner a woman of a superior mind, who had gone through all the vicissitudes of life. 'She has been very unfortunate, and I fear very wicked,' added the poor thing, 'but she is my mother, and God knows, with all her faults and failings, she has never been unkind to me. You, madam, have it in your power to save her; but she has wronged you, and therefore if you will not do it for her sake, do it for mine, and the God of the fatherless will reward you.'

Mrs. Logan answered her with a cast of the head, and a hem! and only remarked, that 'the guilty must not always be suffered to escape, or what a world must we be doomed to live in!'

She was admitted to the prison, and found a tall emaciated figure, who appeared to have once possessed a sort of masculine beauty in no ordinary degree, but was now considerably advanced in years. She viewed Mrs. Logan with a stern, steady gaze, as if reading her features as a margin to her intellect; and when she addressed her it was not with that humility, and agonized fervor, which are natural for one in such circumstances to address to another, who has the power of her life and death in her hands.

'I am deeply indebted to you, for this timely visit, Mrs. Logan,' said she. 'It is not that I value life, or because I fear death, that I have sent for you so expressly. But the manner of the death that awaits me, has something peculiarly revolting in it to a female mind. Good God! when I think of being hung up, a spectacle to a gazing, gaping multitude, with numbers of which I have had intimacies and connections, that would render the moment of parting so hideous, that, believe me, it rends to flinders a soul born for another sphere than that in which it has moved, had not the vile selfishness of a lordly fiend ruined all my prospects, and all my hopes. Hear me then; for I do not ask your pity: I only ask of you to look to yourself, and behave with womanly prudence. If you deny this day, that these goods are yours, there is no other evidence whatever against my life, and it is safe for the present. For as for the word of the wretch who has betrayed me, it is of no avail; he has prevaricated so notoriously to save himself. If you deny them, you shall have them all again to the value of a mite, and more to the bargain. If you swear to the identity of them, the process will, one way and another, cost you the half of what they are worth.'

'And what security have I for that?' said Mrs. Logan.

'You have none but *my word*,' said the other proudly, 'and that never yet was violated. If you cannot take that, I know the worst you can do—But I had forgot—I have a poor helpless child without, waiting, and starving about the prison door—Surely it was of her that I wished to speak. This shameful death of mine will leave her in a deplorable state.'

'The girl seems to have candour and strong affections,' said Mrs. Logan; 'I grievously mistake if such a child would not be a thousand times better without such a guardian and director.'

'Then will you be so kind as come to the Grass Market,* and see me put down?' said the prisoner. 'I thought a woman would estimate a woman's and a mother's feelings, when such a dreadful throw was at

stake, at least in part. But you are callous, and have never known any
feelings but those of subordination to your old unnatural master. Alas,
I have no cause of offence! I have wronged you; and justice must take
its course. Will you forgive me before we part?'

Mrs. Logan hesitated, for her mind ran on something else: On
which the other subjoined, 'No, you will not forgive me, I see. But you
will pray to God to forgive me? I know you will *do that.*'

Mrs. Logan heard not this jeer, but looking at the prisoner with an
absent and stupid stare, she said, 'Did you know my late master?'

'Ay, that I did, and never for any good,' said she. 'I knew the old
and the young spark both, and was by when the latter was slain.'

This careless sentence affected Mrs. Logan in a most peculiar
manner. A shower of tears burst from her eyes ere it was done, and
when it was, she appeared like one bereaved of her mind. She first
turned one way and then another, as if looking for something she had
dropped. She seemed to think she had lost her eyes, instead of her
tears, and at length, as by instinct, she tottered close up to the prisoner's face, and looking wistfully and joyfully in it, said, with breathless earnestness, 'Pray, mistress, what is your name?'

'My name is Arabella Calvert,' said the other: 'Miss, mistress, or
widow, as you chuse, for I have been all the three, and that not once
nor twice only—Ay, and something beyond all these. But as for you,
you have never been any thing!'

'Ay, ay! and so you are Bell Calvert? Well, I thought so—I thought
so,' said Mrs. Logan; and helping herself to a seat, she came and sat
down close by the prisoner's knee. 'So you are indeed Bell Calvert, so
called once. Well, of all the world you are the woman whom I have
longed and travailed the most to see. But you were invisible; a being
to be heard of, not seen.'

'There have been days, madam,' returned she, 'when I *was* to be
seen, and when there were few to be seen like me. But since that time
there have indeed been days on which I was not to be seen. My crimes
have been great, but my sufferings have been greater. So great, that
neither you nor the world can ever either know or conceive them.
I hope they will be taken into account by the Most High. Mine have
been crimes of utter desperation. But whom am I speaking to? You
had better leave me to myself, mistress.'

'Leave you to yourself? That I will be loth to do, till you tell me
where you were that night my young master was murdered?'

'Where the devil would, I was! Will that suffice you? Ah, it was a vile action! A night to be remembered that was! Won't you be going? I want to trust my daughter with a commission.'

'No, Mrs. Calvert, you and I part not, till you have divulged that mystery to me.'

'You must accompany me to the other world, then, for you shall not have it in this.'

'If you refuse to answer me, I can have you before a tribunal, where you shall be sifted to the soul.'

'Such miserable inanity! What care I for your threatenings of a tribunal? I who must so soon stand before my last earthly one? What could the word of such a culprit avail? Or if it could, where is the judge that could enforce it?'

'Did you not say that there was some mode of accommodating matters on that score?'

'Yes, I prayed you to grant me my life, which is in your power. The saving of it would not have cost you a plack, yet you refused to do it. The taking of it will cost you a great deal, and yet to that purpose you adhere. I can have no parley with such a spirit. I would not have my life in a present from its motions, nor would I exchange courtesies with its possessor.'

'Indeed, Mrs. Calvert, since ever we met, I have been so busy thinking about who you might be, that I know not what you have been proposing. I believe, I meant to do what I could to save you. But once for all, tell me every thing that you know concerning that amiable young gentleman's death, and here is my hand there shall be nothing wanting that I can effect for you.'

'No, I despise all barter with such mean and selfish curiosity; and, as I believe *that* passion is stronger with you, than fear is with me, we part on equal terms. Do your worst; and my secret shall go to the gallows and the grave with me.'

Mrs. Logan was now greatly confounded, and after proffering in vain to concede every thing she could ask in exchange, for the particulars relating to the murder, she became the suppliant in her turn. But the unaccountable culprit, exulting in her advantage, laughed her to scorn; and finally, in a paroxysm of pride and impatience, called in the jailor and had her expelled, ordering him in her hearing not to grant her admittance a second time, on any pretence.

Mrs. Logan was now hard put to it, and again driven almost to despair. She might have succeeded in the attainment of that she thirsted for most in life so easily, had she known the character which she had to deal with—Had she known to have soothed her high and afflicted spirit: but that opportunity was past, and the hour of examination at hand. She once thought of going and claiming her articles, as she at first intended; but then, when she thought again of the Wringhims swaying it at Dalcastle, where she had been wont to hear them held in such contempt, if not abhorrence, and perhaps of holding it by the most diabolical means, she was withheld from marring the only chance that remained of having a glimpse into that mysterious affair.

Finally, she resolved not to answer to her name in the court, rather than to appear and assert a falsehood, which she might be called on to certify by oath. She did so; and heard the Sheriff give orders to the officers to make inquiry for Miss Logan from Edinburgh, at the various places of entertainment in town, and to expedite her arrival in court, as things of great value were in dependence. She also heard the man who had turned king's evidence* against the prisoner, examined for the second time, and sifted most cunningly. His answers gave any thing but satisfaction to the Sheriff, though Mrs. Logan believed them to be mainly truth. But there were a few questions and answers that struck her above all others.

'How long is it since Mrs. Calvert and you became acquainted?'

'About a year and a half.'

'State the precise time, if you please; the day, or night, according to your remembrance.'

'It was on the morning of the 28th of February, 1705.'

'What time of the morning?'

'Perhaps about one.'

'So early as that? At what place did you meet then?'

'It was at the foot of one of the north wynds of Edinburgh.'

'Was it by appointment that you met?'

'No, it was not.'

'For what purpose was it then?'

'For no purpose.'

'How is it that you chance to remember the day and hour so minutely, if you met that woman, whom you have accused, merely by chance, and for no manner of purpose, as you must have met others that night, perhaps to the amount of hundreds, in the same way?'

'I have good cause to remember it, my lord.'

'What was that cause?—No answer?—You don't choose to say what that cause was?'

'I am not at liberty to tell.'

The Sheriff then descended to other particulars, all of which tended to prove that the fellow was an accomplished villain, and that the principal share of the atrocities had been committed by him. Indeed the Sheriff hinted, that he suspected the only share Mrs. Calvert had in them, was in being too much in his company, and too true to him. The case was remitted to the Court of Justiciary;* but Mrs. Logan had heard enough to convince her that the culprits first met at the very spot, and the very hour, on which George Colwan was slain; and she had no doubt that they were incendiaries set on by his mother, to forward her own and her darling son's way to opulence. Mrs. Logan was wrong, as will appear in the sequel; but her antipathy to Mrs. Colwan made her watch the event with all care. She never quitted Peebles as long as Bell Calvert remained there, and when she was removed to Edinburgh, the other followed. When the trial came on, Mrs. Logan and her maid were again summoned as witnesses before the jury, and compelled by the prosecutor for the Crown to appear.

The maid was first called; and when she came into the witnesses' box, the anxious and hopeless looks of the prisoner were manifest to all: but the girl, whose name, she said, was Bessy Gillies, answered in so flippant and fearless a way, that the auditors were much amused. After a number of routine questions, the depute-advocate* asked her if she was at home on the morning of the fifth of September last, when her mistress's house was robbed?

'Was I at hame, say ye? Na, faith-ye, lad! An I had been at hame, there had been mair to dee. I wad hae raised sic a yelloch!'

'Where were you that morning?'

'Where was I, say you? I was in the house where my mistress was, sitting dozing an' half sleeping in the kitchen. I thought aye she would be setting out every minute, for twa hours.'

'And when you went home, what did you find?'

'What found we? Be my sooth, we found a broken lock, an' toom kists.'

'Relate some of the particulars, if you please.'

'O, sir, the thieves didna stand upon particulars: they were halesale dealers in a' our best wares.'

'I mean, what passed between your mistress and you on the occasion?'

'What passed, say ye? O, there wasna muckle: I was in a great passion, but she was dung doitrified a wee. When she gaed to put the key i' the door, up it flew to the fer wa'.—"Bess, ye jaud, what's the meaning o' this?" quo she. "Ye hae left the door open, ye tawpie!" quo she. "The ne'er o' that I did," quo I, "or may my shakel bane never turn another key." When we got the candle lightit, a' the house was in a hoad-road. "Bessy, my woman," quo she, "we are baith ruined and undone creatures." "The deil a bit," quo I; "that I deny positively. H'mh! to speak o' a lass o' my age being ruined and undone! I never had muckle except what was within a good jerkin, an' let the thief ruin me there wha can."'

'Do you remember ought else that your mistress said on the occasion? Did you hear her blame any person?'

'O, she made a great deal o' grumphing an' groaning about the *misfortune*, as she ca'd it, an' I think she said it was a part o' the ruin wrought by the Ringans, or some sic name,—"they'll hae't a'! they'll hae't a'!" cried she, wringing her hands; "they'll hae't a', an' hell wi't, an' they'll get them baith." "Aweel, that's aye some satisfaction," quo I.'

'Whom did she mean by the Ringans, do you know?'

'I fancy they are some creatures that she has dreamed about, for I think there canna be as ill folks living as she ca's them.'

'Did you never hear her say that the prisoner at the bar there, Mrs. Calvert, or Bell Calvert, was the robber of her house; or that she was one of the Ringans?'

'Never. Somebody tauld her lately, that ane Bell Calvert robbed her house, but she disna believe it. Neither do I.'

'What reasons have you for doubting it?'

'Because it was nae woman's fingers that broke up the bolts an' the locks that were torn open that night.'

'Very pertinent, Bessy. Come then within the bar, and look at these articles on the table. Did you ever see these silver spoons before?'

'I hae seen some very like them, and whaever has seen siller spoons, has done the same.'

'Can you swear you never saw them before?'

'Na, na, I wadna swear to ony siller spoons that ever war made, unless I had put a private mark on them wi' my ain hand, an' that's what I never did to ane.'

'See, they are all marked with a C.'

'Sae are a' the spoons in Argyle,* an' the half o' them in Edinburgh I think. A C is a very common letter, an' so are a' the names that begin wi't. Lay them by, lay them by, an' gie the poor woman her spoons again. They are marked wi' her ain name, an' I hae little doubt they are hers, an' that she has seen better days.'

'Ah, God bless her heart!' sighed the prisoner; and that blessing was echoed in the breathings of many a feeling breast.

'Did you ever see this gown before, think you?'

'I hae seen ane very like it.'

'Could you not swear that gown was your mistress's once?'

'No, unless I saw her hae't on, an' kend that she had paid for't. I am very scrupulous about an oath. *Like* is an ill mark.* Sae ill indeed, that I wad hardly swear to ony thing.'

'But you say that gown is *very like* one your mistress used to wear.'

'I never said sic a thing. It is like one I hae seen her hae out airing on the hay raip i' the back green. It is very like ane I hae seen Mrs. Butler in the Grass Market wearing too; I rather think it is the same. Bless you, sir, I wadna swear to my ain fore finger, if it had been as lang out o' my sight, an' brought in an' laid on that table.'

'Perhaps you are not aware, girl, that this scrupulousness of yours is likely to thwart the purposes of justice, and bereave your mistress of property to the amount of a thousand merks?' (*From the Judge.*)

'I canna help that, my lord: that's her lookout. For my part, I am resolved to keep a clear conscience, till I be married, at any rate.'

'Look over these things and see if there is any one article among them which you can fix on as the property of your mistress.'

'No ane o' them, sir, no ane o' them. An oath is an awfu' thing, especially when it is for life or death. Gie the poor woman her things again, an' let my mistress pick up the next she finds: that's my advice.'

When Mrs. Logan came into the box, the prisoner groaned, and laid down her head. But how she was astonished when she heard her deliver herself something to the following purport!—That whatever penalties she was doomed to abide, she was determined she would not bear witness against a woman's life, from a certain conviction that it could not be a woman who broke her house. 'I have no doubt that I may find some of my own things there,' added she, 'but if they were found in her possession, she has been made a tool, or the dupe, of an infernal set, who shall be nameless here. I believe she *did not* rob me, and for that reason I will have no hand in her condemnation.'

The Judge. 'This is the most singular perversion I have ever witnessed. Mrs. Logan, I entertain strong suspicions that the prisoner, or her agents, have made some agreement with you on this matter, to prevent the course of justice.'

'So far from that, my lord, I went into the jail at Peebles to this woman, whom I had never seen before, and proffered to withdraw my part in the prosecution, as well as my evidence, provided she would tell me a few simple facts; but she spurned at my offer, and had me turned insolently out of the prison, with orders to the jailor never to admit me again on any pretence.'

The prisoner's counsel, taking hold of this evidence, addressed the jury with great fluency; and finally, the prosecution was withdrawn, and the prisoner dismissed from the bar, with a severe reprimand for her past conduct, and an exhortation to keep better company.

It was not many days till a caddy came with a large parcel to Mrs. Logan's house, which parcel he delivered into her hands, accompanied with a sealed note, containing an inventory of the articles, and a request to know if the unfortunate Arabella Calvert would be admitted to converse with Mrs. Logan.

Never was there a woman so much overjoyed as Mrs. Logan was at this message. She returned compliments: Would be most happy to see her; and no article of the parcel should be looked at, or touched, till her arrival.—It was not long till she made her appearance, dressed in somewhat better style than she had yet seen her; delivered her over the greater part of the stolen property, besides many things that either never had belonged to Mrs. Logan, or that she thought proper to deny, in order that the other might retain them.

The tale that she told of her misfortunes was of the most distressing nature, and was enough to stir up all the tender, as well as abhorrent feelings in the bosom of humanity. She had suffered every deprivation in fame, fortune, and person. She had been imprisoned; she had been scourged, and branded as an impostor; and all on account of her resolute and unmoving fidelity and truth to *several* of the very worst of men, every one of whom had abandoned her to utter destitution and shame. But this story we cannot enter on at present, as it would perhaps mar the thread of our story, as much as it did the anxious anticipations of Mrs. Logan, who sat pining and longing for the relation that follows.

'Now I know, Mrs. Logan, that you are expecting a detail of the circumstances relating to the death of Mr. George Colwan; and in gratitude for your unbounded generosity, and disinterestedness, I will tell you all that I know, although, for causes that will appear obvious to you, I had determined never in life to divulge one circumstance of it. I can tell you, however, that you will be disappointed, for it was not the gentleman who was accused, found guilty, and would have suffered the utmost penalty of the law, had he not made his escape. *It was not he*, I say, who slew your young master, nor had he any hand in it.'

'I never thought he had. But, pray, how do you come to know this?'

'You shall hear. I had been abandoned in York, by an artful and consummate fiend; found guilty of being art and part concerned in the most heinous atrocities, and, in his place, suffered what I yet shudder to think of. I was banished the county—begged my way with my poor outcast child up to Edinburgh, and was there obliged, for the second time in my life, to betake myself to the most degrading of all means to support two wretched lives. I hired a dress, and betook me, shivering, to the High Street, too well aware that my form and appearance would soon draw me suitors enow at that throng and intemperate time of the parliament. On my very first stepping out to the street, a party of young gentlemen was passing. I heard by the noise they made, and the tenor of their speech, that they were more than mellow, and so I resolved to keep near them, in order, if possible, to make some of them my prey. But just as one of them began to eye me, I was rudely thrust into a narrow close by one of the guardsmen. I had heard to what house the party was bound, for the men were talking exceedingly loud, and making no secret of it: so I hasted down the close, and round below to the one where their rendezvous was to be; but I was too late, they were all housed and the door bolted. I resolved to wait, thinking they could not all stay long; but I was perishing with famine, and was like to fall down. The moon shone as bright as day, and I perceived, by a sign at the bottom of the close, that there was a small tavern of a certain description up two stairs there. I went up and called, telling the mistress of the house my plan. She approved of it mainly, and offered me her best apartment, provided I could get one of these noble mates to accompany me. She abused Lucky Sudds, as she called her, at the inn where the party was, envying her huge profits, no doubt, and giving me afterward something to drink, for which I really felt exceedingly grateful in my need. I stepped down stairs in order to be on the alert. The moment that I reached the ground, the door of Lucky Sudds' house opened and shut, and down came the Honourable Thomas Drummond, with hasty and impassioned strides, his sword rattling at his heel. I accosted him in a soft and soothing tone. He was taken with my address; for he instantly stood still and gazed intently at me, then at the place, and then at me again. I beckoned him to follow me, which he did without farther ceremony, and we soon found ourselves together in the best room of a house where every thing was wretched. He still looked about him, and at me; but all this while he had never spoken a word. At length, I asked if he would take any refreshment? "If you please," said he. I asked what he would have? but he only answered, "Whatever you choose, madam." If he was taken with my address, I was much more taken with his; for he was a complete gentleman, and a gentleman will ever act as one. At length, he began as follows:

'"I am utterly at a loss to account for this adventure, madam. It seems to me like enchantment, and I can hardly believe my senses. An English lady, I judge, and one, who from her manner and address should belong to the first class of society, in such a place as this, is indeed matter of wonder to me. At the foot of a close in Edinburgh! and at this time of the night! Surely it must have been no common reverse of fortune that reduced you to this?" I wept, or pretended to do so; on which he added, "Pray, madam, take heart. Tell me what has befallen you; and if I can do any thing for you, in restoring you to your country or your friends, you shall command my interest."

'I had great need of a friend then, and I thought now was the time to secure one. So I began and told him the moving tale I have told you. But I soon perceived that I had kept by the naked truth too unvarnishedly, and thereby quite overshot my mark. When he learned that he was sitting in a wretched corner of an irregular house, with a felon, who had so lately been scourged, and banished as a swindler and impostor, his modest nature took the alarm, and he was shocked, instead of being moved with pity. His eye fixed on some of the casual stripes on my arm, and from that moment he became restless and impatient to be gone. I tried some gentle arts to retain him, but in vain;

so, after paying both the landlady and me for pleasures he had neither tasted nor asked, he took his leave.

'I showed him down stairs; and just as he turned the corner of the next land, a man came rushing violently by him; exchanged looks with him, and came running up to me. He appeared in great agitation, and was quite out of breath; and, taking my hand in his, we ran up stairs together without speaking, and were instantly in the apartment I had left, where a stoup of wine still stood untasted. "Ah, this is fortunate!" said my new spark, and helped himself. In the mean while, as our apartment was a corner one, and looked both east and north, I ran to the easter casement to look after Drummond. Now, note me well: I saw him going eastward in his tartans and bonnet, and the gilded hilt of his claymore glittering in the moon; and, at the very same time, I saw two men, the one in black, and the other likewise in tartans, coming toward the steps from the opposite bank, by the foot of the loch; and I saw Drummond and they eying each other as they passed. I kept view of *him* till he vanished towards Leith Wynd,* and by that time the two strangers had come close up under our window. This is what I wish you to pay particular attention to. I had only lost sight of Drummond, (who had given me his name and address,) for the short space of time that we took in running up one pair of short stairs; and during that space he had halted a moment, for, when I got my eye on him again, he had not crossed the mouth of the next entry, nor proceeded above ten or twelve paces, and, *at the same time,* I saw the two men coming down the bank on the opposite side of the loch, at about three hundred paces distance. Both he and they were distinctly in my view, and never within speech of each other, until he vanished into one of the wynds leading toward the bottom of the High Street, at which precise time the two strangers came below my window; so that it was quite clear he neither could be one of them, nor have any communication with them.

'Yet, mark me again; for of all things I have ever seen, this was the most singular. When I looked down at the two strangers, *one of them was extremely like Drummond.* So like was he, that there was not one item in dress, form, feature, nor voice, by which I could distinguish the one from the other. I was certain it was not he, because I had seen the one going and the other approaching at the same time, and my impression at the moment was, that I looked upon some spirit, or demon, in his likeness. I felt a chillness creep all round my heart,

my knees tottered, and, withdrawing my head from the open casement that lay in the dark shade, I said to the man who was with me,
"Good God, what is this!"

'"What is it, my dear?" said he, as much alarmed as I was.

'"As I live, there stands an apparition!" said I.

'He was not so much afraid when he heard me say so, and peeping
cautiously out, he looked and listened a-while, and then drawing
back, he said in a whisper, "They are both living men, and one of
them is he I passed at the corner."

'"That he is not," said I, emphatically. "To that I will make
oath."

'He smiled and shook his head, and then added, "I never then saw
a man before, whom I could not know again, particularly if he was the
very last I had seen. But what matters it whether it be or not? As it is
no concern of ours, let us sit down and enjoy ourselves."

'"But it *does* matter a very great deal with me, sir," said I.—"Bless
me, my head is giddy—my breath quite gone, and I feel as if I were
surrounded with fiends. Who are you, sir?"

'"You shall know that ere we two part, my love," said he: "I cannot
conceive why the return of this young gentleman to the spot he so
lately left, should discompose you? I suppose he got a glance of you as
he passed, and has returned to look after you, and that is the whole
secret of the matter."

'"If you will be so civil as to walk out and join him then, it will
oblige me hugely," said I, "for I never in my life experienced such
boding apprehensions of evil company. I cannot conceive how you
should come up here without asking my permission? Will it please
you to begone, sir?"—I was within an ace of prevailing. He took out
his purse—I need not say more—I was bribed to let him remain. Ah,
had I kept by my frail resolution of dismissing him at that moment,
what a world of shame and misery had been evited! But that, though
uppermost still in my mind, has nothing ado here.

'When I peeped over again, the two men were disputing in a whisper, the one of them in violent agitation and terror, and the other
upbraiding him, and urging him on to some desperate act. At length
I heard the young man in the Highland garb say indignantly, "Hush,
recreant! It is God's work which you are commissioned to execute,
and it must be done. But if you positively decline it, I will do it myself,
and do you beware of the consequences."

' "Oh, I will, I will!" cried the other in black clothes, in a wretched beseeching tone. "You shall instruct me in this, as in all things else."

'I thought all this while I was closely concealed from them, and wondered not a little when he in tartans gave me a sly nod, as much as to say, "What do you think of this?" or, "Take note of what you see," or something to that effect, from which I perceived, that whatever he was about, he did not wish it to be kept a secret. For all that, I was impressed with a terror and anxiety that I could not overcome, but it only made me mark every event with the more intense curiosity. The Highlander, whom I still could not help regarding as the evil genius of Thomas Drummond, performed every action, as with the quickness of thought. He concealed the youth in black in a narrow entry, a little to the westward of my windows, and as he was leading him across the moonlight green by the shoulder, I perceived, for the first time, that both of them were armed with rapiers. He pushed him without resistance into the dark shaded close, made another signal to me, and hasted up the close to Lucky Sudds' door. The city and the morning were so still, that I heard every word that was uttered, on putting my head out a little. He knocked at the door sharply, and after waiting a considerable space, the bolt was drawn, and the door, as I conceived, edged up as far as the massy chain would let it. "Is young Dalcastle still in the house?" said he sharply.

'I did not hear the answer, but I heard him say, shortly after, "If he is, pray tell him to speak with me for a few minutes." He then withdrew from the door, and came slowly down the close, in a lingering manner, looking oft behind him. Dalcastle came out; advanced a few steps after him, and then stood still, as if hesitating whether or not he should call out a friend to accompany him; and that instant the door behind him was closed, chained, and the iron bolt drawn; on hearing of which, he followed his adversary without farther hesitation. As he passed below my window, I heard him say, "I beseech you, Tom, let us do nothing in this matter rashly;" but I could not hear the answer of the other, who had turned the corner.

'I roused up my drowsy companion, who was leaning on the bed, and we both looked together from the north window. We were in the shade, but the moon shone full on the two young gentlemen. Young Dalcastle was visibly the worse of liquor, and his back being turned toward us, he said something to the other which I could not make out, although he spoke a considerable time, and, from his tones and gestures, appeared to be reasoning. When he had done, the tall young man in the tartans drew his sword, and his face being straight to us, we heard him say distinctly, "No more words about it, George, if you please; but if you be a man, as I take you to be, draw your sword, and let us settle it here."

'Dalcastle drew his sword, without changing his attitude; but he spoke with more warmth, for we heard his words, "Think you that I fear you, Tom? Be assured, sir, I would not fear ten of the best of your name, at each other's backs: all that I want is to have friends with us to see fair play, for if you close with me, you are a dead man."

'The other stormed at these words. "You are a braggart, sir," cried he, "a wretch—a blot on the cheek of nature—a blight on the Christian world—a reprobate—I'll have your soul, sir—You must play at tennis, and put down elect brethren in another world to-morrow." As he said this, he brandished his rapier, exciting Dalcastle to offence. He gained his point: The latter, who had previously drawn, advanced in upon his vapouring and licentious antagonist, and a fierce combat ensued. My companion was delighted beyond measure, and I could not keep him from exclaiming, loud enough to have been heard, "that's grand! that's excellent!" For me, my heart quaked like an aspen. Young Dalcastle either had a decided advantage over his adversary, or else the other thought proper to let him have it; for he shifted, and wore, and flitted from Dalcastle's thrusts like a shadow, uttering ofttimes a sarcastic laugh, that seemed to provoke the other beyond all bearing. At one time, he would spring away to a great distance, then advance again on young Dalcastle with the swiftness of lightning. But that young hero always stood his ground, and repelled the attack: he never gave way, although they fought nearly twice round the bleaching green,* which you know is not a very small one. At length they fought close up to the mouth of the dark entry, where the fellow in black stood all this while concealed, and then the combatant in tartans closed with his antagonist, or pretended to do so; but the moment they began to grapple, he wheeled about, turning Colwan's back towards the entry, and then cried out, "Ah, hell has it! My friend, my friend!"

'That moment the fellow in black rushed from his cover with his drawn rapier, and gave the brave young Dalcastle two deadly wounds in the back, as quick as arm could thrust, both of which I thought pierced through his body. He fell, and rolling himself on his back, he perceived who it was that had slain him thus foully, and said, with a dying emphasis, which I never heard equalled, "Oh, dog of hell, is it you who has done this!"

'He articulated some more, which I could not hear for other sounds; for the moment that the man in black inflicted the deadly wound, my companion called out, "That's unfair, you rip! That's damnable! to strike a brave fellow behind! One at a time, you cowards! &c." to all which the unnatural fiend in the tartans answered with a loud exulting laugh; and then, taking the poor paralysed murderer by the bow of the arm, he hurried him into the dark entry once more, where I lost sight of them for ever.'

Before this time, Mrs. Logan had risen up; and when the narrator had finished, she was standing with her arms stretched upward at their full length, and her visage turned down, on which were pourtrayed the lines of the most absolute horror. 'The dark suspicions of my late benefactor have been just, and his last prediction is fulfilled,' cried she. 'The murderer of the accomplished George Colwan has been his own brother, set on, there is little doubt, by her who bare them both, and her directing angel, the self-justified bigot. Aye, and yonder they sit, enjoying the luxuries so dearly purchased, with perfect impunity! If the Almighty do not hurl them down, blasted with shame and confusion, there is no hope of retribution in this life. And, by his might, I will be the agent to accomplish it! Why did the man not pursue the foul murderers? Why did he not raise the alarm, and call the watch?'

'He? The wretch! He durst not move from the shelter he had obtained,—no, not for the soul of him. He was pursued for his life, at the moment when he first flew into my arms. But I did not know it; no, I did not *then* know him. May the curse of heaven, and the blight of hell, settle on the detestable wretch! He pursue for the sake of justice! No; his efforts have all been for evil, but never for good. But *I* raised the alarm; miserable and degraded as I was, I pursued and raised the watch myself. Have you not heard the name of Bell Calvert coupled with that hideous and mysterious affair?'

'Yes, I have. In secret often I have heard it. But how came it that you could never be found? How came it that you never appeared in defence of the Honourable Thomas Drummond; you, the only person who could have justified him?'

'I could not, for I then fell under the power and guidance of a wretch, who durst not for the soul of him be brought forward in the affair. And what was worse, his evidence would have overborne mine, for he would have sworn, that the man who called out and fought Colwan, was the same he met leaving my apartment, and there was an end of it. And moreover, it is well known, that this same man,—this wretch of whom I speak, never mistook one man for another in his life, which makes the mystery of the likeness between this incendiary and Drummond the more extraordinary.'

'If it was Drummond, after all that you have asserted, then are my surmises still wrong.'

'There is nothing of which I can be more certain, than that it was not Drummond. We have nothing on earth but our senses to depend upon:* if these deceive us, what are we to do. I own I cannot account for it; nor ever shall be able to account for it as long as I live.'

'Could you know the man in black, if you saw him again?'

'I think I could, if I saw him walk or run: his gait was very particular: He walked as if he had been flat-soled, and his legs made of steel, without any joints in his feet or ancles.'

'The very same! The very same! The very same! Pray will you take a few days' journey into the country with me, to look at such a man?'

'You have preserved my life, and for you I will do any thing. I will accompany you with pleasure: and I think I can say that I will know him, for his form left an impression on my heart not soon to be effaced. But of this I am sure, that my unworthy companion *will* recognize him, and that he will be able to swear to his identity every day as long as he lives.'

'Where is he? Where is he? O! Mrs. Calvert, where is he?'

'Where is he? He is the wretch whom you heard giving me up to the death; who, after experiencing every mark of affection that a poor ruined being could confer, and after committing a thousand atrocities of which she was ignorant, became an informer to save his diabolical life, and attempted to offer up mine as a sacrifice for all. We will go by ourselves first, and I will tell you if it is necessary to send any farther.'

The two dames, the very next morning, dressed themselves like country goodwives; and, hiring two stout ponies furnished with pillions, they took their journey westward, and the second evening after leaving Edinburgh they arrived at the village about two miles below Dalcastle, where they alighted. But Mrs. Logan, being anxious to have Mrs. Calvert's judgment, without either hint or preparation, took care not to mention that they were so near to the end of their journey. In conformity with this plan, she said, after they had sat a while, 'Heigh-ho, but I am weary! What suppose we should rest a day here before we proceed farther on our journey?'

Mrs. Calvert was leaning on the casement, and looking out when her companion addressed these words to her, and by far too much engaged to return any answer, for her eyes were riveted on two young men who approached from the farther end of the village; and at length, turning round her head, she said, with the most intense interest, 'Proceed farther on our journey, did you say? That we need not do; for, as I live, here comes the very man!'

Mrs. Logan ran to the window, and behold, there was indeed Robert Wringhim Colwan (now the Laird of Dalcastle) coming forward almost below their window, walking arm in arm with another young man; and as the two passed, the latter looked up and made a sly signal to the two dames, biting his lip, winking with his left eye, and nodding his head. Mrs. Calvert was astonished at this recognizance, the young man's former companion having made exactly such another signal on the night of the duel, by the light of the moon, and it struck her, moreover, that she had somewhere seen this young man's face before. She looked after him, and he winked over his shoulder to her; but she was prevented from returning his salute by her companion, who uttered a loud cry, between a groan and shriek, and fell down on the floor with a rumble like a wall that had suddenly been undermined. She had fainted quite away, and required all her companion's attention during the remainder of the evening, for she had scarcely ever well recovered out of one fit before she fell into another, and in the short intervals she raved like one distracted, or in a dream. After falling into a sound sleep by night, she recovered her equanimity, and the two began to converse seriously on what they had seen. Mrs. Calvert averred that the young man who passed next to the window, *was* the very man who stabbed George Colwan in the back, and she said she was willing to take her oath on it at any time when required, and was certain if the wretch Ridsley saw him, that he would make oath to the same purport, for that his walk was so peculiar, no one of common discernment could mistake it.

Mrs. Logan was in great agitation, and said, 'It is what I have suspected all along, and what I am sure my late master and benefactor was persuaded of, and the horror of such an idea cut short his days. That wretch, Mrs. Calvert, is the born brother of him he murdered, sons of the same mother they were, whether or not of the same father, the Lord only knows. But, O Mrs. Calvert, that is not the main thing that has discomposed me, and shaken my nerves to pieces at this time. Who do you think the young man was who walked in his company to night?'

'I cannot for my life recollect, but am convinced I have seen the same fine form and face before.'

'And did not he seem to know us, Mrs. Calvert? You who are able to recollect things as they happened, did he not seem to recollect us, and make signs to that effect?'

'He did, indeed, and apparently with great good humour.'

'O, Mrs. Calvert, hold me, else I shall fall into hysterics again! Who is he? Who is he? Tell me who you suppose he is, for I cannot say my own thought.'

'On my life, I cannot remember.'

'Did you note the appearance of the young gentleman you saw slain that night? Do you recollect aught of the appearance of my young master, George Colwan?'

Mrs. Calvert sat silent, and stared the other mildly in the face. Their looks encountered, and there was an unearthly amazement that gleamed from each, which, meeting together, caught real fire, and returned the flame to their heated imaginations, till the two associates became like two statues, with their hands spread, their eyes fixed, and their chops fallen down upon their bosoms. An old woman who kept the lodging-house, having been called in before when Mrs. Logan was faintish, chanced to enter at this crisis with some cordial; and, seeing the state of her lodgers, she caught the infection, and fell into the same rigid and statue-like appearance. No scene more striking was ever exhibited; and if Mrs. Calvert had not resumed strength of mind to speak, and break the spell, it is impossible to say how long it might have continued. 'It is he, I believe,' said she, uttering the words as it were inwardly. 'It can be none other but he. But, no, it is impossible! I saw him stabbed through and through the heart; I saw him roll backward on the green in his own blood, utter his last words, and groan away his soul. Yet, if it is not he, who can it be?'

'It *is* he!' cried Mrs. Logan, hysterically.

'Yes, yes, it *is* he!' cried the landlady, in unison.

'It is who?' said Mrs. Calvert; 'whom do you mean, mistress?'

'Oh, I don't know! I don't know! I was affrighted.'

'Hold your peace then till you recover your senses, and tell me, if you can, who that young gentleman is, who keeps company with the new Laird of Dalcastle?'

'Oh, it is he! it is he!' screamed Mrs. Logan, wringing her hands.

'Oh, it is he! it is he!' cried the landlady, wringing hers.

Mrs. Calvert turned the latter gently and civilly out of the apartment, observing that there seemed to be some infection in the air of the room, and she would be wise for herself to keep out of it.

The two dames had a restless and hideous night. Sleep came not to their relief; for their conversation was wholly about the dead, who seemed to be alive, and their minds were wandering and groping in a chaos of mystery. 'Did you attend to his corpse, and know that he positively died and was buried?' said Mrs. Calvert.

'O, yes, from the moment that his fair but mangled corpse was brought home, I attended it till that when it was screwed in the coffin. I washed the long stripes of blood from his lifeless form, on both sides of the body—I bathed the livid wound that passed through his generous and gentle heart. There was one through the flesh of his left side too, which had bled most outwardly of them all. I bathed them, and bandaged them up with wax and perfumed ointment, but still the blood oozed through all, so that when he was laid in the coffin he was like one newly murdered. My brave, my generous young master! he was always as a son to me, and no son was ever more kind or more respectful to a mother. But he was butchered—he was cut off from the earth ere he had well reached to manhood—most barbarously and unfairly slain. And how is it, how can it be, that we again see him here, walking arm in arm with his murderer?'

'The thing cannot be, Mrs. Logan. It is a phantasy of our disturbed imaginations, therefore let us compose ourselves till we investigate this matter farther.'

'It cannot be in nature, that is quite clear,' said Mrs. Logan; 'yet how it should be that I should *think* so—I who knew and nursed him from his infancy—there lies the paradox. As you said once before, we have nothing but our senses to depend on, and if you and I believe that we see a person, why, we do see him. Whose word, or whose reasoning can convince us against our own senses? We will disguise ourselves, as poor women selling a few country wares, and we will go up to the Hall, and see what is to see, and hear what we can hear, for this is a weighty business in which we are engaged, namely, to turn the vengeance of the law upon an unnatural monster; and we will farther learn, if we can, who this is that accompanies him.'

Mrs. Calvert acquiesced, and the two dames took their way to Dalcastle, with baskets well furnished with trifles. They did not take the common path from the village, but went about, and approached the mansion by a different way. But it seemed as if some overruling power ordered it, that they should miss no chance of attaining the information they wanted. For ere ever they came within half a mile of Dalcastle, they perceived the two youths coming, as to meet them, on the same path. The road leading from Dalcastle toward the north-east, as all the country knows, goes along a dark bank of brushwood called the Bogle-heuch.* It was by this track that the two women were going; and when they perceived the two gentlemen meeting them, they turned back, and the moment they were out of their sight, they concealed themselves in a thicket close by the road. They did this because Mrs. Logan was terrified for being discovered, and because they wished to reconnoitre without being seen. Mrs. Calvert now charged her, whatever she saw, or whatever she heard, to put on a resolution, and support it, for if she fainted there and was discovered, what was to become of her!

The two young men came on, in earnest and vehement conversation; but the subject they were on was a terrible one, and hardly fit to be repeated in the face of a Christian community. Wringhim was disputing the boundlessness of the true Christian's freedom, and expressing doubts, that, chosen as he knew he was from all eternity, still it might be possible for him to commit acts that would exclude him from the limits of the covenant. The other argued, with mighty fluency, that the thing was utterly impossible, and altogether inconsistent with eternal predestination. The arguments of the latter prevailed, and the laird was driven to sullen silence. But, to the women's utter surprise, as the conquering disputant passed, he made a signal of recognizance through the brambles to them, as formerly, and that he might expose his associate fully, and in his true colours, he led him backward and forward by the women more than twenty times, making him to confess both the crimes that he had done, and those he had in contemplation. At length he said to him, 'Assuredly I saw some strolling vagrant women on this walk, my dear friend: I wish we could find them, for there is little doubt that they are concealed here in your woods.'

'I wish we *could* find them,' answered Wringhim; 'we would have fine sport maltreating and abusing them.'

'That we should, that we should! Now tell me, Robert, if you found a malevolent woman, the latent enemy of your prosperity, lurking in these woods to betray you, what would you inflict on her?'

'I would tear her to pieces with my dogs, and feed them with her flesh. O, my dear friend, there is an old strumpet who lived with my unnatural father, whom I hold in such utter detestation, that I stand constantly in dread of her, and would sacrifice the half of my estate to shed her blood!'

'What will you give me if I will put her in your power, and give you a fair and genuine excuse for making away with her; one for which you shall answer at any bar, here or hereafter?'

'I should like to see the vile hag put down. She is in possession of the family plate, that is mine by right, as well as a thousand valuable relics, and great riches besides, all of which the old profligate gifted shamefully away. And it is said, besides all these, that she has sworn my destruction.'

'She has, she has. But I see not how she can accomplish that, seeing the deed was done so suddenly, and in the silence of the night?'

'It was said there were some on-lookers.—But where shall we find that disgraceful Miss Logan?'

'I will show you her by and by. But will you then consent to the other meritorious deed? Come, be a man, and throw away scruples.'

'If you can convince me that the promise is binding,* I will.'

'Then step this way, till I give you a piece of information.'

They walked a little way out of hearing, but went not out of sight; therefore, though the women were in a terrible quandary, they durst not stir, for they had some hopes that this extraordinary person was on a mission of the same sort with themselves, knew of them, and was going to make use of their testimony. Mrs. Logan was several times on the point of falling into a swoon, so much did the appearance of the young man impress her, until her associate covered her face that she might listen without embarrassment. But this latter dialogue aroused different feelings within them; namely, those arising from imminent personal danger. They saw his waggish associate point out the place of their concealment to Wringhim, who came toward them, out of curiosity to see what his friend meant by what he believed to be a joke, manifestly without crediting it in the least degree. When he came running away, the other called after him, 'If she is too hard for you, call to me.' As he said this, he hasted out of sight, in the contrary direction, apparently much delighted with the joke.

Wringhim came rushing through the thicket impetuously, to the very spot where Mrs. Logan lay squatted. She held the wrapping close about her head, but he tore it off and discovered her. 'The curse of God be on thee!' said he: 'What fiend has brought thee here, and for what purpose art thou come? But, whatever has brought thee, *I have thee!*' and with that he seized her by the throat. The two women, when they heard what jeopardy they were in from such a wretch, had squatted among the underwood at a small distance from each other, so that he had never observed Mrs. Calvert; but no sooner had he seized her benefactor, than, like a wild cat, she sprung out of the thicket, and had both her hands fixed at his throat, one of them twisted in his stock, in a twinkling. She brought him back-over among the brushwood, and the two, fixing on him like two harpies, mastered him with ease. Then indeed was he wofully beset. He deemed for a while that his friend was at his back, and turning his bloodshot eyes toward the path, he attempted to call; but there was no friend there, and the women cut short his cries by another twist of his stock. 'Now, gallant and rightful Laird of Dalcastle,' said Mrs. Logan, 'what hast thou to say for thyself? Lay thy account to dree the weird thou hast so well earned. Now shalt thou suffer due penance for murdering thy brave and only brother.'

'Thou liest, thou hag of the pit! I touched not my brother's life.'

'I saw thee do it with these eyes that now look thee in the face; ay, when his back was to thee too, and while he was hotly engaged with thy friend,' said Mrs. Calvert.

'I heard thee confess it again and again this same hour,' said Mrs. Logan.

'Ay, and so did I,' said her companion.—'Murder will out, though the Almighty should lend hearing to the ears of the willow, and speech to the seven tongues of the woodriff.'*

'You are liars, and witches!' said he, foaming with rage, 'and creatures fitted from the beginning for eternal destruction. I'll have your bones and your blood sacrificed on your cursed altars! O, Gil-Martin!

Gil-Martin!* where art thou now? Here, here is the proper food for blessed vengeance!—Hilloa!'

There was no friend, no Gil-Martin there to hear or assist him: he was in the two women's mercy, but they used it with moderation. They mocked, they tormented, and they threatened him; but, finally, after putting him in great terror, they bound his hands behind his back, and his feet fast with long straps of garters which they chanced to have in their baskets, to prevent him from pursuing them till they were out of his reach. As they left him, which they did in the middle of the path, Mrs. Calvert said, 'We could easily put an end to thy sinful life, but our hands shall be free of thy blood. Nevertheless thou art still in our power, and the vengeance of thy country shall overtake thee, thou mean and cowardly murderer, ay, and that more suddenly than thou art aware!'

The women posted to Edinburgh; and as they put themselves under the protection of an English merchant, who was journeying thither with twenty horses loaden, and armed servants, so they had scarcely any conversation on the road. When they arrived at Mrs. Logan's house, then they spoke of what they had seen and heard, and agreed that they had sufficient proof to condemn young Wringhim, who they thought richly deserved the severest doom of the law.

'I never in my life saw any human being,' said Mrs. Calvert, 'whom I thought so like a fiend. If a demon could inherit flesh and blood, that youth is precisely such a being as I could conceive that demon to be. The depth and the malignity of his eye is hideous. His breath is like the airs from a charnel house, and his flesh seems fading from his bones, as if the worm that never dies* were gnawing it away already.'

'He was always repulsive, and every way repulsive,' said the other; 'but he is now indeed altered greatly to the worse. While we were hand-fasting him, I felt his body to be feeble and emaciated; but yet I know him to be so puffed up with spiritual pride, that I believe he weens every one of his actions justified before God, and instead of having stings of conscience for these, he takes great merit to himself in having effected them. Still my thoughts are less about him than the extraordinary being who accompanies him. He does every thing with so much ease and indifference, so much velocity and effect, that all bespeak him an adept in wickedness. The likeness to my late hapless young master is so striking, that I can hardly believe it to be a chance model; and I think he imitates him in every thing, for some purpose, or some effect on his sinful associate. Do you know that he is so like in every lineament, look, and gesture, that, against the clearest light of reason, I cannot in my mind separate the one from the other, and have a certain indefinable impression on my mind, that they are one and the same being, or that the one was a prototype of the other.'

'If there is an earthly crime,' said Mrs. Calvert, 'for the due punishment of which the Almighty may be supposed to subvert the order of nature, it is fratricide. But tell me, dear friend, did you remark to what the subtile and hellish villain was endeavouring to prompt the assassin?'

'No, I could not comprehend it. My senses were altogether so bewildered, that I thought they had combined to deceive me, and I gave them no credit.'

'Then hear me: I am almost certain he was using every persuasion to induce him to make away with his mother; and I likewise conceive that I heard the incendiary give his consent!'

'This is dreadful. Let us speak and think no more about it, till we see the issue. In the meantime, let us do that which is our bounden duty,—go and divulge all that we know relating to this foul murder.'

Accordingly the two women went to Sir Thomas Wallace of Craigie, the Lord Justice Clerk, (who was, I think, either uncle or grandfather to young Drummond,* who was outlawed, and obliged to fly his country on account of Colwan's death,) and to that gentleman they related every circumstance of what they had seen and heard. He examined Calvert very minutely, and seemed deeply interested in her evidence—said he knew she was relating the truth, and in testimony of it, brought a letter of young Drummond's from his desk, wherein that young gentleman, after protesting his innocence in the most forcible terms, confessed having been with such a woman in such a house, after leaving the company of his friends; and that on going home, Sir Thomas's servant had let him in, in the dark, and from these circumstances he found it impossible to prove an *alibi*. He begged of his relative, if ever an opportunity offered, to do his endeavour to clear up that mystery, and remove the horrid stigma from his name in his country, and among his kin, of having stabbed a friend behind his back.

Lord Craigie, therefore, directed the two women to the proper authorities, and after hearing their evidence there, it was judged proper to apprehend the present Laird of Dalcastle, and bring him to his trial. But before that, they sent the prisoner in the tolbooth, he who had seen the whole transaction along with Mrs. Calvert, to take a view of Wringhim privately; and his discrimination being so well known as to be proverbial all over the land, they determined secretly to be ruled by his report. They accordingly sent him on a pretended mission of legality to Dalcastle, with orders to see and speak with the proprietor, without giving him a hint what was wanted. On his return, they examined him, and he told them that he found all things at the place in utter confusion and dismay; that the lady of the place was missing, and could not be found, dead or alive. On being asked if he had ever seen the proprietor before, he looked astounded, and unwilling to answer. But it came out that he had; and that he had once seen him kill a man on such a spot at such an hour.

Officers were then despatched, without delay, to apprehend the monster, and bring him to justice. On these going to the mansion, and inquiring for him, they were told he was at home; on which they stationed guards, and searched all the premises, but he was not to be found. It was in vain that they overturned beds, raised floors, and broke open closets: Robert Wringhim Colwan was lost once and for ever. His mother also was lost; and strong suspicions attached to some of the farmers and house servants, to whom she was obnoxious, relating to her disappearance. The Honourable Thomas Drummond became a distinguished officer in the Austrian service, and died in the memorable year for Scotland, 1715;* and this is all with which history, justiciary records, and tradition, furnish me relating to these matters.

––––––––––

I have now the pleasure of presenting my readers with an original document of a most singular nature, and preserved for their perusal in a still more singular manner. I offer no remarks on it, and make as few additions to it, leaving every one to judge for himself. We have heard much of the rage of fanaticism in former days, but nothing to this.

PRIVATE MEMOIRS
AND
CONFESSIONS OF A SINNER

WRITTEN BY HIMSELF

PRIVATE MEMOIRS

AND

CONFESSIONS OF A SINNER

MY life has been a life of trouble and turmoil; of change and vicissitude; of anger and exultation; of sorrow and of vengeance. My sorrows have all been for a slighted gospel, and my vengeance has been wreaked on its adversaries. Therefore, in the might of heaven I will sit down and write: I will let the wicked of this world know what I have done in the faith of the promises, and justification by grace, that they may read and tremble, and bless their gods of silver and of gold,* that the minister of heaven was removed from their sphere before their blood was mingled with their sacrifices.

I was born an outcast in the world, in which I was destined to act so conspicuous a part. My mother was a burning and a shining light,* in the community of Scottish worthies, and in the days of her virginity had suffered much in the persecution of the saints.* But it so pleased Heaven, that, as a trial of her faith, she was married to one of the wicked; a man all over spotted with the leprosy of sin. As well might they have conjoined fire and water together, in hopes that they would consort and amalgamate, as purity and corruption: She fled from his embraces the first night after their marriage, and from that time forth, his iniquities so galled her upright heart, that she quitted his society altogether, keeping her own apartments in the same house with him.

I was the second son of this unhappy marriage, and, long ere ever I was born, my father according to the flesh* disclaimed all relation or connection with me, and all interest in me, save what the law compelled him to take, which was to grant me a scanty maintenance; and had it not been for a faithful minister of the gospel, my mother's early instructor, I should have remained an outcast from the church visible. He took pity on me, admitting me not only into that, but into the bosom of his own household and ministry also, and to him am I indebted, under Heaven, for the high conceptions and glorious discernment between good and evil, right and wrong, which I attained even at an early age. It was he who directed my studies aright, both in the learning of the ancient fathers, and the doctrines of the reformed church, and designed me for his assistant and successor in the holy office. I missed no opportunity of perfecting myself particularly in all the minute points of theology in which my reverend father and mother took great delight; but at length I acquired so much skill, that I astonished my teachers, and made them gaze at one another.* I remember that it was the custom, in my patron's house, to ask the questions of the Single Catechism* round every Sabbath night. He asked the first, my mother the second, and so on, every one saying the question asked, and then asking the next. It fell to my mother to ask Effectual Calling* at me. I said the answer with propriety and emphasis. 'Now, madam,' added I, 'my question to you is, What is *In*effectual Calling?'

'Ineffectual Calling? There is no such thing, Robert,' said she.

'But there is, madam,' said I; 'and that answer proves how much you say these fundamental precepts by rote, and without any consideration. Ineffectual Calling is, *the outward call of the gospel* without any effect on the hearts of unregenerated and impenitent sinners. Have not all these the same calls, warnings, doctrines, and reproofs, that we have? and is not this Ineffectual Calling? Has not Ardinferry the same? Has not Patrick M'Lure the same? *Has not the Laird of Dalcastle and his reprobate heir* the same? And will any tell me, that *this is not In*effectual Calling?'

'What a wonderful boy he is!' said my mother.

'I'm feared he turn out to be a conceited gowk,' said old Barnet, the minister's man.

'No,' said my pastor, and *father*, (as I shall henceforth denominate him,) 'No, Barnet, he *is* a wonderful boy; and no marvel, for I have prayed for these talents to be bestowed on him from his infancy: and do you think that Heaven would refuse a prayer so disinterested? No, it is impossible. But my dread is, madam,' continued he, turning to my mother, 'that he is yet in the bond of iniquity.'*

'God forbid!' said my mother.

'I have struggled with the Almighty long and hard,'* continued he; 'but have as yet had no certain token of acceptance in his behalf. I have indeed fought a hard fight, but have been repulsed by him who hath seldom refused my request; although I cited his own words against him, and endeavoured to hold him at his promise, he hath so many turnings in the supremacy of his power, that I have been rejected. How dreadful is it to think of our darling being still without the pale of the covenant! But I have vowed a vow, and in that there is hope.'

My heart quaked with terror, when I thought of being still living in a state of reprobation, subjected to the awful issues of death, judgment, and eternal misery, by the slightest accident or casualty, and I set about the duty of prayer myself with the utmost earnestness. I prayed three times every day, and seven times on the Sabbath; but the more frequently and fervently that I prayed, I sinned still the more. About this time, and for a long period afterwards, amounting to several years, I lived in a hopeless and deplorable state of mind; for I said to myself, 'If my name is not written in the book of life from all eternity,* it is in vain for me to presume that either vows or prayers of mine, or those of all mankind combined, can ever procure its insertion now.' I had come under many vows, most solemnly taken, every one of which I had broken; and I saw with the intensity of juvenile grief, that there was no hope for me. I went on sinning every hour, and all the while most strenuously warring against sin, and repenting of every one transgression, as soon after the commission of it as I got leisure to think. But O what a wretched state this unregenerated state is, in which every effort after righteousness only aggravates our offences! I found It vanity to contend; for after communing with my heart, the conclusion was as follows: 'If I could repent me of all my sins, and shed tears of blood for them, still have I not a load of original transgression* pressing on me, that is enough to crush me to the lowest hell. I may be angry with my first parents for having sinned, but how I shall repent me of their sin, is beyond what I am able to comprehend.'

Still, in those days of depravity and corruption, I had some of those principles implanted in my mind, which were afterward to spring up with such amazing fertility among the heroes of the faith and the promises. In particular, I felt great indignation against all the wicked of this world, and often wished for the means of ridding it of such a noxious burden. I liked John Barnet, my reverend father's serving-man, extremely ill; but, from a supposition that he might be one of the justified, I refrained from doing him any injury. He gave always his word against me, and when we were by ourselves, in the barn or the fields, he rated me with such severity for my faults, that my heart could brook it no longer. He discovered some notorious lies that I had framed, and taxed me with them in such a manner that

I could in nowise get off. My cheek burnt with offence, rather than shame; and he, thinking he had got the mastery of me, exulted over me most unmercifully, telling me I was a selfish and conceited blackguard, who made great pretences towards religious devotion to cloak a disposition tainted with deceit, and that it would not much astonish him if I brought myself to the gallows.

I gathered some courage from his over severity, and answered him as follows: 'Who made thee a judge of the actions or dispositions of the Almighty's creatures—thou who art a worm, and no man in his sight?* How it befits thee to deal out judgments and anathemas! Hath he not made one vessel to honour, and another to dishonour,* as in the case with myself and thee? Hath he not builded his stories in the heavens, and laid the foundations thereof in the earth,* and how can a being like thee judge between good and evil, that are both subjected to the workings of his hand; or of the opposing principles in the soul of man, correcting, modifying, and refining one another?'

I said this with that strong display of fervor for which I was remarkable at my years, and expected old Barnet to be utterly confounded; but he only shook his head, and, with the most provoking grin, said, 'There he goes! sickan sublime and ridiculous sophistry I never heard come out of another mouth but ane. There needs nae aiths to be sworn afore the session* wha is your father, young goodman. I ne'er, for my part, saw a son sae like a dad, sin' my een first opened.' With that he went away, saying, with an ill-natured wince, 'You made to honour and me to dishonour! Dirty bow-kail thing that thou be'st!'

'I will have the old rascal on the hip for this, if I live,' thought I. So I went and asked my mother if John was a righteous man? She could not tell, but supposed he was, and therefore I got no encouragement from her. I went next to my reverend father, and inquired his opinion, expecting as little from that quarter. He knew the elect as it were by instinct, and could have told you of all those in his own, and some neighbouring parishes, who were born within the boundaries of the covenant of promise, and who were not.

'I keep a good deal in company with your servant, old Barnet, father,' said I.

'You do, boy; you do, I see,' said he.

'I wish I may not keep too much in his company,' said I, 'not knowing what kind of society I am in;—is John a good man, father?'

'Why, boy, he is but so, so. A morally good man John is, but very little of the leaven of true righteousness,* which is faith, within. I am afraid old Barnet, with all his stock of morality, will be a cast-away.'

My heart was greatly cheered by this remark; and I sighed very deeply, and hung my head to one side. The worthy father observed me, and inquired the cause? when I answered as follows: 'How dreadful the thought, that I have been going daily in company and fellowship with one, whose name is written on the red-letter side of the book of life;* whose body and soul have been, from all eternity, consigned over to everlasting destruction, and to whom the blood of the atonement can never, never reach! Father, this is an awful thing, and beyond my comprehension.'

'While we are in the world, we must mix with the inhabitants thereof,' said he; 'and the stains which adhere to us by reason of this admixture, which is unavoidable, shall all be washed away. It is our duty, however, to shun the society of wicked men as much as possible, lest we partake of their sins, and become sharers with them in punishment. John, however, is a morally good man, and may yet get a cast of grace.'

'I always thought him a good man till to day,' said I, 'when he threw out some reflections on your character, so horrible that I quake to think of the wickedness and malevolence of his heart. He was rating me very impertinently for some supposed fault, which had no being save in his own jealous brain, when I attempted to reason him out of his belief in the spirit of calm Christian argument. But how do you think he answered me? He did so, sir, by twisting his mouth at me, and remarking that such sublime and ridiculous sophistry never came out of another mouth but one, (meaning yours,) and that no oath before a kirk session was necessary to prove who was my dad, for that he had never seen a son so like a father as I was like mine.'

'He durst not for his soul's salvation, and for his daily bread, which he values much more, say such a word, boy; therefore take care what you assert,' said my reverend father.

'He said these very words, and will not deny them, sir,' said I.

My reverend father turned about in great wrath and indignation, and went away in search of John; but I kept out of the way, and listened at a back window; for John was dressing the plot of ground behind the house; and I hope it was no sin in me that I did rejoice in the dialogue which took place, it being the victory of righteousness over error.

'Well, John, this is a fine day for your delving work.'

'Ey, it's a tolerable day, sir.'

'Are you thankful in your heart, John, for such temporal mercies as these?'

'Aw doubt we're a' ower little thankfu', sir, baith for temporal an' speeritual mercies; but it isna aye the maist thankfu' heart that maks the greatest fraze wi' the tongue.'

'I hope there is nothing personal under that remark, John?'

'Gin the bannet fits ony body's head, they're unco welcome to it, sir, for me.'

'John, I do not approve of these innuendoes. You have an arch malicious manner of vending your aphorisms, which the men of the world are too apt to read the wrong way, for your dark hints are sure to have *one* very bad meaning.'

'Hout na, sir, it's only bad folks that think sae. They find ma bits o' gibes come hame to their hearts wi' a kind o' yerk, an' that gars them wince.'

'That saying is ten times worse than the other, John; it is a manifest insult: it is just telling me to my face, that you think me a bad man.'

'A body canna help his thoughts, sir.'

'No, but a man's thoughts are generally formed from observation. Now I should like to know, even from the mouth of a misbeliever, what part of my conduct warrants such a conclusion?'

'Nae particular pairt, sir; I draw a' my conclusions frae the haill o' a man's character, an' I'm no that aften far wrang.'

'Well, John, and what sort of general character do you suppose mine to be?'

'Yours is a Scripture character, sir, an' I'll prove it.'

'I hope so, John. Well, which of the Scripture characters do you think approximates nearest to my own?'

'Guess, sir, guess; I wish to lead a proof.'*

'Why, if it be an Old Testament character, I hope it is Melchizedek,* for at all events you cannot deny there is one point of resemblance: I, like him, am a preacher of righteousness. If it be a New Testament character, I suppose you mean the Apostle of the Gentiles,* of whom I am an unworthy representative.'

'Na, na, sir, better nor that still, an' fer closer is the resemblance. When ye bring me to the point, I maun speak. Ye are the just Pharisee, sir, that gaed up wi' the poor publican to pray in the Temple;* an' ye're acting the very same pairt at this time, an' saying i' your heart, "God, I thank thee that I am not as other men are, an' in nae way like this poor misbelieving unregenerate sinner, John Barnet." '

'I hope I may say so indeed.'

'There now! I tauld you how it was! But, d'ye hear, maister: Here stands the poor sinner, John Barnet, your beadle an' servant-man, wha wadna change chances wi' you in the neist world, nor consciences in this, for ten times a' that you possess,—your justification by faith an' awthegither.'

'You are extremely audacious and impertinent, John; but the language of reprobation cannot affect me: I came only to ask you one question, which I desire you to answer candidly. Did you ever say to any one that I was the boy Robert's natural father?'

'Hout na, sir! Ha—ha—ha! Aih, fie na, sir! I durstna say that for my life. I doubt the black stool, an' the sack gown, or maybe the juggs* wad hae been my portion had I said sic a thing as that. Hout, hout! Fie, fie! Unco-like doings thae for a Melchizedek or a Saint Paul!'

'John, you are a profane old man, and I desire that you will not presume to break your jests on me. Tell me, dare you say, or dare you think, that I am the natural father of that boy?'

'Ye canna hinder me to think whatever I like, sir, nor can I hinder mysel.'

'But did you ever *say* to any one, that he resembled me, and fathered himself well enough?'

'I hae said mony a time, that he resembled you, sir. Naebody can mistake that.'

'But, John, there are many natural reasons for such likenesses, besides that of consanguinity. They depend much on the thoughts and affections of the mother; and, it is probable, that the mother of this boy, being deserted by her worthless husband, having turned her thoughts on me, as likely to be her protector, may have caused this striking resemblance.'

'Ay, it may be, sir. I coudna say.'

'I have known a lady, John, who was delivered of a blackamoor child, merely from the circumstance of having got a start by the sudden entrance of her negro servant, and not being able to forget him for several hours.'*

'It may be, sir; but I ken this;—an I had been the laird, I wadna hae ta'en that story in.'

'So, then, John, you positively think, from a casual likeness, that this boy is my son?'

'Man's thoughts are vanity,* sir; they come unasked, an' gang away without a dismissal, an' he canna help them. I'm neither gaun to say that I *think* he's your son, nor that I think he's *no* your son: sae ye needna pose me nae mair about it.'

'Hear then my determination, John: If you do not promise to me, in faith and honour, that you never will say, or insinuate such a thing again in your life, as that that boy is my natural son, I will take the keys of the church from you, and dismiss you my service.'

John pulled out the keys, and dashed them on the gravel at the reverend minister's feet. 'There are the keys o' your kirk, sir! I hae never had muckle mense o' them sin' ye entered the door o't. I hae carried them this three an thretty year, but they hae aye been like to burn a hole i' my pouch sin' ever they were turned for your admittance. Tak them again, an' gie them to wha you will, and muckle gude may he get o' them. Auld John may dee a beggar in a hay barn, or at the back of a dike, but he sall aye be master o' his ain thoughts, an' gie them vent or no, as he likes.'

He left the manse that day, and I rejoiced in the riddance; for I disdained to be kept so much under, by one who was in the bond of iniquity, and of whom there seemed no hope, as he rejoiced in his frowardness, and refused to submit to that faithful teacher, his master.

It was about this time that my reverend father preached a sermon, one sentence of which affected me most disagreeably: It was to the purport, that every unrepented sin was productive of a new sin with each breath that a man drew; and every one of these new sins added to the catalogue in the same manner. I was utterly confounded at the multitude of my transgressions; for I was sensible that there were great numbers of sins of which I had never been able thoroughly to repent, and these momentary ones, by a moderate calculation, had, I saw, long ago, amounted to a hundred and fifty thousand in the minute, and I saw no end to the series of repentances to which I had subjected myself. A life-time was nothing to enable me to accomplish the sum, and then being, for any thing I was certain of, in my state of nature, and the grace of repentance withheld from me,—what was I to do, or what was to become of me? In the meantime, I went on sinning without measure; but I was still more troubled about the multitude than the magnitude of my transgressions, and the small minute ones puzzled me more than those that were more heinous, as the latter had generally some good effects in the way of punishing wicked men, froward boys, and deceitful women; and I rejoiced, even then in my early youth, at being used as a scourge in the hand of the Lord; another Jehu, a Cyrus, or a Nebuchadnezzar.*

On the whole, I remember that I got into great confusion relating to my sins and repentances, and knew neither where to begin nor how to proceed, and often had great fears that I was wholly without Christ, and that I would find God a consuming fire* to me. I could not help running into new sins continually; but then I was mercifully dealt with, for I was often made to repent of them most heartily, by reason of bodily chastisements received on these delinquencies being discovered. I was particularly prone to lying, and I cannot but admire the mercy that has freely forgiven me all these juvenile sins. Now that I know them all to be blotted out, and that I am an accepted person, I may the more freely confess them: the truth is, that one lie always paved the way for another, from hour to hour, from day to day, and from year to year; so that I found myself constantly involved in a labyrinth of deceit, from which it was impossible to extricate myself. If I knew a person to be a godly one, I could almost have kissed his feet; but against the carnal portion of mankind, I set my face continually. I esteemed the true ministers of the gospel; but the prelatic party, and the preachers up of good works* I abhorred, and to this hour I account them the worst and most heinous of all transgressors.

There was only one boy at Mr. Wilson's class who kept always the upper hand of me in every part of education. I strove against him from year to year, but it was all in vain; for he was a very wicked boy, and I was convinced he had dealings with the devil. Indeed it was believed all over the country that his mother was a witch; and I was at length convinced that it was no human ingenuity that beat me with so much ease in the Latin, after I had often sat up a whole night with my reverend father, studying my lesson in all its bearings. I often read as well and sometimes better than he; but the moment Mr. Wilson began to examine us, my opponent popped up above me. I determined, (as I knew him for a wicked person, and one of the devil's hand-fasted children,) to be revenged on him, and to humble him by some means or other. Accordingly I lost no opportunity of setting the Master against him, and succeeded several times in getting him severely beaten for faults of which he was innocent. I can hardly describe the joy that it gave to my heart to see a wicked creature suffering, for though he deserved it not for one thing, he richly deserved it for others. This may be by some people accounted a great sin in me; but I deny it, for I did it as a duty, and what a man or boy does for the right, will never be put into the sum of his transgressions.

This boy, whose name was M'Gill, was, at all his leisure hours, engaged in drawing profane pictures of beasts, men, women, houses, and trees, and, in short, of all things that his eye encountered. These profane things the Master often smiled at, and admired; therefore I began privately to try my hand likewise. I had scarcely tried above once to draw the figure of a man, ere I conceived that I had hit the very features of Mr. Wilson. They were so particular, that they could not be easily mistaken, and I was so tickled and pleased with the droll likeness that I had drawn, that I laughed immoderately at it. I tried no other figure but this; and I tried it in every situation in which a man and a schoolmaster could be placed. I often wrought for hours together at this likeness, nor was it long before I made myself so much master of the outline, that I could have drawn it in any situation whatever, almost off hand. I then took M'Gill's account book of algebra home with me, and at my leisure put down a number of gross caricatures of Mr. Wilson here and there, several of them in situations notoriously ludicrous. I waited the discovery of this treasure with great impatience; but the book, chancing to be one that M'Gill was not using, I saw it might be long enough before I enjoyed the consummation of my grand scheme: therefore, with all the ingenuity I was master of, I brought it before our dominie's eye. But never shall I forget the rage that gleamed in the tyrant's phiz! I was actually terrified to look at him, and trembled at his voice. M'Gill was called upon, and examined relating to the obnoxious figures. He denied flatly that any of them were of his doing. But the Master inquiring at him whose they were, he could not tell, but affirmed it to be some trick. Mr. Wilson at one time, began, as I thought, to hesitate; but the evidence was so strong against M'Gill, that at length his solemn asseverations of innocence only proved an aggravation of his crime.

There was not one in the school who had ever been known to draw a figure but himself, and on him fell the whole weight of the tyrant's vengeance. It was dreadful; and I was once in hopes that he would not leave life in the culprit. He, however, left the school for several months, refusing to return to be subjected to punishment for the faults of others, and I stood king of the class.

Matters were at last made up between M'Gill's parents and the schoolmaster, but by that time I had got the start of him, and never in my life did I exert myself so much as to keep the mastery. It was in vain; the powers of enchantment prevailed, and I was again turned down with the tear in my eye. I could think of no amends but one, and being driven to desperation, I put it in practice. I told a lie of him. I came boldly up to the master, and told him that M'Gill had in my hearing cursed him in a most shocking manner, and called him vile names. He called M'Gill, and charged him with the crime, and the proud young coxcomb was so stunned at the atrocity of the charge, that his face grew as red as crimson, and the words stuck in his throat as he feebly denied it. His guilt was manifest, and he was again flogged most nobly, and dismissed the school for ever in disgrace, as a most incorrigible vagabond.

This was a great victory gained, and I rejoiced and exulted exceedingly in it. It had, however, very nigh cost me my life; for not long thereafter, I encountered M'Gill in the fields, on which he came up and challenged me for a liar, daring me to fight him. I refused, and said that I looked on him as quite below my notice; but he would not quit me, and finally told me that he should either *lick me*, or I should *lick him*, as he had no other means of being revenged on such a scoundrel. I tried to intimidate him, but it would not do; and I believe I would have given all that I had in the world to be quit of him. He at length went so far as first to kick me, and then strike me on the face; and, being both older and stronger than he, I thought it scarcely became me to take such insults patiently. I was, nevertheless, well aware that the devilish powers of his mother would finally prevail; and either the dread of this, or the inward consciousness of having wronged him, certainly unnerved my arm, for I fought wretchedly, and was soon wholly overcome. I was so sore defeated, that I kneeled, and was going to beg his pardon; but another thought struck me momentarily, and I threw myself on my face, and inwardly begged aid from heaven; at the same time I felt as if assured that my prayer was heard, and would be answered. While I was in this humble attitude, the villain kicked me with his foot and cursed me; and I being newly encouraged, arose and encountered him once more. We had not fought long at this second turn, before I saw a man hastening toward us; on which I uttered a shout of joy, and laid on valiantly; but my very next look assured me, that the man was old John Barnet, whom I had likewise wronged all that was in my power, and between these two wicked persons I expected any thing but justice. My arm was again enfeebled, and that of my adversary prevailed. I was knocked down and mauled most grievously, and while the ruffian was kicking and cuffing me at his will and pleasure, up came old John Barnet, breathless with running and at one blow with his open hand, levelled my opponent with the earth. 'Tak ye that, maister!' says John, 'to learn ye better breeding. Hout awa, man! an ye will fight, fight fair. Gude sauf us, ir ye a gentleman's brood, that ye will kick an' cuff a lad when he's down?'

When I heard this kind and unexpected interference, I began once more to value myself on my courage, and springing up, I made at my adversary; but John, without saying a word, bit his lip, and seizing me by the neck, threw me down. M'Gill begged of him to stand and see fair play, and suffer us to finish the battle; for, added he, 'he is a liar, and a scoundrel, and deserves ten times more than I can give him.'

'I ken he's a' that ye say, an' mair, my man,' quoth John: 'But am I sure that ye're no as bad, an' waur? It says nae muckle for ony o' ye to be tearing like tikes at ane anither here.'

John cocked his cudgel and stood between us, threatening to knock the one dead, who first offered to lift his hand against the other; but, perceiving no disposition in any of us to separate, he drove me home before him like a bullock, keeping close guard behind me, lest M'Gill had followed. I felt greatly indebted to John, yet I complained of his interference to my mother, and the old officious sinner got no thanks for his pains.

As I am writing only from recollection, so I remember of nothing farther in these early days, in the least worthy of being recorded. That I was a great, a transcendent sinner, I confess. But still I had hopes of forgiveness, because I never sinned from principle, but accident; and then I always *tried* to repent of these sins by the slump, for individually it was impossible; and though not always successful in my endeavours, I could not help that; the grace of repentance being withheld from me, I regarded myself as in no degree accountable for the failure. Moreover, there were many of the most deadly sins into which I never fell, for I dreaded those mentioned in the Revelations as excluding sins,* so that I guarded against them continually. In particular, I brought myself to despise, if not to abhor, the beauty of women, looking on it as the greatest snare to which mankind are subjected, and though young men and maidens, and even old women, (my mother among the rest,) taxed me with being an unnatural wretch, I gloried in my acquisition; and to this day, am thankful for having escaped the most dangerous of all snares.

I kept myself also free of the sins of idolatry, and misbelief, both of a deadly nature; and, upon the whole, I think I had not then broken, that is, absolutely broken, above four out of the ten commandments; but for all that, I had more sense than to regard either my good works, or my evil deeds, as in the smallest degree influencing the eternal decrees of God concerning me, either with regard to my acceptance or reprobation. I depended entirely on the bounty of free grace, holding all the righteousness of man as filthy rags,* and believing in the momentous and magnificent truth, that the more heavily loaden with transgressions, the more welcome was the believer at the throne of grace. And I have reason to believe that it was this dependence and this belief that at last ensured my acceptance there.

I come now to the most important period of my existence,—the period that has modelled my character, and influenced every action of my life,—without which, this detail of my actions would have been as a tale that hath been told—a monotonous *farrago*—an uninteresting harangue—in short, a thing of nothing. Whereas, lo! it must now be a relation of great and terrible actions, done in the might, and by the commission of heaven. *Amen.*

Like the sinful king of Israel, I had been walking softly before the Lord for a season.* I had been humbled for my transgressions, and, as far as I recollect, sorry on account of their numbers and heinousness. My reverend father had been, moreover, examining me every day regarding the state of my soul, and my answers sometimes appeared to give him satisfaction, and sometimes not. As for my mother, she would harp on the subject of my faith for ever; yet, though I knew her to be a Christian, I confess that I always despised her motley instructions, nor had I any great regard for her person. If this was a crime in me, I never could help it. I confess it freely, and believe it was a judgment from heaven inflicted on her for some sin of former days, and that I had no power to have acted otherwise toward her than I did.

In this frame of mind was I, when my reverend father one morning arose from his seat, and, meeting me as I entered the room, he embraced me, and welcomed me into the community of the just upon earth. I was struck speechless, and could make no answer save by looks of surprise. My mother also came to me, kissed, and wept over me; and after showering unnumbered blessings on my head, she also welcomed me into the society of *the just made perfect.** Then each of them took me by a hand, and my reverend father explained to me how he had wrestled with God, as the patriarch of old had done,* not for a night, but for days and years, and that in bitterness and anguish of spirit, on my account; but that *he* had at last prevailed, and had now gained the long and earnestly desired assurance of my acceptance with the Almighty, in and through the merits and sufferings of his Son: That I was now a justified person, adopted among the number of God's children—my name written in the Lamb's book of life,* and that no bypast transgression, nor any future act of my own, or of other men, could be instrumental in altering the decree. 'All the powers of darkness,' added he, 'shall never be able to pluck you again out of your Redeemer's hand. And now, my son, be strong and sted-fast in the truth. Set your face against sin, and sinful men, and resist even to blood,* as many of the faithful of this land have done, and your reward shall be double. I am assured of your acceptance by the word and spirit of him who cannot err, and your sanctification and repentance unto life* will follow in due course. Rejoice and be thank-ful, for you are plucked as a brand out of the burning,* and now your redemption is sealed and sure.'

I wept for joy to be thus assured of my freedom from all sin, and of the impossibility of my ever again falling away from my new state. I bounded away into the fields and the woods, to pour out my spirit in prayer before the Almighty for his kindness to me: my whole frame seemed to be renewed; every nerve was buoyant with new life; I felt as if I could have flown in the air, or leaped over the tops of the trees. An exaltation of spirit lifted me, as it were, far above the earth, and the sinful creatures crawling on its surface; and I deemed myself as an eagle among the children of men, soaring on high, and looking down with pity and contempt on the grovelling creatures below.

As I thus wended my way, I beheld a young man of a mysterious appearance coming towards me. I tried to shun him, being bent on my own contemplations; but he cast himself in my way, so that I could not well avoid him; and more than that, I felt a sort of invisible power that drew me towards him, something like the force of enchantment, which I could not resist. As we approached each other, our eyes met, and I can never describe the strange sensations that thrilled through my whole frame at that impressive moment; a moment to me fraught with the most tremendous consequences; the beginning of a series of adventures which has puzzled myself, and will puzzle the world when I am no more in it. That time will now soon arrive, sooner than any one can devise who knows not the tumult of my thoughts, and the labour of my spirit; and when it hath come and passed over,—when my flesh and my bones are decayed, and my soul has passed to its everlasting home, then shall the sons of men ponder on the events of my life; wonder and tremble, and tremble and wonder how such things should be.

That stranger youth and I approached each other in silence, and slowly, with our eyes fixed on each other's eyes. We approached till not more than a yard intervened between us, and then stood still and gazed, measuring each other from head to foot. What was my astonishment, on perceiving that he was the same being as myself! The clothes were the same to the smallest item. The form was the same; the apparent age; the colour of the hair; the eyes; and, as far as recollection could serve me from viewing my own features in a glass, the features too were the very same. I conceived at first, that I saw a vision, and that my guardian angel had appeared to me at this important era of my life; but this singular being read my thoughts in my looks, anticipating the very words that I was going to utter.

'You think I am your brother,' said he; 'or that I am your second self.* I am indeed your brother, not according to the flesh, but in my belief of the same truths, and my assurance in the same mode of redemption, than which, I hold nothing so great or so glorious on earth.'

'Then you are an associate well adapted to my present state,' said I. 'For this time is a time of great rejoicing in spirit to me. I am on my way to return thanks to the Most High for my redemption from the bonds of sin and misery. If you will join with me heart and hand in youthful thanksgiving, then shall we two go and worship together; but if not, go your way, and I shall go mine.'

'Ah, you little know with how much pleasure I will accompany you, and join with you in your elevated devotions,' said he fervently. 'Your state is a state to be envied indeed; but I have been advised of it, and am come to be a humble disciple of yours; to be initiated into the true way of salvation by conversing with you, and perhaps by being assisted by your prayers.'

My spiritual pride being greatly elevated by this address, I began to assume the preceptor, and questioned this extraordinary youth with regard to his religious principles, telling him plainly, if he was one who expected acceptance with God at all, on account of good works, that I would hold no communion with him. He renounced these at once, with the greatest vehemence, and declared his acquiescence in my faith. I asked if he believed in the eternal and irrevocable decrees of God, regarding the salvation and condemnation of all mankind? He answered that he did so: aye, what would signify all things else that he believed, if he did not believe in that? We then went on to commune about all our points of belief; and in every thing that I suggested, he acquiesced, and, as I thought that day, often carried them to extremes, so that I had a secret dread he was advancing blasphemies. Yet he had such a way with him, and paid such a deference to all my opinions, that I was quite captivated, and, at the same time, I stood in a sort of awe of him, which I could not account for, and several times was seized with an involuntary inclination to escape from his presence, by making a sudden retreat. But he seemed constantly to anticipate my thoughts, and was sure to divert my purpose by some turn in the conversation that particularly interested me. He took care to dwell much on the theme of the impossibility of those ever falling away, who were once accepted and received into covenant with God, for he seemed to know, that in that confidence, and that trust, my whole hopes were centred.

We moved about from one place to another, until the day was wholly spent. My mind had all the while been kept in a state of agitation resembling the motion of a whirlpool, and when we came to separate, I then discovered that the purpose for which I had sought the fields had been neglected, and that I had been diverted from the worship of God, by attending to the quibbles and dogmas of this singular and unaccountable being, who seemed to have more knowledge and information than all the persons I had ever known put together.

We parted with expressions of mutual regret, and when I left him I felt a deliverance, but at the same time a certain consciousness that I was not thus to get free of him, but that he was like to be an acquaintance that was to stick to me for good or for evil. I was astonished at his acuteness and knowledge about every thing; but as for his likeness to me, that was quite unaccountable. He was the same person in every respect, but yet he was not always so; for I observed several times, when we were speaking of certain divines and their tenets, that his face assumed something of the appearance of theirs; and it struck me, that by setting his features to the mould of other people's, he entered at once into their conceptions and feelings.* I had been greatly flattered, and greatly interested by his conversation; whether I had been the better for it or the worse, I could not tell. I had been diverted from returning thanks to my gracious Maker for his great kindness to me, and came home as I went away, but not with the same buoyancy and lightness of heart. Well may I remember that day in which I was first received into the number, and made an heir to all the privileges of the children of God, and on which I first met this mysterious associate, who from that day forth contrived to wind himself into all my affairs, both spiritual and temporal, to this day on which I am writing the account of it. It was on the 25th day of March 1704, when I had just entered the eighteenth year of my age.* Whether it behoves me to bless God for the events of that day, or to deplore them, has been hid from my discernment, though I have inquired into it with fear and trembling; and I have now lost all hopes of ever discovering the true import of these events until that day when my accounts are to make up and reckon for in another world.

When I came home, I went straight into the parlour, where my mother was sitting by herself. She started to her feet, and uttered a smothered scream. 'What ails you, Robert?' cried she. 'My dear son, what is the matter with you?'

'Do you see any thing the matter with me?' said I. 'It appears that the ailment is with yourself, and either in your crazed head or your dim eyes, for there is nothing the matter with me.'

'Ah, Robert, you are ill!' cried she; 'you are very ill, my dear boy; you are quite changed; your very voice and manner are changed. Ah, Jane, haste you up to the study, and tell Mr. Wringhim to come here on the instant and speak to Robert.'

'I beseech you, woman, to restrain yourself,' said I. 'If you suffer your frenzy to run away with your judgment in this manner, I will leave the house. What do you mean? I tell you, there is nothing ails me: I never was better.'

She screamed, and ran between me and the door, to bar my retreat: in the meantime my reverend father entered, and I have not forgot how he gazed, through his glasses, first at my mother, and then at me. I imagined that his eyes burnt like candles, and was afraid of him, which I suppose made my looks more unstable than they would otherwise have been.

'What is all this for?' said he. 'Mistress! Robert! What is the matter here?'

'Oh, sir, our boy!' cried my mother; 'our dear boy, Mr. Wringhim! Look at him, and speak to him: he is either dying or translated,* sir!'

He looked at me with a countenance of great alarm; mumbling some sentences to himself, and then taking me by the arm, as if to feel my pulse, he said, with a faltering voice, 'Something has indeed befallen you, either in body or mind, boy, for you are transformed, since the morning, that I could not have known you for the same person. Have you met with any accident?'

'No.'

'Have you seen any thing out of the ordinary course of nature?'

'No.'

'Then, Satan, I fear, has been busy with you, tempting you in no ordinary degree at this momentous crisis of your life?'

My mind turned on my associate for the day, and the idea that he might be an agent of the devil, had such an effect on me, that I could make no answer.

'I see how it is,' said he; 'you are troubled in spirit,* and I have no doubt that the enemy of our salvation has been busy with you. Tell me this, has he overcome you, or has he not?'

'He has not, my dear father,' said I. 'In the strength of the Lord, I hope I have withstood him. But indeed, if he has been busy with me, I knew it not. I have been conversant this day with one stranger only, whom I took rather for an angel of light.'

'It is one of the devil's most profound wiles to appear like one,'* said my mother.

'Woman, hold thy peace!' said my reverend father: 'thou pretendest to teach what thou knowest not. Tell me this, boy: Did this stranger, with whom you met, adhere to the religious principles in which I have educated you?'

'Yes, to every one of them, in their fullest latitude,' said I.

'Then he was no agent of the wicked one with whom you held converse,' said he; 'for that is the doctrine that was made to overturn the principalities and powers, the might and dominion* of the kingdom of darkness.—Let us pray.'

After spending about a quarter of an hour in solemn and sublime thanksgiving, this saintly man and minister of Christ Jesus, gave out that the day following should be kept by the family as a day of solemn thanksgiving, and spent in prayer and praise, on account of the calling and election of one of its members; or rather for the election of that individual being revealed on earth, as well as confirmed in heaven.

The next day was with me a day of holy exultation. It was begun by my reverend father laying his hands upon my head and blessing me, and then dedicating me to the Lord in the most awful and impressive manner. It was in no common way that he exercised this profound rite, for it was done with all the zeal and enthusiasm of a devotee to the true cause, and a champion on the side he had espoused. He used these remarkable words, which I have still treasured up in my heart:—'I give him unto Thee only, to Thee wholly, and to Thee for ever. I dedicate him unto Thee, soul, body, and spirit. Not as the wicked of this world, or the hirelings of a church profanely called by Thy name, do I dedicate this Thy servant to Thee:* Not in words and form, learned by rote, and dictated by the limbs of Antichrist, but, Lord, I give him into Thy hand, as a captain putteth a sword into the hand of his sovereign, wherewith to lay waste his enemies. May he be a two-edged weapon in Thy hand, and a spear coming out of Thy mouth,* to destroy, and overcome, and pass over; and may the enemies of Thy church fall down before him, and be as dung to fat the land!'

From that moment, I conceived it decreed, not that I should be a minister of the gospel, but a champion of it, to cut off the enemies of the Lord from the face of the earth; and I rejoiced in the commission, finding it more congenial to my nature to be cutting sinners off with the sword, than to be haranguing them from the pulpit, striving to produce an effect, which God, by his act of absolute predestination, had for ever rendered impracticable. The more I pondered on these things, the more I saw of the folly and inconsistency of ministers, in spending their lives, striving and remonstrating with sinners, in order to induce them to do that which they had it not in their power to do. Seeing that God had from all eternity decided the fate of every individual that was to be born of woman, how vain was it in man to endeavour to save those whom their Maker had, by an unchangeable decree, doomed to destruction. I could not disbelieve the doctrine which the best of men had taught me, and toward which he made the whole of the Scriptures to bear, and yet it made the economy of the Christian world appear to me as an absolute contradiction. How much more wise would it be, thought I, to begin and cut sinners off with the sword! for till that is effected, the saints can never inherit the earth in peace. Should I be honoured as an instrument to begin this great work of purification, I should rejoice in it. But then, where had I the means, or under what direction was I to begin? There was one thing clear, I was now the Lord's, and it behoved me to bestir myself in his service. O that I had an host at my command, then would I be as a devouring fire among the workers of iniquity!*

Full of these great ideas, I hurried through the city, and sought again the private path through the field and wood of Finnieston,* in which my reverend preceptor had the privilege of walking for study, and to which he had a key that was always at my command. Near one of the stiles, I perceived a young man sitting in a devout posture, reading on a Bible. He rose, lifted his hat, and made an obeisance to me, which I returned and walked on. I had not well crossed the stile, till it struck me I knew the face of the youth, and that he was some intimate acquaintance, to whom I ought to have spoken. I walked on, and returned, and walked on again, trying to recollect who he was; but for my life I could not. There was, however, a fascination in his look and manner, that drew me back toward him in spite of myself, and I resolved to go to him, if it were merely to speak and see who he was.

I came up to him and addressed him, but he was so intent on his book, that, though I spoke, he lifted not his eyes. I looked on the book also, and still it seemed a Bible, having columns, chapters, and verses; but it was in a language of which I was wholly ignorant, and all intersected with red lines, and verses.* A sensation resembling a stroke of electricity came over me, on first casting my eyes on that mysterious book, and I stood motionless. He looked up, smiled, closed his book, and put it in his bosom. 'You seem strangely affected, dear sir, by looking on my book,' said he mildly.

'In the name of God, what book is that?' said I: 'Is it a Bible?'

'It is *my* Bible, sir,' said he; 'but I will cease reading it, for I am glad to see you. Pray, is not this a day of holy festivity with you?'

I stared in his face, but made no answer, for my senses were bewildered.

'Do you not know me?' said he. 'You appear to be somehow at a loss. Had not you and I some sweet communion and fellowship yesterday?'

'I beg your pardon, sir,' said I. 'But surely if you are the young gentleman with whom I spent the hours yesterday, you have the cameleon art of changing your appearance; I never could have recognized you.'

'My countenance changes with my studies and sensations,' said he. 'It is a natural peculiarity in me, over which I have not full control. If I contemplate a man's features seriously, mine own gradually assume the very same appearance and character. And what is more, by contemplating a face minutely, I not only attain the same likeness, but, with the likeness, I attain the very same ideas as well as the same mode of arranging them, so that, you see, by looking at a person attentively, I by degrees assume his likeness, and by assuming his likeness I attain to the possession of his most secret thoughts. This, I say, is a peculiarity in my nature, a gift of the God that made me; but whether or not given me for a blessing, he knows himself, and so do I. At all events, I have this privilege,—I can never be mistaken of a character in whom I am interested.'

'It is a rare qualification,' replied I, 'and I would give worlds to possess it. Then, it appears, that it is needless to dissemble with you, since you can at any time extract our most secret thoughts from our bosoms. You already know my natural character?'

'Yes,' said he, 'and it is that which attaches me to you. By assuming your likeness yesterday, I became acquainted with your character, and was no less astonished at the profundity and range of your thoughts, than at the heroic magnanimity with which these were combined. And now, in addition to these, you are dedicated to the great work of the Lord; for which reasons I have resolved to attach myself as closely to you as possible, and to render you all the service of which my poor abilities are capable.'

I confess that I was greatly flattered by these compliments paid to my abilities by a youth of such superior qualifications; by one who, with a modesty and affability rare at his age, combined a height of genius and knowledge almost above human comprehension. Nevertheless, I began to assume a certain superiority of demeanour toward him, as judging it incumbent on me to do so, in order to keep up his idea of my exalted character. We conversed again till the day was near a close; and the things that he strove most to inculcate on my mind, were the infallibility of the elect, and the pre-ordination of all things that come to pass. I pretended to controvert the first of these, for the purpose of showing him the extent of my argumentative powers, and said, that 'indubitably there were degrees of sinning which would induce the Almighty to throw off the very elect.' But behold my hitherto humble and modest companion took up the argument with such warmth, that he put me not only to silence, but to absolute shame.

'Why, sir,' said he, 'by vending such an insinuation, you put discredit on the great atonement, in which you trust. Is there not enough of merit in the blood of Jesus to save thousands of worlds, if it was for these worlds that he died? Now, when you know, as you do, (and as every one of the elect may know of himself,) that this Saviour died for you, namely and particularly, dare you say that there is not enough of merit in his great atonement to annihilate all your sins, let them be as heinous and atrocious as they may? And, moreover, do you not acknowledge that God hath pre-ordained and decreed whatsoever comes to pass? Then, how is it that you should deem it in your power to eschew one action of your life, whether good or evil? Depend on it, the advice of the great preacher is genuine: "What thine hand findeth to do, do it with all thy might, for none of us knows what a day may bring forth?"* That is, none of us knows what is pre-ordained, but whatever is pre-ordained we *must* do, and none of these things will be laid to our charge.'

I could hardly believe that these sayings were genuine or orthodox; but I soon felt, that, instead of being a humble disciple of mine, this new acquaintance was to be my guide and director, and all under the humble guise of one stooping at my feet to learn the right. He said that he saw I was ordained to perform some great action for the cause of Jesus and his church, and he earnestly coveted being a partaker with me; but he besought of me never to think it possible for me to fall from the truth, or the favour of him who had chosen me, else that misbelief would baulk every good work to which I set my face.

There was something so flattering in all this, that I could not resist it. Still, when he took leave of me, I felt it as a great relief; and yet, before the morrow, I wearied and was impatient to see him again. We carried on our fellowship from day to day, and all the while I knew not who he was, and still my mother and reverend father kept insisting that I was an altered youth, changed in my appearance, my manners, and my whole conduct; yet something always prevented me from telling them more about my new acquaintance than I had done on the first day we met. I rejoiced in him, was proud of him, and soon could not live without him; yet, though resolved every day to disclose the whole history of my connection with him, I had it not in my power: Something always prevented me, till at length I thought no more of it, but resolved to enjoy his fascinating company in private, and by all means to keep my own with him. The resolution was vain: I set a bold face to it, but my powers were inadequate to the task; my adherent, with all the suavity imaginable, was sure to carry his point. I sometimes fumed, and sometimes shed tears at being obliged to yield to proposals against which I had at first felt every reasoning power of my soul rise in opposition; but, for all that, he never failed in carrying conviction along with him in effect, for he either forced me to acquiesce in his measures, and assent to the truth of his positions, or he put me so completely down, that I had not a word left to advance against them.

After weeks, and I may say months of intimacy, I observed, somewhat to my amazement, that we had never once prayed together; and more than that, that he had constantly led my attentions away from that duty, causing me to neglect it wholly. I thought this a bad mark of a man seemingly so much set on inculcating certain important points of religion, and resolved next day to put him to the test, and request of him to perform that sacred duty in name of us both. He objected boldly; saying there were very few people indeed, with whom he could join in prayer, and he made a point of never doing it, as he was sure they were to ask many things of which he disapproved, and that if he were to officiate himself, he was as certain to allude to many things that came not within the range of their faith. He disapproved of prayer altogether, in the manner it was generally gone about, he said. Man made it merely a selfish concern, and was constantly employed asking, asking, for every thing. Whereas it became all God's creatures to be content with their lot, and only to kneel before him in order to thank him for such benefits as he saw meet to bestow. In short, he argued with such energy, that before we parted I acquiesced, as usual, in his position, and never mentioned prayer to him any more.

Having been so frequently seen in his company, several people happened to mention the circumstance to my mother and reverend father; but at the same time had all described him differently. At length, they began to examine me with respect to the company I kept, as I absented myself from home day after day. I told them I kept company only with one young gentleman, whose whole manner of thinking on religious subjects, I found so congenial with my own, that I could not live out of his society. My mother began to lay down some of her old hackneyed rules of faith, but I turned from hearing her with disgust; for, after the energy of my new friend's reasoning, hers appeared so tame I could not endure it. And I confess with shame, that my reverend preceptor's religious dissertations began, about this time, to lose their relish very much, and by degrees became exceedingly tiresome to my ear. They were so inferior, in strength and sublimity, to the most common observations of my young friend, that in drawing a comparison the former appeared as nothing. He, however, examined me about many things relating to my companion, in all of which I satisfied him, save in one: I could neither tell him who my friend was, what was his name, nor of whom he was descended; and I wondered at myself how I had never once adverted to such a thing, for all the time we had been intimate.

I inquired the next day what his name was; as I said I was often at a loss for it, when talking with him. He replied, that there was no occasion for any one friend ever naming another, when their society was held in private, as ours was; for his part he had never once named me since we first met, and never intended to do so, unless by my own request. 'But if you cannot converse without naming me, you may call me Gil for the present,' added he; 'and if I think proper to take another name at any future period, it shall be with your approbation.'

'Gil!'* said I; 'Have you no name but Gil? Or which of your names is it? Your Christian or surname?'

'O, you must have a surname too, must you!' replied he, 'Very well, you may call me Gil-Martin. It is not my *Christian* name; but it *is* a name which may serve your turn.'

'This is very strange!' said I. 'Are you ashamed of your parents, that you refuse to give your real name?'

'I have no parents save one, whom I do not acknowledge,' said he proudly; 'therefore, pray drop that subject, for it is a disagreeable one. I am a being of a very peculiar temper, for though I have servants and subjects more than I can number, yet, to gratify a certain whim, I have left them, and retired to this city, and for all the society it contains, you see I have attached myself only to you. This is a secret, and I tell it you only in friendship, therefore pray let it remain one, and say not another word about the matter.'

I assented, and said no more concerning it; for it instantly struck me that this was no other than the Czar Peter of Russia,* having heard that he had been travelling through Europe in disguise, and I cannot say that I had not thenceforward great and mighty hopes of high preferment, as a defender and avenger of the oppressed Christian Church, under the influence of this great potentate. He had hinted as much already, as that it was more honourable, and of more avail to put down the wicked with the sword, than try to reform them, and I thought myself quite justified in supposing that he intended me for some great employment, that he had thus selected me for his companion out of all the rest in Scotland, and even pretended to learn the great truths of religion from my mouth. From that time I felt disposed to yield to such a great prince's suggestions without hesitation.

Nothing ever astonished me so much, as the uncommon powers with which he seemed invested. In our walk one day, we met with a Mr. Blanchard, who was reckoned a worthy, pious divine, but quite of the moral cast,* who joined us; and we three walked on, and rested together in the fields. My companion did not seem to like him, but, nevertheless, regarded him frequently with deep attention, and there were several times, while he seemed contemplating him, and trying to find out his thoughts, that his face became so like Mr. Blanchard's, that it was impossible to have distinguished the one from the other. The antipathy between the two was mutual, and discovered itself quite palpably in a short time. When my companion the prince was gone, Mr. Blanchard asked me anent him, and I told him that he was a stranger in the city, but a very uncommon and great personage. Mr. Blanchard's answer to me was as follows: 'I never saw any body I disliked so much in my life, Mr. Robert; and if it be true that he is a stranger here, which I doubt, believe me he is come for no good.'

'Do you not perceive what mighty powers of mind he is possessed of?' said I, 'and also how clear and unhesitating he is on some of the most interesting points of divinity?'

'It is for his great mental faculties that I dread him,' said he. 'It is incalculable what evil such a person as he may do, if so disposed. There is a sublimity in his ideas, with which there is to me a mixture of terror; and when he talks of religion, he does it as one that rather dreads its truths than reverences them. He, indeed, pretends great strictness of orthodoxy regarding some of the points of doctrine embraced by the reformed church; but you do not seem to perceive, that both you and he are carrying these points to a dangerous extremity. Religion is a sublime and glorious thing, the bond of society on earth, and the connector of humanity with the Divine nature;* but there is nothing so dangerous to man as the wresting of any of its principles, or forcing them beyond their due bounds: this is of all others the readiest way to destruction. Neither is there any thing so easily done. There is not an error into which a man can fall, which he may not press Scripture into his service as proof of the probity of, and though your boasted theologian shunned the full discussion of the subject before me, while you pressed it, I can easily see that both you and he are carrying your ideas of absolute predestination, and its concomitant appendages, to an extent that overthrows all religion and revelation together; or, at least, jumbles them into a chaos, out of which human capacity can never select what is good. Believe me, Mr. Robert, the less you associate with that illustrious stranger the better, for it appears to me that your creed and his carries damnation on the very front of it.'

I was rather stunned at this; but I pretended to smile with disdain, and said, it did not become youth to control age; and, as I knew our principles differed fundamentally, it behoved us to drop the subject. He, however, would not drop it, but took both my principles and me fearfully to task, for Blanchard was an eloquent and powerful-minded old man; and, before we parted, I believe I promised to drop my new acquaintance, and was *all but* resolved to do it.

As well might I have laid my account with shunning the light of day. He was constant to me as my shadow, and by degrees he acquired such an ascendency over me, that I never was happy out of his company, nor greatly so in it. When I repeated to him all that Mr. Blanchard had said, his countenance kindled with indignation and rage; and then by degrees his eyes sunk inward, his brow lowered, so that I was awed, and withdrew my eyes from looking at him. A while afterward, as I was addressing him, I chanced to look him again in the face, and the sight of him made me start violently. He had made himself so like Mr. Blanchard, that I actually believed I had been addressing that gentleman, and that I had done so in some absence of mind that I could not account for. Instead of being amused at the quandary I was in, he seemed offended: indeed, he never was truly amused with any thing. And he then asked me sullenly, if I conceived such personages as he to have no other endowments than common mortals?

I said I never conceived that princes or potentates had any greater share of endowments than other men, and frequently not so much. He shook his head, and bade me think over the subject again; and there was an end of it. I certainly felt every day the more disposed to acknowledge such a superiority in him, and from all that I could gather, I had now no doubt that he was Peter of Russia. Every thing combined to warrant the supposition, and, of course, I resolved to act in conformity with the discovery I had made.

For several days the subject of Mr. Blanchard's doubts and doctrines formed the theme of our discourse. My friend deprecated them most devoutly; and then again he would deplore them, and lament the great evil that such a man might do among the human race. I joined with him in allowing the evil in its fullest latitude; and, at length, after he thought he had fully prepared my nature for such a trial of its powers and abilities, he proposed calmly that we two should make away with Mr. Blanchard. I was so shocked, that my bosom became as it were a void, and the beatings of my heart sounded loud and hollow in it; my breath cut, and my tongue and palate became dry and speechless. He mocked at my cowardice, and began a-reasoning on the matter with such powerful eloquence, that before we parted, I felt fully convinced that it was my bounden duty to slay Mr. Blanchard; but my will was far, very far from consenting to the deed.

I spent the following night without sleep, or nearly so; and the next morning, by the time the sun arose, I was again abroad, and in the company of my illustrious friend. The same subject was resumed, and again he reasoned to the following purport: That supposing me placed at the head of an army of Christian soldiers, all bent on putting down the enemies of the church, would I have any hesitation in destroying and rooting out these enemies?—None surely.—Well then, when I saw and was convinced, that here was an individual who was doing more detriment to the church of Christ on earth, than tens of thousands of such warriors were capable of doing, was it not my duty to cut him off, and save the elect? 'He, who would be a champion in the cause of Christ and his Church, my brave young friend,' added he, 'must begin early, and no man can calculate to what an illustrious eminence small beginnings may lead. If the man Blanchard is worthy, he is only changing his situation for a better one; and if unworthy, it is better that one fall, than that a thousand souls perish.* Let us be up and doing in our vocations. For me, my resolution is taken; I have but one great aim in this world, and I never for a moment lose sight of it.'

I was obliged to admit the force of his reasoning; for though I cannot from memory repeat his words, his eloquence was of that overpowering nature, that the subtilty of other men sunk before it; and there is also little doubt that the assurance I had that these words were spoken by a great potentate, who could raise me to the highest eminence, (provided that I entered into his extensive and decisive measures,) assisted mightily in dispelling my youthful scruples and qualms of conscience; and I thought moreover, that having such a powerful back friend to support me, I hardly needed to be afraid of the consequences. I consented! But begged a little time to think of it. He said the less one thought of a duty the better; and we parted.

But the most singular instance of this wonderful man's power over my mind was, that he had as complete influence over me by night as by day. All my dreams corresponded exactly with his suggestions; and when he was absent from me, still his arguments sunk deeper in my heart than even when he was present. I dreamed that night of a great triumph obtained, and though the whole scene was but dimly and confusedly defined in my vision, yet the overthrow and death of Mr. Blanchard was the first step by which I attained the eminent station I occupied. Thus, by dreaming of the event by night, and discoursing of it by day, it soon became so familiar to my mind, that I almost conceived it as done. It was resolved on: which was the first and greatest victory gained; for there was no difficulty in finding opportunities enow of cutting off a man, who, every good day, was to be found walking by himself in private grounds. I went and heard him preach for two days, and in fact I held his tenets scarcely short of blasphemy; they were such as I had never heard before, and his congregation, which was numerous, were turning up their ears and drinking in his doctrines with the utmost delight; for O, they suited their carnal natures and self-sufficiency to a hair! He was actually holding it forth, as a fact, that 'it was every man's own blame if he was not saved!' What horrible misconstruction! And then he was alleging, and trying to prove from nature and reason, that no man ever was guilty of a sinful action, who might not have declined it had he so chosen! 'Wretched controvertist!' thought I to myself an hundred times, 'shall not the sword of the Lord* be moved from its place of peace for such presumptuous and absurd testimonies as these!'

When I began to tell the prince about these false doctrines, to my astonishment I found that he had been in the church himself, and had every argument that the old divine had used *verbatim*; and he remarked on them with great concern, that these were not the tenets that corresponded with his views in society, and that he had agents in every city, and every land, exerting their powers to put them down. I asked, with great simplicity, 'Are all your subjects Christians, prince?'

'All my European subjects are, or deem themselves so,' returned he; 'and they are the most faithful and true subjects I have.'

Who could doubt, after this, that he was the Czar of Russia? I have nevertheless had reasons to doubt of his identity since that period, and which of my conjectures is right, I believe the God of heaven only knows, for I do not. I shall go on to write such things as I remember, and if any one shall ever take the trouble to read over these confessions, such a one will judge for himself. It will be observed, that since ever I fell in with this extraordinary person, I have written about him only, and I must continue to do so to the end of this memoir, as I have performed no great or interesting action in which he had not a principal share.

He came to me one day and said, 'We must not linger thus in executing what we have resolved on. We have much before our hands to perform for the benefit of mankind, both civil as well as religious. Let us do what we have to do here, and then we must wend our way to other cities, and perhaps to other countries. Mr. Blanchard is to hold forth in the high church of Paisley* on Sunday next, on some particularly great occasion: this must be defeated; he must not go there. As he will be busy arranging his discourses, we may expect him to be walking by himself in Finnieston Dell the greater part of Friday and Saturday. Let us go and cut him off. What is the life of a man more than the life of a lamb, or any guiltless animal? It is not half so much, especially when we consider the immensity of the mischief this old fellow is working among our fellow-creatures. Can there be any doubt that it is the duty of one consecrated to God, to cut off such a mildew?'

'I fear me, great sovereign,' said I, 'that your ideas of retribution are too sanguine, and too arbitrary for the laws of this country. I dispute not that your motives are great and high; but have you debated the consequences, and settled the result?'

'I have,' returned he, 'and hold myself amenable for the action, to the laws of God and of equity; as to the enactments of men I despise them. Fain would I see the weapon of the Lord of Hosts,* begin the work of vengeance that awaits it to do!'

I could not help thinking, that I perceived a little derision of countenance on his face as he said this, nevertheless I sunk dumb before such a man, and aroused myself to the task, seeing he would not have it deferred. I approved of it in theory, but my spirit stood aloof from the practice. I saw and was convinced that the elect of God would be happier, and purer, were the wicked and unbelievers all cut off from troubling and misleading them, but if it had not been the instigations of this illustrious stranger, I should never have presumed to begin so great a work myself. Yet, though he often aroused my zeal to the highest pitch, still my heart at times shrunk from the shedding of lifeblood, and it was only at the earnest and unceasing instigations of my enlightened and voluntary patron, that I at length put my hand to the conclusive work. After I said all that I could say, and all had been overborne, (I remember my actions and words as well as it had been yesterday,) I turned round hesitatingly, and looked up to Heaven for direction; but there was a dimness came over my eyes that I could not see. The appearance was as if there had been a veil drawn over me, so nigh that I put up my hand to feel it; and then Gil-Martin (as this great sovereign was pleased to have himself called,) frowned, and asked me what I was grasping at? I knew not what to say, but answered, with fear and shame, 'I have no weapons, not one; nor know I where any are to be found.'

'The God whom thou servest will provide these,' said he; 'if thou provest worthy of the trust committed to thee.'

I looked again up into the cloudy veil that covered us, and thought I beheld golden weapons of every description let down in it, but all with their points towards me.* I kneeled, and was going to stretch out my hand to take one, when my patron seized me, as I thought, by the clothes, and dragged me away with as much ease as I had been a lamb, saying, with a joyful and elevated voice,—'Come, my friend, let us depart: thou art dreaming—thou art dreaming. Rouse up all the energies of thy exalted mind, for thou art an highly-favoured one;* and doubt thou not, that he whom *thou* servest, will be ever at thy right and left hand, to direct and assist thee.'

These words, but particularly the vision I had seen, of the golden weapons descending out of Heaven, inflamed my zeal to that height that I was as one beside himself; which my parents perceived that night, and made some motions toward confining me to my room. I joined in the family prayers, and then I afterwards sung a psalm and prayed by myself; and I had good reasons for believing that that small oblation of praise and prayer was not turned to sin. But there are strange things, and unaccountable agencies in nature. He only who dwells between the Cherubim* can unriddle them, and to him the honour must redound for ever. *Amen.*

I felt greatly strengthened and encouraged that night, and the next morning I ran to meet my companion, out of whose eye I had now no life. He rejoiced at seeing me so forward in the great work of reformation by blood, and said many things to raise my hopes of future fame and glory; and then, producing two pistols of pure beaten gold, he held them out and proffered me the choice of one, saying, 'See what thy master hath provided thee!' I took one of them eagerly, for I perceived at once that they were two of the very weapons that were let down from Heaven in the cloudy veil, the dim tapestry of the firmament; and I said to myself, 'Surely this is the will of the Lord.'

The little splendid and enchanting piece was so perfect, so complete, and so ready for executing the will of the donor, that I now longed to use it in his service. I loaded it with my own hand, as Gil-Martin did the other, and we took our stations behind a bush of hawthorn and bramble on the verge of the wood, and almost close to the walk. My patron was so acute in all his calculations that he never mistook an event. We had not taken our stand above a minute and a half, till old Mr. Blanchard appeared, coming slowly on the path. When we saw this, we cowered down, and leaned each of us a knee upon the ground, pointing the pistols through the bush, with an aim so steady, that it was impossible to miss our victim.

He came deliberately on, pausing at times so long, that we dreaded
he was going to turn. Gil-Martin dreaded it, and I said I did, but
wished in my heart that he might. He, however, came onward, and I
will never forget the manner in which he came! No—I don't believe I
ever can forget it, either in the narrow bounds of time or the ages of
eternity! He was a boardly ill-shaped man, of a rude exterior, and a
little bent with age; his hands were clasped behind his back, and below
his coat, and he walked with a slow swinging air that was very peculiar.
When he paused and looked abroad on nature, the act was highly
impressive: he seemed conscious of being all alone, and conversant
only with God and the elements of his creation. Never was there such
a picture of human inadvertency! a man approaching step by step to
the one that was to hurl him out of one existence into another, with as
much ease and indifference as the ox goeth to the stall.* Hideous
vision, wilt thou not be gone from my mental sight! If not, let me bear
with thee as I can!

When he came straight opposite to the muzzles of our pieces, Gil-
Martin called out 'Eh!' with a short quick sound. The old man, without starting, turned his face and breast toward us, and looked into the
wood, but looked over our heads. 'Now!' whispered my companion,
and fired. But my hand refused the office, for I was not at that moment
sure about becoming an assassin in the cause of Christ and his Church.
I thought I heard a sweet voice behind me, whispering me to beware,
and I was going to look round, when my companion exclaimed,
'Coward, we are ruined!'

I had no time for an alternative: Gil-Martin's ball had not taken
effect, which was altogether wonderful, as the old man's breast was
within a few yards of him. 'Hilloa!' cried Blanchard; 'what is that for,
you dog!' and with that he came forward to look over the bush. I
hesitated, as I said, and attempted to look behind me; but there was
no time: the next step discovered two assassins lying in covert, waiting for blood. 'Coward, we are ruined!' cried my indignant friend;
and that moment my piece was discharged. The effect was as might
have been expected: the old man first stumbled to one side, and then
fell on his back. We kept our places, and I perceived my companion's
eyes gleaming with an unnatural joy. The wounded man raised himself from the bank to a sitting posture, and I beheld his eyes swim-
ming; he, however, appeared sensible, for we heard him saying in a
low and rattling voice, 'Alas, alas! whom have I offended, that they

should have been driven to an act like this! Come forth and shew yourselves, that I may either forgive you before I die, or curse you in the name of the Lord.' He then fell a-groping with both hands on the ground, as if feeling for something he had lost, manifestly in the agonies of death; and, with a solemn and interrupted prayer for forgiveness, he breathed his last.

I had become rigid as a statue, whereas my associate appeared to be elevated above measure. 'Arise, thou faint-hearted one, and let us be going,' said he. 'Thou hast done well for once; but wherefore hesitate in such a cause? This is but a small beginning of so great a work as that of purging the Christian world. But the first victim is a worthy one, and more of such lights must be extinguished immediately.'

We touched not our victim, nor any thing pertaining to him, for fear of staining our hands with his blood; and the firing having brought three men within view, who were hasting towards the spot, my undaunted companion took both the pistols, and went forward as with intent to meet them, bidding me shift for myself. I ran off in a contrary direction, till I came to the foot of the Pearman Sike, and then, running up the hollow of that, I appeared on the top of the bank as if I had been another man brought in view by hearing the shots in such a place. I had a full view of a part of what passed, though not of all. I saw my companion going straight to meet the men, apparently with a pistol in every hand, waving in a careless manner. They seemed not quite clear of meeting with him, and so he went straight on, and passed between them. They looked after him, and came onward; but when they came to the old man lying stretched in his blood, then they turned and pursued my companion, though not so quickly as they might have done; and I understood that from the first they saw no more of him.

Great was the confusion that day in Glasgow. The most popular of all their preachers of morality was (what they called) murdered in cold blood, and a strict and extensive search was made for the assassin. Neither of the accomplices was found, however, that is certain, nor was either of them so much as suspected; but another man was apprehended under circumstances that warranted suspicion.—This was one of the things that I witnessed in my life, which I never understood, and it surely was one of my patron's most dexterous tricks, for I must still say, what I have thought from the beginning, that like him there never was a man created. The young man who was taken up was a preacher; and it was proved that he had purchased fire arms in town, and gone out with them that morning. But the far greatest mystery of the whole was, that two of the men, out of the three who met my companion, swore, that that unfortunate preacher was the man whom they met with a pistol in each hand, fresh from the death of the old divine. The poor fellow made a confused speech himself, which there is not the least doubt was quite true; but it was laughed to scorn, and an expression of horror ran through both the hearers and jury. I heard the whole trial, and so did Gil-Martin; but we left the journeyman preacher to his fate, and from that time forth I have had no faith in the justice of criminal trials. If once a man is prejudiced on one side, he will swear any thing in support of such prejudice. I tried to expostulate with my mysterious friend on the horrid injustice of suffering this young man to die for our act, but the prince exulted in it more than the other, and said the latter was the most dangerous man of the two.

The alarm in and about Glasgow was prodigious. The country being divided into two political parties, the court and the country party,* the former held meetings, issued proclamations, and offered rewards, ascribing all to the violence of party spirit, and deprecating the infernal measures of their opponents. I did not understand their political differences; but it was easy to see that the true Gospel preachers joined all on one side, and the upholders of pure morality and a blameless life on the other, so that this division proved a test to us, and it was forthwith resolved, that we two should pick out some of the leading men of this unsaintly and heterodox cabal, and cut them off one by one, as occasion should suit.

Now, the ice being broke, I felt considerable zeal in our great work, but pretended much more; and we might soon have kidnapped them all through the ingenuity of my patron, had not our next attempt miscarried, by some awkwardness or mistake of mine. The consequence was, that he was discovered fairly, and very nigh seized. I also was seen, and suspected so far, that my reverend father, my mother, and myself were examined privately. I denied all knowledge of the matter; and they held it in such a ridiculous light, and their conviction of the complete groundlessness of the suspicion was so perfect, that their testimony prevailed, and the affair was hushed. I was obliged, however, to walk circumspectly, and saw my companion the prince very seldom, who was prowling about every day, quite unconcerned about his safety. He was every day a new man, however, and needed not to be alarmed at any danger; for such a facility had he in disguising himself, that if it had not been for a pass-word which we had between us, for the purposes of recognition, I never could have known him myself.

It so happened that my reverend father was called to Edinburgh about this time, to assist with his council in settling the national affairs. At my earnest request I was permitted to accompany him, at which both my associate and I rejoiced, as we were now about to move in a new and extensive field. All this time I never knew where my illustrious friend resided. He never once invited me to call on him at his lodgings, nor did he ever come to our house, which made me sometimes to suspect, that if any of our great efforts in the cause of true religion were discovered, he intended leaving me in the lurch. Consequently, when we met in Edinburgh (for we travelled not in company) I proposed to go with him to look for lodgings, telling him at the same time what a blessed religious family my reverend instructor and I were settled in. He said he rejoiced at it, but he made a rule of never lodging in any particular house, but took these daily, or hourly, as he found it convenient, and that he never was at a loss in any circumstance.

'What a mighty trouble you put yourself to, great sovereign!' said I, 'and all, it would appear, for the purpose of seeing and knowing more and more of the human race.'

'I never go but where I have some great purpose to serve,' returned he, 'either in the advancement of my own power and dominion, or in thwarting my enemies.'

'With all due deference to your great comprehension, my illustrious friend,' said I, 'it strikes me that you can accomplish very little either the one way or the other here, in the humble and private capacity you are pleased to occupy.'

'It is your own innate modesty that prompts such a remark,' said he. 'Do you think the gaining of *you* to my service, is not an attainment worthy of being envied by the greatest potentate in Christendom? Before I had missed such a prize as the attainment of your services, I would have travelled over one half of the habitable globe.'—I bowed with great humility, but at the same time how could I but feel proud and highly flattered? He continued. 'Believe me, my dear friend, for such a prize I account no effort too high. For a man who is not only dedicated to the King of Heaven, in the most solemn manner, soul, body, and spirit, but also chosen of him from the beginning, justified, sanctified, and received into a communion that never shall be broken, and from which no act of his shall ever remove him,—the possession of such a man, I tell you, is worth kingdoms; because every deed that he performs, he does it with perfect safety to himself and honour to me.'—I bowed again, lifting my hat, and he went on.—'I am now going to put his courage in the cause he has espoused, to a severe test—to a trial at which common nature would revolt, but he who is dedicated to be the sword of the Lord, must raise himself above common humanity. You have a father and a brother according to the flesh, what do you know of them?'

'I am sorry to say I know nothing good,' said I. 'They are reprobates, cast-aways, beings devoted to the wicked one, and, like him, workers of every species of iniquity with greediness.'

'They must both fall!' said he, with a sigh and melancholy look: 'It is decreed in the councils above, that they must both fall by your hand.'

'The God of heaven forbid it!' said I. 'They are enemies to Christ and his church, that I know and believe; but they shall live and die in their iniquity for me, and reap their guerdon when their time cometh. There my hand shall not strike.'

'The feeling is natural, and amiable,' said he; 'but you *must* think again. Whether are the bonds of carnal nature, or the bonds and vows of the Lord, strongest?'

'I will not reason with you on this head, mighty potentate,' said I, 'for whenever I do so it is but to be put down. I shall only express my determination, not to take vengeance out of the Lord's hand in this instance. It availeth not. These are men that have the mark of the beast in their foreheads and right hands;* they are lost beings themselves, but have no influence over others. Let them perish in their sins; for they shall not be meddled with by me.'

'How preposterously you talk, my dear friend!' said he. These people are your greatest enemies; they would rejoice to see you annihilated. And now that you have taken up the Lord's cause of being avenged on *his* enemies, wherefore spare those that are your own as well as his? Besides, you ought to consider what great advantages would be derived to the cause of righteousness and truth, were the estate and riches of that opulent house in your possession, rather than in that of such as oppose the truth and all manner of holiness.'

This was a portion of the consequence of following my illustrious adviser's summary mode of procedure, that had never entered into my calculation—I disclaimed all idea of being influenced by it; however, I cannot but say that the desire of being enabled to do so much good, by the possession of these bad men's riches, made some impression on my heart, and I said I would consider of the matter. I did consider it, and that right seriously as well as frequently; and there was scarcely an hour in the day on which my resolves were not animated by my great friend, till at length I began to have a longing desire to kill my brother, in particular. Should any man ever read this scroll, he will wonder at this confession, and deem it savage and unnatural. So it appeared to me at first, but a constant thinking of an event changes every one of its features. I have done all for the best, and as I was prompted, by one who knew right and wrong much better than I did. I *had* a desire to slay him, it is true, and such a desire too as a thirsty man has to drink; but at the same time, this longing desire was mingled with a certain terror, as if I had dreaded that the drink for which I longed was mixed with deadly poison. My mind was so much weakened, or rather softened about this time, that my faith began a little to give way, and I doubted most presumptuously of the least tangible of all Christian tenets, namely, of *the infallibility of the elect.* I hardly comprehended the great work I had begun, and doubted of *my own* infallibility, or that of any created being. But I was brought over again by the unwearied diligence of my friend to repent of my backsliding, and view once more the superiority of the Almighty's counsels in its fullest latitude. *Amen.*

I prayed very much in secret about this time, and that with great fervor of spirit, as well as humility; and my satisfaction at finding all my requests granted is not to be expressed.

My illustrious friend still continuing to sound in my ears the imperious duty to which I was called, of making away with my sinful relations, and quoting many parallel actions out of the Scriptures, and the writings of the holy Fathers, of the pleasure the Lord took in such as executed his vengeance on the wicked, I was obliged to acquiesce in his measures, though with certain limitations. It was not easy to answer his arguments, and yet I was afraid that he soon perceived a leaning to his will on my part. 'If the acts of Jehu, in rooting out the whole house of his master, were ordered and approved of by the Lord,' said he, 'would it not have been more praiseworthy if one of

Ahab's own sons had stood up for the cause of the God of Israel, and rooted out the sinners and their idols out of the land?'*

'It would certainly,' said I. 'To our duty to God all other duties must yield.'

'Go thou then and do likewise,'* said he. 'Thou art called to a high vocation; to cleanse the sanctuary of thy God in this thy native land by the shedding of blood; go thou forth then like a ruling energy, a master spirit of desolation in the dwellings of the wicked,* and high shall be your reward both here and hereafter.'

My heart now panted with eagerness to look my brother in the face: On which my companion, who was never out of the way, conducted me to a small square in the suburbs of the city, where there were a number of young noblemen and gentlemen playing at a vain, idle, and sinful game, at which there was much of the language of the accursed going on; and among these blasphemers he instantly pointed out my brother to me. I was fired with indignation at seeing him in such company, and so employed; and I placed myself close beside him to watch all his motions, listen to his words, and draw inferences from what I saw and heard. In what a sink of sin was he wallowing! I resolved to take him to task, and if he refused to be admonished, to inflict on him some condign punishment; and knowing that my illustrious friend and director was looking on, I resolved to show some spirit. Accordingly, I waited until I heard him profane his Maker's name three times, and then, my spiritual indignation being roused above all restraint, I went up and kicked him. Yes, I went boldly up and struck him with my foot, and meant to have given him a more severe blow than it was my fortune to inflict. It had, however, the effect of rousing up his corrupt nature to quarrelling and strife, instead of taking the chastisement of the Lord in humility and meekness. He ran furiously against me in the choler that is always inspired by the wicked one; but I overthrew him, by reason of impeding the natural and rapid progress of his unholy feet, running to destruction. I also fell slightly; but his fall proving a severe one, he arose in wrath, and struck me with the mall which he held in his hand, until my blood flowed copiously; and from that moment I vowed his destruction in my heart. But I chanced to have no weapon at that time, nor any means of inflicting due punishment on the caitiff, which would not have been returned double on my head, by him and his graceless associates. I mixed among them at the suggestion of my friend, and following them to their den of voluptuousness and sin, I strove to be admitted among them, in hopes of finding some means of accomplishing my great purpose, while I found myself moved by the spirit within me so to do. But I was not only debarred, but, by the machinations of my wicked brother and his associates, cast into prison.

I was not sorry at being thus honoured to suffer in the cause of righteousness, and at the hands of sinful men; and as soon as I was alone, I betook myself to prayer, deprecating the long-suffering of God toward such horrid sinners. My jailer came to me, and insulted me. He was a rude unprincipled fellow, partaking much of the loose and carnal manners of the age; but I remembered of having read, in the Cloud of Witnesses,* of such men formerly, having been converted by the imprisoned saints; so I set myself, with all my heart, to bring about this man's repentance and reformation.

'Fat the deil* are ye yoolling an' praying that gate for, man?' said he, coming angrily in. 'I thought the days o' praying prisoners had been a' ower. We had rowth o' them aince; an' they were the poorest an' the blackest bargains that ever poor jailers saw. Gie up your crooning, or I'll pit you to an in-by place, where ye sall get plenty o't.'

'Friend,' said I, 'I am making my appeal at that bar where all human actions are seen and judged, and where you shall not be forgot, sinful as you are. Go in peace,* and let me be.'

'Hae ye naebody nearer-hand hame to mak your appeal to, man?' said he; 'because an ye haena, I dread you an' me may be unco weel acquaintit by an' by?'

I then opened up the mysteries of religion to him in a clear and perspicuous manner, but particularly the great doctrine of the election of grace; and then I added, 'Now, friend, you must tell me if you pertain to this chosen number. It is in every man's power to ascertain this, and it is every man's duty to do it.'

'An' fat the better wad you be for the kenning o' this, man?' said he.

'Because, if you are one of my brethren, I will take you into sweet communion and fellowship,' returned I; 'but if you belong to the unregenerate, I have a commission to slay you.'

'The deil you hae, callant!' said he, gaping and laughing. 'An' pray now, fa was it that gae you siccan a braw commission?'

'My commission is sealed by the signet above,' said I, 'and that I will let you and all sinners know. I am dedicated to it by the most solemn vows and engagements. I am the sword of the Lord, and

Famine and Pestilence* are my sisters. Wo then to the wicked of this land, for they must fall down dead together, that the church may be purified!'

'Oo, foo, foo! I see how it is,' said he; 'yours is a very braw commission, but you will have the small opportunity of carrying it through here. Take my advising, and write a bit of a letter to your friends, and I will send it, for this is no place for such a great man. If you cannot steady your hand to write, as I see you have been at your great work, a word of a mouth may do; for I do assure you this is not the place at all, of any in the world, for your operations.'

The man apparently thought I was deranged in my intellect. He could not swallow such great truths at the first morsel. So I took his advice, and sent a line to my reverend father, who was not long in coming, and great was the jailer's wonderment when he saw all the great Christian noblemen of the land sign my bond of freedom.

My reverend father took this matter greatly to heart, and bestirred himself in the good cause till the transgressors were ashamed to shew their faces. My illustrious companion was not idle: I wondered that he came not to me in prison, nor at my release; but he was better employed, in stirring up the just to the execution of God's decrees; and he succeeded so well, that my brother and all his associates had nearly fallen victims to their wrath: But many were wounded, bruised, and imprisoned, and much commotion prevailed in the city. For my part, I was greatly strengthened in my resolution by the anathemas of my reverend father, who, privately, (that is in a family capacity,) in his prayers, gave up my father and brother, according to the flesh, to Satan, making it plain to all my senses of perception, that they were beings given up of God, to be devoured by fiends or men, at their will and pleasure, and that *whosoever* should slay them, would do God good service.

The next morning my illustrious friend met me at an early hour, and he was greatly overjoyed at hearing my sentiments now chime so much in unison with his own. I said, 'I longed for the day and the hour that I might look my brother in the face at Gilgal,* and visit on him the iniquity of his father and himself, for that I was now strengthened and prepared for the deed.'

'I have been watching the steps and movements of the profligate one,' said he; 'and lo, I will take you straight to his presence. Let your heart be as the heart of the lion, and your arms strong as the shekels of brass,* and swift to avenge as the bolt that descendeth from Heaven, for the blood of the just and the good hath long flowed in Scotland. But already is the day of their avengement begun; the hero is at length arisen, who shall send all such as bear enmity to the true church, or trust in works of their own, to Tophet!'*

Thus encouraged, I followed my friend, who led me directly to the same court in which I had chastised the miscreant on the foregoing day; and behold, there was the same group again assembled. They eyed me with terror in their looks, as I walked among them and eyed them with looks of disapprobation and rebuke; and I saw that the very eye of a chosen one lifted on these children of Belial,* was sufficient to dismay and put them to flight. I walked aside to my friend, who stood at a distance looking on, and he said to me, 'What thinkest thou now?' and I answered in the words of the venal prophet, 'Lo now, if I had a sword into mine hand, I would even kill him.'*

'Wherefore lackest thou it?' said he. 'Dost thou not see that they tremble at thy presence, knowing that the avenger of blood* is among them.'

My heart was lifted up* on hearing this, and again I strode into the midst of them, and eyeing them with threatening looks, they were so much confounded, that they abandoned their sinful pastime, and fled every one to his house!

This was a palpable victory gained over the wicked, and I thereby knew that the hand of the Lord was with me. My companion also exulted, and said, 'Did not I tell thee? Behold thou dost not know one half of thy might, or of the great things thou art destined to do. Come with me and I will show thee more than this, for these young men cannot subsist without the exercises of sin. I listened to their councils, and I know where they will meet again.'

Accordingly he led me a little farther to the south, and we walked aside till by degrees we saw some people begin to assemble; and in a short time we perceived the same group stripping off their clothes to make them more expert in the practice of madness and folly. Their game was begun before we approached, and so also were the oaths and cursing. I put my hands in my pockets, and walked with dignity and energy into the midst of them. It was enough: Terror and astonishment seized them. A few of them cried out against me, but their voices were soon hushed amid the murmurs of fear. One of them, in the name of the rest, then came and besought of me to grant them liberty to amuse themselves; but I refused peremptorily, dared the whole multitude so much as to touch me with one of their fingers, and dismissed them in the name of the Lord.

Again they all fled and dispersed at my eye, and I went home in triumph, escorted by my friend, and some well-meaning young Christians, who, however, had not learned to deport themselves with soberness and humility. But my ascendency over my enemies was great indeed; for wherever I appeared I was hailed with approbation, and wherever my guilty brother made his appearance, he was hooted and held in derision, till he was forced to hide his disgraceful head, and appear no more in public.

Immediately after this I was seized with a strange distemper, which neither my friends nor physicians could comprehend, and it confined me to my chamber for many days; but I knew, myself, that I was bewitched, and suspected my father's reputed concubine of the deed. I told my fears to my reverend protector, who hesitated concerning them, but I knew by his words and looks that he was conscious I was right. I generally conceived myself to be two people. When I lay in bed, I deemed there were two of us in it; when I sat up, I always beheld another person, and always in the same position from the place where I sat or stood, which was about three paces off me towards my left side. It mattered not how many or how few were present: this my second self was sure to be present in his place; and this occasioned a confusion in all my words and ideas that utterly astounded my friends, who all declared, that instead of being deranged in my intellect, they had never heard my conversation manifest so much energy or sublimity of conception; but for all that, over the singular delusion that I was two persons, my reasoning faculties had no power. The most perverse part of it was, that I rarely conceived *myself* to be any of the two persons. I thought for the most part that my companion was one of them, and my brother the other; and I found, that to be obliged to speak and answer in the character of another man, was a most awkward business at the long run.

Who can doubt, from this statement, that I was bewitched, and that my relatives were at the ground of it? The constant and unnatural persuasion that I was my brother, proved it to my own satisfaction, and must, I think, do so to every unprejudiced person. This victory of the wicked one over me kept me confined in my chamber, at Mr. Millar's house, for nearly a month, until the prayers of the faithful prevailed, and I was restored. I knew it was a chastisement for my pride, because my heart was lifted up at my superiority over the enemies of the church; nevertheless, I determined to make short work with the aggressor, that the righteous might not be subjected to the effect of his diabolical arts again.

I say I was confined a month. I beg he that readeth to take note of this, that he may estimate how much the word, or even the oath, of a wicked man, is to depend on. For a month I saw no one but such as came into my room, and for all that, it will be seen, that there were plenty of the same set to attest upon oath that I saw my brother every day during that period; that I persecuted him with my presence day and night, while all the time I never saw his face, save in a delusive dream. I cannot comprehend what manœuvres my illustrious friend was playing off with them about this time; for he, having the art of personating whom he chose, had peradventure deceived them, else so many of them had never all attested the same thing. I never saw any man so steady in his friendships and attentions as he; but as he made a rule of never calling at private houses, for fear of some discovery being made of his person, so I never saw him while my malady lasted; but as soon as I grew better, I knew I had nothing ado but to attend at some of our places of meeting, to see him again. He was punctual, as usual, and I had not to wait.

My reception was precisely as I apprehended. There was no flaring, no flummery, nor bombastical pretensions, but a dignified return to my obeisance, and an immediate recurrence, in converse, to the important duties incumbent on us, in our stations, as reformers and purifiers of the Church.

'I have marked out a number of most dangerous characters in this city,' said he, 'all of whom must be cut off from cumbering the true vineyard* before we leave this land. And if you bestir not yourself in the work to which you are called, I must raise up others who shall have the honour of it.'

'I am, most illustrious prince, wholly at your service,' said I. 'Show but what ought to be done, and here is the heart to dare, and the hand to execute. You pointed out my relations, according to the flesh, as brands fitted to be thrown into the burning. I approve peremptorily of the award; nay, I thirst to accomplish it; for I myself have suffered severely from their diabolical arts. When once that trial of my devotion to the faith is accomplished, then be your future operations disclosed.'

'You are free of your words and promises,' said he.

'So will I be of my deeds in the service of my master, and that shalt thou see,' said I. 'I lack not the spirit, nor the will, but I lack experience wofully; and because of that shortcoming, must bow to your suggestions.'

'Meet me here to-morrow betimes,' said he, 'and perhaps you may hear of some opportunity of displaying your zeal in the cause of righteousness.'

I met him as he desired me; and he addressed me with a hurried and joyful expression, telling me that my brother was astir, and that a few minutes ago he had seen him pass on his way to the mountain. 'The hill is wrapped in a cloud,' added he, 'and never was there such an opportunity of executing divine justice on a guilty sinner. You may trace him in the dew, and shall infallibly find him on the top of some precipice; for it is only in secret that he dares show his debased head to the sun.'

'I have no arms, else assuredly I would pursue him and discomfit him,' said I.

'Here is a small dagger,' said he; 'I have nothing of weapon-kind about me save that, but it is a potent one; and should you require it, there is nothing more ready or sure.'

'Will not you accompany me?' said I: 'Sure you will?'

'I will be with you, or near you,' said he. 'Go you on before.'

I hurried away as he directed me, and imprudently asked some of Queensberry's guards if such and such a young man passed by them going out from the city. I was answered in the affirmative, and till then had doubted of my friend's intelligence, it was so inconsistent with a profligate's life to be so early astir. When I got the certain intelligence that my brother was before me, I fell a-running, scarcely knowing what I did; and looking several times behind me, I perceived nothing of my zealous and arbitrary friend. The consequence of this was, that by the time I reached St. Anthony's well, my resolution began to give way. It was not my courage, for now that I had once shed blood in the cause of the true faith, I was exceedingly bold and ardent; but whenever I was left to myself, I was subject to sinful doubtings. These always hankered on one point: I doubted if the elect were infallible, and if the Scripture promises to them were binding in all situations and relations. I confess this, and that it was a sinful and shameful weakness in me, but my nature was subject to it, and I could not eschew it. I never doubted that I was one of the elect myself; for, besides the strong inward and spiritual conviction that I possessed, I had my kind father's assurance; and these had been revealed to him in that way and measure that they could not be doubted.

In this desponding state, I sat myself down on a stone, and bethought me of the rashness of my understanding. I tried to ascertain, to my own satisfaction, whether or not I really had been commissioned of God to perpetrate these crimes in his behalf, for in the eyes, and by the laws of men, they were great and crying transgressions. While I sat pondering on these things, I was involved in a veil of white misty vapour, and looking up to heaven, I was just about to ask direction from above, when I heard as it were a still small voice* close by me, which uttered some words of derision and chiding. I looked intensely in the direction whence it seemed to come, and perceived a lady, robed in white, who hasted toward me. She regarded me with a severity of look and gesture that appalled me so much, I could not address her; but she waited not for that, but coming close to my side, said, without stopping, 'Preposterous wretch! how dare you lift your eyes to heaven with such purposes in your heart? Escape homeward, and save your soul, or farewell for ever!'

These were all the words that she uttered, as far as I could ever recollect, but my spirits were kept in such a tumult that morning, that something might have escaped me. I followed her eagerly with my eyes, but in a moment she glided over the rocks above the holy well, and vanished. I persuaded myself that I had seen a vision, and that the radiant being that had addressed me was one of the good angels, or guardian spirits, commissioned by the Almighty to watch over the steps of the just. My first impulse was to follow her advice, and make my escape home; for I thought to myself, 'How is this interested and mysterious foreigner, a proper judge of the actions of a free Christian?'

The thought was hardly framed, nor had I moved in a retrograde direction six steps, when I saw my illustrious friend and great adviser descending the ridge towards me with hasty and impassioned strides. My heart fainted within me; and when he came up and addressed me, I looked as one caught in a trespass. 'What hath detained thee, thou desponding trifler?' said he. 'Verily now shall the golden opportunity be lost which may never be recalled. I have traced the reprobate to his sanctuary in the cloud, and lo he is perched on the pinnacle of a precipice an hundred fathoms high. One ketch with thy foot, or toss with thy finger, shall throw him from thy sight into the foldings of the cloud, and he shall be no more seen, till found at the bottom of the cliff dashed to pieces. Make haste therefore, thou loiterer, if thou wouldst ever prosper and rise to eminence in the work of thy Lord and master.'

'I go no farther on this work,' said I, 'for I have seen a vision that has reprimanded the deed.'

'A vision?' said he: 'Was it that wench who descended from the hill?'

'The being that spake to me, and warned me of my danger, was indeed in the form of a lady,' said I.

'She also approached me and said a few words,' returned he; 'and I thought there was something mysterious in her manner. Pray, what did she say? for the words of such a singular message, and from such a messenger, ought to be attended to. If I understood her aright, she was chiding us for our misbelief and preposterous delay.'

I recited her words, but he answered that I had been in a state of sinful doubting at the time, and it was to these doubtings she had adverted. In short, this wonderful and clear-sighted stranger soon banished all my doubts and despondency, making me utterly ashamed of them, and again I set out with him in the pursuit of my brother. He showed me the traces of his footsteps in the dew, and pointed out the spot where I should find him. 'You have nothing more to do than go softly down behind him,' said he; 'which you can do to within an ell of him, without being seen; then rush upon him, and throw him from his seat, where there is neither footing nor hold. I will go, meanwhile, and amuse his sight by some exhibition in the contrary direction, and he shall neither know nor perceive who has done him this *kind office*: for, exclusive of more weighty concerns, be assured of this, that the sooner he falls, the fewer crimes will he have to answer for, and his estate in the other world will be proportionally more tolerable, than if he spent a long unregenerate life steeped in iniquity to the loathing of the soul.'

'Nothing can be more plain or more pertinent,' said I: 'therefore I fly to perform that which is both a duty toward God and toward man!'

'You shall yet rise to great honour and preferment,' said he.

'I value it not, provided I do honour and justice to the cause of my master here,' said I.

'You shall be lord of your father's riches and demesnes,' added he.

'I disclaim and deride every selfish motive thereto relating,' said I, 'farther than as it enables me to do good.'

'Ay, but that is a great and a heavenly consideration, that *longing for ability to do good*,' said he;—and as he said so, I could not help remarking a certain derisive exultation of expression which I could not comprehend; and indeed I have noted this very often in my illustrious friend, and sometimes mentioned it civilly to him, but he has never failed to disclaim it. On this occasion I said nothing, but concealing his poniard in my clothes, I hasted up the mountain, determined to execute my purpose before any misgivings should again visit me; and I never had more ado, than in keeping firm my resolution. I could not help my thoughts, and there are certain trains and classes of thoughts that have great power in enervating the mind. I thought of the awful thing of plunging a fellow creature from the top of a cliff into the dark and misty void below—of his being dashed to pieces on the protruding rocks, and of hearing his shrieks as he descended the cloud, and beheld the shagged points on which he was to alight. Then I thought of plunging a soul so abruptly into hell, or, at the best, sending it to hover on the confines of that burning abyss—of its appearance at the bar of the Almighty to receive its sentence. And then I thought, 'Will there not be a sentence pronounced against me there, by a jury of the just made perfect, and written down in the registers of heaven?'

These thoughts, I say, came upon me unasked, and instead of being able to dispel them, they mustered, upon the summit of my imagination, in thicker and stronger array: and there was another that impressed me in a very particular manner, though, I have reason to believe, not so strongly as those above written. It was this: 'What if I should fail in my first effort? Will the consequence not be that I am tumbled from the top of the rock myself?' and then all the feelings anticipated, with regard to both body and soul, must happen to me! This was a spine-breaking reflection; and yet, though the probability was rather on that side, my zeal in the cause of godliness was such that it carried me on, maugre all danger and dismay.

I soon came close upon my brother, sitting on the dizzy pinnacle, with his eyes fixed stedfastly in the direction opposite to me. I descended the little green ravine behind him with my feet foremost, and every now and then raised my head, and watched his motions. His posture continued the same, until at last I came so near him

I could have heard him breathe, if his face had been towards me. I laid my cap aside, and made me ready to spring upon him, and push him over. I could not for my life accomplish it! I do not think it was that *I durst not*, for I have always felt my courage equal to any thing in a good cause. But I had not the heart, or something that I ought to have had. In short, it was not done in time, as it easily might have been. These THOUGHTS are hard enemies wherewith to combat! And I was so grieved that I could not effect my righteous purpose, that I laid me down on my face and shed tears. Then, again, I thought of what my great enlightened friend and patron would say to me, and again my resolution rose indignant, and indissoluble save by blood. I arose on my right knee and left foot, and had just begun to advance the latter forward: the next step my great purpose had been accomplished, and the culprit had suffered the punishment due to his crimes. But what moved him I knew not: in the critical moment he sprung to his feet, and dashing himself furiously against me, he overthrew me, at the imminent peril of my life. I disencumbered myself by main force, and fled, but he overhied me, knocked me down, and threatened, with dreadful oaths, to throw me from the cliff. After I was a little recovered from the stunning blow, I aroused myself to the combat; and though I do not recollect the circumstances of that deadly scuffle very minutely, I know that I vanquished him so far as to force him to ask my pardon, and crave a reconciliation. I spurned at both, and left him to the chastisements of his own wicked and corrupt heart.

My friend met me again on the hill, and derided me, in a haughty and stern manner, for my imbecility and want of decision. I told him how nearly I had effected my purpose, and excused myself as well as I was able. On this, seeing me bleeding, he advised me to swear the peace against my brother, and have him punished in the mean time, he being the first aggressor. I promised compliance, and we parted, for I was somewhat ashamed of my failure, and was glad to be quit for the present of one of whom I stood so much in awe.

When my reverend father beheld me bleeding a second time by the hand of a brother, he was moved to the highest point of displeasure; and, relying on his high interest and the justice of his cause, he brought the matter at once before the courts. My brother and I were first examined face to face. His declaration was a mere romance: mine was not the truth; but as it was by the advice of my reverend father, and that of my illustrious friend, both of whom I knew to be sincere

Christians and true believers, that I gave it, I conceived myself completely justified on that score. I said, I had gone up into the mountain early on the morning to pray, and had withdrawn myself, for entire privacy, into a little sequestered dell—had laid aside my cap, and was in the act of kneeling, when I was rudely attacked by my brother, knocked over, and nearly slain. They asked my brother if this was true. He acknowledged that it was; that I was bare-headed, and in the act of kneeling when he ran foul of me without any intent of doing so. But the judge took him to task on the improbability of this, and put the profligate sore out of countenance. The rest of his tale told still worse, insomuch that he was laughed at by all present, for the judge remarked to him, that granting it was true that he had at first run against me on an open mountain, and overthrown me by accident, how was it, that after I had extricated myself and fled, that he had pursued, overtaken, and knocked me down a second time? Would he pretend that all that was likewise by chance? The culprit had nothing to say for himself on this head, and I shall not forget my exultation and that of my reverend father, when the sentence of the judge was delivered. It was, that my wicked brother should be thrown into prison, and tried on a criminal charge of assault and battery, with the intent of committing murder. This was a just and righteous judge, and saw things in their proper bearings, that is, he could discern between a righteous and a wicked man, and then there could be no doubt as to which of the two were acting right, and which wrong.

Had I not been sensible that a justified person could do nothing wrong, I should not have been at my ease concerning the statement I had been induced to give on this occasion. I could easily perceive, that by rooting out the weeds from the garden of the Church, I heightened the growth of righteousness; but as to the tardy way of giving false evidence on matters of such doubtful issue, I confess I saw no great propriety in it from the beginning. But I now only moved by the will and mandate of my illustrious friend: I had no peace or comfort when out of his sight, nor have I ever been able to boast of much in his presence; so true is it that a Christian's life is one of suffering.

My time was now much occupied, along with my reverend preceptor, in making ready for the approaching trial, as the prosecutors. Our counsel assured us of a complete victory, and that banishment would be the mildest award of the law on the offender. Mark how different was the result! From the shifts and ambiguities of a wicked Bench, who had a fellow-feeling of iniquity with the defenders,—my suit was cast, the graceless libertine was absolved, and I was incarcerated, and bound over to keep the peace, with heavy penalties, before I was set at liberty.

I was exceedingly disgusted at this issue, and blamed the counsel of my friend to his face. He expressed great grief, and expatiated on the wickedness of our judicatories, adding, 'I see I cannot depend on you for quick and summary measures, but for your sake I shall be revenged on that wicked judge, and that you shall see in a few days.' The Lord Justice Clerk died that same week!* But he died in his own house and his own bed, and by what means my friend effected it, I do not know. He would not tell me a single word of the matter, but the judge's sudden death made a great noise, and I made so many curious inquiries regarding the particulars of it, that some suspicions were like to attach to our family, of some unfair means used. For my part I know nothing, and rather think he died by the visitation of Heaven, and that my friend had foreseen it, by symptoms, and soothed me by promises of complete revenge.

It was some days before he mentioned my brother's meditated death to me again, and certainly he then found me exasperated against him personally to the highest degree. But I told him that I could not now think any more of it, owing to the late judgment of the court, by which, if my brother were missing or found dead, I would not only forfeit my life, but my friends would be ruined by the penalties.

'I suppose you know and believe in the perfect safety of your soul,' said he, 'and that that is a matter settled from the beginning of time, and now sealed and ratified both in heaven and earth?'

'I believe in it thoroughly and perfectly,' said I; 'and whenever I entertain doubts of it, I am sensible of sin and weakness.'

'Very well, so then am I,' said he. 'I think I can now divine, with all manner of certainty, what will be the high and merited guerdon of your immortal part. Hear me then farther: I give you my solemn assurance, and bond of blood, that no human hand shall ever henceforth be able to injure your life, or shed one drop of your precious blood, but it is on the condition that you walk always by my directions.'

'I will do so with cheerfulness,' said I; 'for without your enlightened counsel, I feel that I can do nothing. But as to your power of protecting my life, you must excuse me for doubting of it. Nay, were we in your own proper dominions, you could not ensure that.'

'In whatever dominion or land I am, my power accompanies me,' said he; 'and it is only against human might and human weapon that I ensure your life; on that will I keep an eye, and on that you may depend. I have never broken word or promise with you. Do you credit me?'

'Yes, I do,' said I; 'for I see you are in earnest. I believe, though I do not comprehend you.'

'Then why do you not at once challenge your brother to the field of honour? Seeing you now act without danger, cannot you also act without fear?'

'It is not fear,' returned I; 'believe me, I hardly know what fear is. It is a doubt, that on all these emergencies constantly haunts my mind, that in performing such and such actions I may fall from my upright state. This makes fratricide a fearful task.'

'This is imbecility itself,' said he. 'We have settled, and agreed on that point an hundred times. I would therefore advise that you challenge your brother to single combat. I shall ensure your safety, and he cannot refuse giving you satisfaction.'

'But then the penalties?' said I.

'We will try to evade these,' said he; 'and supposing you should be caught, if once you are Laird of Dalcastle and Balgrennan, what are the penalties to you?'

'Might we not rather pop him off in private and quietness, as we did the deistical divine?' said I.

'The deed would be alike meritorious, either way,' said he. 'But may we not wait for years before we find an opportunity? My advice is to challenge him, as privately as you will, and there cut him off.'

'So be it then,' said I. 'When the moon is at the full, I will send for him forth to speak with one, and there will I smite him and slay him, and he shall trouble the righteous no more.'

'Then this is the very night,' said he. 'The moon is nigh to the full, and this night your brother and his sinful mates hold carousal; for there is an intended journey to-morrow. The exulting profligate leaves town, where we must remain till the time of my departure hence; and then is he safe, and must live to dishonour God, and not only destroy his own soul, but those of many others. Alack, and wo is me! The sins that he and his friends will commit this very night, will cry to heaven against us for our shameful delay! When shall our great work of cleansing the sanctuary be finished, if we proceed at this puny rate?'

'I see the deed *must* be done, then,' said I; 'and since it is so, it shall be done. I will arm myself forthwith, and from the midst of his wine and debauchery you shall call him forth to me, and there will I smite him with the edge of the sword,* that our great work be not retarded.'

'If thy execution were equal to thy intent, how great a man you soon might be!' said he. 'We shall make the attempt once more; and if it fail again, why, I must use other means to bring about my high purposes relating to mankind.—Home and make ready. I will go and procure what information I can regarding their motions, and will meet you in disguise twenty minutes hence, at the first turn of Hewie's lane beyond the loch.'

'I have nothing to make ready,' said I; 'for I do not choose to go home. Bring me a sword, that we may consecrate it with prayer and vows, and if I use it not to the bringing down of the wicked and profane, then may the Lord do so to me, and more also!'

We parted, and there was I left again to the multiplicity of my own thoughts for the space of twenty minutes, a thing my friend never failed in subjecting me to, and these were worse to contend with than hosts of sinful men. I prayed inwardly, that these deeds of mine might never be brought to the knowledge of men who were incapable of appreciating the high motives that led to them; and then I sung part of the 10th Psalm,* likewise in spirit; but for all these efforts, my sinful doubts returned, so that when my illustrious friend joined me, and proffered me the choice of two gilded rapiers, I declined accepting any of them, and began, in a very bold and energetic manner, to express my doubts regarding the justification of all the deeds of perfect men. He chided me severely, and branded me with cowardice, a thing that my nature never was subject to; and then he branded me with falsehood, and breach of the most solemn engagements both to God and man.

I was compelled to take the rapier, much against my inclination; but for all the arguments, threats, and promises that he could use, I would not consent to send a challenge to my brother by his mouth. There was one argument only that he made use of which had some weight with me, but yet it would not preponderate. He told me my brother was gone to a notorious and scandalous habitation of women, and that if I left him to himself for ever so short a space longer, it might embitter his state through ages to come. This was a trying concern to me; but I resisted it, and reverted to my doubts. On this he said that he had meant to do me honour, but since I put it out of his power, he would do the deed, and take the responsibility on himself. 'I have with sore travail procured a guardship of your life,' added he. 'For my own, I have not; but, be that as it will, I shall not be baffled in my attempts to benefit my friends without a trial. You will at all events accompany me, and see that I get justice?'

'Certes, I will do thus much,' said I; 'and wo be to him if his arm prevail against my friend and patron!'

His lip curled with a smile of contempt, which I could hardly brook; and I began to be afraid that the eminence to which I had been destined by him was already fading from my view. And I thought what I should then do to ingratiate myself again with him, for without his countenance I had no life. 'I will be a man in act,' thought I, 'but in sentiment I will not yield, and for this he must surely admire me the more.'

As we emerged from the shadowy lane into the fair moonshine, I started so that my whole frame underwent the most chilling vibrations of surprise. I again thought I had been taken at unawares, and was conversing with another person. My friend was equipped in the Highland garb, and so completely translated into another being, that, save by his speech, all the senses of mankind could not have recognized him. I blessed myself, and asked whom it was his pleasure to personify to-night? He answered me carelessly, that it was a spark whom he meant should bear the blame of whatever might fall out to-night; and that was all that passed on the subject.

We proceeded by some stone steps at the foot of the North Loch, in hot argument all the way. I was afraid that our conversation might be overheard, for the night was calm and almost as light as day, and we saw sundry people crossing us as we advanced. But the zeal of my friend was so high, that he disregarded all danger, and continued to argue fiercely and loudly on my delinquency, as he was pleased to call it. I stood on one argument alone, which was, 'that I did not think the Scripture promises to the elect, taken in their utmost latitude, warranted the assurance that they could do no wrong; and that, therefore, it behoved every man to look well to his steps.'

There was no religious scruple that irritated my enlightened friend and master so much as this. He could not endure it. And the sentiments of our great covenanted reformers being on his side, there is not a doubt that I was wrong. He lost all patience on hearing what I advanced on this matter, and taking hold of me, he led me into a darksome booth in a confined entry; and, after a friendly but cutting reproach, he bade me remain there in secret and watch the event; 'and if I fall,' said he, 'you will not fail to avenge my death?'

I was so entirely overcome with vexation that I could make no answer, on which he left me abruptly, a prey to despair; and I saw or heard no more, till he came down to the moonlight green followed by my brother. They had quarrelled before they came within my hearing, for the first words I heard were those of my brother, who was in a state of intoxication, and he was urging a reconciliation, as was his wont on such occasions. My friend spurned at the suggestion, and dared him to the combat; and after a good deal of boastful altercation, which the turmoil of my spirits prevented me from remembering, my brother was compelled to draw his sword and stand on the defensive. It was a desperate and terrible engagement. I at first thought that the royal stranger and great champion of the faith would overcome his opponent with ease, for I considered heaven as on his side, and nothing but the arm of sinful flesh against him. But I was deceived: The sinner stood firm as a rock, while the assailant flitted about like a shadow, or rather like a spirit. I smiled inwardly, conceiving that these lightsome manœuvres were all a sham to show off his art and mastership in the exercise, and that whenever they came to close fairly, that instant my brother would be overcome. Still I was deceived: My brother's arm seemed invincible, so that the closer they fought the more palpably did it prevail. They fought round the green to the very edge of the water, and so round, till they came close up to the covert where I stood. There being no more room to shift ground, my brother then forced him to come to close quarters, on which, the former still having the decided advantage, my friend quitted his sword, and called out. I could resist no longer; so, springing from my concealment, I rushed between them with my sword drawn, and parted them as if they had been two schoolboys: then turning to my brother, I addressed him as follows:—'Wretch! miscreant! knowest thou what thou art attempting? Wouldst thou lay thine hand on the Lord's anointed, or shed his precious blood?* Turn thee to me, that I may chastise thee for all thy wickedness, and not for the many injuries thou hast done to me!' To it we went, with full thirst of vengeance on every side. The duel was fierce; but the might of heaven prevailed, and not my might.

The ungodly and reprobate young man fell, covered with wounds, and with curses and blasphemy in his mouth, while I escaped uninjured. Thereto his power extended not.

I will not deny, that my own immediate impressions of this affair in some degree differed from this statement. But this is precisely as my illustrious friend described it to me afterwards, and I can rely implicitly on his information, as he was at that time a looker-on, and my senses all in a state of agitation, and he could have no motive for saying what was not the positive truth.

Never till my brother was down did we perceive that there had been witnesses to the whole business. Our ears were then astounded by rude challenges of unfair play, which were quite appalling to me; but my friend laughed at them, and conducted me off in perfect safety. As to the unfairness of the transaction, I can say thus much, that my royal friend's sword was down ere ever mine was presented. But if it still be accounted unfair to take up a conqueror, and punish him in his own way, I answer; That if a man is sent on a positive mission by his master, and hath laid himself under vows to do his work, he ought not to be too nice in the means of accomplishing it; and farther, I appeal to holy writ, wherein many instances are recorded of the pleasure the Lord takes in the final extinction of the wicked and profane;* and this position I take to be unanswerable.

I was greatly disturbed in my mind for many days, knowing that the transaction had been witnessed, and sensible also of the perilous situation I occupied, owing to the late judgment of the court against me. But, on the contrary, I never saw my enlightened friend in such high spirits. He assured me there was no danger; and again repeated, that he warranted my life against the power of man. I thought proper, however, to remain in hiding for a week; but, as he said, to my utter amazement, the blame fell on another, who was not only accused, but pronounced guilty by the general voice, and outlawed for non-appearance! how could I doubt, after this, that the hand of heaven was aiding and abetting me? The matter was beyond my comprehension; and as for my friend, he never explained any thing that was past, but his activity and art were without a parallel.

He enjoyed our success mightily; and for his sake I enjoyed it somewhat, but it was on account of his comfort only, for I could not for my life perceive in what degree the church was better or purer than before these deeds were done. He continued to flatter me with great things, as to honours, fame, and emolument; and, above all, with the blessing and protection of him to whom my body and soul were dedicated. But after these high promises, I got no longer peace; for he began to urge the death of my father with such an unremitting earnestness, that I found I had nothing for it but to comply. I did so; and cannot express his enthusiasm of approbation. So much did he hurry and press me in this, that I was forced to devise some of the most openly violent measures, having no alternative. Heaven spared me the deed, taking, in that instance, the vengeance in its own hand; for before my arm could effect the sanguine but meritorious act, the old man followed his son to the grave. My illustrious and zealous friend seemed to regret this somewhat; but he comforted himself with the reflection, that still I had the merit of it, having not only consented to it, but in fact effected it, for by doing the one action I had brought about both.

No sooner were the obsequies of the funeral over, than my friend and I went to Dalcastle, and took undisputed possession of the houses, lands, and effects that had been my father's; but his plate, and vast treasures of ready money, he had bestowed on a voluptuous and unworthy creature, who had lived long with him as a mistress. Fain would I have sent her after her lover, and gave my friend some hints on the occasion; but he only shook his head, and said that we must lay all selfish and interested motives out of the question.

For a long time, when I awaked in the morning, I could not believe my senses, that I was indeed the undisputed and sole proprietor of so much wealth and grandeur; and I felt so much gratified, that I immediately set about doing all the good I was able, hoping to meet with all approbation and encouragement from my friend. I was mistaken: He checked the very first impulses towards such a procedure, questioned my motives, and uniformly made them out to be wrong. There was one morning that a servant said to me, there was a lady in the back chamber who wanted to speak with me, but he could not tell me who it was, for all the old servants had left the mansion, every one on hearing of the death of the late laird, and those who had come knew none of the people in the neighbourhood. From several circumstances, I had suspicions of private confabulations with women, and refused to go to her, but bid the servant inquire what she wanted. She would not tell; she could only state the circumstances to me; so I, being sensible that a little dignity of manner became me in my elevated situation, returned for answer, that if it was business that could not be transacted by my steward, it must remain untransacted. The answer which the servant brought back was of a threatening nature. She stated that she *must* see me, and if I refused her satisfaction there, she would compel it where I should not evite her.

My friend and director appeared pleased with my dilemma, and rather advised that I should hear what the woman had to say; on which I consented, provided she would deliver her mission in his presence. She came in with manifest signs of anger and indignation, and began with a bold and direct charge against me of a shameful assault on one of her daughters; of having used the basest of means in order to lead her aside from the paths of rectitude; and on the failure of these, of having resorted to the most unqualified measures.

I denied the charge in all its bearings, assuring the dame that I had never so much as seen either of her daughters to my knowledge, far less wronged them; on which she got into great wrath, and abused me to my face as an accomplished vagabond, hypocrite, and sensualist; and she went so far as to tell me roundly, that if I did not *marry* her daughter, she would bring me to the gallows, and that in a very short time.

'Marry your daughter, honest woman!' said I, 'on the faith of a Christian, I never saw your daughter; and you may rest assured in this, that I will neither marry you nor her. Do you consider how short a time I have been in this place? How much that time has been occupied? And how there was even a *possibility* that I could have accomplished such villainies?'

'And how long does your Christian reverence suppose you have remained in this place since the late laird's death?' said she.

'That is too well known to need recapitulation,' said I: 'only a very few days, though I cannot at present specify the exact number; perhaps from thirty to forty, or so. But in all that time, certes, I have never seen either you or any of your two daughters that you talk of. You must be quite sensible of that.'

My friend shook his head three times during this short sentence, while the woman held up her hands in amazement and disgust, exclaiming, 'There goes the self-righteous one! There goes the consecrated youth, who cannot err! You, sir, know, and the world shall know of the faith that is in this most just, devout, and religious miscreant! Can you deny that you have already been in this place four months and seven days? Or that in that time you have been forbid my house twenty times? Or that you have persevered in your endeavours to effect the basest and most ungenerous of purposes? Or that you *have* attained them? hypocrite and deceiver as you are! Yes, sir; I say, dare you deny that you *have* attained your vile, selfish, and degrading purposes towards a young, innocent, and unsuspecting creature, and thereby ruined a poor widow's only hope in this world? No, you cannot look in my face, and deny aught of this.'

'The woman is raving mad!' said I. 'You, illustrious sir, know, that in the first instance, I have not yet been in this place *one* month.' My friend shook his head again, and answered me, 'You are wrong, my dear friend; you are wrong. It is indeed the space of time that the lady hath stated, to a day, since you came here, and I came with you; and I am sorry that I know for certain that you have been frequently haunting her house, and have often had private correspondence with one of the young ladies too. Of the nature of it I presume not to know.'

'You are mocking me,' said I. 'But as well may you try to reason me out of my existence, as to convince me that I have been here even one month, or that any of those things you allege against me has the shadow of truth or evidence to support it. I will swear to you, by the great God that made me; and by——'

'Hold, thou most abandoned profligate!' cried she violently, 'and do not add perjury to your other detestable crimes. Do not, for mercy's sake, any more profane that name whose attributes you have wrested and disgraced. But tell me what reparation you propose offering to my injured child?'

'I again declare, before heaven, woman, that to the best of my knowledge and recollection, I never saw your daughter. I now think I have some faint recollection of having seen your face, but where, or in what place, puzzles me quite.'

'And, why?' said she. 'Because for months and days you have been in such a state of extreme inebriety, that your time has gone over like a dream that has been forgotten. I believe, that from the day you came first to my house, you have been in a state of utter delirium, and that principally from the fumes of wine and ardent spirits.'

'It is a manifest falsehood!' said I; 'I have never, since I entered on the possession of Dalcastle, tasted wine or spirits, saving once, a few evenings ago; and, I confess to my shame, that I was led too far; but I have craved forgiveness and obtained it. I take my noble and distinguished friend there for a witness to the truth of what I assert; a man who has done more, and sacrificed more for the sake of genuine Christianity, than any this world contains. Him you will believe.'

'I hope you have attained forgiveness,' said he, seriously. 'Indeed it would be next to blasphemy to doubt it. But, of late, you have been very much addicted to intemperance. I doubt if, from the first night you tasted the delights of drunkenness, that you have ever again been in your right mind until Monday last. Doubtless you have been for a good while most diligent in your addresses to this lady's daughter.'

'This is unaccountable,' said I. 'It is impossible that I can have been doing a thing, and not doing it at the same time. But indeed, honest woman, there have several incidents occurred to me in the course of my life which persuade me I have a second self; or that there is some other being who appears in my likeness.'

Here my friend interrupted me with a sneer, and a hint that I was talking insanely; and then he added, turning to the lady, 'I know my friend Mr. Colwan will do what is just and right. Go and bring the young lady to him, that he may see her, and he will then recollect all his former amours with her.'

'I humbly beg your pardon, sir,' said I. 'But the mention of such a thing as *amours* with any woman existing, to me, is really so absurd, so far from my principles, so far from the purity of nature and frame to which I was born and consecrated, that I hold it as an insult, and regard it with contempt.'

I would have said more in reprobation of such an idea, had not my servant entered, and said, that a gentleman wanted to see me on business. Being glad of an opportunity of getting quit of my lady visitor, I ordered the servant to show him in; and forthwith a little lean gentleman, with a long acquiline nose, and a bald head, daubed all over with powder and pomatum, entered. I thought I recollected having seen him too, but could not remember his name, though he spoke to me with the greatest familiarity; at least, that sort of familiarity that an official person generally assumes. He bustled about and about, speaking to every one, but declined listening for a single moment to any. The lady offered to withdraw, but he stopped her.

'No, no, Mrs. Keeler, you need not go; you need not go; you *must* not go, madam. The business I came about, concerns you—yes, that it does—Bad business yon of Walker's? Eh? Could not help it—did all I could, Mr. Wringhim. Done your business. Have it all cut and dry here, sir—No, this is not it—Have it among them, though—I'm at a little loss for your name, sir, (addressing my friend,)—seen you very often, though—exceedingly often—quite well acquainted with you.'

'No, sir, you are not,' said my friend, sternly.—The intruder never regarded him; never so much as lifted his eyes from his bundle of law papers, among which he was bustling with great hurry and import-ance, but went on—

'*Im*possible! Have seen a face very like it, then—what did you say your name was, sir?—very like it indeed. Is it not the young laird who was murdered whom you resemble so much?'

Here Mrs. Keeler uttered a scream, which so much startled me, that it seems I grew pale. And on looking at my friend's face, there was something struck me so forcibly in the likeness between him and my late brother, that I had very nearly fainted. The woman exclaimed, that it was my brother's spirit that stood beside me.

'Im*poss*ible!' exclaimed the attorney; 'at least I hope not, else his signature is not worth a pin. There is some balance due on yon busi-ness, madam. Do you wish your account? because I have it here, ready discharged, and it does not suit letting such things lie over. This busi-ness of Mr. Colwan's will be a severe one on you, madam,—*ra*ther a severe one.'

'What business of mine, if it be your will, sir,' said I. 'For my part I never engaged you in business of any sort, less or more.' He never regarded me, but went on. 'You may appeal, though: Yes, yes, there are such things as appeals for the refractory. Here it is, gentlemen,—here they are all together—Here is, in the first place, sir, your power of attorney, regularly warranted, sealed, and signed with your own hand.'

'I declare solemnly that I never signed that document,' said I.

'Ay, ay, the system of denial is not a bad one in general,' said my attorney; 'but at present there is no occasion for it. You do not deny your own hand?'

'I deny every thing connected with the business,' cried I; 'I dis-claim it *in toto*, and declare that I know no more about it than the child unborn.'

'That is exceedingly good!' exclaimed he; 'I like your pertinacity vastly! I have three of your letters, and three of your signatures; that part is all settled, and I hope so is the whole affair; for here is the original grant to your father, which he has never thought proper to put in requisition. Simple gentleman! But here have I, Lawyer Linkum,* in one hundredth part of the time that any other notary, writer, attorney, or writer to the signet in Britain, would have done it, procured the signature of his Majesty's commissioner, and thereby confirmed the charter to you and your house, sir, for ever and ever,—Begging your pardon, madam.' The lady, as well as myself, tried several times to interrupt the loquacity of Linkum, but in vain: he only raised his hand with a quick flourish, and went on:—

'Here it is:*—"JAMES, by the grace of God, King of Great Britain, France, and Ireland, to his right trusty cousin, sendeth greeting: And whereas his right leal and trust-worthy cousin, George Colwan, of Dalcastle and Balgrennan, hath suffered great losses, and undergone much hardship, on behalf of his Majesty's rights and titles; he therefore, for himself, and as prince and steward of Scotland, and by the consent of his right trusty cousins and councillors, hereby grants to the said George Colwan, his heirs and assignees whatsomever, herit ably and irrevocably, all and haill, the lands and others underwritten: *To wit*, All and haill, the five merk land of Kipplerig; the five pound land of Easter Knockward, with all the towers, fortalices, manorplaces, houses, biggings, yards, orchards, tofts, crofts, mills, woods, fishings, mosses, muirs, meadows, communities, pasturages, coals, coalheughs, tenants, tenantries, services of free tenants, annexes, connexes, dependencies, parts, pendicles, and pertinents of the same whatsomever; to be peaceably brooked, joysed, set, used, and disposed of by him and his aboves, as specified, heritably and irrevocably, in all time coming: And, in testimony thereof, His Majesty, for himself, and as prince and steward of Scotland, with the advice and consent of his foresaids, knowledge, proper motive, and kingly power, makes, erects, creates, unites, annexes, and incorporates, the whole lands above mentioned in an haill and free barony, by all the rights, miethes, and marches thereof, old and divided, as the same lies, in length and breadth, in houses, biggings, mills, multures, hawking, hunting, fishing; with court, plaint, herezeld, fock, fork, sack, sock, thole, thame, vert, wraik, waith, wair, venison, outfang thief, infang thief, pit and gallows, and all and sundry other commodities. Given at our Court of Whitehall, &c. &c. God save the King.

"Compositio 5 *lib.* 13. 8.

"Registrate 26th September, 1687."*

'See, madam, here are ten signatures of privy councillors of that year, and here are other ten of the present year, with his Grace the Duke of Queensberry* at the head. All right—See here it is, sir,—all right—done your work. So you see, madam, this gentleman is the true and sole heritor of all the land that your father possesses, with all the rents thereof for the last twenty years, and upwards—Fine job for my employers!—sorry on your account, madam—can't help it.'

I was again going to disclaim all interest or connection in the matter, but my friend stopped me; and the plaints and lamentations of the dame became so overpowering, that they put an end to all farther colloquy; but Lawyer Linkum followed me, and stated his great outlay, and the important services he had rendered me, until I was obliged to subscribe an order to him for £100 on my banker.

I was now glad to retire with my friend, and ask seriously for some explanation of all this. It was in the highest degree unsatisfactory. He confirmed all that had been stated to me; assuring me, that I had not only been assiduous in my endeavours to seduce a young lady of great beauty, which it seemed I had effected, but that I had taken counsel, and got this supposed, old, false, and forged grant, raked up and new signed, to ruin the young lady's family quite, so as to throw her entirely on myself for protection, and be wholly at my will.

This was to me wholly incomprehensible. I could have freely made oath to the contrary of every particular. Yet the evidences were against me, and of a nature not to be denied. Here I must confess, that, highly as I disapproved of the love of women, and all intimacies and connections with the sex, I felt a sort of indefinite pleasure, an ungracious delight in having a beautiful woman solely at my disposal. But I thought of her spiritual good in the meantime. My friend spoke of my backslidings with concern; requesting me to make sure of my forgiveness, and to forsake them; and then he added some words of sweet comfort. But from this time forth I began to be sick at times of my existence. I had heart-burnings, longings, and yearnings, that would not be satisfied; and I seemed hardly to be an accountable creature; being thus in the habit of executing transactions of the utmost moment, without being sensible that I did them. I was a being incomprehensible to myself. Either I had a second self, who transacted business in my likeness, or else my body was at times possessed by a spirit over which it had no controul, and of whose actions my own soul was wholly unconscious. This was an anomaly not to be accounted for by any philosophy of mine, and I was many times, in contemplating it, excited to terrors and mental torments hardly describable. To be in a state of consciousness and unconsciousness, at the same time, in the same body and same spirit, was impossible. I was under the greatest anxiety, dreading some change would take place momently in my nature; for of dates I could make nothing: one-half, or two-thirds of my time, seemed to me to be totally lost. I often, about this time, prayed with great fervour, and lamented my hopeless condition, especially in being liable to the commission of crimes, which I was not sensible of, and could not eschew. And I confess, notwithstanding the promises on which I had been taught to rely, I began to have secret terrors, that the great enemy of man's salvation was exercising powers over me, that might eventually lead to my ruin. These were but temporary and sinful fears, but they added greatly to my unhappiness.

The worst thing of all was, what hitherto I had never felt, and, as yet, durst not confess to myself, that the presence of my illustrious and devoted friend was becoming irksome to me. When I was by myself, I breathed freer, and my step was lighter; but, when he approached, a pang went to my heart, and, in his company, I moved and acted as if under a load that I could hardly endure. What a state to be in! And yet to shake him off was impossible—we were incorporated together—identified with one another, as it were, and the power was not in me to separate myself from him. I still knew nothing who he was, farther than that he was a potentate of some foreign land, bent on establishing some pure and genuine doctrines of Christianity, hitherto only half understood, and less than half exercised. Of this I could have no doubts, after all that he had said, done, and suffered in the cause. But, alongst with this, I was also certain, that he was possessed of some supernatural power, of the source of which I was wholly ignorant. That a man could be a Christian, and at the same time a powerful necromancer, appeared inconsistent, and adverse to every principle taught in our church; and from this I was led to believe, that he inherited his powers from on high, for I could not doubt either of the soundness of his principles, or that he accomplished things impossible to account for.

Thus was I sojourning in the midst of a chaos of confusion. I looked back on my bypast life with pain, as one looks back on a perilous journey, in which he has attained his end, without gaining any advantage either to himself, or others; and I looked forward, as on a darksome waste, full of repulsive and terrific shapes, pitfalls, and precipices, to which there was no definite bourne, and from which I turned with disgust. With my riches, my unhappiness was increased tenfold; and here, with another great acquisition of property, for which I had pleaed, and which I had gained in a dream, my miseries and difficulties were increasing. My principal feeling, about this time, was an insatiable longing for something that I cannot describe or denominate properly, unless I say it was for *utter oblivion* that I longed. I desired to sleep; but it was for a deeper and longer sleep, than that in which the senses were nightly steeped. I longed to be at rest and quiet, and close my eyes on the past and the future alike, as far as this frail life was concerned. But what had been formerly and finally settled in the counsels above, I presumed not to call in question.

In this state of irritation and misery, was I dragging on an existence, disgusted with all around me, and in particular with my mother, who, with all her love and anxiety, had such an insufferable mode of manifesting them, that she had by this time rendered herself exceedingly obnoxious to me. The very sound of her voice at a distance, went to my heart like an arrow, and made all my nerves to shrink; and as for the beautiful young lady of whom they told me I had been so much enamoured, I shunned all intercourse with her or hers, as I would have done with the devil. I read some of their letters and burnt them, but refused to see either the young lady or her mother, on any account.

About this time it was, that my worthy and reverend parent came with one of his elders to see my mother and myself. His presence always brought joy with it into our family, for my mother was uplifted, and I had so few who cared for me, or for whom I cared, that I felt rather gratified at seeing him. My illustrious friend was also much more attached to him, than any other person, (except myself,) for their religious principles tallied in every point, and their conversation was interesting, serious, and sublime. Being anxious to entertain well and highly the man to whom I had been so much indebted, and knowing that with all his integrity and righteousness, he disdained not the good things of this life, I brought from the late laird's well-stored cellars, various fragrant and salubrious wines, and we drank and became merry, and I found that my miseries and overpowering calamities, passed away over my head like a shower that is driven by the wind.

I became elevated and happy, and welcomed my guests an hundred times; and then I joined them in religious conversation, with a zeal and enthusiasm which I had not often experienced, and which made all their hearts rejoice, so that I said to myself, 'Surely every gift of God is a blessing, and ought to be used with liberality and thankfulness.'

The next day I waked from a profound and feverish sleep, and called for something to drink. There was a servant answered whom I had never seen before, and he was clad in my servant's clothes and livery. I asked for Andrew Handyside, the servant who had waited at table the night before; but the man answered with a stare and a smile.

'What do you mean, sirrah,' said I. 'Pray what do you here? or what are you pleased to laugh at? I desire you to go about your business, and send me up Handyside. I want him to bring me something to drink.'

'Ye sanna want a drink, maister,' said the fellow: 'Tak a hearty ane, and see if it will wauken ye up something, sae that ye dinna ca' for ghaists through your sleep. Surely ye hacna forgotten that Andrew Handyside has been in his grave these six months?'

This was a stunning blow to me. I could not answer farther, but sunk back on my pillow as if I had been a lump of lead, refusing to take a drink or any thing else at the fellow's hand, who seemed thus mocking me with so grave a face. The man seemed sorry, and grieved at my being offended, but I ordered him away, and continued sullen and thoughtful. Could I have again been for a season in utter oblivion to myself, and transacting business which I neither approved of, nor had any connection with! I tried to recollect something in which I might have been engaged, but nothing was pourtrayed on my mind subsequent to the parting with my friends at a late hour the evening before. The evening before it certainly was: but if so, how came it, that Andrew Handyside, who served at table that evening, should have been in his grave six months! This was a circumstance somewhat equivocal; therefore, being afraid to arise lest accusations of I knew not what might come against me, I was obliged to call once more in order to come at what intelligence I could. The same fellow appeared to receive my orders as before, and I set about examining him with regard to particulars. He told me his name was Scrape; that I hired him myself; of whom I hired him; and at whose recommendation.

I smiled, and nodded so as to let the knave see I understood he was telling me a chain of falsehoods, but did not choose to begin with any violent asseverations to the contrary.

'And where is my noble friend and companion?' said I. 'How has he been engaged in the interim?'

'I dinna ken him, sir,' said Scrape; 'but have heard it said, that the strange mysterious person that attended you, him that the maist part of folks countit uncanny, had gane awa wi' a Mr. Ringan o' Glasko last year, and had never returned.'

I thanked the Lord in my heart for this intelligence, hoping that the illustrious stranger had returned to his own land and people, and that I should thenceforth be rid of his controlling and appalling presence. 'And where is my mother?' said I.—The man's breath cut short, and he looked at me without returning any answer.—'I ask you where my mother is?' said I.

'God only knows, and not I, where she is,' returned he. 'He knows where her soul is, and as for her body, if you dinna ken something o' it, I suppose nae man alive does.'

'What do you mean, you knave?' said I. 'What dark hints are these you are throwing out? Tell me precisely and distinctly what you know of my mother?'

'It is unco queer o' ye to forget, or pretend to forget every thing that gate, the day, sir,' said he. 'I'm sure you heard enough about it yestreen; an' I can tell you, there are some gayan ill-faurd stories gaun about that business. But as the thing is to be tried afore the circuit lords,* it wad be far wrang to say either this or that to influence the public mind; it is best just to let justice tak its swee. I hae naething to say, sir. Ye hae been a good enough maister to me, and paid my wages regularly, but ye hae muckle need to be innocent, for there are some heavy accusations rising against you.'

'I fear no accusations of man,' said I, 'as long as I can justify my cause in the sight of Heaven; and that I can do this I am well aware. Go you and bring me some wine and water, and some other clothes than these gaudy and glaring ones.'

I took a cup of wine and water; put on my black clothes, and walked out. For all the perplexity that surrounded me, I felt my spirits considerably buoyant. It appeared that I was rid of the two greatest bars to my happiness, by what agency I knew not. My mother, it seemed, was gone, who had become a grievous thorn in my side of late, and my great companion and counsellor, who tyrannized over every spontaneous movement of my heart, had likewise taken himself off. This last was an unspeakable relief; for I found that for a long season I had only been able to act by the motions of his mysterious mind and spirit. I therefore thanked God for my deliverance, and strode through my woods with a daring and heroic step; with independence in my eye, and freedom swinging in my right hand.

At the extremity of the Colwan wood, I perceived a figure approaching me with slow and dignified motion. The moment that I beheld it, my whole frame received a shock as if the ground on which I walked had sunk suddenly below me. Yet, at that moment, I knew not who it was; it was the air and motion of some one that I dreaded, and from whom I would gladly have escaped; but this I even had not power to attempt. It came slowly onward, and I advanced as slowly to meet it; yet when we came within speech, I still knew not who it was. It bore the figure, air, and features of my late brother, I thought, exactly, yet in all these there were traits so forbidding, so mixed with an appearance of misery, chagrin, and despair, that I still shrunk from the view, not knowing on whose face I looked. But when the being spoke, both my mental and bodily frame received another shock more terrible than the first, for it was the voice of the great personage I had so long denominated my friend, of whom I had deemed myself for ever freed, and whose presence and counsels I now dreaded more than hell. It was his voice, but so altered—I shall never forget it till my dying day. Nay, I can scarce conceive it possible that any earthly sounds could be so discordant, so repulsive to every feeling of a human soul, as the tones of the voice that grated on my ear at that moment. They were the sounds of the pit, wheezed through a grated cranny, or seemed so to my distempered imagination.

'So! Thou shudderest at my approach now, dost thou?' said he. 'Is this all the gratitude that you deign for an attachment of which the annals of the world furnish no parallel? An attachment which has caused me to forego power and dominion, might, homage, conquest and adulation, all that I might gain one highly valued and sanctified spirit, to my great and true principles of reformation among mankind. Wherein have I offended? What have I done for evil, or what have I not done for your good, that you would thus shun my presence?'

'Great and magnificent prince,' said I humbly, 'let me request of you to abandon a poor worthless wight to his own wayward fortune, and return to the dominion of your people. I am unworthy of the sacrifices you have made for my sake; and after all your efforts, I do not feel that you have rendered me either more virtuous or more happy. For the sake of that which is estimable in human nature, depart from me to your own home, before you render me a being either altogether above, or below the rest of my fellow creatures. Let me plod on towards heaven and happiness in my own way, like those that have gone before me, and I promise to stick fast by the great principles which you have so strenuously inculcated, on condition that you depart and leave me for ever.'

'Sooner shall you make the mother abandon the child of her bosom; nay, sooner cause the shadow to relinquish the substance, than separate me from your side. Our beings are amalgamated, as it were, and consociated in one, and never shall I depart from this country until I can carry you in triumph with me.'

I can in nowise describe the effect this appalling speech had on me. It was like the announcement of death to one who had of late deemed himself free, if not of something worse than death, and of longer continuance. There was I doomed to remain in misery, subjugated, soul and body, to one whose presence was become more intolerable to me than ought on earth could compensate: And at that moment, when he beheld the anguish of my soul, he could not conceal that he enjoyed it. I was troubled for an answer, for which he was waiting: it became incumbent on me to say something after such a protestation of attachment; and, in some degree to shake the validity of it, I asked, with great simplicity, where he had been all this while?

'Your crimes and your extravagancies forced me from your side for a season,' said he; 'but now that I hope the day of grace is returned, I am again drawn towards you by an affection that has neither bounds nor interest; an affection for which I receive not even the poor return of gratitude, and which seems to have its radical sources in fascination. I have been far, far abroad, and have seen much, and transacted much, since I last spoke with you. During that space, I grievously suspect that you have been guilty of great crimes and misdemeanours, crimes that would have sunk an unregenerated person to perdition; but as I knew it to be only a temporary falling off, a specimen of that liberty by which the chosen and elected ones are made free, I closed my eyes on the wilful debasement of our principles, knowing that the transgressions could never be accounted to your charge, and that in good time you would come to your senses, and throw the whole weight of your crimes on the shoulders that had voluntarily stooped to receive the load.'

'Certainly I will,' said I, 'as I and all the justified have a good right to do. But what crimes? What misdemeanours and transgressions do you talk about? For my part, I am conscious of none, and am utterly amazed at insinuations which I do not comprehend.'

'You have certainly been left to yourself for a season,' returned he, 'having gone on rather like a person in a delirium, than a Christian in his sober senses. You are accused of having made away with your mother privately; as also of the death of a beautiful young lady, whose affections you had seduced.'

'It is an intolerable and monstrous falsehood!' cried I, interrupting him; 'I never laid a hand on a woman to take away her life, and have even shunned their society from my childhood: I know nothing of my mother's exit, nor of that young lady's whom you mention—Nothing whatever.'

'I hope it is so,' said he. 'But it seems there are some strong presumptuous proofs against you, and I came to warn you this day that a precognition* is in progress, and that unless you are perfectly convinced, not only of your innocence, but of your ability to prove it, it will be the safest course for you to abscond, and let the trial go on without you.'

'Never shall it be said that I shrunk from such a trial as this,' said I. 'It would give grounds for suspicions of guilt that never had existence, even in thought. I will go and show myself in every public place, that no slanderous tongue may wag against me. I have shed the blood of sinners, but of these deaths I am guiltless; therefore, I will face every tribunal, and put all my accusers down.'

'Asseveration will avail you but little,' answered he, composedly: 'It is, however, justifiable in its place, although to me it signifies nothing, who know too well that you *did* commit both crimes, in your own person, and with your own hands. Far be it from me to betray you; indeed, I would rather endeavour to palliate the offences; for though adverse to nature, I can prove them not to be so to the cause of pure Christianity, by the mode of which we have approved of it, and which we wish to promulgate.'

'If this that you tell me be true,' said I, 'then is it as true that I have two souls, which take possession of my bodily frame by turns,* the one being all unconscious of what the other performs; for as sure as I have at this moment a spirit within me, fashioned and destined to eternal felicity, as sure am I utterly ignorant of the crimes you now lay to my charge.'

'Your supposition may be true in effect,' said he. 'We are all subjected to two distinct natures in the same person. I myself have suffered grievously in that way. The spirit that now directs my energies is not that with which I was endowed at my creation. It is changed within me, and so is my whole nature. My former days were those of grandeur and felicity. But, would you believe it? *I was not then a Christian.* Now I am. I have been converted to its truths by passing through the fire, and since my final conversion, my misery has been extreme. You complain that I have not been able to render you more happy than you were. Alas! do you expect it in the difficult and exterminating career which you have begun. I, however, promise you this—a portion of the only happiness which I enjoy, sublime in its motions, and splendid in its attainments—I will place you on the right hand of my throne, and show you the grandeur of my domains, and the felicity of my millions of true professors.'

I was once more humbled before this mighty potentate, and promised to be ruled wholly by his directions, although at that moment my nature shrunk from the concessions, and my soul longed rather to be inclosed in the deeps of the sea,* or involved once more in utter oblivion. I was like Daniel in the den of lions,* without his faith in divine support, and wholly at their mercy. I felt as one round whose body a deadly snake is twisted, which continues to hold him in its fangs, without injuring him, farther than in moving its scaly infernal folds with exulting delight, to let its victim feel to whose power he has subjected himself; and thus did I for a space drag an existence from day to day, in utter weariness and helplessness; at one time worshipping with great fervour of spirit, and at other times so wholly left to myself, as to work all manner of vices and follies with greediness. In these my enlightened friend never accompanied me, but I always observed that he was the first to lead me to every one of them, and then leave me in the lurch. The next day, after these my fallings off, he never failed to reprove me gently, blaming me for my venial transgressions; but then he had the art of reconciling all, by reverting to my justified and infallible state, which I found to prove a delightful healing salve for every sore.

But, of all my troubles, this was the chief: I was every day and every hour assailed with accusations of deeds of which I was wholly ignorant; of acts of cruelty, injustice, defamation, and deceit; of pieces of business which I could not be made to comprehend; with law-suits, details, arrestments of judgment, and a thousand interminable quibbles from the mouth of my loquacious and conceited attorney. So miserable was my life rendered by these continued attacks, that I was often obliged to lock myself up for days together, never seeing any person save my man Samuel Scrape, who was a very honest blunt fellow, a staunch Cameronian,* but withal very little conversant in religious matters. He said he came from a place called Penpunt,* which I thought a name so ludicrous, that I called him by the name of his native village, an appellation of which he was very proud, and answered every thing with more civility and perspicuity when I denominated him Penpunt, than Samuel, his own Christian name. Of this peasant was I obliged to make a companion on sundry occasions, and strange indeed were the details which he gave me concerning myself, and the ideas of the country people concerning me. I took down a few of these in writing, to put off the time, and here leave them on record to show how the best and greatest actions are misconstrued among sinful and ignorant men.

'You say, Samuel, that I hired you myself—that I have been a good enough master to you, and have paid you your weekly wages punctually. Now, how is it that you say this, knowing, as you do, that I never hired you, and never paid you a sixpence of wages in the whole course of my life, excepting this last month?'

'Ye may as weel say, master, that water's no water, or that stanes are no stanes. But that's just your gate, an' it is a great pity aye to do a thing an' profess the clean contrair. Weel then, since you havena paid me ony wages, an' I can prove day and date when I was hired, an' came hame to your service, will you be sae kind as to pay me now? That's the best way o' curing a man o' the mortal disease o' leasing-making that I ken o'.'

'I should think that Penpunt and Cameronian principles, would not admit of a man taking twice payment for the same article.'

'In sic a case as this, sir, it disna hinge upon principles, but a piece o' good manners; an' I can tell you that at sic a crisis, a Cameronian is a gayan weel-bred man. He's driven to this, that he maun either make a breach in his friend's good name, or in his purse; an' O, sir, whilk o' thae, think you, is the most precious?* For instance, an a Galloway drover had comed to the town o' Penpunt, an' said to a Cameronian, (the folk's a' Cameronians there,) "Sir, I want to buy your cow." "Vera weel," says the Cameronian, "I just want to sell the cow, sae gie me twanty punds Scots, an' take her w'ye." It's a bargain. The drover takes away the cow, an' gies the Cameronian his twanty pund Scots. But after that, he meets him again on the white sands, amang a' the drovers an' dealers o' the land, an' the Gallowayman, he says to the Cameronian, afore a' thae witnesses, "Come, Master Whiggam,* I hae never paid you for yon bit useless cow, that I bought, I'll pay her the day, but you maun mind the luck-penny; there's muckle need for't,"—or something to that purpose. The Cameronian then turns out to be a civil man, an' canna bide to make the man baith a feele an' liar at the same time, afore a' his associates; an' therefore he pits his principles aff at the side, to be a kind o' sleepin partner, as it war, an' brings up his good breeding to stand at the counter: he pockets the money, gies the Galloway drover time o' day, an' comes his way. An' wha's to blame? *Man mind yoursel* is the first commandment. A Cameronian's principles never came atween him an' his purse, nor sanna in the present case; for as I canna bide to make you out a leear, I'll thank you for my wages.'

'Well, you shall have them, Samuel, if you declare to me that I hired you myself in this same person, and bargained with you with this same tongue, and voice, with which I speak to you just now.'

'That I do declare, unless ye hae twa persons o' the same appearance, and twa tongues to the same voice. But, od saif us, sir, do you ken what the auld wives o' the clachan say about you?'

'How should I, when no one repeats it to me?'

'Oo, I trow it's a' stuff;—folk shouldna heed what's said by auld crazy kimmers. But there are some o' them weel kend for witches too; an' they say,—lord have a care o' us!—they say the deil's often seen gaun sidie for sidie w'ye, whiles in ae shape, an' whiles in another. An' they say that he whiles takes your ain shape, or else enters into you, and then you turn a deil yoursel.'

I was so astounded at this terrible idea that had gone abroad, regarding my fellowship with the prince of darkness, that I could make no answer to the fellow's information, but sat like one in a stupor; and if it had not been for my well-founded faith, and conviction that I was a chosen and elected one before the world was made,

I should at that moment have given into the popular belief, and fallen into the sin of despondency; but I was preserved from such a fatal error by an inward and unseen supporter. Still the insinuation was so like what I felt myself, that I was greatly awed and confounded.

The poor fellow observed this, and tried to do away the impression by some farther sage remarks of his own.

'Hout, dear sir, it is balderdash, there's nae doubt o't. It is the crownhead o' absurdity to tak in the havers o' auld wives for gospel. I told them that my master was a peeous man, an' a sensible man; an' for praying, that he could ding auld Macmillan* himsel. "Sae could the deil," they said, "when he liket, either at preaching or praying, if these war to answer his ain ends." "Na, na," says I, "but he's a strick believer in a' the truths o' Christianity, my master." They said, sae was Satan, for that he was the firmest believer in a' the truths of Christianity that was out o' heaven; an' that, sin' the Revolution that the gospel had turned sae rife, he had been often driven to the shift o' preaching it himsel, for the purpose o' getting some wrang tenets introduced into it, and thereby turning it into blasphemy and ridicule.'

I confess, to my shame, that I was so overcome by this jumble of nonsense, that a chillness came over me, and in spite of all my efforts to shake off the impression it had made, I fell into a faint. Samuel soon brought me to myself, and after a deep draught of wine and water, I was greatly revived, and felt my spirit rise above the sphere of vulgar conceptions, and the restrained views of unregenerate men. The shrewd but loquacious fellow, perceiving this, tried to make some amends for the pain he had occasioned to me, by the following story, which I noted down, and which was brought on by a conversation to the following purport:—

'Now, Penpunt, you may tell me all that passed between you and the wives of the clachan. I am better of that stomach qualm, with which I am sometimes seized, and shall be much amused by hearing the sentiments of noted witches regarding myself and my connections.'

'Weel, you see, sir, I says to them, "It will be lang afore the deil intermeddle wi' as serious a professor, and as fervent a prayer as my master, for gin he gets the upper hand o' sickan men, wha's to be safe?" An', what think ye they said, sir? There was ane Lucky Shaw set up her lang lantern chafts, an' answered me, an' a' the rest shanned and noddit in assent an' approbation: "Ye silly, sauchless,

Cameronian cuif!" quo she, "is that a' that ye ken about the wiles and doings o' the prince o' the air, that rules an' works in the bairns of disobedience? Gin ever he observes a proud professor, wha has mae than ordinary pretensions to a divine calling, and that reards and prays till the very howlets learn his preambles, *that's* the man Auld Simmie* fixes on to mak a dishclout o'. He canna get rest in hell, if he sees a man, or a set of men o' this stamp, an' when he sets fairly to wark, it is seldom that he disna bring them round till his ain measures by hook or by crook. Then, O it is a grand prize for him, an' a proud deil he is, when he gangs hame to his ain ha', wi' a batch o' the souls o' sic strenuous professors* on his back. Ay, I trow, auld Ingleby, the Liverpool packman, never came up Glasco street* wi' prouder pomp, when he had ten horse-laids afore him o' Flanders lace, an' Hollin lawn, an' silks an' satins frae the eastern Indians, than Satan wad strodge into hell with a pack-laid o' the souls o' proud professors on his braid shoulders. Ha, ha, ha! I think I see how the auld thief wad be gaun through his gizened dominions, crying his wares, in derision, 'Wha will buy a fresh, cauler divine, a bouzy bishop, a fasting zealot, or a piping priest? For a' their prayers an' their praises, their aumuses, an' their penances, their whinings, their howlings, their rantings, an' their ravings, here they come at last! Behold the end! Here go the rare and precious wares! A fat professor for a bodle, an' a lean ane for half a merk!'" I declare, I trembled at the auld hag's ravings, but the lave o' the kimmers applauded the sayings as sacred truths. An' then Lucky went on: "There are many wolves in sheep's claithing,* among us, my man; mony deils aneath the masks o' zealous professors, roaming about in kirks and meeting-houses o' the land. It was but the year afore the last, that the people o' the town o' Auchtermuchty* grew so rigidly righteous, that the meanest hind among them became a shining light in ither towns an' parishes. There was nought to be heard, neither night nor day, but preaching, praying, argumentation, an' catechising in a' the famous town o' Auchtermuchty. The young men wooed their sweethearts out o' the Song o' Solomon, an' the girls returned answers in strings o' verses out o' the Psalms. At the lint-swinglings, they said questions round;* and read chapters, and sang hymns at bridals; auld and young prayed in their dreams, an' prophesied in their sleep, till the deils in the farrest nooks o' hell were alarmed, and moved to commotion. Gin it hadna been an auld carl, Robin Ruthven, Auchtermuchty wad at that time hae been ruined and lost for ever. But Robin was a cunning man, an' had rather mae wits than his ain, for he had been in the hands o' the fairies when he was young, an' a' kinds o' spirits were visible to his een, an' their language as familiar to him as his ain mother tongue.* Robin was sitting on the side o' the West Lowmond,* ae still gloomy night in September, when he saw a bridal o' corbie craws* coming east the lift, just on the edge o' the gloaming. The moment that Robin saw them, he kenned, by their movements, that they were craws o' some ither warld than this; so he signed himself,* and crap into the middle o' his bourock. The corbie craws came a' an' sat down round about him, an' they poukit their black sooty wings, an' spread them out to the breeze to cool; and Robin heard ae corbie speaking, an' another answering him; and the tane said to the tither: 'Where will the ravens find a prey the night?'—'On the lean crazy souls o' Auchtermuchty,' quo the tither.—'I fear they will be o'er weel wrappit up in the warm flannens o' faith, an' clouted wi' the dirty duds o' repentance, for us to mak a meal o',' quo the first.—'Whaten vile sounds are these that I hear coming bumming up the hill?' 'O these are the hymns and praises o' the auld wives and creeshy louns o' Auchtermuchty, wha are gaun crooning their way to heaven; an' gin it warna for the shame o' being beat, we might let our great enemy tak them. For sic a prize as he will hae! Heaven, forsooth! What shall we think o' heaven, if it is to be filled wi' vermin like thae, amang whom there is mair poverty and pollution, than I can name.' 'No matter for that,' said the first, 'we cannot have our power set at defiance; though we should put them in the thief's hole, we must catch them, and catch them with their own bait too. Come all to church to-morrow, and I'll let you hear how I'll gull the saints of Auchtermuchty. In the mean time, there is a feast on the Sidlaw hills to-night, below the hill of Macbeth,—Mount, Diabolus, and fly.'* Then, with loud croaking and crowing, the bridal of corbies again scaled the dusky air, and left Robin Ruthven in the middle of his cairn.

'"The next day the congregation met in the kirk of Auchtermuchty, but the minister made not his appearance. The elders ran out and in, making inquiries; but they could learn nothing, save that the minister was missing. They ordered the clerk to sing a part of the 119th Psalm, until they saw if the minister would cast up. The clerk did as he was ordered, and by the time he reached the 77th verse'* a strange divine entered the church, by the *western door*,* and advanced solemnly up to the pulpit. The eyes of all the congregation were riveted on the sublime stranger, who was clothed in a robe of black sackcloth, that flowed all around him, and trailed far behind, and they weened him an angel, come to exhort them, in disguise. He read out his text from the Prophecies of Ezekiel, which consisted of these singular words: 'I will overturn, overturn, overturn it; and it shall be no more, until he come, whose right it is, and I will give it him.'*

' "From these words he preached such a sermon as never was heard by human ears, at least never by ears of Auchtermuchty. It was a true, sterling, gospel sermon—it was striking, sublime, and awful in the extreme. He finally made out the IT, mentioned in the text, to mean, properly and positively, the notable town of Auchtermuchty. He proved all the people in it, to their perfect satisfaction, to be in the gall of bitterness and bond of iniquity,* and he assured them, that God would overturn them, their principles, and professions; and that they should be no more, until the devil, the town's greatest enemy, came, and then it should be given unto him for a prey, for it was his right, and to him it belonged, if there was not forthwith a radical change made in all their opinions and modes of worship.

' "The inhabitants of Auchtermuchty were electrified—they were charmed; they were actually raving mad about the grand and sublime truths delivered to them, by this eloquent and impressive preacher of Christianity. 'He is a prophet of the Lord,' said one, 'sent to warn us, as Jonah was sent to the Ninevites.'* 'O, he is an angel sent from heaven, to instruct this great city,' said another, 'for no man ever uttered truths so sublime before.' The good people of Auchtermuchty were in perfect raptures with the preacher, who had thus sent them to hell by the slump, tag, rag, and bobtail! Nothing in the world delights a truly religious people so much, as consigning them to eternal damnation. They wondered after the preacher—they crowded together, and spoke of his sermon with admiration, and still as they conversed, the wonder and the admiration increased; so that honest Robin Ruthven's words would not be listened to. It was in vain that he told them he heard a raven speaking, and another raven answering him: the people laughed him to scorn, and kicked him out of their assemblies, as a one who spoke evil of dignities;* and they called him a warlock, an' a daft body, to think to mak language out o' the crouping o' craws.

' "The sublime preacher could not be heard of, although all the country was sought for him, even to the minutest corner of

St. Johnston and Dundee; but as he had announced another sermon on the same text, on a certain day, all the inhabitants of that populous country, far and near, flocked to Auchtermuchty. Cupar, Newburgh, and Strathmiglo, turned out men, women, and children. Perth and Dundee gave their thousands; and from the East Nook of Fife to the foot of the Grampian hills,* there was nothing but running and riding that morning to Auchtermuchty. The kirk would not hold the thousandth part of them. A splendid tent* was erected on the brae north of the town, and round that the countless congregation assembled. When they were all waiting anxiously for the great preacher, behold, Robin Ruthven set up his head in the tent, and warned his countrymen to beware of the doctrines they were about to hear, for he could prove, to their satisfaction, that they were all false, and tended to their destruction!

'"The whole multitude raised a cry of indignation against Robin, and dragged him from the tent, the elders rebuking him, and the multitude threatening to resort to stronger measures; and though he told them a plain and unsophisticated tale of the black corbies, he was only derided. The great preacher appeared once more, and went through his two discourses with increased energy and approbation. All who heard him were amazed, and many of them went into fits, writhing and foaming in a state of the most horrid agitation. Robin Ruthven sat on the outskirts of the great assembly, listening with the rest, and perceived what they, in the height of their enthusiasm, perceived not,—the ruinous tendency of the tenets so sublimely inculcated. Robin kenned the voice of his friend the corby-craw again, and was sure he could not be wrang: sae when public worship was finished, a' the elders an' a' the gentry flocked about the great preacher, as he stood on the green brae in the sight of the hale congregation, an' a' war alike anxious to pay him some mark o' respect. Robin Ruthven came in amang the thrang, to try to effect what he had promised; and, with the greatest readiness and simplicity, just took haud o' the side an' wide gown, an' in sight of a' present, held it aside as high as the preacher's knee, and behold, there was a pair o' cloven feet! The auld thief was fairly catched in the very height o' his proud conquest, an' put down by an auld carl. He could feign nae mair, but gnashing on Robin wi' his teeth, he dartit into the air like a fiery dragon, an' keust a reid rainbow our the taps o' the Lowmonds.

' "A' the auld wives an' weavers o' Auchtermuchty fell down flat wi' affright, an' betook them to their prayers aince again, for they saw the dreadfu' danger they had escapit, an' frae that day to this it is a hard matter to gar an Auchtermuchty man listen to a sermon at a', an' a harder ane still to gar him applaud ane, for he thinks aye that he sees the cloven foot peeping out frae aneath ilka sentence.

' "Now, this is a true story, my man," quo the auld wife; "an' whenever you are doubtfu' of a man, take auld Robin Ruthven's plan, an' look for the cloven foot, for it's a thing that winna weel hide; an' it appears whiles where ane wadna think o't. It will keek out frae aneath the parson's gown, the lawyer's wig, and the Cameronian's blue bannet; but still there is a gouden rule* whereby to detect it, an' that never, never fails."—The auld witch didna gie me the rule, an' though I hae heard tell o't often an' often, shame fa' me an I ken what it is! But ye will ken it well, an' it wad be nae the waur of a trial on some o' your friends, maybe; for they say there's a certain gentleman seen walking wi' you whiles, that, wherever he sets his foot, the grass withers as gin it war scoudered wi' a het ern. His presence be about us! What's the matter wi' you, master? Are ye gaun to take the calm o' the stamock again?'

The truth is, that the clown's absurd story, with the still more ridiculous application, made me sick at heart a second time. It was not because I thought my illustrious friend was the devil, or that I took a fool's idle tale as a counterbalance to divine revelation, that had assured me of my justification in the sight of God before the existence of time. But, in short, it gave me a view of my own state, at which I shuddered, as indeed I now always did, when the image of my devoted friend and ruler presented itself to my mind. I often communed with my heart on this, and wondered how a connection, that had the well-being of mankind solely in view, could be productive of fruits so bitter. I then went to try my works by the Saviour's golden rule, as my servant had put it into my head to do; and, behold, not one of them would stand the test. I had shed blood on a ground on which I could not admit that any man had a right to shed mine; and I began to doubt the motives of my adviser once more, not that they were intentionally bad, but that his was some great mind led astray by enthusiasm, or some overpowering passion.

He seemed to comprehend every one of these motions of my heart, for his manner towards me altered every day. It first became any thing but agreeable, then supercilious, and finally, intolerable; so that I resolved to shake him off, cost what it would, even though I should be reduced to beg my bread in a foreign land. To do it at home was impossible, as he held my life in his hands, to sell it whenever he had a mind; and besides, his ascendancy over me was as complete as that of a huntsman over his dogs. I was even so weak, as, the next time I met with him, to look stedfastly at his foot, to see if it was not cloven into two hoofs. It was the foot of a gentleman, in every respect, so far as appearances went, but the form of his counsels was somewhat equivocal, and if not double, they were amazingly crooked.

But, if I had taken my measures to abscond and fly from my native place, in order to free myself of this tormenting, intolerant, and bloody reformer, he had likewise taken his to expel me, or throw me into the hands of justice. It seems, that about this time, I was haunted by some spies connected with my late father and brother, of whom the mistress of the former was one. My brother's death had been witnessed by two individuals; indeed, I always had an impression that it was witnessed by more than one, having some faint recollection of hearing voices and challenges close beside me; and this woman had searched about until she found these people; but, as I shrewdly suspected, not without the assistance of the only person in my secret,—my own warm and devoted friend. I say this, because I found that he had them concealed in the neighbourhood, and then took me again and again where I was fully exposed to their view, without being aware. One time in particular, on pretence of gratifying my revenge on that base woman, he knew so well where she lay concealed, that he led me to her, and left me to the mercy of two viragos, who had very nigh taken my life. My time of residence at Dalcastle was wearing to a crisis. I could no longer live with my tyrant, who haunted me like my shadow; and besides, it seems there were proofs of murder leading against me from all quarters. Of part of these I deemed myself quite free, but the world deemed otherwise; and how the matter would have gone, God only knows, for, the case never having undergone a judicial trial, I do not. It perhaps, however, behoves me here to relate all that I know of it, and it is simply this:

On the first of June 1712, (well may I remember the day,) I was sitting locked in my secret chamber, in a state of the utmost despondency, revolving in my mind what I ought to do to be free of my persecutors, and wishing myself a worm, or a moth, that I might be crushed and at rest, when behold Samuel entered, with eyes like to start out of his head, exclaiming, 'For God's sake, master, fly and hide yourself, for your mother's found, an' as sure as you're a living soul, the blame is gaun to fa' on you!'

'My mother found!' said I. 'And, pray, where has she been all this while?' In the mean time, I was terribly discomposed at the thoughts of her return.

'Been, sir! Been? Why, she has been where ye pat her, it seems,—lying buried in the sands o' the linn. I can tell you, ye will see her a frightsome figure, sic as I never wish to see again. An' the young lady is found too, sir: an' it is said the devil—I beg pardon sir, *your friend*, I mean,—it is said your *friend* has made the discovery, an' the folk are away to raise officers, an' they will be here in an hour or two at the farthest, sir; an' sae you hae not a minute to lose, for there's proof, sir, strong proof, an' sworn proof, that ye were last seen wi' them baith; sae, unless ye can gie a' the better an account o' baith yoursel an' them, either hide, or flee for your bare life.'

'I will neither hide nor fly,' said I; 'for I am as guiltless of the blood of these women as the child unborn.'

'The country disna think sae, master; an' I can assure you, that should evidence fail, you run a risk o' being torn limb frae limb. They are bringing the corpse here, to gar ye touch them baith afore witnesses,* an' plenty o' witnesses there will be!'

'They shall not bring them here,' cried I, shocked beyond measure at the experiment about to be made: 'Go, instantly, and debar them from entering my gate with their bloated and mangled carcases.'

'The body of your own mother, sir!' said the fellow emphatically. I was in terrible agitation; and, being driven to my wit's end, I got up and strode furiously round and round the room. Samuel wist not what to do, but I saw by his staring he deemed me doubly guilty. A tap came to the chamber door: we both started like guilty creatures; and as for Samuel, his hairs stood all on end with alarm, so that when I motioned to him, he could scarcely advance to open the door. He did so at length, and who should enter but my illustrious friend, manifestly in the utmost state of alarm. The moment that Samuel admitted him, the former made his escape by the prince's side as he entered, seemingly in a state of distraction. I was little better, when I saw this dreaded personage enter my chamber, which he had never before attempted; and being unable to ask his errand, I suppose I stood and gazed on him like a statue.

'I come with sad and tormenting tidings to you, my beloved and ungrateful friend,' said he; 'but having only a minute left to save your life, I have come to attempt it. There is a mob coming towards you with two dead bodies, which will place you in circumstances disagreeable enough: but that is not the worst, for of that you may be able to clear yourself. At this moment there is a party of officers, with a Justiciary warrant from Edinburgh, surrounding the house, and about to begin the search of it, for you. If you fall into their hands, you are inevitably lost; for I have been making earnest inquiries, and find that every thing is in train for your ruin.'

'Ay, and who has been the cause of all this?' said I, with great bitterness. But he stopped me short, adding, 'There is no time for such reflections at present. I gave you my word of honour that your life should be safe from the hand of man. So it shall, if the power remain with me to save it. I am come to redeem my pledge, and to save your life by the sacrifice of my own. Here,—Not one word of expostulation, change habits with me, and you may then pass by the officers, and guards, and even through the approaching mob, with the most perfect temerity. There is a virtue in this garb, and instead of offering to detain you, they shall pay you obeisance. Make haste, and leave this place for the present, flying where you best may, and if I escape from these dangers that surround me, I will endeavour to find you out, and bring you what intelligence I am able.'

I put on his green frock coat, buff belt, and a sort of a turban that he always wore on his head, somewhat resembling a bishop's mitre: he drew his hand thrice across my face, and I withdrew as he continued to urge me. My hall door and postern gate were both strongly guarded, and there were sundry armed people within, searching the closets; but all of them made way for me, and lifted their caps as I passed by them. Only one superior officer accosted me, asking if I had seen the culprit? I knew not what answer to make, but chanced to say, with great truth and propriety, 'He is safe enough.' The man beckoned with a smile, as much as to say, 'Thank you, sir, that is quite sufficient;' and I walked deliberately away.

I had not well left the gate, till, hearing a great noise coming from the deep glen toward the east, I turned that way, deeming myself quite secure in this my new disguise, to see what it was, and if matters were as had been described to me. There I met a great mob, sure enough, coming with two dead bodies stretched on boards, and decently covered with white sheets. I would fain have examined their appearance, had I not perceived the apparent fury in the looks of the men, and judged from that how much more safe it was for me not to intermeddle in the affray. I cannot tell how it was, but I felt a strange and unwonted delight in viewing this scene, and a certain pride of heart in being supposed the perpetrator of the unnatural crimes laid to my charge. This was a feeling quite new to me; and if there were virtues in the robes of the illustrious foreigner, who had without all dispute preserved my life at this time; I say, if there was any inherent virtue in these robes of his, as he had suggested, this was one of their effects, that they turned my heart towards that which was evil, horrible, and disgustful.

I mixed with the mob to hear what they were saying. Every tongue was engaged in loading me with the most opprobrious epithets! One called me a monster of nature; another an incarnate devil; and another a creature made to be cursed in time and eternity. I retired from them, and winded my way southward, comforting myself with the assurance, that so mankind had used and persecuted the greatest fathers and apostles of the Christian church, and that their vile opprobrium could not alter the counsels of heaven concerning me.

On going over that rising ground called Dorington Moor, I could not help turning round and taking a look of Dalcastle. I had little doubt that it would be my last look, and nearly as little ambition that it should not. I thought how high my hopes of happiness and advancement had been on entering that mansion, and taking possession of its rich and extensive domains, and how miserably I had been disappointed. On the contrary, I had experienced nothing but chagrin, disgust, and terror; and I now consoled myself with the hope that I should henceforth shake myself free of the chains of my great tormentor, and for that privilege was I willing to encounter any earthly distress. I could not help perceiving, that I was now on a path which was likely to lead me into a species of distress hitherto unknown, and hardly dreamed of by me, and that was total destitution. For all the riches I had been possessed of a few hours previous to this, I found that here I was turned out of my lordly possessions without a single merk, or the power of lifting and commanding the smallest sum, without being thereby discovered and seized. Had it been possible for me to have escaped in my own clothes, I had a considerable sum secreted in these, but, by the sudden change, I was left without a coin for present necessity. But I had hope in heaven, knowing that the just man would not be left destitute;* and that though many troubles surrounded him, he would at last be set free from them all. I was possessed of strong and brilliant parts, and a liberal education; and though I had somehow unaccountably suffered my theological qualifications to fall into desuetude, since my acquaintance with the ablest and most rigid of all theologians, I had nevertheless hopes that, by preaching up redemption by grace, pre-ordination, and eternal purpose, I should yet be enabled to benefit mankind in some country, and rise to high distinction.

These were some of the thoughts by which I consoled myself as I posted on my way southward, avoiding the towns and villages, and falling into the cross ways that led from each of the great roads passing east and west, to another. I lodged the first night in the house of a country weaver, into which I stepped at a late hour, quite overcome with hunger and fatigue, having travelled not less than thirty miles from my late home. The man received me ungraciously, telling me of a gentleman's house at no great distance, and of an inn a little farther away; but I said I delighted more in the society of a man like him, than that of any gentleman of the land, for my concerns were with the poor of this world, it being easier for a camel to go through the eye of a needle, than for a rich man to enter into the kingdom of heaven.* The weaver's wife, who sat with a child on her knee, and had not hitherto opened her mouth, hearing me speak in that serious and religious style, stirred up the fire, with her one hand; then drawing a chair near it, she said, 'Come awa, honest lad, in by here; sin' it be sae that you belang to Him wha gies us a' that we hae, it is but right that you should share a part. You are a stranger, it is true, but *them* that winna entertain a stranger will never entertain an angel unawares.'*

I never was apt to be taken with the simplicity of nature; in general I despised it; but, owing to my circumstances at the time, I was deeply affected by the manner of this poor woman's welcome. The weaver continued in a churlish mood throughout the evening, apparently dissatisfied with what his wife had done in entertaining me, and spoke to her in a manner so crusty that I thought proper to rebuke him, for the woman was comely in her person, and virtuous in her conversation; but the weaver her husband was large of make, ill-favoured, and pestilent; therefore did I take him severely to task for the tenor of his conduct; but the man was froward, and answered me rudely, with sneering and derision, and, in the height of his caprice, he said to his wife, 'Whan focks are sae keen of a chance o' entertaining angels, gudewife, it wad maybe be worth their while to tak tent what kind o' angels they are. It wadna wonder me vera muckle an ye had entertained your friend the deil the night, for aw thought aw fand a saur o' reek an' brimstane about him. *He's* nane o' the best o' angels, an' focks winna hae muckle credit by entertaining him.'

Certainly, in the assured state I was in, I had as little reason to be alarmed at mention being made of the devil as any person on earth: of late, however, I felt that the reverse was the case, and that any allusion to my great enemy, moved me exceedingly. The weaver's speech had such an effect on me, that both he and his wife were alarmed at my looks. The latter thought I was angry, and chided her husband gently for his rudeness; but the weaver himself rather seemed to be confirmed in his opinion that I was the devil, for he looked round like a startled roe-buck, and immediately betook him to the family Bible.

I know not whether it was on purpose to prove my identity or not, but I think he was going to desire me either to read a certain portion of Scripture that he had sought out, or to make family worship, had not the conversation at that instant taken another turn; for the weaver, not knowing how to address me, abruptly asked my name, as he was about to put the Bible into my hands. Never having considered myself in the light of a malefactor, but rather as a champion in the cause of truth, and finding myself perfectly safe under my disguise, I had never once thought of the utility of changing my name, and when the man asked me, I hesitated; but being compelled to say something, I said my name was Cowan. The man stared at me, and then at his wife, with a look that spoke a knowledge of something alarming or mysterious.

'Ha! Cowan?' said he. 'That's most extrordinar! Not Colwan, I hope?'

'No: Cowan is my sirname,' said I. 'But why not Colwan, there being so little difference in the sound?'

'I was feared ye might be that waratch that the deil has taen the possession o', an' eggit him on to kill baith his father an' his mother, his only brother, an' his sweetheart,' said he; 'an' to say the truth, I'm no that sure about you yet, for I see you're gaun wi' arms on ye.'

'Not I, honest man,' said I; 'I carry no arms; a man conscious of his innocence and uprightness of heart, needs not to carry arms in his defence now.'

'Ay, ay, maister,' said he; 'an' pray what div ye ca' this bit windlestrae that's appearing here?' With that he pointed to something on the inside of the breast of my frock-coat. I looked at it, and there certainly was the gilded haft of a poniard, the same weapon I had seen and handled before, and which I knew my illustrious companion always carried about with him; but till that moment I knew not that I was in possession of it. I drew it out: a more dangerous or insidious looking weapon could not be conceived. The weaver and his wife were both frightened, the latter in particular; and she being my friend, and I dependant on their hospitality, for that night, I said, 'I declare I knew not that I carried this small rapier, which has been in my coat by chance, and not by any design of mine. But lest you should think that I meditate any mischief to any under this roof, I give it into your hands, requesting of you to lock it by till to-morrow, or when I shall next want it.'

The woman seemed rather glad to get hold of it; and, taking it from me, she went into a kind of pantry out of my sight, and locked the weapon up; and then the discourse went on.

'There cannot be such a thing in reality,' said I, 'as the story you were mentioning just now, of a man whose name resembles mine.'

'It's likely that you ken a wee better about the story than I do, maister,' said he, 'suppose you do leave the *L* out of your name. An' yet I think sic a waratch, an' a murderer, wad hae taen a name wi' some gritter difference in the sound. But the story is just that true, that there were twa o' the Queen's officers here nae mair than an hour ago, in pursuit o' the vagabond, for they gat some intelligence that he had fled this gate; yet they said he had been last seen wi' black claes on, an' they supposed he was clad in black. His ain servant is wi' them, for the purpose o' kennin the scoundrel, an' they're galloping through the country like mad-men. I hope in God they'll get him, an' rack his neck for him!'

I could not say *Amen* to the weaver's prayer, and therefore tried to compose myself as well as I could, and made some religious comment on the causes of the nation's depravity. But suspecting that my potent friend had betrayed my flight and disguise, to save his life, I was very uneasy, and gave myself up for lost. I said prayers in the family, with the tenor of which the wife was delighted, but the weaver still dissatis-fied; and, after a supper of the most homely fare, he tried to start an argument with me, proving, that every thing for which I had interceded in my prayer, was irrelevant to man's present state. But I, being weary and distressed in mind, shunned the contest, and requested a couch whereon to repose.

I was conducted into the other end of the house, among looms, treadles, pirns, and confusion without end; and there, in a sort of box, was I shut up for my night's repose, for the weaver, as he left me, cautiously turned the key of my apartment, and left me to shift for myself among the looms, determined that I should escape from the house with nothing. After he and his wife and children were crowded into their den, I heard the two mates contending furiously about me in suppressed voices, the one maintaining the probability that I was the murderer, and the other proving the impossibility of it. The husband, however, said as much as let me understand, that he had locked me up on purpose to bring the military, or officers of justice, to seize me. I was in the utmost perplexity, yet, for all that, and the imminent danger I was in, I fell asleep, and a more troubled and tormenting sleep never enchained a mortal frame. I had such dreams that they will not bear repetition, and early in the morning I awaked, feverish, and parched with thirst.

I went to call mine host, that he might let me out to the open air, but before doing so, I thought it necessary to put on some clothes. In attempting to do this, a circumstance arrested my attention, (for which I could in nowise account, which to this day I cannot unriddle, nor shall I ever be able to comprehend it while I live,) the frock and turban, which had furnished my disguise on the preceding day, were both removed, and my own black coat and cocked hat laid down in their place. At first I thought I was in a dream, and felt the weaver's beam, web, and treadle-strings with my hands, to convince myself that I was awake. I was certainly awake; and there was the door locked firm and fast as it was the evening before. I carried my own black coat to the small window, and examined it. It was my own in verity; and the sums of money, that I had concealed in case of any emergency, remained untouched. I trembled with astonishment; and on my return from the small window, went doiting in amongst the weaver's looms, till I entangled myself, and could not get out again without working great deray amongst the coarse linen threads that stood in warp from one end of the apartment unto the other. I had no knife whereby to cut the cords of this wicked man, and therefore was obliged to call out lustily for assistance. The weaver came half naked, unlocked the door, and, setting in his head and long neck, accosted me thus:

'What now, Mr. Satan? What for are ye roaring that gate? Are you fawn inna little hell, instead o' the big muckil ane? Deil be in your reistit trams! What for have ye abscondit yoursel into ma leddy's wab for?'

'Friend, I beg your pardon,' said I; 'I wanted to be at the light, and have somehow unfortunately involved myself in the intricacies of your web, from which I cannot get clear without doing you a great injury. Pray do, lend your experienced hand to extricate me.'

'May aw the pearls o' damnation* light on your silly snout, an I dinna estricat ye weel enough! Ye ditit, donnart, deil's burd that ye be! what made ye gang howkin in there to be a poor man's ruin? Come out, ye vile rag-of-a-muffin, or I gar ye come out wi' mair shame and disgrace, an' fewer haill banes in your body.'

My feet had slipped down through the double warpings of a web, and not being able to reach the ground with them, (there being a small pit below,) I rode upon a number of yielding threads, and there being nothing else that I could reach, to extricate myself was impossible. I was utterly powerless; and besides, the yarn and cords hurt me very much. For all that, the destructive weaver seized a loomspoke, and began a-beating me most unmercifully, while, entangled as I was, I could do nothing but shout aloud for mercy, or assistance, whichever chanced to be within hearing. The latter, at length, made its appearance, in the form of the weaver's wife, in the same state of dishabille with himself, who instantly interfered, and that most strenuously, on my behalf. Before her arrival, however, I had made a desperate effort to throw myself out of the entanglement I was in; for the weaver continued repeating his blows and cursing me so, that I determined to get out of his meshes at any risk. This effect made my case worse; for my feet being wrapt among the nether threads, as I threw myself from my saddle on the upper ones, my feet brought the others up through these, and I hung with my head down, and my feet as firm as they had been in a vice. The predicament of the web being thereby increased, the weaver's wrath was doubled in proportion, and he laid on without mercy.

At this critical juncture the wife arrived, and without hesitation rushed before her offended lord, withholding his hand from injuring me farther, although then it was uplifted along with the loomspoke in overbearing ire. 'Dear Johnny! I think ye be gaen dementit this morning. Be quiet, my dear, an' dinna begin a Boddel Brigg* business in your ain house. What for ir ye persecutin' a servant o' the Lord's that gate, an' pitting the life out o' him wi' his head down an' his heels up?'

'Had ye said a servant o' the deil's, Nans, ye wad hae been nearer the nail, for gin he binna the auld ane himsel, he's gayan sib till him. There, didna I lock him in on purpose to bring the military on him; an' in place o' that, hasna he keepit me in a sleep a' this while as deep as death? An' here do I find him abscondit like a speeder i' the mids o' my leddy's wab, an' me dreamin' a' the night that I had the deil i' my house, an' that he was clapper-clawin me ayont the loom. Have at you, ye brunstane thief!' and, in spite of the good woman's struggles, he lent me another severe blow.

'Now, Johnny Dods, my man! O Johnny Dods, think if that be like a Christian, and ane o' the heroes o' Boddel Brigg, to entertain a stranger, an' then bind him in a web wi' his head down, an' mell him to death! O Johnny Dods, think what you are about! Slack a pin, an' let the good honest religious lad out.'

The weaver was rather overcome, but still stood to his point that I was the deil, though in better temper; and as he slackened the web to release me, he remarked, half laughing, 'Wha wad hae thought that John Dods should hae escapit a' the snares an' dangers that circum-fauldit him, an' at last should hae weaved a net to catch the deil.'

The wife released me soon, and carefully whispered me, at the same time, that it would be as well for me to dress and be going. I was not long in obeying, and dressed myself in my black clothes, hardly knowing what I did, what to think, or whither to betake myself. I was sore hurt by the blows of the desperate ruffian; and, what was worse, my ankle was so much strained, that I could hardly set my foot to the ground. I was obliged to apply to the weaver once more, to see if I could learn any thing about my clothes, or how the change was effected. 'Sir,' said I, 'how comes it that you have robbed me of my clothes, and put these down in their place over night?'

'Ha! thae claes? Me pit down thae claes!' said he, gaping with astonishment, and touching the clothes with the point of his fore-finger; 'I never saw them afore, as I have death to meet wi': So help me God!'

He strode into the work-house where I slept, to satisfy himself that my clothes were not there, and returned perfectly aghast with con-sternation. 'The doors were baith fast lockit,' said he. 'I could hae defied a rat either to hae gotten out or in. My dream has been true! My dream has been true! The Lord judge between thee and me; but, in his name, I charge you to depart out o' this house; an', gin it be your will, dinna tak the braidside o't w'ye, but gang quietly out at the door wi' your face foremost.* Wife, let nought o' this enchanter's remain i' the house, to be a curse, an' a snare to us; gang an' bring him his gildit weapon, an' may the Lord protect a' his ain against its hellish an' deadly point!'

The wife went to seek my poniard, trembling so excessively that she could hardly walk, and shortly after, we heard a feeble scream from the pantry. The weapon had disappeared with the clothes, though under double lock and key; and the terror of the good people having now reached a disgusting extremity, I thought proper to make a sudden retreat, followed by the weaver's anathemas.

My state both of body and mind was now truly deplorable. I was hungry, wounded, and lame; an outcast and a vagabond in society; my life sought after with avidity, and all for doing that to which I was predestined by him who fore-ordains whatever comes to pass. I knew not whither to betake me. I had purposed going into England, and there making some use of the classical education I had received, but my lameness rendered this impracticable for the present. I was therefore obliged to turn my face towards Edinburgh, where I was little known—where concealment was more practicable than by skulking in the country, and where I might turn my mind to something that was great and good. I had a little money, both Scots and English, now in my possession, but not one friend in the whole world on whom I could rely. One devoted friend, it is true, I had, but he was become my greatest terror. To escape from him, I now felt that I would willingly travel to the farthest corners of the world, and be subjected to every deprivation; but after the certainty of what had taken place last night, after I had travelled thirty miles by secret and bye-ways, I saw not how escape from him was possible.

Miserable, forlorn, and dreading every person that I saw, either behind or before me, I hasted on towards Edinburgh, taking all the bye and unfrequented paths; and the third night after I left the weaver's house, I reached the West Port,* without meeting with any thing remarkable. Being exceedingly fatigued and lame, I took lodgings in the first house I entered, and for these I was to pay two groats a-week, and to board and sleep with a young man who wanted a companion to make his rent easier. I liked this; having found from experience, that the great personage who had attached himself to me, and was now become my greatest terror among many surrounding evils, generally haunted me when I was alone, keeping aloof from all other society.

My fellow lodger came home in the evening, and was glad at my coming. His name was Linton, and I changed mine to Elliot.* He was a flippant unstable being, one to whom nothing appeared a difficulty, in his own estimation, but who could effect very little, after all. He was what is called by some a compositor, in the Queen's printing house, then conducted by a Mr. James Watson.* In the course of our conversation that night, I told him that I was a first-rate classical scholar, and would gladly turn my attention to some business wherein my education might avail me something; and that there was nothing would delight me so much as an engagement in the Queen's printing office. Linton made no difficulty in bringing about that arrangement. His answer was, 'Oo, gud sir, you are the very man we want. Gud bless your breast and your buttons, sir! Ay, that's neither here nor there—That's all very well—Ha-ha-ha—A byeword in the house, sir. But, as I was saying, you are the very *man* we want—You will get any money you like to ask, sir—*Any* money you like, sir. God bless your buttons!—That's settled—All done—Settled, settled—I'll do it, I'll do it—No more about it; no more about it. Settled, settled.'

The next day I went with him to the office, and he presented me to Mr. Watson as the most wonderful genius and scholar ever known. His recommendation had little sway with Mr. Watson, who only smiled at Linton's extravagancies, as one does at the prattle of an infant. I sauntered about the printing office for the space of two or three hours, during which time Watson bustled about with green spectacles on his nose, and took no heed of me. But seeing that I still lingered, he addressed me at length, in a civil gentlemanly way, and inquired concerning my views. I satisfied him with all my answers, in particular those to his questions about the Latin and Greek languages; but when he came to ask testimonials of my character and acquirements, and found that I could produce none, he viewed me with a jealous eye, and said he dreaded I was some ne'er-do-weel, run from my parents or guardians, and he did not chuse to employ any such. I said my parents were both dead; and that being thereby deprived of the means of following out my education, it behoved me to apply to some business in which my education might be of some use to me.

He said he would take me into the office, and pay me according to the business I performed, and the manner in which I deported myself; but he could take no man into her Majesty's printing office upon a regular engagement, who could not produce the most respectable references with regard to morals.

I could not but despise the man in my heart who laid such a stress upon morals, leaving grace out of the question; and viewed it as a deplorable instance of human depravity and self conceit; but for all that, I was obliged to accept of his terms, for I had an inward thirst and longing to distinguish myself in the great cause of religion, and I thought if once I could print my own works, how I would astonish mankind, and confound their self wisdom and their esteemed morality—blow up the idea of any dependence on good works, and *morality*, forsooth! And I weened that I might thus get me a name even higher than if I had been made a general of the Czar Peter's troops against the infidels.

I attended the office some hours every day, but got not much encouragement, though I was eager to learn every thing, and could soon have set types considerably well. It was here that I first conceived the idea of writing this journal, and having it printed, and applied to Mr. Watson to print it for me, telling him it was a religious parable such as the Pilgrim's Progress.* He advised me to print it close, and make it a pamphlet, and then if it did not sell, it would not cost me much; but that religious pamphlets, especially if they had a shade of allegory in them, were the very rage of the day. I put my work to the press, and wrote early and late; and encouraging my companion to work at odd hours, and on Sundays, before the press-work of the second sheet was begun, we had the work all in types, corrected, and a clean copy thrown off for farther revisal. The first sheet was wrought off;* and I never shall forget how my heart exulted when at the printing house this day, I saw what numbers of my works were to go abroad among mankind, and I determined with myself that I would not put the Border name of Elliot, which I had assumed, to the work.

———————

THUS far have my History and Confessions been carried.

I must now furnish my Christian readers with a key to the process, management, and winding up of the whole matter; which I propose, by the assistance of God, to limit to a very few pages.

Chesters,* July 27, 1712.—My hopes and prospects are a wreck. My precious journal is lost! consigned to the flames! My enemy hath found me out, and there is no hope of peace or rest for me on this side the grave.

In the beginning of the last week, my fellow lodger came home, running in a great panic, and told me a story of the devil having appeared twice in the printing house, assisting the workmen at the printing of my book, and that some of them had been frightened out of their wits. That the story was told to Mr. Watson, who till that time had never paid any attention to the treatise, but who, out of curiosity, began and read a part of it, and thereupon flew into a great rage, called my work a medley of lies and blasphemy, and ordered the whole to be consigned to the flames, blaming his foreman, and all connected with the press, for letting a work go so far, that was enough to bring down the vengeance of heaven on the concern.

If ever I shed tears through perfect bitterness of spirit it was at that time, but I hope it was more for the ignorance and folly of my countrymen than the overthrow of my own hopes. But my attention was suddenly aroused to other matters, by Linton mentioning that it was said by some in the office the devil had inquired for me.

'Surely you are not such a fool,' said I, 'as to believe that the devil really was in the printing office?'*

'Oo, gud bless you sir! saw him myself, gave him a nod, and good-day. Rather a gentlemanly personage—Green Circassian hunting coat and turban*—Like a foreigner—Has the power of vanishing in one moment though—Rather a suspicious circumstance that. Otherwise, his appearance not much against him.'

If the former intelligence thrilled me with grief, this did so with terror. I perceived who the personage was that had visited the printing house in order to further the progress of my work; and at the approach of every person to our lodgings, I from that instant trembled every bone, lest it should be my elevated and dreaded friend. I could not say I had ever received an office at his hand that was not friendly, yet these offices had been of a strange tendency; and the horror with which I now regarded him was unaccountable to myself. It was beyond description, conception, or the soul of man to bear. I took my printed sheets, the only copy of my unfinished work existing; and, on pretence of going straight to Mr. Watson's office, decamped from my lodgings at Portsburgh* a little before the fall of evening, and took the road towards England.

As soon as I got clear of the city, I ran with a velocity I knew not before I had been capable of. I flew out the way towards Dalkeith so swiftly, that I often lost sight of the ground, and I said to myself, 'O that I had the wings of a dove, that I might fly to the farthest corners of the earth, to hide me from those against whom I have no power to stand!*

I travelled all that night and the next morning, exerting myself beyond my power; and about noon the following day I went into a yeoman's house, the name of which was Ellanshaws, and requested of the people a couch of any sort to lie down on, for I was ill, and could not proceed on my journey. They showed me to a stable-loft where there were two beds, on one of which I laid me down; and, falling into a sound sleep, I did not awake till the evening, that other three men came from the fields to sleep in the same place, one of whom lay down beside me, at which I was exceedingly glad. They fell all sound asleep, and I was terribly alarmed at a conversation I overheard somewhere outside the stable. I could not make out a sentence, but trembled to think I knew one of the voices at least, and rather than not be mistaken, I would that any man had run me through with a sword. I fell into a cold sweat, and once thought of instantly putting hand to my own life, as my only means of relief, (May the rash and sinful thought be in mercy forgiven!) when I heard as it were two persons at the door, contending, as I thought, about their right and interest in me. That the one was forcibly preventing the admission of the other, I could hear distinctly, and their language was mixed with something dreadful and mysterious. In an agony of terror, I awakened my snoring companion with great difficulty, and asked him, in a low whisper, who these were at the door? The man lay silent, and listening, till fairly awake, and then asked if I had heard any thing? I said I had heard strange voices contending at the door.

'Then I can tell you, lad, it has been something neither good nor canny,' said he: 'It's no for naething that our horses are snorking that gate.'

For the first time, I remarked that the animals were snorting and rearing as if they wished to break through the house. The man called to them by their names, and ordered them to be quiet; but they raged still the more furiously. He then roused his drowsy companions, who were alike alarmed at the panic of the horses, all of them declaring that they had never seen either Mause or Jolly start in their lives before. My bed-fellow and another then ventured down the ladder, and I heard one of them then saying, 'Lord be wi' us! What can be i' the house? The sweat's rinning off the poor beasts like water.'

They agreed to sally out together, and if possible to reach the kitchen and bring a light. I was glad at this, but not so much so when I heard the one man saying to the other, in a whisper, 'I wish that stranger man may be canny enough.'

'God kens!' said the other: 'It doesnae look unco weel.'

The lad in the other bed, hearing this, set up his head in manifest affright as the other two departed for the kitchen; and, I believe, he would have been glad to have been in their company. This lad was next the ladder, at which I was extremely glad, for had he not been there, the world should not have induced me to wait the return of these two men. They were not well gone, before I heard another distinctly enter the stable, and come towards the ladder. The lad who was sitting up in his bed, intent on the watch, called out, 'Wha's that there? Walker, is that you? Purdie, I say, is it you?'

The darkling intruder paused for a few moments, and then came towards the foot of the ladder. The horses broke loose, and snorting and neighing for terror, raged through the house. In all my life I never heard so frightful a commotion. The being that occasioned it all, now began to mount the ladder toward our loft, on which the lad in the bed next the ladder sprung from his couch, crying out, 'the L——d A——y preserve us! What can it be?' With that he sped across the loft, and by my bed, praying lustily all the way; and, throwing himself from the other end of the loft into a manger, he darted, naked as he was, through among the furious horses, and making the door, that stood open, in a moment he vanished and left me in the lurch. Powerless with terror, and calling out fearfully, I tried to follow his example; but not knowing the situation of the places with regard to one another, I missed the manger, and fell on the pavement in one of the stalls. I was both stunned and lamed on the knee; but terror prevailing, I got up and tried to escape. It was out of my power; for there were divisions and cross divisions in the house, and mad horses smashing every thing before them, so that I knew not so much as on what side of the house the door was. Two or three times was I knocked down by the animals, but all the while I never stinted crying out with all my power. At length, I was seized by the throat and hair of the head, and dragged away, I wist not whither. My voice was now laid, and all my powers, both mental and bodily, totally overcome; and I remember no more till I found myself lying naked on the kitchen table of the farm house, and something like a horse's rug thrown over me. The only hint that I got from the people of the house on coming to myself was, that my absence would be good company; and that they had got me in a woful state, one which they did not chuse to describe, or hear described.

As soon as day-light appeared, I was packed about my business, with the hisses and execrations of the yeoman's family, who viewed me as a being to be shunned, ascribing to me the visitations of that unholy night. Again was I on my way southward, as lonely, hopeless, and degraded a being as was to be found on life's weary round. As I limped out the way, I wept, thinking of what I might have been, and what I really had become: of my high and flourishing hopes, when I set out as the avenger of God on the sinful children of men; of all that I had dared for the exaltation and progress of the truth; and it was with great difficulty that my faith remained unshaken, yet was I preserved from that sin, and comforted myself with the certainty, that the believer's progress through life is one of warfare and suffering.

My case was indeed a pitiable one. I was lame, hungry, fatigued, and my resources on the very eve of being exhausted. Yet these were but secondary miseries, and hardly worthy of a thought, compared with those I suffered inwardly. I not only looked around me with terror at every one that approached, but I was become a terror to myself; or rather, my body and soul were become terrors to each other; and, had it been possible, I felt as if they would have gone to war. I dared not look at my face in a glass, for I shuddered at my own image and likeness. I dreaded the dawning, and trembled at the approach of night, nor was there one thing in nature that afforded me the least delight.

In this deplorable state of body and mind, was I jogging on towards the Tweed, by the side of the small river called Ellan, when, just at the narrowest part of the glen, whom should I meet full in the face, but the very being in all the universe of God I would the most gladly have shunned. I had no power to fly from him, neither durst I, for the spirit within me, accuse him of falsehood, and renounce his fellowship.

I stood before him like a condemned criminal, staring him in the face, ready to be winded, twisted, and tormented as he pleased. He regarded me with a sad and solemn look. How changed was now that majestic countenance,* to one of haggard despair—changed in all save the extraordinary likeness to my late brother, a resemblance which misfortune and despair tended only to heighten. There were no kind greetings passed between us at meeting, like those which pass between the men of the world; he looked on me with eyes that froze the currents of my blood, but spoke not, till I assumed as much courage as to articulate—'You here! I hope you have brought me tidings of comfort?'

'Tidings of despair!' said he. 'But such tidings as the timid and the ungrateful deserve, and have reason to expect. You are an outlaw, and a vagabond in your country, and a high reward is offered for your apprehension. The enraged populace have burnt your house, and all that is within it; and the farmers on the land bless themselves at being rid of you. So fare it with every one who puts his hand to the great work of man's restoration to freedom, and draweth back, contemning the light that is within him! Your enormities caused me to leave you to yourself for a season, and you see what the issue has been. You have given some evil ones power over you, who long to devour you, both soul and body, and it has required all my power and influence to save you. Had it not been for my hand, you had been torn in pieces last night; but for once I prevailed. We must leave this land forthwith, for here there is neither peace, safety, nor comfort for us. Do you now, and here, pledge yourself to one who has so often saved your life, and has put his own at stake to do so? Do you pledge yourself that you will henceforth be guided by my counsel, and follow me whithersoever I chuse to lead?'

'I have always been swayed by your counsel,' said I, 'and for your sake, principally, am I sorry, that all our measures have proved abortive. But I hope still to be useful in my native isle, therefore let me plead that your highness will abandon a poor despised and outcast wretch to his fate, and betake you to your realms, where your presence cannot but be greatly wanted.'

'Would that I could do so!' said he wofully. 'But to talk of that is to talk of an impossibility. I am wedded to you so closely, that I feel as if I were the same person. Our essences are one, our bodies and spirits being united, so, that I am drawn towards you as by magnetism, and wherever you are, there must my presence be with you.'

Perceiving how this assurance affected me, he began to chide me most bitterly for my ingratitude; and then he assumed such looks, that it was impossible for me longer to bear them; therefore I staggered out the way, begging and beseeching of him to give me up to my fate, and hardly knowing what I said; for it struck me, that, with all his assumed appearance of misery and wretchedness, there were traits of exultation in his hideous countenance, manifesting a secret and inward joy at my utter despair.

It was long before I durst look over my shoulder, but when I did so, I perceived this ruined and debased potentate coming slowly on the same path, and I prayed that the Lord would hide me in the bowels of the earth, or depths of the sea.* When I crossed the Tweed, I perceived him still a little behind me; and my despair being then at its height, I cursed the time I first met with such a tormentor; though, on a little recollection it occurred, that it was at that blessed time when I was solemnly dedicated to the Lord, and assured of my final election, and confirmation, by an eternal decree never to be annulled. This being my sole and only comfort, I recalled my curse upon the time, and repented me of my rashness.

After crossing the Tweed, I saw no more of my persecutor that day,* and had hopes that he had left me for a season; but, alas, what hope was there of my relief after the declaration I had so lately heard! I took up my lodgings that night in a small miserable inn in the village of Ancrum, of which the people seemed alike poor and ignorant. Before going to bed, I asked if it was customary with them to have family worship of evenings? The man answered, that they were so hard set with the world, they often could not get time, but if I would be so kind as officiate they would be much obliged to me. I accepted the invitation, being afraid to go to rest lest the commotions of the foregoing night might be renewed, and continued the worship as long as in decency I could. The poor people thanked me, hoped my prayers would be heard both on their account and my own, seemed much taken with my abilities, and wondered how a man of my powerful eloquence chanced to be wandering about in a condition so forlorn. I said I was a poor student of theology, on my way to Oxford. They stared at one another with expressions of wonder, disappointment, and fear. I afterwards came to learn, that the term *theology* was by them quite misunderstood, and that they had some crude conceptions that nothing was taught at Oxford but the *black arts*,* which ridiculous idea prevailed over all the south of Scotland. For the present I could not understand what the people meant, and less so, when the man asked me, with deep concern, 'If I was serious in my intentions of going to Oxford? He hoped not, and that I would be better guided.'

I said my education wanted finishing;—but he remarked, that the Oxford arts were a bad finish for a religious man's education.—Finally, I requested him to sleep with me, or in my room all the night, as I wanted some serious and religious conversation with him, and likewise to convince him that the study of the fine arts, though not absolutely necessary, were not incompatible with the character of a Christian divine. He shook his head, and wondered how I could call them *fine arts*—hoped I did not mean to convince him by any ocular demonstration, and at length reluctantly condescended to sleep with me, and let the lass and wife sleep together for one night. I believe he would have declined it, had it not been some hints from his wife, stating, that it was a good arrangement, by which I understood there were only two beds in the house, and that when I was preferred to the lass's bed, she had one to shift for.

The landlord and I accordingly retired to our homely bed, and conversed for some time about indifferent matters, till he fell sound asleep. Not so with me: I had that within which would not suffer me to close my eyes; and about the dead of night, I again heard the same noises and contention begin outside the house, as I had heard the night before; and again I heard it was about a sovereign and peculiar right in me. At one time the noise was on the top of the house, straight above our bed, as if the one party were breaking through the roof, and the other forcibly preventing it; at another time it was at the door, and at a third time at the window; but still mine host lay sound by my side, and did not waken. I was seized with terrors indefinable,* and prayed fervently, but did not attempt rousing my sleeping companion until I saw if no better could be done. The women, however, were alarmed, and, rushing into our apartment, exclaimed that all the devils in hell were besieging the house. Then, indeed, the landlord awoke, and it was time for him, for the tumult had increased to such a degree, that it shook the house to its foundations, being louder and more furious than I could have conceived the heat of battle to be when the volleys of artillery are mixed with groans, shouts, and blasphemous cursing. It thundered and lightened; and there were screams, groans, laughter, and execrations, all intermingled.

I lay trembling and bathed in a cold perspiration, but was soon obliged to bestir myself, the inmates attacking me one after the other.

'O, Tam Douglas! Tam Douglas! haste ye an' rise out fra-yont that incarnal devil!' cried the wife: 'Ye are in ayont the auld ane himsel, for our lass Tibbie saw his cloven cloots last night.'

'Lord forbid!' roared Tam Douglas, and darted over the bed like a flying fish. Then, hearing the unearthly tumult with which he was surrounded, he returned to the side of the bed, and addressed me thus, with long and fearful intervals:

'If ye be the deil, rise up, an' depart in peace out o' this house—afore the bedstrae take kindling about ye, an' than it'll maybe be the waur for ye—Get up—an' gang awa out amang your cronies, like a good—lad—There's nae body here wishes you ony ill—D'ye hear me?'

'Friend,' said I, 'no Christian would turn out a fellow creature on such a night as this, and in the midst of such a commotion of the villagers.'

'Na, if ye be a mortal man,' said he, 'which I rather think, from the use you made of the holy book—Nane o' your practical jokes on strangers an' honest foks. These are some o' your Oxford tricks, an' I'll thank you to be ower wi' them.—Gracious heaven, they are brikkin through the house at a' the four corners at the same time!'

The lass Tibby, seeing the innkeeper was not going to prevail with me to rise, flew toward the bed in desperation, and seizing me by the waist, soon landed me on the floor, saying: 'Be ye deil, be ye chiel, ye's no lie there till baith the house an' us be swallowed up!'

Her master and mistress applauding the deed, I was obliged to attempt dressing myself, a task to which my powers were quite inadequate in the state I was in, but I was readily assisted by every one of the three; and as soon as they got my clothes thrust on in a loose way, they shut their eyes lest they should see what might drive them distracted, and thrust me out to the street, cursing me, and calling on the fiends to take their prey and begone.

The scene that ensued is neither to be described, nor believed, if it were. I was momently surrounded by a number of hideous fiends, who gnashed on me with their teeth, and clenched their crimson paws in my face; and at the same instant I was seized by the collar of my coat behind, by my dreaded and devoted friend, who pushed me on, and, with his gilded rapier waving and brandishing around me, defended me against all their united attacks. Horrible as my assailants were in appearance, (and they had all monstrous shapes,) I felt that I would rather have fallen into their hands, than be thus led away captive by my defender at his will and pleasure, without having the right or power to say my life, or any part of my will, was my own. I could not even thank him for his potent guardianship, but hung down my head, and moved on I knew not whither, like a criminal led to execution, and still the infernal combat continued, till about the dawning, at which time I looked up, and all the fiends were expelled but one, who kept at a distance; and still my persecutor and defender pushed me by the neck before him.

At length he desired me to sit down and take some rest, with which I complied, for I had great need of it, and wanted the power to withstand what he desired. There, for a whole morning did he detain me, tormenting me with reflections on the past, and pointing out the horrors of the future, until a thousand times I wished myself non-existent. 'I have attached myself to your wayward fortune,' said he; 'and it has been my ruin as well as thine. Ungrateful as you are, I cannot give you up to be devoured; but this is a life that it is impossible to brook longer. Since our hopes are blasted in this world, and all our schemes of grandeur overthrown; and since our everlasting destiny is settled by a decree which no act of ours can invalidate, let us fall by our own hands, or by the hands of each other; die like heroes;* and, throwing off this frame of dross and corruption, mingle with the pure ethereal essence of existence, from which we derived our being.'

I shuddered at a view of the dreadful alternative, yet was obliged to confess that in my present circumstances existence was not to be borne. It was in vain that I reasoned on the sinfulness of the deed, and on its damning nature; he made me condemn myself out of my own mouth, by allowing the absolute nature of justifying grace, and the impossibility of the elect ever falling from the faith, or the glorious end to which they were called; and then he said, this granted, self-destruction was the act of a hero, and none but a coward would shrink from it, to suffer a hundred times more every day and night that passed over his head.

I said I was still contented to be that coward; and all that I begged of him was, to leave me to my fortune for a season, and to the just judgment of my creator; but he said his word and honour were engaged on my behoof, and these, in such a case, were not to be violated. 'If you will not pity yourself, have pity on me,' added he: 'turn your eyes on me, and behold to what I am reduced.'

Involuntarily did I turn round at the request, and caught a half glance of his features. May no eye destined to reflect the beauties of the New Jerusalem* inward upon the beatific soul, behold such a sight as mine then beheld! My immortal spirit, blood, and bones, were all withered at the blasting sight; and I arose and withdrew, with groanings which the pangs of death shall never wring from me.

Not daring to look behind me, I crept on my way, and that night reached this hamlet on the Scottish border; and being grown reckless of danger, and hardened to scenes of horror, I took up my lodging with a poor hind, who is a widower, and who could only accommodate me with a bed of rushes at his fire-side. At midnight I heard some strange sounds, too much resembling those to which I had of late been inured; but they kept at a distance, and I was soon persuaded that there was a power protected that house superior to those that contended for, or had the mastery over me. Overjoyed at finding such an asylum, I remained in the humble cot. This is the third day I have lived under the roof, freed of my hellish assailants, spending my time in prayer, and writing out this my journal, which I have fashioned to stick in with my printed work, and to which I intend to add portions while I remain in this pilgrimage state, which, I find too well, cannot be long.

August 3, 1712.—This morning the hind has brought me word from Redesdale,* whither he had been for coals, that a stranger gentleman had been traversing that country, making the most earnest inquiries after me, or one of the same appearance; and from the description that he brought of this stranger, I could easily perceive who it was. Rejoicing that my tormentor has lost traces of me for once, I am making haste to leave my asylum, on pretence of following this stranger, but in reality to conceal myself still more completely from his search. Perhaps this may be the last sentence ever I am destined to write. If so, farewell Christian reader! May God grant to thee a happier destiny than has been allotted to me here on earth, and the same assurance of acceptance above! *Amen.*

Ault-Righ, *August* 24, 1712.—Here am I, set down on the open moor to add one sentence more to my woful journal; and then, farewell all beneath the sun!

On leaving the hind's cottage on the Border, I hasted to the northwest, because in that quarter I perceived the highest and wildest hills before me. As I crossed the mountains above Hawick, I exchanged clothes with a poor homely shepherd, whom I found lying on a hill side, singing to himself some woful love ditty. He was glad of the change, and proud of his saintly apparel; and I was no less delighted with mine, by which I now supposed myself completely disguised; and I found moreover that in this garb of a common shepherd I was made welcome in every house. I slept the first night in a farm-house nigh to the church of Roberton, without hearing or seeing aught extraordinary; yet I observed next morning that all the servants kept aloof from me, and regarded me with looks of aversion. The next night I came to this house, where the farmer engaged me as a shepherd; and finding him a kind, worthy, and religious man, I accepted of his terms with great gladness. I had not, however, gone many times to the sheep, before all the rest of the shepherds told my master, that I knew nothing about herding, and begged of him to dismiss me. He perceived too well the truth of their intelligence; but being much taken with my learning, and religious conversation, he would not put me away, but set me to herd his cattle.

It was lucky for me, that before I came here, a report had prevailed, perhaps for an age, that this farm-house was haunted at certain seasons by a ghost. I say it was lucky for me, for I had not been in it many days before the same appalling noises began to prevail around me about midnight, often continuing till near the dawning. Still they kept aloof, and without doors; for this gentleman's house, like the cottage I was in formerly, seemed to be a sanctuary from all demoniacal power. He appears to be a good man and a just, and mocks at the idea of supernatural agency, and he either does not hear these persecuting spirits, or will not acknowledge it, though of late he appears much perturbed.

The consternation of the menials has been extreme. They ascribe all to the ghost, and tell frightful stories of murders having been committed there long ago. Of late, however, they are beginning to suspect that it is I that am haunted; and as I have never given them any satisfactory account of myself, they are whispering that I am a murderer, and haunted by the spirits of those I have slain.

August 30.—This day I have been informed, that I am to be banished the dwelling-house by night, and to sleep in an out-house by myself, to try if the family can get any rest when freed of my presence. I have peremptorily refused acquiescence, on which my master's brother struck me, and kicked me with his foot. My body being quite exhausted by suffering, I am grown weak and feeble both in mind and bodily frame, and actually unable to resent any insult or injury. I am the child of earthly misery and despair, if ever there was one existent. My master is still my friend; but there are so many masters here, and every one of them alike harsh to me, that I wish myself in my grave every hour of the day. If I am driven from the family sanctuary by night, I know I shall be torn in pieces before morning; and then who will deign or dare to gather up my mangled limbs, and give them honoured burial.

My last hour is arrived: I see my tormentor once more approaching me in this wild. Oh, that the earth would swallow me up, or the hill fall and cover me!* Farewell for ever!

September 7, 1712.—My devoted, princely, but sanguine friend, has been with me again and again. My time is expired, and I find a relief beyond measure, for he has fully convinced me that no act of mine can mar the eternal counsel, or in the smallest degree alter or extenuate one event which was decreed before the foundations of the world were laid. He said he had watched over me with the greatest anxiety, but perceiving my rooted aversion towards him, he had forborn troubling me with his presence. But now, seeing that I was certainly to be driven from my sanctuary that night, and that there would be a number of infernals watching to make a prey of my body, he came to caution me not to despair, for that he would protect me at all risks, if the power remained with him. He then repeated an ejaculatory prayer,* which I was to pronounce, if in great extremity. I objected to the words as equivocal, and susceptible of being rendered in a meaning perfectly dreadful; but he reasoned against this, and all reasoning with him is to no purpose. He said he did not ask me to repeat the words, unless greatly straitened; and that I saw his strength and power giving way, and when perhaps nothing else could save me.

The dreaded hour of night arrived; and, as he said, I was expelled from the family residence, and ordered to a byre, or cow-house, that stood parallel with the dwelling-house behind, where, on a divot loft, my humble bedstead stood, and the cattle grunted and puffed below me. How unlike the splendid halls of Dalcastle! And to what I am now reduced, let the reflecting reader judge. Lord, thou knowest all that I have done for thy cause on earth! Why then art thou laying thy hand so sore upon me? Why hast thou set me as a butt of thy malice? But thy will must be done! Thou wilt repay me in a better world. *Amen.*

September 8.——My first night of trial in this place is overpast! Would that it were the last that I should ever see in this detested world! If the horrors of hell are equal to those I have suffered, eternity will be of short duration there, for no created energy can support them for one single month, or week. I have been buffeted as never living creature was. My vitals have all been torn, and every faculty and feeling of my soul racked, and tormented into callous insensibility. I was even hung by the locks over a yawning chasm, to which I could perceive no bottom, and then——not till then, did I repeat the tremendous prayer!——I was instantly at liberty; and what I now am, the Almighty knows! *Amen.*

September 18, 1712.——Still am I living, though liker to a vision than a human being; but this is my last day of mortal existence. Unable to resist any longer, I pledged myself to my devoted friend, that on this day we should die together, and trust to the charity of the children of men for a grave. I am solemnly pledged; and though I dared to repent, I am aware he will not be gainsaid, for he is raging with despair at his fallen and decayed majesty, and there is some miserable comfort in the idea that my tormentor shall fall with me. Farewell, world, with all thy miseries; for comforts or enjoyments hast thou none! Farewell, woman, whom I have despised and shunned; and man, whom I have hated; whom, nevertheless, I desire to leave in charity! And thou, sun, bright emblem of a far brighter effulgence, I bid farewell to thee also!* I do not now take my last look of thee, for to thy glorious orb shall a poor suicide's last earthly look be raised. But, ah! who is yon that I see approaching furiously——his stern face blackened with horrid despair! My hour is at hand.*——Almighty God, what is this that I am about to do! The hour of repentance is past, and now my fate is inevitable.—— *Amen, for ever!* I will now seal up my little book, and conceal it; and cursed be he who trieth to alter or amend!*

END OF THE MEMOIR

————

WHAT can this work be? Sure, you will say, it must be an allegory; or (as the writer calls it) a religious PARABLE, showing the dreadful danger of self-righteousness? I cannot tell. Attend to the sequel: which is a thing so extraordinary, so unprecedented, and so far out of the common course of human events, that if there were not hundreds of living witnesses to attest the truth of it, I would not bid any rational being believe it.

In the first place, take the following extract from an authentic letter, published in *Blackwood's Magazine for August*, 1823.*

'On the top of a wild height called Cowanscroft,* where the lands of three proprietors meet all at one point, there has been for long and many years the grave of a suicide marked out by a stone standing at the head, and another at the feet. Often have I stood musing over it myself, when a shepherd on one of the farms,* of which it formed the extreme boundary, and thinking what could induce a young man, who had scarcely reached the prime of life, to brave his Maker, and rush into his presence by an act of his own erring hand, and one so unnatural and preposterous. But it never once occurred to me, as an object of curiosity, to dig up the mouldering bones of the culprit, which I considered as the most revolting of all objects. The thing was, however, done last month, and a discovery made of one of the greatest natural phenomena that I have heard of in this country.

'The little traditionary history that remains of this unfortunate youth, is altogether a singular one. He was not a native of the place, nor would he ever tell from what place he came; but he was remarkable for a deep, thoughtful, and sullen disposition. There was nothing against his character that any body knew of here, and he had been a considerable time in the place. The last service he was in was with a Mr. Anderson of Eltrive, (Ault-Righ, *the King's burn*,*) who died about 100 years ago, and who had hired him during the summer to herd a stock of young cattle in Eltrive Hope. It happened one day in the month of September, that James Anderson,* his master's son, went with this young man to the Hope to divert himself. The herd had his dinner along with him, and about one o'clock, when the boy proposed going home, the former pressed him very hard to stay and take share of his dinner; but the boy refused, for fear his parents might be alarmed about him, and said he *would* go home: on which the herd said to him, "Then, if ye winna stay with me, James, ye may depend on't I'll cut my throat afore ye come back again."

'I have heard it likewise reported, but only by one person, that there had been some things stolen out of his master's house a good while before, and that the boy had discovered a silver knife and fork, that was a part of the stolen property, in the herd's possession that day, and that it was this discovery that drove him to despair.

'The boy did not return to the Hope that afternoon; and, before evening, a man coming in at the pass called *The Hart Loup*, with a drove of lambs, on the way for Edinburgh, perceived something like a man standing in a strange frightful position at the side of one of Eldinhope hay-ricks.* The driver's attention was riveted on this strange uncouth figure, and as the drove-road passed at no great distance from the spot, he first called, but receiving no answer, he went up to the spot, and behold it was the above-mentioned young man, who had hung himself in the hay rope that was tying down the rick.

'This was accounted a great wonder; and every one said, if the devil had not assisted him it was impossible the thing could have been done; for, in general, these ropes are so brittle, being made of green hay, that they will scarcely bear to be bound over the rick. And the more to horrify the good people of this neighbourhood, the driver said, when he first came in view, *he could almost give his oath* that he saw two people busily engaged at the hay-rick, going round it and round it, and he thought they were dressing it.

'If this asseveration approximated at all to truth, it makes this evident at least, that the unfortunate young man had hanged himself after the man with the lambs came in view. He was, however, quite dead when he cut him down. He had fastened two of the old hay-ropes at the bottom of the rick on one side, (indeed they are all fastened so when first laid on,) so that he had nothing to do but to loosen two of the ends on the other side. These he had tied in a knot round his neck, and then slackening his knees, and letting himself down gradually, till the hay-rope bore all his weight, he had contrived to put an end to his existence in that way. Now the fact is, that if you try all the ropes that are thrown over all the outfield hay-ricks in Scotland, there is not one among a thousand of them will hang a colley dog; so that the manner of this wretch's death was rather a singular circumstance.

'Early next morning, Mr. Anderson's servants went reluctantly away, and, taking an old blanket with them for a winding sheet, they rolled up the body of the deceased, first in his own plaid, letting the hay-rope still remain about his neck, and then rolling the old blanket over all, they bore the loathed remains away to the distance of three miles or so, on spokes, to the top of Cowan's-Croft, at the very point where the Duke of Buccleuch's land, the Laird of Drummelzier's, and Lord Napier's,* meet, and there they buried him, with all that he had on and about him, silver knife and fork and altogether. Thus far went tradition, and no one ever disputed one jot of the disgusting oral tale.

'A nephew of that Mr. Anderson's who was with the hapless youth that day he died, says, that, as far as he can gather from the relations of friends that he remembers, and of that same uncle in particular, it is one hundred and five years next month, (that is September, 1823,) since that event happened; and I think it likely that this gentleman's information is correct. But sundry other people, much older than he, whom I have consulted, pretend that it is six or seven years more. They say they have heard that Mr. James Anderson was then a boy ten years of age; that he lived to an old age, upwards of fourscore, and it is two and forty years since he died. Whichever way it may be, it was about that period some way, of that there is no doubt.

'It so happened, that two young men, William Shiel and W. Sword,* were out, on an adjoining height, this summer, casting peats, and it came into their heads to open this grave in the wilderness, and see if there were any of the bones of the suicide of former ages and centuries remaining. They did so, but opened only one half of the grave, beginning at the head and about the middle at the same time. It was not long till they came upon the old blanket—I think they said not much more than a foot from the surface. They tore that open, and there was the hay rope lying stretched down alongst his breast, so fresh that they saw at first sight that it was made of *risp*, a sort of long sword-grass that grows about marshes and the sides of lakes. One of the young men seized the rope and pulled by it, but the old enchantment of the devil remained,—it would not break; and so he pulled and pulled at it, till behold the body came up into a sitting posture, with a broad blue bonnet on its head, and its plaid around it, all as fresh as that day it was laid in! I never heard of a preservation so wonderful, if it be true as was related to me, for still I have not had the curiosity to go and view the body myself. The features were all so plain, that an acquaintance might easily have known him. One of the lads gripped the face of the corpse with his finger and thumb, and the cheeks felt quite soft and fleshy, but the dimples remained and did not spring out again. He had fine yellow hair, about nine inches long; but not a hair of it could they pull out till they cut part of it off with a knife. They also cut off some portions of his clothes, which were all quite fresh, and distributed them among their acquaintances, sending a portion to me, among the rest, to keep as natural curiosities. Several gentlemen have in a manner forced me to give them fragments of these enchanted garments: I have, however, retained a small portion for you, which I send along with this, being a piece of his plaid, and another of his waistcoat breast, which you will see are still as fresh as that day they were laid in the grave.

'His broad blue bonnet was sent to Edinburgh several weeks ago, to the great regret of some gentlemen connected with the land, who wished to have it for a keep-sake. For my part, fond as I am of blue bonnets, and broad ones in particular, I declare I durst not have worn that one. There was nothing of the silver knife and fork discovered, that I heard of, nor was it very likely it should: but it would appear he had been very near run of cash, which I daresay had been the cause of his utter despair; for, on searching his pockets, nothing was found but three old Scots halfpennies. These young men meeting with another shepherd afterwards, his curiosity was so much excited that they went and digged up the curious remains a second time, which was a pity, as it is likely that by these exposures to the air, and from the impossibility of burying it up again as closely as it was before, the flesh will now fall to dust.'

*　　*　　*

The letter from which the above is an extract, is signed JAMES HOGG, and dated from Altrive Lake, *August 1st,* 1823. It bears the stamp of authenticity in every line; yet, so often had I been hoaxed by the ingenious fancies displayed in that Magazine, that when this relation met my eye, I did not believe it; but from the moment that I perused it, I half formed the resolution of investigating these wonderful remains personally, if any such existed; for, in the immediate vicinity of the scene, as I supposed, I knew of more attractive metal* than the dilapidated remains of mouldering suicides.

Accordingly, having some business in Edinburgh in September last, and being obliged to wait a few days for the arrival of a friend from London, I took that opportunity to pay a visit to my townsman and fellow collegian, Mr. L——t of C——d,* advocate. I mentioned to him Hogg's letter, asking him if the statement was founded at all on truth. His answer was, 'I suppose so. For my part I never doubted the thing, having been told that there has been a deal of talking about it up in the Forest for some time past. But, God knows! Hogg has imposed as ingenious lies on the public ere now.'*

I said, if it was within reach, I should like exceedingly to visit both the Shepherd and the Scots mummy he had described. Mr. L——t assented at the first proposal, saying he had no objections to take a ride that length with me, and make the fellow produce his credentials: That we would have a delightful jaunt through a romantic and now classical country,* and some good sport into the bargain, provided he could procure a horse for me, from his father-in-law, next day. He sent up to a Mr. L——w* to inquire, who returned for answer, that there was an excellent pony at my service, and that he himself would accompany us, being obliged to attend a great sheep fair at Thirlestane;* and that he was certain the Shepherd would be there likewise.

Mr. L——t said that was the very man we wanted to make our party complete; and at an early hour next morning we started for the ewe fair of Thirlestane, taking Blackwood's Magazine for August along with us. We rode through the ancient royal burgh of Selkirk,— halted and corned our horses at a romantic village,* nigh to some deep linns on the Ettrick, and reached the market ground at Thirlestane-green a little before mid-day. We soon found Hogg, standing near the *foot* of the market, as he called it, beside a great drove of *paulies,* a species of stock that I never heard of before. They were small sheep, striped on the backs with red chalk. Mr. L——t introduced me to him as a great wool-stapler, come to raise the price of that article; but he eyed me with distrust, and turning his back on us, answered, 'I hae sell'd mine.'

I followed, and shewing him the above-quoted letter, said I was exceedingly curious to have a look of these singular remains he had so ingeniously described; but he only answered me with the remark, that 'It was a queer fancy for a woo-stapler to tak.'

His two friends then requested him to accompany us to the spot, and to take some of his shepherds with us to assist in raising the body; but he spurned at the idea, saying, 'Od bless ye, lad! I hae ither matters to mind. I hae a' thae paulies to sell, an' a' yon Highland stotts down on the green every ane; an' then I hae ten scores o' yowes to buy after, an' if I canna first sell my ain stock, I canna buy nae ither body's. I hae mair ado than I can manage the day, foreby ganging to houk up hunder-year-auld banes.'

Finding that we could make nothing of him, we left him with his *paulies*, Highland stotts, grey jacket, and broad blue bonnet, to go in search of some other guide. L——w soon found one, for he seemed acquainted with every person in the fair. We got a fine old shepherd, named W——m B——e,* a great original, and a very obliging and civil man, who asked no conditions but that we should not speak of it, because he did not wish it to come to his master's ears, that he had been engaged in *sic a profane thing*. We promised strict secrecy; and accompanied by another farmer, Mr. S—t,* and old B——e, we proceeded to the grave, which B——e described as about a mile and a half distant from the market ground.

We went into a shepherd's cot to get a drink of milk, when I read to our guide Mr. Hogg's description, asking him if he thought it correct? He said there was hardly a bit o't correct, for the grave was not on the hill of Cowan's-Croft, nor yet on the point where three lairds' lands met, but on the top of a hill called the Faw-Law,* where there was no land that was not the Duke of Buccleuch's within a quarter of a mile. He added that it was a wonder how the poet could be mistaken there, who once herded the very ground where the grave is, and saw both hills from his own window. Mr. L——w testified great surprise at such a singular blunder, as also how the body came *not* to be buried at the meeting of three or four lairds' lands, which had always been customary in the south of Scotland.* Our guide said he had always heard it reported, that the Eltrive men, with Mr. David Anderson at their head, had risen before day on the Monday morning, it having been on the Sabbath day that the man *put down* himself; and that they set out with the intention of burying him on Cowan's-Croft, where three marches met at a point. But it having been an invariable rule to bury such *lost sinners* before the rising of the sun, these five men were overtaken by day-light, as they passed the house of Berry-Knowe; and by the time they reached the top of the Faw-Law, the sun was beginning to skair the east. On this they laid down the body, and digged a deep grave with all expedition; but when they had done, it was too short, and the body being stiff, it would not go down, on which Mr. David Anderson looking to the east, and perceiving that the sun would be up on them in a few minutes, set his foot on the suicide's brow, and tramped down his head into the grave with his iron-heeled shoe, until his nose and skull crashed again, and at the same time uttered a terrible curse on the wretch who had disgraced the family, and given them all this trouble. This anecdote, our guide said, he had heard when a boy, from the mouth of Robert Laidlaw,* one of the five men who buried the body.

We soon reached the spot, and I confess I felt a singular sensation, when I saw the grey stone* standing at the head, and another at the feet, and the one half of the grave manifestly new digged, and closed up again as had been described. I could still scarcely deem the thing to be a reality, for the ground did not appear to be wet, but a kind of dry rotten moss. On looking around, we found some fragments of clothes, some teeth, and part of a pocket-book, which had not been returned into the grave, when the body had been last raised, for it had been twice raised before this, but only from the loins upward.

To work we fell with two spades, and soon cleared away the whole of the covering. The part of the grave that had been opened before, was filled with mossy mortar, which impeded us exceedingly, and entirely prevented a proper investigation of the fore parts of the body. I will describe every thing as I saw it before four respectable witnesses, whose names I shall publish at large if permitted. A number of the bones came up separately; for with the constant flow of liquid stuff into the deep grave, we could not see to preserve them in their places. At length great loads of coarse clothes, blanketing, plaiding, &c. appeared; we tried to lift these regularly up, and on doing so, part of a skeleton came up, but no flesh, save a little that was hanging in dark flitters about the spine, but which had no consistence; it was merely the appearance of flesh without the substance. The head was wanting; and I being very anxious to possess the skull, the search was renewed among the mortar and rags. We first found a part of the scalp, with the long hair firm on it; which, on being cleaned, is neither black nor fair, but of a darkish dusk, the most common of any other colour. Soon afterwards we found the skull, but it was not complete. A spade had damaged it, and one of the temple quarters was wanting. I am no phrenologist, not knowing one organ from another, but I thought the skull of that wretched man no study. If it was particular for any thing, it was for a smooth, almost perfect rotundity, with only a little protuberance above the vent of the ear.*

When we came to that part of the grave that had never been opened before, the appearance of every thing was quite different. There the remains lay under a close vault of moss, and within a vacant space;

and I suppose, by the digging in the former part of the grave, that part had been deepened, and drawn the moisture away from this part, for here all was perfect. The breeches still suited the thigh, the stocking the leg, and the garters were wrapt as neatly and as firm below the knee as if they had been newly tied. The shoes were all opened in the seams, the hemp having decayed, but the soles, upper leathers, and wooden heels, which were made of birch, were all as fresh as any of those we wore. There was one thing I could not help remarking, that in the inside of one of the shoes there was a layer of cow's dung, about one eighth of an inch thick, and in the hollow of the sole fully one fourth of an inch. It was firm, green, and fresh; and proved that he had been working in a byre. His clothes were all of a singular ancient cut, and no less singular in their texture. Their durability certainly would have been prodigious; for in thickness, coarseness, and strength, I never saw any cloth in the smallest degree to equal them. His coat was a frock coat, of a yellowish drab colour, with wide sleeves. It is tweeled, milled, and thicker than a carpet. I cut off two of the skirts and brought them with me. His vest was of striped serge, such as I have often seen worn by country people. It was lined and backed with white stuff. The breeches were a sort of striped plaiding, which I never saw worn, but which our guide assured us was very common in the country once, though, from the old clothes which he had seen remaining of it, he judged that it could not be less than 200 years since it was in fashion. His garters were of worsted, and striped with black or blue; his stockings gray, and wanting the feet. I brought samples of all along with me. I have likewise now got possession of the bonnet, which puzzles me most of all. It is not conformable with the rest of the dress. It is neither a broad bonnet, nor a Border bonnet; for there is an open behind, for tying, which no genuine Border bonnet, I am told, ever had. It seems to have been a Highland bonnet, worn in a flat way like a scone on the crown, such as is sometimes still seen in the west of Scotland. All the limbs, from the loins to the toes, seemed perfect and entire, but they could not bear handling. Before we got them returned again into the grave, they were all shaken to pieces, except the thighs, which continued to retain a kind of flabby form.

All his clothes that were sewed with linen yarn were lying in separate portions, the thread having rotten; but such as were sewed with worsted remained perfectly firm and sound. Among such a confusion, we had hard work to find out all his pockets, and our guide supposed, that, after all, we did not find above the half of them. In his vest pocket was a long clasp knife, very sharp; the haft was thin, and the scales shone as if there had been silver inside. Mr. Sc—t took it with him, and presented it to his neighbour, Mr. R——n of W—n L—e,* who still has it in his possession. We found a comb, a gimblet, a vial, a small neat square board, a pair of plated knee-buckles, and several samples of cloth of different kinds, rolled neatly up within one another. At length, while we were busy on the search, Mr. L——t picked up a leathern case, which seemed to have been wrapped round and round by some ribbon, or cord, that had been rotten from it, for the swaddling marks still remained. Both L——w and B——e called out that 'it was the tabacco spleuchan, and a well-filled ane too;' but on opening it out, we found, to our great astonishment, that it contained a *printed pamphlet*. We were all curious to see what sort of a pamphlet such a person would read; what it could contain that he seemed to have had such a care about? for the slough in which it was rolled, was fine chamois leather; what colour it had been, could not be known. But the pamphlet was wrapped so close together, and so damp, rotten, and yellow, that it seemed one solid piece. We all concluded, from some words that we could make out, that it was a religious tract, but that it would be impossible to make any thing of it. Mr. L——w remarked that it was a great pity if a few sentences could not be made out, for that it was a question what might be contained in that little book; and then he requested Mr. L——t to give it to me, as he had so many things of literature and law to attend to, that he would never think more of it. He replied, that either of us were heartily welcome to it, for that he had thought of returning it into the grave, if he could have made out but a line or two, to have seen what was its tendency.

'Grave, man!' exclaimed L——w, who speaks excellent strong broad Scots: 'My truly, but ye grave weel! I wad esteem the contents o' that spleuchan as the most precious treasure. I'll tell you what it is, sir: I hae often wondered how it was that this man's corpse has been miraculously preserved frae decay, a hunder times langer than ony other body's, or than even a tanner's. But now I could wager a guinea, it has been for the preservation o' that little book. And Lord kens what may be in't! It will maybe reveal some mystery that mankind disna ken naething about yet.'

'If there be any mysteries in it,' returned the other, 'it is not for your handling, my dear friend, who are too much taken up about mysteries already.' And with these words he presented the mysterious pamphlet to me. With very little trouble, save that of a thorough drying, I unrolled it all with ease, and found the very tract which I have here ventured to lay before the public, part of it in small bad print, and the remainder in manuscript. The title page is written, and is as follows:

THE PRIVATE MEMOIRS
AND CONFESSIONS
OF A JUSTIFIED SINNER:

WRITTEN BY HIMSELF.

FIDELI CERTA MERCES.*

And, alongst the head, it is the same as given in the present edition of the work. I altered the title to *A Self-justified Sinner,* but my booksellers did not approve of it; and there being a curse pronounced by the writer on him that should dare to alter or amend, I have let it stand as it is. Should it be thought to attach discredit to any received principle of our church, I am blameless. The printed part ends at page 165, and the rest is in a fine old hand, extremely small and close. I have ordered the printer to procure a fac-simile of it, to be bound in with the volume.*

With regard to the work itself, I dare not venture a judgment, for I do not understand it. I believe no person, man or woman, will ever peruse it with the same attention that I have done, and yet I confess that I do not comprehend the writer's drift. It is certainly impossible that these scenes could ever have occurred, that he describes as having himself transacted. I think it *may be* possible that he had some hand in the death of his brother, and yet I am disposed greatly to doubt it; and the numerous distorted traditions, &c. which remain of that event, may be attributable to the work having been printed and burnt, and of course the story known to all the printers, with their families and gossips. That the young Laird of Dalcastle came by a violent death, there remains no doubt; but that this wretch slew him, there is to me a good deal. However, allowing this to have been the case, I account all the rest either dreaming or madness; or, as he says to Mr. Watson, a religious parable, on purpose to illustrate something scarcely tangible, but to which he seems to have attached great weight. Were the relation at all consistent with reason, it corresponds so minutely with traditionary facts, that it could scarcely have missed to have been received as authentic; but in this day, and with the present generation, it will not go down, that a man should be daily tempted by the devil, in the semblance of a fellow-creature; and at length lured to self-destruction, in the hopes that this same fiend and tormentor was to suffer and fall along with him. It was a bold theme for an allegory, and would have suited that age well had it been taken up by one fully qualified for the task, which this writer was not. In short, we must either conceive him not only the greatest fool, but the greatest wretch, on whom was ever stamped the form of humanity; or, that he was a religious maniac, who wrote and wrote about a deluded creature, till he arrived at that height of madness, that he believed himself the very object whom he had been all along describing. And in order to escape from an ideal tormentor, committed that act for which, according to the tenets he embraced, there was no remission, and which consigned his memory and his name to everlasting detestation.

FINIS

EXPLANATORY NOTES

These notes are indebted to Peter Garside's edition of *The Private Memoirs and Confessions of a Justified Sinner* (Edinburgh, 2001), cited here as 'Garside'. Other sources frequently consulted include John Carey's 1969 Oxford English Novels edition of the novel (Carey), *Blackwood's Edinburgh Magazine* (*Blackwood's*), the *Oxford English Dictionary* (*OED*), *Scottish National Dictionary* (*SND*), Calvin's *Institutes of the Christian Religion*, trans. Henry Beveridge (2 vols., Edinburgh, 1845), the Westminster Confession of Faith and Westminster Shorter Catechism (consulted on-line at http://www.reformed.org/documents), the King James Bible, and Oxford Complete Works of Shakespeare. Short title references are given to sources cited in the Select Bibliography. Hogg's biblical literacy was exceptional even by nineteenth-century standards, and Wringhim's memoir, in particular, is dense with scriptural references. I have identified as many of these as possible, since the interpretation and manipulation of Scripture are crucial to the novel's effect. A few locations mentioned in the novel have not been identified, and are not annotated.

3   *[dedication] Lord Provost of Glasgow*: William Smith (1786–1871), West India merchant, Lord Provost of Glasgow from 1822 to 1824. Evidently Hogg did not know him personally.

THE EDITOR'S NARRATIVE

5   *Dalcastle . . . Dalchastel*: apparently a fictitious estate (like 'Balgrennan', below); in the west of Scotland, not far from Glasgow.

    Colwan . . . Colquhoun . . . Cowans: Colquhoun (pronounced 'Cohoon') and Cowan are both west-of-Scotland names; the Cowans originally came from Ayrshire (to the south-west of Glasgow), the Colquhouns from Dumbartonshire (north-west, on the edge of the Highlands).

    the year 1687: i.e. on the eve of the 1688–9 Revolution. The coup which replaced James II (of England) and VII (of Scotland) with William of Orange (William III) installed a new order, Whig in politics and (in Scotland) Presbyterian in religion. (See Introduction.)

    Reformation principles: as formulated by French Protestant theologian Jean Calvin (1509–64), adopted by the mid-sixteenth-century Scottish Reformers, and codified in the Westminster Confession of Faith (1646), which became the doctrinal standard of the Church of Scotland (with its pedagogical supplements, the Shorter and Larger Catechisms) when Presbyterianism was re-established in 1690. Reformation principles included democratic Church governance (and a rejection of the authority of the sovereign and bishops over forms of worship); theological doctrines of original depravity, election, and justification by faith; and a strict personal morality.

5 *court party*: supporting the absolutist prerogative of the king. The Restoration court was notorious for its licentious manners.

6 *doctrines . . . a stumbling-block*: a key tenet of Calvin's *Institutes of the Christian Religion* is election—God's unconditional choice of those who will be saved—and its corollaries, predestination and justification by faith (i.e. the agency of grace rather than good works in determining salvation). Calvin calls the doctrine of election 'a stumbling-block to the profane' (*Institutes*, bk. III, ch. 21 (vol. ii, p. 528), echoing 1 Corinthians 23: 'Christ crucified, unto the Jews a stumbling-block'. Here, as elsewhere, the Pauline epistles provide the main scriptural source for the doctrine of election.

   despised . . . in her heart: compare 1 Chronicles 15: 29: 'Michal the daughter of Saul . . . saw king David dancing and playing: and she despised him in her heart'.

7 *parson*: Anglican term, revealing the editor's distance from Presbyterian usage; 'pastor' or 'minister' would be a more appropriate title for the Revd Wringhim.

   the Amorite, the Hittite, and the Girgashite: enemies of Israel (Deuteronomy 7: 1; Joshua 3: 10 and 24: 11; Nehemiah 9: 1); like 'Moabite' (2 Kings 3; Ezra 9: 10), below, p. 14.

   broad way that leadeth to destruction: Matthew 7: 13.

8 *concord of sweet sounds*: Shakespeare, *Merchant of Venice*, v. i. 84.

   Morphean: associated with Morpheus, classical god of dreams (as in Ovid, *Metamorphoses*, ii).

9 *had held*: had taken place.

10 *man of Belial . . . promiscuous dancer*: worthless or wicked man (1 Samuel 25: 25; 2 Samuel 16: 7, 20: 1). 'Promiscuous' (mixed-sex) dancing at weddings was a staple theme of pulpit censure: see H. G. Graham, *The Social Life of Scotland in the Eighteenth Century* (1909), 187, 243.

   stage-coaches and steam-boats . . . in that quarter: stagecoaches began running between Glasgow and Edinburgh in 1749, and between Glasgow and London in 1788; the first commercial steamboat began plying the Clyde between Glasgow and Greenock in 1812.

12 *standard doctrine of absolute predestination*: articulated by Calvin in *Institutes*, bk. III, ch. 21: 'Of the eternal election, by which God has predestinated some to salvation, and others to destruction'; adopted in the Westminster Confession of Faith, ch. 3, 'Of God's Eternal Decree'.

   Antichrist: 'he that denieth the father and the son', 1 John 2: 22; a 'deceiver' (2 John 1: 7). 'Limb of Antichrist' is not a scriptural expression.

regenerated: by God's grace from original sin: technical term, adopted by the Westminster Confession (ch. 23: i) from Calvin's *Institutes* (bk. III, ch. 3).

civil wars: the series of armed conflicts and insurrections in Scotland (part of a larger British struggle) involving Covenanter, Royalist, and Parliamentarian forces between 1644 and the Stuart Restoration in 1660.

Canaanitish woman: i.e. heathen woman: Genesis 46: 10, Exodus 6: 15; Abraham forbade his son to take a wife from among the women of Canaan (Genesis 24: 3).

13 *twelve in all*: the total is thirteen—the proverbial 'Devil's dozen'. The sum was corrected, despite its fitness to the context, in the 1837 edition of the novel. Calvin stresses the unity of faith, although he distinguishes the temporary faith of the reprobate from the lasting faith of the elect (*Institutes*, bk. III, ch. 2).

nature, utility, and common sense: keywords of Scottish Enlightenment moral philosophy, associated with the 'Moderate' ascendancy in the later eighteenth-century Church of Scotland, and abhorrent to the evangelicals.

To the wicked . . . all things are just and right: compare Titus 1: 15: 'Unto the pure all things are pure: but unto them that are defiled and unbelieving is nothing pure; but even their mind and conscience is defiled'.

the liberty wherewith we are made free: compare Galatians 5: 1. The Calvinist doctrine of election holds that a sinner cannot earn salvation by good works; rather, salvation is God's unconditional gift. However this does not release the elect from the moral law. Calvin insists that justification by faith will dispose the elect to observe the moral law, and refutes as a 'calumny' the argument 'that men are invited to sin when we affirm that the pardon in which we hold that justification consists is gratuitous' (bk. III, ch. 16, sect. 4). See also the Westminster Confession, ch. 29: v: 'The moral law doth forever bind all, as well justified persons as others, to the obedience thereof'. See Introduction.

dung . . . fatten the land: phrase frequent in Jeremiah.

15 *backslidings*: in the context of (figurative) adultery, see Jeremiah 3.

mildew . . . canker-worm: compare e.g. 1 Kings 8: 37, Deuteronomy 28: 22 (mildew); Joel 1: 4, Nahum 3: 15 (canker-worm).

Go thou . . . no more: echoing Jesus' dismissal of the woman taken in adultery, 'go, and sin no more', John 8: 11.

on the hip: at a disadvantage (metaphor from wrestling).

Supreme Being: an epithet associated with eighteenth-century deism.

16 *children of adoption*: 'Adoption is an act of God's free grace, whereby we are received into the number, and have a right to all the privileges of, the sons of God' (Shorter Catechism, 34): never to be 'cast off, but sealed to the day of redemption' (Westminster Confession, ch. 12). Again, St Paul is the scriptural source: Romans 8: 14–15.

16 *sweet spiritual converse*: compare Milton, *Paradise Lost*, viii. 909: 'Thy
    sweet Converse and Love so dearly joyn'd'.

    final election: not a term specified in Calvin's *Institutes* or in the Westminster
    Confession; perhaps a synonym for 'sanctification', or an example of 'split-
    ting the doctrines of Calvin'.

17 *an alien from the visible church*: baptism was one of only two sacraments
    admitted by the Presbyterian Church; the child could not be saved until
    the ceremony took place. The 'visible church' refers to the church's earthly
    congregation, as distinct from the transcendental 'invisible church' con-
    stituted by the elect. The banquet following the baptism ceremony was a
    pre-Reformation custom, still popular despite disapproval by the stricter
    presbyteries.

    doom all . . . to destruction: as in Psalm 109, later recited by the Wringhims.
    (King David was the supposed author of the Psalms.)

    cut off . . . carried quick into hell: Jeremiah 51: 6, with (as Garside notes) a
    reminiscence of *Hamlet*—foreboding fratricide as well as a murdered
    father: 'Thus was I, sleeping, by a brother's hand, ... | Cut off even in the
    blossoms of my sin, ... | No reckoning made, but sent to my account |
    With all my imperfections on my head' (I. v. 74–9).

18 *Covenanters*: radical Presbyterians who defended the principles of the
    National Covenant (1638) and Solemn League and Covenant (1643),
    affirming the Presbyterian forms of worship and church governance
    against the authority of the king and bishops, after the Stuart Restoration
    in 1660. The re-establishment of episcopacy under Charles II and James II
    and VII provoked a chain reaction of Covenanter resistance and govern-
    ment repression which culminated in a Whig insurgency in the south-west
    of Scotland (1679) followed by a state terror, the 'killing time' (1680–5).

    cavalier party: the Jacobite and Episcopalian party, supporting the claims
    of James II and VII, ousted in 1688.

    Earls of Seafield and Tullibardine: James Ogilvy (1663–1730), 1st Earl of
    Seafield, Lord High Chancellor of Scotland in 1703, and John Murray
    (1659–1724), Earl of Tullibardine, Lord Privy Seal. Joint secretaries
    of state under William III, they shifted from pro-Unionist and Whig
    positions to favouring the ascendant Cavalier party in the parliamentary
    session of 1703.

    famous session . . . such an extremity: the editor's account describes the par-
    liamentary session of 1703, although Wringhim's memoir sets these events
    one year later: 1703 was the first session of the first Scottish Parliament to
    be elected since 1689 and the last to be elected before the Union of the
    Parliaments of Scotland and England in 1707. Scottish feeling ran high
    against the Union, negotiations for which had begun the previous year.
    James Douglas, 2nd Duke of Queensberry and Dover (1662–1711), was
    Lord High Commissioner, the representative of the Crown in Scotland;
    he led the minority, pro-Union 'court party', opposed by the Cavaliers

(who made significant gains in the 1703 elections). Angry at the proposed conditions of Union and the English failure to consult them over the succession of William III, the Scots put forward an Act of Security containing measures to safeguard the country's political, religious, and commercial liberties (including the right to choose their own sovereign should Queen Anne die without issue). When Parliament reconvened in July 1704 Queen Anne replaced Queensberry with the Marquess of Tweeddale.

revolutionary principles: that is, of the 'Glorious Revolution' of 1688–9.

19 *Duke of Argyle*: Archibald Campbell (d. 1703), 1st Duke of Argyll, a powerful supporter of the 1688–9 Revolution and the Presbyterian interest. At this time he was 'engaged in setting up his own group from discontented elements in the court party' (*Oxford DNB*).

tennis: real or royal tennis, played in Scotland since the sixteenth century. Garside mentions two courts known to exist in Edinburgh in the period: one at the lower end of the Canongate, near Holyrood Palace, and one near the Fleshmarket, on the north side of the High Street.

20 *Black Bull tavern*: apparently a fictitious establishment, located (as we later learn) amid the narrow streets between the High Street and the Cowgate, south of the Market Cross. The High Street, descending from the Castle Hill to the Canongate, is the main thoroughfare of the Edinburgh Old Town.

on his brother's right hand: compare Zechariah 3: 1: 'Joshua the high priest standing before the angel of the Lord, and Satan standing at his right hand to resist him'. See also Psalm 109: 6, recited by the Revd Wringhim, below (p. 27).

22 *guard-house*: headquarters of the Edinburgh Town Guard, in the middle of the High Street between St Giles's and the Tron kirk; demolished in 1785.

Marquis of Annandale: William Johnstone (1664–1721), 1st Marquess of Annandale, Lord President of the Privy Council; at this time a strong advocate of the Presbyterian Church and the Hanoverian succession, despite his earlier involvement in a Jacobite plot.

23 *Canongate*: eastern extension of the High Street, from the Netherbow to Holyrood, comprising the burgh of the Canongate.

set the mountain on fire: variant of proverb, 'set the heather on fire'—cause an uproar (*SND*).

24 *Jacobite . . . Episcopal side*: supporters of the claims of James II and VII and his son (who were Roman Catholics), or the Scottish Episcopal Church ('High Church'); opponents of the 1689–90 Whig and Presbyterian ('Revolutionist') settlement.

barterers of the liberties . . . most sacred trust: because they would restore the absolutist Stuarts and undermine Protestantism.

25 *the Cross*: the Mercat (or Market) Cross, in the High Street near St Giles's church.

25 *abominable weapons of offence*: the Edinburgh Old Town was notorious
    for the nightly emptying of chamber pots from the upper storeys of
    tenements.

26 *town-guard*: proverbially ineffectual urban police force, consisting mainly
    of military veterans; abolished in 1817.

    Cameronian regiment . . . Hon. Captain Douglas: a regiment consisting of
    the adherents of Richard Cameron (d. 1680), radical Covenanter leader,
    had been raised by James Douglas (d. 1692), Earl of Angus, in support of
    William III in 1689. In 1703–4 however the Cameronians were in the Low
    Countries, fighting in Marlborough's campaigns in the War of the Spanish
    Succession.

    lord-commissioner . . . sheriffs of Edinburgh and Linlithgow: the Duke of
    Queensberry (see above, note to p. 18), responsible for maintaining civil
    order; chief county magistrates or legal officers.

27 *vials of wrath*: to be discharged on a sinful earth: Revelation 15: 7, 16: 1.

    the following verses: Psalm 109, verses 6–8, 14, 17–18 (reading 'remem-
    bered' for 'condemned', l. 6): from *The Psalms of David in Metre*, approved
    for use in the Church of Scotland in 1650. Michael Henchard sings verses
    10–13 of the same psalm (in the Book of Common Prayer version) in chap-
    ter 33 of Thomas Hardy's *The Mayor of Casterbridge* (1886).

29 *Links . . . a game at cricket*: Bruntsfield Links, open ground south-west of
    the city walls, used as a public golf course. Cricket does not seem to have
    been played in Scotland until late in the eighteenth century; it was imported
    by English soldiers after the 1745 rebellion.

30 *Adam Gordon*: evidently a fictitious character, although, as Garside notes,
    the Gordons (Earls of Aberdeen) were a prominent Jacobite family in the
    north-east of Scotland.

31 *High Church*: St Giles's, the High Kirk of Edinburgh, in Parliament
    Square on the High Street.

    Grey-Friars: major Presbyterian kirk, where the National Covenant was
    signed (1638), on the south side of the city.

    devoted: 'formally or surely consigned to evil or destruction; doomed'
    (*OED*, 'devoted', 3).

32 *Arthur's Seat*: extinct volcanic formation, 823 feet (251 m) high, overlook-
    ing Edinburgh from the south-east. A wild, rugged landscape close to the
    city centre, it had been featured as a site of uncanny encounters in Walter
    Scott's *The Heart of Mid-Lothian* (1818). In the episode that follows,
    George goes along the South Back of the Canongate (now Holyrood Rd.)
    towards Holyrood Palace, then around the southern perimeter of the
    King's Park to the ruined chapel of St Anthony ('the Saint's chapel and
    well') on the north-western flank of Arthur's Seat. From there he hikes to
    the summit, where he looks west across the hollow between himself and
    the adjacent basalt ridge of Salisbury Crags ('rocks of Salisbury').

lord-commissioner's house: Queensberry House, a seventeenth-century mansion at the foot of the Canongate; now part of the Scottish Parliament complex.

blue haze, like a dense smoke: 'haar' or sea fog, to which Edinburgh is prone.

33 *ghost of the rainbow*: Hogg later recounted his own sightings of the 'glory' in his youth as a shepherd in an essay, 'Nature's Magic Lantern', published in *Chambers's Edinburgh Journal*, 28 September 1833 (273–4). The 'glory' accompanies rather than precedes the optical phenomenon next witnessed by George, the so-called 'Brocken Spectre' (also discussed in 'Nature's Magic Lantern').

34 *fear and trembling*: ironical echo of Philippians 2: 12, 'work out your own salvation with fear and trembling'.

dilated frame of embodied air: Hogg accurately evokes the pneumatology of the turn of the eighteenth century, when there was an epidemic of apparition sightings. Apparitions were 'often most exactly painted in the nascent language of natural philosophy, as a simple configuration of the air. . . . The northernmost latitudes, from Scotland up to Lapland, were supposedly most conducive to such displays because the air there was held to be exceptionally rigid, hence especially apt to support and preserve apparitional forms': Jayne Elizabeth Lewis, 'Spectral Currencies in the Air of Reality: *A Journal of the Plague Year* and the History of Apparitions', *Representations* 87/1 (2004), 82–101 (87) The phenomenon described here is a version of the famous 'Brocken Spectre', the seemingly gigantic shadow of a human figure cast across a low cloud-bank by the sun shining from behind, observed in the Harz Mountains, Germany, and much discussed in the Romantic period. Early nineteenth-century Edinburgh saw a flurry of materialist explanations of apparitions as optical illusions or physiologically induced hallucinations. A note on the Brocken Spectre in John Ferriar's *An Essay Towards a Theory of Apparitions* (1813), 21–8, may inform the present description, as well as Hogg's later account in 'Nature's Magic Lantern'.

39 *upon his own head sevenfold*: echoing God's curse on Cain, Genesis 4: 15.

coals of juniper . . . children of the promise: for the threats of destruction, see Psalms 120: 4 and 144: 6, 1; for the 'children of the promise', Romans 9: 8, Galatians 4: 28.

opposite political principles: rivalry between the governing Tory party and the opposition Whigs was especially fierce in Edinburgh literary circles, issuing in libels, lawsuits, brawls, and even duels, in the decade following the Napoleonic Wars (1815–25). Hogg himself was associated with the intemperately Tory *Blackwood's Edinburgh Magazine*.

40 *High Court of Justiciary*: Scotland's supreme criminal court, presided over by the Lord Justice Clerk (referred to below as the 'Lord Justice').

Lord Advocate: senior legal officer for the Crown in Scotland and chief public prosecutor.

41   *evening cup of joy . . . sorrow in the morning*: compare Psalm 30: 5, 'weeping may endure for a night, but joy cometh in the morning'.

     Mr. Drummond . . . a nobleman of distinction: as becomes clear later, this is Thomas Drummond (d. 1715), second son by a second marriage to the exiled Jacobite peer John Drummond (1649–1714), 1st Earl and titular 1st Duke of Melfort.

42   *North Loch*: shallow lake north of Castle Hill, drained in the later eighteenth century; now the site of Princes Street Gardens.

     Guard-house: see note to p. 22, 'guard-house'.

43   *lived abroad with . . . the Stuarts*: as Secretary of State for Scotland under James II and VII, Melfort had been a notable persecutor of Whigs; he followed James into exile in 1688 and was outlawed by the new regime.

     an uncle . . . a Lord of Session: i.e. one of the thirteen judges of the Court of Session, the supreme civil court of Scotland. Hogg (or the editor) confuses Sir Thomas Wallace of Craigie (c.1630–80), who was a Lord of Session and grandfather of Thomas Drummond, with Craigie's second son of the same name (1665–c.1730), who was Drummond's uncle and an advocate, but not a judge (Garside).

44   *Emperor Charles VI*: Thomas Drummond joined the service of Charles VI, who would not succeed to the title of Holy Roman Emperor until 1711.

     bring it to light: compare 1 Corinthians 4: 'until the Lord come, who . . . will bring to light the hidden things of darkness'.

45   *controller of Nature*: like 'Supreme Being', a title carrying connotations of deism.

     the mole . . . hidden truths to light: compare Isaiah 45: 3 ('I will give thee the treasures of darkness, and hidden riches of secret places'); Psalm 8: 1, Matthew 21: 16 ('babes and sucklings'); 1 Corinthians 4 ('until the Lord come, who . . . will bring to light the hidden things of darkness'). Folk belief held that moles knew the whereabouts of precious minerals and buried treasure.

46   *cue*: thus (for 'clue') in the original, and elsewhere in Hogg.

     libelled in the indictment: specified in the written statement of the charge.

47   *Grass Market*: open square beneath the Castle Rock, used for public executions until 1784. Garside speculates that the fate in store for Bell Calvert may recall the hanging of Mary M'Kinnon (for knifing a client in a brothel) before an immense crowd in Edinburgh in April 1823.

50   *turned king's evidence*: given information in return for a reduced sentence.

51   *Court of Justiciary*: see note to p. 40, above.

     depute-advocate: legal officer appointed by the Lord Advocate to conduct a criminal prosecution.

53   *a' the spoons in Argyle*: Argyllshire was the hereditary domain of the Campbells, Dukes of Argyll, so names beginning with C would be ubiquitous there.

Like is an ill mark: proverbial phrase, recorded in Allan Ramsay, *A Collection of Scots Proverbs* (1736).

57 *Leith Wynd*: alley leading northwards, towards the port of Leith, from the eastern end of the High Street.

60 *bleaching green*: open space where laundry was spread out to bleach in the sun (earlier, a 'washing-green').

62 *We have nothing on earth but our senses to depend upon*: fundamental tenet of eighteenth-century empiricism, given notable philosophical amplification in David Hume's *A Treatise of Human Nature* (1739–40).

66 *Bogleheuch*: i.e. 'ghost-bank'.

67 *the promise is binding*: the promise (of salvation) cannot be broken.

68 *ears of the willow . . . seven tongues of the woodriff*: the lobes of the willow catkin and the leaves of the herb sweet woodruff (Garside).

69 *Gil-Martin*: in Gaelic 'Gille Martuinn' is a nickname for the fox: see *Dictionarium Scoto-Celticum* (1828), i. 482, and ii. 523. The 'Gille Mairtean', the fox, a shape-shifting trickster, appears in the tale 'Mac Iain Diareach', collected by J. F. Campbell in *Popular Tales of the West Highlands* (1860), ii. 328–40. See MacLachlan, 'The Name "Gil-Martin"'. In British folklore the Devil is supposed to come from the north.

worm that never dies: compare Isaiah 66: 24, Mark 9: 44–8.

70 *uncle or grandfather to young Drummond*: see note to p. 41. The elder Craigie, Drummond's grandfather, was Lord Justice Clerk from 1675 until his death in 1680.

71 *memorable year . . . 1715*: memorable because of a major Jacobite rising. Two other Thomas Drummonds fought on the Jacobite side at the battle of Sherriffmuir: Thomas Drummond, younger brother of Lord Strathallan, and Thomas Drummond of Logiealmond.

PRIVATE MEMOIRS AND CONFESSIONS OF A SINNER

75 *gods of silver and of gold*: heathen idols: Exodus 20: 23, Psalm 135: 15. The 'promises' are the successive covenants with God.

a burning and a shining light: see John 5: 35; but also recalling Robert Burns, 'Holy Willie's Prayer' (1786): 'I am here afore thy sight, | For gifts an' grace, | A burnin' an' a shinin' light, | To a' this place' (ll. 9–12).

Scottish worthies . . . persecution of the saints: echo of *The Scots Worthies*, the popular title of John Howie's *Biographia Scoticana* (1774), a much-reprinted compilation of the lives of heroes and martyrs of the Scottish Reformation and Covenant. 'Persecution of the saints' refers to the tribulations of the Presbyterian faithful during the Stuart restoration.

according to the flesh: a catchphrase in the Pauline epistles: see esp. Romans 1: 3, 9: 3.

76   *I astonished my teachers . . . gaze at one another*: like the 12-year-old Jesus in
      the temple, Luke 2: 46–7. Several of Wringhim's scriptural allusions
      sustain the blasphemous analogy.

      Single Catechism: or Shorter Catechism, approved by the Westminster
      Confession; much used in teaching children.

      Effectual Calling: question no. 31 in the Shorter Catechism, which gives
      the answer: 'the work of God's Spirit, whereby, convincing us of our sin
      and misery, enlightening our minds in the knowledge of Christ, and
      renewing our wills, he doth persuade and enable us to embrace Jesus
      Christ, freely offered to us in the gospel'. 'Ineffectual calling' (below), a
      conviction of election that turns out to be illusory, was discussed by
      Calvinist theologians Theodore Beza and William Perkins (Garside).
      Presbyterian theologians also distinguished between the elect (recipients
      of effectual calling) and those who were called but not chosen: see Gordon
      Marshall, *Presbyteries and Profits: Calvinism and the Development of
      Capitalism in Scotland, 1560–1707* (Oxford, 1980), 73–6. (I thank Hans de
      Groot for this reference.)

      bond of iniquity: Acts 8: 23.

      struggled with the Almighty long and hard: as in Jacob's all-night wrestling
      match, Genesis 32: 24–30.

77   *written in the book of life from all eternity*: see Revelation 13: 8, 17: 8, 20: 15.

      original transgression: original sin, committed by Adam and Eve ('my first
      parents', below).

78   *a worm, and no man in his sight*: compare Psalm 22: 6.

      one vessel . . . to dishonour: compare Romans 9: 21: 'Hath not the potter
      power over the clay, of the same lump to make one vessel unto honour, and
      another unto dishonour?'

      stories in the heavens . . . foundations . . . in the earth: compare Amos 9: 6.

      afore the session: the Kirk Session, a local ecclesiastical court comprising
      the minister and lay elders of the parish, regulated parishioners' sexual
      morality (among other duties) and imposed penalties for fornication.

79   *leaven of true righteousness*: the scriptural phrase is 'leaven of the Pharisees,
      which is hypocrisy' (Luke 12: 3; see also Matthew 16: 6, 11 and Mark
      8: 15) or 'leaven of malice and wickedness' (1 Corinthians 5: 8).

      red-letter side of the book of life: for 'the book of life' see note to p. 77, above.
      While it is tempting to detect an association with debit or loss in double-
      entry book-keeping, red ink does not appear to have been used to mark
      deficits in Scottish account books before the twentieth century. The phrase
      suggests a diabolical reversal of 'red-letter day', a saint's day or church
      festival marked with red letters in the pre-Reformation calendar, 'hence,
      any memorable, fortunate, or specially happy day'; also (likewise reversed)
      'rubric', 'a direction for the conduct of divine service inserted in liturgical
      books, and properly written or printed in red' (*OED*). Garside notes the

precedent of a contract with the Devil signed in blood in Christopher Marlowe's *Dr Faustus* (compare also Matthew Lewis's *The Monk*). The 'blood of the atonement', below, is Christ's blood, shed for the redemption of mankind.

80 *lead a proof*: produce proof or evidence (Scots legal term: *SND*).

Melchizedek: archetypal 'priest of the most high God' (Genesis 14: 18; Psalm 110: 4).

Apostle of the Gentiles: St Paul (Romans 11: 13), whose epistles are the main source for the Calvinist doctrines of predestination and justification by faith.

81 *Pharisee . . . in the Temple*: in Luke 18: 10–14, the Pharisee thanks God that he is 'not as other men [are], extortioners, unjust, adulterers, or even as this publican'. The publican, whose prayer is 'God be merciful to me a sinner', is the one deemed by Jesus to be 'justified'.

black stool . . . sack gown . . . juggs: instruments of penance for fornication in Presbyterian church discipline. Sinners would be obliged to stand before the congregation on the pillory ('juggs') or sit on a stool, wearing a sackcloth gown, and bear the rebukes of the minister during Sunday service (see Graham, *Social Life*, 321–4).

82 *not being able to forget him for several hours*: the power of the maternal imagination to influence foetal development was widely credited in the eighteenth century. Gillian Hughes has suggested that Hogg may be recalling an anecdote in the *Edinburgh Evening Courant*, 2 March 1813 ('London News'), regarding the birth of a black baby to the wife of an Irish landlord: 'The lady accounts for this extraordinary accident by saying, that she was the victim of curiosity, and could not avoid looking attentively at the face of a black servant, whenever he came into the room' (private communication).

thoughts are vanity: compare Psalm 94: 11.

83 *Jehu . . . Cyrus . . . Nebuchadnezzar*: usurping or heathen kings whom God makes instruments of his wrath: 2 Kings: 9–10, Ezra 5: 14–15, 2 Kings 25: 11–20.

a consuming fire: Deuteronomy 4: 24, Hebrews 12: 29.

the prelatic party, and the preachers up of good works: the Episcopalian party, and the Presbyterian moderates, who argue that good works as well as faith are requisite for salvation.

87 *excluding sins*: sins that exclude the sinner from salvation. Revelation 21: 8 lists 'the fearful, and unbelieving, and the abominable, and murderers, and whoremongers, and sorcerers, and idolators, and all liars' as so excluded; see also 22: 15.

filthy rags: from Isaiah 64: 6.

sinful king of Israel . . . before the Lord for a season: Ahab, in 1 Kings 21: 27.

88   *the just made perfect*: those already in heaven, or as good as there: see Hebrews 12: 23.

as the patriarch of old had done: Jacob, in Genesis 24–8.

Lamb's book of life: Revelation 21: 27.

resist even to blood: Hebrews 12: 4.

sanctification and repentance unto life: those who are 'called and regenerated', according to the Westminster Confession, 'are further sanctified, really and personally, through the virtue of Christ's death and resurrection, by his Word and Spirit dwelling in them' (ch. 13); for 'repentance unto life' see Acts 11: 18 (referring to the admission of Gentiles into the Christian covenant).

plucked as a brand out of the burning: Amos 4: 11.

89   *second self*: proverbial phrase for 'a friend who agrees absolutely with one's tastes and opinions, or for whose welfare one cares as much as for one's own' (*OED*).

91   *he entered at once into their conceptions and feelings*: see the Introduction for a discussion of a possible source for this passage in Edmund Burke's *A Philosophical Inquiry into the Origin of Our Ideas of the Sublime and the Beautiful* (1757).

25th day of March 1704 . . . eighteenth year of my age: contradicting the 'Editor's Narrative', according to which Robert is born at least eighteen months after George Colwan senior succeeds to the Dalcastle estate in 1687. Garside points out that 25 March is Lady Day, i.e. the Feast of the Annunciation, commemorating the angel Gabriel's appearance to the Virgin Mary to tell her she would be the mother of Christ. The analogy is reiterated, below, p. 105.

92   *translated*: as in Hebrews 11: 5: 'By faith Enoch was translated that he should not see death'.

troubled in spirit: John 13: 21 (of Jesus).

to appear like one: 'Satan himself is transformed into an angel of light', 2 Corinthians 11: 14.

93   *principalities . . . dominion*: compare Ephesians 1: 21; subsequently titles of angelic orders.

laying his hands . . . I dedicate this Thy servant to Thee: the Revd Wringhim's blessing mixes, to ironic effect, motifs from 2 Timothy 1: 6 ('Wherefore I put thee in remembrance that thou stir up the gift of God, which is in thee by the putting on of my hands'), 1 Thessalonians 5: 23 ('I pray God your whole spirit and soul and body be preserved blameless unto the coming of our Lord Jesus Christ'), and John 10: 12–13 ('hirelings'). Douglas Mack suggests (private communication) that the episode recalls the dedication of the young Samuel to the Lord in 1 Samuel 1–3, and thus another overweening analogy: Samuel goes on to be God's agent in choosing David as King of Israel, prefiguring the role of John the Baptist in relation to Christ.

two-edged weapon . . . spear coming out of Thy mouth: compare Psalm 149: 6–7 (calling for the saints to be given 'a two-edged sword in their hand; | To execute vengeance upon the heathen, and punishments upon the people') and Revelation 1: 16 ('out of his mouth went a sharp two-edged sword'); in Psalm 57: 4, however, 'the sons of men, whose teeth are spears and arrows, and their tongue a sharp sword' are enemies of the righteous. For 'dung to fat the land' see note to p. 13, above.

94 *a devouring fire . . . workers of iniquity*: common biblical phrases. See Isaiah 29: 6, 30: 27 and 30, 33: 14 ('devouring fire'); Job 31: 3, 34: 8 and 22, Psalms 5: 5, 6: 8, 14: 4, 24: 3, etc. ('workers of iniquity').

Finnieston: countryside 1 mile (1.6 km) west of Glasgow, now part of the city centre.

intersected with red lines, and verses: seventeenth-century bibles were often 'ruled in red', usually along the margins of the text. See also 'red-letter side of the book of life', above, p. 79.

96 *great preacher . . . what a day may bring forth*: conflation of Ecclesiastes 9: 10 and Proverbs 27: 1.

98 *Gil*: suggesting 'gillie', a male follower or attendant (from the Gaelic, 'Gille'). For 'Gil-Martin' see note to p. 69, above.

99 *Czar Peter of Russia*: Peter I ('the Great', 1672–1725) visited England—but not Scotland—for four months in 1698, in the course of his 'Grand Embassy' through Europe to strengthen political alliances and gather information about naval technology. The Czar accompanied his ambassadors under an incognito. Anecdotes about Peter, who was at once a ferocious despot and a modernizing reformer, were popular in the British press following the alliance with Russia in the Napoleonic Wars. His reputation as a defender of Christianity derived from his campaigns against the Ottoman Empire.

of the moral cast: i.e. a proponent of the moral law, a preacher of salvation by good works as well as by faith.

100 *connector of humanity with the Divine nature*: Garside notes an analogous passage in Hogg's *A Series of Lay Sermons* (1834): 'Wo to him who would weaken the bonds with which true Christianity connects us with Heaven and with one another!' (ed. Gillian Hughes (Edinburgh, 1997), 83).

102 *better that one fall, than that a thousand souls perish*: a diabolical reversal of Luke 15: 4–7: 'joy shall be in heaven over one sinner that repenteth, more than over ninety and nine just persons, which need no repentance'.

103 *sword of the Lord*: Judges 7: 18, 20.

Paisley: town about 8 miles (13 km) west of Glasgow.

104 *weapon of the Lord of Hosts*: Compare Jeremiah 51: 19–20: 'the Lord of hosts is his name. | Thou art my battle axe and weapons of war: for with thee will I break in pieces the nations, and with thee will I destroy kingdoms'.

105 *their points towards me*: perhaps an echo, as Garside suggests, of Peter's
    vision in Acts 10: 10–16. '[He] saw heaven opened, and a certain vessel
    descending unto him, as it had been a great sheet knit at the four corners,
    and let down to the earth' (10: 11). The vessel contains different animals,
    not weapons, in a revelation of the obsolescence of Jewish dietary law as a
    condition for the salvation of the Gentiles.

    highly-favoured one: as Garside points out, a perversion of Gabriel's
    address to Mary at the Annunciation ('thou that art highly favoured',
    Luke 1: 28).

    between the Cherubim: biblical commonplace for God's station: see e.g.
    Ezekiel 10: 2, 6, and 7.

106 *as the ox goeth to the stall*: compare Proverbs 7: 22, 'as an ox goeth to the
    slaughter'.

108 *the court and the country party*: broadly speaking, the government and the
    opposition; in the 1703 session of the Scottish Parliament the Cavalier
    and Country parties, representing different interests, joined forces against
    the pro-Union Court party (see note to p. 18, above).

110 *mark of the beast . . . foreheads and right hands*: the seal of the Antichrist on
    his followers: Revelation 13: 16, 16: 2, 19: 20.

112 *acts of Jehu . . . out of the land*: See 2 Kings 10. Ahab's seventy sons, com-
    plicit in the worship of Baal in Israel, are exterminated (along with the
    disciples of Baal) by Ahab's former servant Jehu.

    Go thou then and do likewise: Jesus' directive to his disciples, Luke 10: 37,
    John 13: 27.

    a ruling energy . . . dwellings of the wicked: 'ruling energy' and 'master
    spirit' are terms with demonological associations, according to Garside,
    who notes their usage in other tales of the supernatural by Hogg. The
    remainder of the phrase echoes a common Old Testament curse, e.g. in
    Jeremiah, Isaiah, Zephaniah 1 and 2; for 'desolation of the wicked' see
    Proverbs 3: 25.

113 *Cloud of Witnesses*: the phrase (from Hebrews 12: 1), used for the title of
    a mid-seventeenth-century Protestant martyrology, is most often associ-
    ated with *A Cloud of Witnesses, for the Prerogatives of Jesus Christ; or, The
    Last Speeches and Testimonies of those who have Suffered for the Truth, in
    Scotland, since the Year 1680*, published in Edinburgh in 1714 and
    reprinted well into the nineteenth century. This memorial of the 'killing
    time' ('the days o' praying prisoners') fits the present context, despite the
    light anachronism.

    Fat the deil: 'fat' for 'what' and 'fa' for 'who' (p. 113) suggest a speaker
    from Aberdeenshire, according to a well-established convention.

    Go in peace: echoing the jailer's words to St Paul and Silas after they have
    converted him, Acts 16: 36: an ironical analogue to the present scene, as
    Garside notes.

114 *sword . . . Famine and Pestilence*: Ezekiel 7: 15.

Gilgal: the camp from which Joshua besieged Jericho (Joshua 4–6); also, as Garside notes, where 'Samuel hewed Agag in pieces before the Lord' (1 Samuel 15: 33).

115 *shekels of brass*: the Philistine champion Goliath's armour weighs 'five thousand shekels of brass' (1 Samuel 17: 5).

Tophet: name for hell, after a site near Jerusalem where children were sacrificed to Moloch (2 Kings 23: 10, Isaiah 30: 33).

children of Belial: biblical phrase for wicked, unbelieving, or 'vain men' (2 Chronicles 13: 7).

venal prophet . . . I would even kill him: Balaam issues the threat to his ass when the animal falls down in front of the angel of the Lord, whom Balaam has failed to see standing in his way (Numbers 22: 29). In the New Testament he is rather unfairly denounced as one 'who loved the wages of unrighteousness' (2 Peter 2: 15; see also Jude 1: 11).

avenger of blood: given scriptural sanction (with conditions) in Deuteronomy 19: 12; Joshua 20: 3, 5, 9.

My heart was lifted up: an ambiguous exaltation: compare, e.g., 'his heart was lifted up in the ways of the Lord' (2 Chronicles 17: 6) and 'his heart was lifted up to his destruction' (2 Chronicles 26: 16).

117 *cumbering the true vineyard*: compare Luke 13: 7: 'Then said he unto the dresser of his vineyard, Behold, these three years I come seeking fruit on this fig tree, and find none: cut it down; why cumbereth it the ground?', and Jesus' declaration in John 15: 1: 'I am the true vine, and my Father is the husbandman. | Every branch in me that beareth not fruit he taketh away: and every branch that beareth fruit, he purgeth it, that it may bring forth more fruit'.

119 *still small voice*: like the voice of God speaking to Elijah, 1 Kings 19: 12.

124 *died that same week*: Sir William Hamilton of Whitelaw died suddenly in December 1704, just two months after his appointment as Lord Justice Clerk (Garside). See p. 43, however, for the Editor's identification of the Lord Justice Clerk as Sir Thomas Wallace of Craigie (d. 1680).

126 *smite him with the edge of the sword*: scriptural formula (like 'cleansing the sanctuary', previous paragraph): Jeremiah 21: 7; Deuteronomy 13: 15, 20: 13, etc.

part of the 10th Psalm: describing the persecution of the poor by the wicked man. Verses 8–10 are ironically apt to Wringhim's situation: 'He sitteth in the lurking places of the villages: in the secret places doth he murder the innocent', etc.

128 *the Lord's anointed . . . precious blood*: injunctions against harming the Lord's anointed recur throughout the books of Samuel (e.g. 1 Samuel 16: 9, 24: 6 and 10, 26: 9, etc.; 2 Samuel 1: 14); for 'the precious blood of Christ' see 1 Peter 1: 19.

129 *extinction of the wicked and profane*: see e.g. Joshua 6: 8–10.

135 *Linkum*: from the Scots 'linkum' or 'linkie', a roguish, untrustworthy person (*SND*, 'linkie', II).

Here it is: the pastiche of charter-style that follows is authentic, and may derive (as Carey and Garside suggest) from a charter of 1636 quoted in William Maitland's *The History of Edinburgh from its Foundation to the Present Time* (1753), 148–51, which includes several of the technical terms listed here. Most of them refer to categories of feudal property and service: *all and haill*: altogether, all included; *tofts*: homesteads; *fortalices*: fortifications; *biggings*: buildings; *commonties*: common lands; *coal-heughs*: coal-pits; *annexes, connexes*: attached and connected properties; *brooked, joysed*: possessed, enjoyed; *miethes, and marches*: boundaries; *multures*: duties on milling grain. The closing list is of baronial rights or privileges: *court, plaint*: the right to hold court and adjudicate grievances; *herezeld*: to claim a tenant's best animal on his death; *fork*: (gallows) the right to hang felons; *vert*: to cut greenwood; *wraik, waith, wair*: to claim flotsam, lost property or stray livestock; *sack, sock*: rights of jurisdiction; *thole, thame*: these terms had lost their original meaning in Anglo-Saxon law and become formulaic appendages of 'sac, soc'; *outfang thief, infang thief*: the right to pursue a thief beyond the boundaries of the domain and bring him back, and to try and punish him there; *pit and gallows*: the right to execute felons. Several of these terms also occur (in Latin) in Scott's *Waverley* (1814), ch. 10.

Compositio . . . 1687: i.e. registered, with payment of a fee of £5. 13s. 8d. Following the Union of Crowns (1604), charters were registered under the Great Seal at the Palace of Whitehall, London, until it burned down in 1698.

136 *privy councillors . . . Queensberry*: the Scottish Privy Council oversaw royal charters until 1707. James Douglas, 2nd Duke of Queensberry (see note to p. 18) was Keeper of the Privy Seal in Scotland, responsible for approving charters up to the affixing of the Great Seal, from 1695 to 1702 and again from 1705 to 1709.

140 *circuit lords*: judges of the Court of Justiciary 'on circuit', i.e. hearing criminal cases in towns outside Edinburgh.

143 *presumptuous proofs . . . precognition*: proofs based on probable inference; preliminary collection of evidence for a prosecution.

I have two souls . . . by turns: an echo of a famous passage in Goethe's *Faust*: compare 'Horae Germanicae, No. V: The Faustus of Goethe', *Blackwood's*, 7 (1820), 235–58: 'In my breast | Alas two souls have taken their abode, | And each is struggling there for mastery' (245).

144 *inclosed in the deeps of the sea*: compare the closing scene of Marlowe's *Dr Faustus*: 'O, soule, be chang'd into small water drops, | And fall into the ocean, ne'er to be found!': quoted in John Wilson, 'Marlowe's Tragical History of the Life and Death of Dr Faustus', *Blackwood's*, 1 (1817), 388–94 (393), which reproduces the whole of Faustus' final soliloquy.

Daniel in the den of lions: see Daniel 6: 16–23; Daniel's faith preserves him from harm during his captivity in the lions' den.

145 *Cameronian*: follower of the militant Covenanter Richard Cameron (killed by government troops in 1680). With the establishment of Presbyterianism in 1690 the Cameronians formed a separate congregation, later (1743) called the Reformed Presbyterians.

Penpunt: Penpont, a village in Upper Nithsdale, Dumfriesshire, also associated with the Cameronians in Hogg's 1831 tale 'The Barber of Duncow'. 'Auld Penpont' is the name of a 'droll' character in 'Recollections of Mark Macrabin, the Cameronian, No. XI: The Harvest Kirn of Lillycross', *Blackwood's*, 8 (1821), 399.

146 *a breach in his friend's good name ... most precious*: compare *Othello*, III. iii, 'Who steals my purse steals trash . . . | But he who filches from me my good name . . . | . . . makes me poor indeed'.

Master Whiggam: 'whiggamore' became an epithet for Presbyterians from the south-west of Scotland after the 1648 'Whiggamore Raid', a Covenanter march on Edinburgh—and hence the later term 'Whig'. An eighteenth-century source derives the word from 'whiggam', a cry used by West-Country drovers to urge on their horses (*SND*).

147 *Macmillan*: 'John Macmillan (1670–1753), minister of Balmaghie, who became minister to the Cameronians in 1706, amid much controversy. They were then known as the Macmillanites until 1743, when he founded the Reformed Presbyterian Church' (Carey). Hogg recounts a story of Macmillan defying a ghost in his tale 'The Wool-gatherer' (1818).

148 *Auld Simmie*: the Devil.

professors: persons 'who [make] open profession of religious faith' (*SND*).

Glasco street: Glasgow High Street, where peddlers ('packmen') sold their wares around the Mercat Cross.

wolves in sheep's claithing: proverbial, from Jesus' warning against false prophets: they 'come to you in sheep's clothing, but inwardly they are ravening wolves' (Matthew 7: 15).

Auchtermuchty: town in central Fife; also a comic Scots shibboleth. The phrase 'rigidly righteous' recalls Burns's poem 'Address to the Unco Guid, or Rigidly Righteous' (1786).

lint-swinglings ... questions round: flax-beating (a stage in the preparation of linen) was an occasion for social gatherings in which songs would be sung, stories told, and so on. '[Saying] questions round' means taking turns to recite the Catechism.

149 *cunning man ... his ain mother tongue*: the figure of Robin Ruthven is reminiscent of Hogg's maternal grandfather (and Ettrick legend) William Laidlaw, 'Will o' Phaup' (d. 1778), reputedly the last man in the Borders to have conversed with the fairies (Gillian Hughes, *James Hogg*, 5–6). Robin's having 'been in the hands o' the fairies when he was young' recalls

traditional lore about changelings, as in the ballad of Thomas the Rhymer.

149   *West Lowmond*: West Lomond, highest (1,713 feet; 522 m) of the Lomond Hills, 4.3 miles (7 km) south-west of Auchtermuchty.

bridal o' corbie-craws: a flock of ravens. The episode echoes the traditional ballad 'The Twa Corbies', collected by Scott in *Minstrelsy of the Scottish Border*: 'As I was walking all alane, | I heard twa corbies making a mane; | The tane unto the t'other say, | Where sall we gang and dine to-day?' The answer yields a gruesome anti-epithalamium: while the ravens feast on the body of a young knight, his lady takes another mate.

signed himself: i.e. crossed himself, a hint that Robin adheres to the pre-Reformation religion.

Sidlaw hills . . . Mount, Diabolus, and fly: Walter Scott quotes the latter phrase, from an unnamed ballad on the warlock Michael Scott, in note 30 to canto II of *The Lay of the Last Minstrel* (1805). 'Diabolus' is a name for the Devil in John Bunyan's *The Holy War* (1682). The Sidlaw hills extend north-east of Perth, along the north bank of the Firth of Tay; 'the hill of Macbeth' is Dunsinane, named in the prophecy in the witches' cavern in *Macbeth*, IV. i.

119th Psalm . . . 77th verse: 'Let thy tender mercies come unto me, that I may live: for thy law is my delight'.

western door: i.e. at the opposite end of the church to the holy altar.

150   *I will give it him*: Ezekiel 21: 27, alluding to the overthrow of a corrupt Israel by the Babylonian king Nebuchadnezzar.

gall of bitterness and bond of iniquity: Acts 8: 23.

as Jonah . . . to the Ninevites: see Jonah 3. The Ninevites repented and were saved.

spoke evil of dignities: compare 2 Peter 2: 10.

151   *St. Johnston and Dundee . . . Grampian hills*: i.e. the whole of Fife and Perthshire east of the Highlands—the low country between the firths of Forth and Tay. St Johnston is the old name for Perth.

A splendid tent: 'a moveable wooden pulpit, with steps and a canopy, erected in the open air, esp. at the half-yearly communion services when the congregation is too large for the church to contain' (*SND*).

152   *gouden rule*: 'Therefore all things whatsoever ye would that men should do to you, do ye even so to them' (Matthew 7: 12).

154   *touch them baith afore witnesses*: according to traditional belief a corpse would bleed when touched by (or even in the presence of) its murderer. Scott's note to 'Earl Richard' in *Minstrelsy of the Scottish Border* cites the admission of the phenomenon as evidence in Scottish criminal trials as late as the seventeenth century, e.g. the case of Philip Standfield, executed for parricide in 1687. Hogg uses the belief in his ballad 'The Pedlar', in *The Mountain Bard* (1807), and the short story 'The Barber of Duncow' (1831).

157   *the just man . . . left destitute*: an echo of Psalm 37: 25, as Garside notes, in
      the Scottish metrical version: 'yet have I never seen | The just man left'.

      easier for a camel . . . kingdom of heaven: see Matthew 19: 24.

      an angel unawares: compare Hebrews 13: 2: 'Be not forgetful to entertain
      strangers: for thereby some have entertained angels unawares'.

161   *pearls o' damnation*: i.e. perils of damnation (sounding alike with the
      rolled 'r').

      Boddel Brigg: Bothwell Bridge, a battle (1679) in which the
      Covenanter army was beaten by government forces under the Duke of
      Monmouth.

163   *dinna tak the braidside . . . wi' your face foremost*: the precise meaning is
      obscure. According to *SND* 'at a / at the braidside' means 'in a hurry,
      suddenly', so the weaver's injunction might mean, 'don't rush out sud-
      denly, but walk quietly out of the door without looking back'; or else,
      more extravagantly, 'don't take the side of the house with you [erupting in
      the shape of a dragon, like the preacher in Samuel Scrape's tale] but leave
      by the door like a human being'. In any case the phrase seems to refer to
      the delicate matter of how evil spirits cross thresholds.

      West Port: western gate in the Edinburgh city walls, south of the castle.

164   *Elliot*: name of one of the great Scottish Border clans.

      James Watson: James Watson (d. 1722), appointed Queen's Printer in
      Scotland in 1711. Books printed by him include Robert Wodrow's *History
      of the Sufferings of the Church of Scotland* (1721–2), a famous memorial of
      the Covenanting martyrs, from which, Garside speculates, Hogg might
      have got Watson's name. At this time Watson's shop was situated across
      from St Giles's, in the High Street.

165   *Pilgrim's Progress*: the great English religious allegory of human life as a
      journey from sin to salvation. Editions of John Bunyan's masterpiece
      (1678) were printed in Edinburgh in 1680 (John Cairns) and 1681
      (Andrew Anderson); none are recorded from James Watson, although he
      did print other Bunyan titles, including *The Holy War*.

      press-work . . . wrought off: i.e. the entire work has been typeset, corrected,
      and a set of proofs run off; now the first sheet (to be folded into pages for
      binding) is printed for publication, and the second sheet is ready to go
      (Garside).

166   *Chesters*: a hamlet about 5 miles (8 km) from the English border, south-
      east of Hawick. In the journal entry that follows, Wringhim recounts his
      flight from Edinburgh to the south-east. Leaving the city in the early
      evening, he passes the town of Dalkeith and keeps walking all night and
      the next morning (along the route of the present-day A7) until he reaches
      Langshaw (Ellanshaws), a farmhouse north of Galashiels, where he
      spends the following night: a journey of roughly 30 miles (50 km). The
      next morning he follows Allan Water ('a small river called Ellan') 5 miles
      (8 km) south to its junction with the Tweed. After crossing the Tweed

he heads south-east again, another 9 miles (15 km) to Ancrum, a village near Jedburgh, where he spends the night. From there he walks 12 miles (20 km) due south to his present location.

166 *devil . . . printing office*: with a pun on 'printer's devil', errand boy or apprentice in a printing office.

Green Circassian hunting coat and turban: Garside notes that the Edinburgh painter William Allan, an associate of J. G. Lockhart's, liked to wear a 'Circassian vest' (i.e. from the Caucasus). The travels of Byron and other Romantic tourists in the Ottoman Empire inspired a fad for 'Oriental' costumes. Gary Kelly suggests that Gil-Martin's dress may recall the Armenian coat and headgear worn by Jean-Jacques Rousseau, recorded in the portrait of him painted by Allan Ramsay in 1766 for David Hume (*English Fiction of the Romantic Period*, 269). Rousseau's reputation as an ideologue of 'incendiary' Jacobinism would make the allusion apposite. Green was associated with magic in Border folklore.

167 *Portsburgh*: Edinburgh suburb (until 1856) outside the West Port.

O that I had the wings of a dove . . . no power to stand: compare Psalm 55: 6, 'Oh that I had wings like a dove! for then would I fly away, and be at rest'; Leviticus 26: 37, 'ye shall have no power to stand before your enemies'.

170 *How changed . . . that majestic countenance*: like the fallen Satan in *Paradise Lost*, i. 84–7.

171 *hide me in the bowels of the earth, or depths of the sea*: another echo of the last speech of Marlowe's Faustus: 'Mountaines and hills, come, come, and fall on me! | And hide me from the heavy wrath of God. | No! Then will I headlong run into the earth!' (*Blackwood's*, i. 392); see also note to p. 177.

no more of my persecutor that day: evil spirits were supposed to be unable to cross running water; compare, e.g., Robert Burns, 'Tam o' Shanter', l. 208.

Oxford . . . the black arts: a witty exaggeration (no doubt) of Presbyterian suspicion of High Church Oxford. The thirteenth-century philosopher and astrologer Michael Scott, notorious in Border tradition as a warlock, was supposed to have studied at Oxford. Some commentators (e.g. Carey, Garside) have detected an allusion to Hogg's literary friends, the 'two devils' (as he dubbed them in private correspondence) John Wilson and John Gibson Lockhart, both former Oxford students.

172 *terrors indefinable*: Gillian Hughes detects a reference here to the night-terrors that afflicted Hogg in his childhood (*James Hogg*, 192).

174 *die like heroes*: mutual suicide does not feature in analogous stories of the pact with the Devil. It is however a topos of Roman (thus pagan) heroism, e.g. in Shakespeare's *Antony and Cleopatra*. Christian theologians condemned suicide as self-murder, therefore a breach of the Sixth

Commandment, or as an act committed in a state of despair, cutting off the possibility of repentance and thus salvation.

175 *beauties of the New Jerusalem*: 'the holy city, new Jerusalem, coming down from God out of heaven, prepared as a bride adorned for her husband' (Revelation 21: 2); its beauties are listed in verses 11–21.

Redesdale: over the border, in Northumberland.

Ault-Righ: Altrive, Altrieve, or Eltrive, a farm to the east of St Mary's Loch, bounded by the drove-road between the Ettrick and Yarrow valleys. For the final stage of his flight Robert turns back from the border and heads north-west across the hills to Roberton, west of Hawick, a journey of about 15.5 miles (25 km). From there he hikes another 15.5 miles (25 km) across rugged country to Altrive, again to the north-west.

177 *fall and cover me*: compare the last hour of Marlowe's Faustus, note to p. 171, above.

ejaculatory prayer: a short prayer 'darted up to God' in an emergency (*OED*).

178 *Farewell, world . . . farewell to thee also*: a parody, Garside suggests, of the 'last speeches and testimonies' of Covenanters from the scaffold in popular martyrologies such as the *Cloud of Witnesses* (see note to p. 113).

My hour is at hand: compare Matthew 26: 45, 'the hour is at hand': Jesus' words at the time of his betrayal.

cursed be he . . . alter or amend: compare the end of the Book of Revelation: 'If any man shall add unto these things, God shall add unto him the plagues that are written in this book: | And if any man shall take away from the words of the book of this prophecy, God shall take away his part out of the book of life, and out of the holy city, and from the things which are written in this book' (22: 18–19).

THE EDITOR'S NARRATIVE

179 *Blackwood's Magazine for August, 1823*: Hogg reprints his own letter, 'A Scots Mummy. To Sir Christopher North', from *Blackwood's*, 14 (Aug. 1823), 188–90, omitting the introduction, conclusion, and a few sentences of expostulation with 'Sir Christy' (i.e. John Wilson, effectively the editor of *Blackwood's*).

Cowanscroft: Cowan's Croft, 1,897 feet (579 m), south of St Mary's Loch and south-west of Altrive. The topography of this last part of the novel is concentrated on the moorland farms around the stream of Altrive Lake and the wild hills south-west of it. Since 1815 Hogg had lived in a cottage at the head of Altrive Lake, by Yarrow Water, on the north-eastern corner of the Altrive farm of the novel. Ettrickhall, his birthplace, is 1.25–2 miles (2–3 km) due south of Cowan's Croft and Fall Law.

179 *a shepherd on one of the farms*: Hogg had been employed as a shepherd at
     nearby Blackhouse, on Yarrow Water (north of Altrive), from 1790 to 1800.
     the King's burn: Gaelic 'allt', a stream, and 'righ', king; a likelier deriva-
     tion is from 'ruighe', the bottom of a valley or stretch of land at the base
     of a hill.
     James Anderson: apparently an actual James Anderson, whose gravestone
     in Ettrick kirkyard identifies him as 'tenant in Altrive', d. 1782, corres-
     ponding with the subsequent assertion that it is 'two and forty years since
     he died' (p. 181); the stone gives his age as 70, however, rather than
     'upwards of fourscore'. In this part of the novel Hogg uses local names,
     some of which have been traced to real people: see Garside's essay, 'Hogg,
     Eltrive, and *Confessions*'.

180 *Hart Loup . . . Eldinhope hay-ricks*: Hart Leap, a pass between the valleys
     of Ettrick and Yarrow; Eldinhope, a farm bordering Altrive to the east.

181 *Duke of Buccleuch's . . . Lord Napier's*: the three great landowners in the
     region at the time.
     William Shiel and W. Sword: local names. Douglas Mack cites late nine-
     teenth-century anecdotal evidence that a William Shiel was one of two
     shepherds who first opened the grave: 'The Suicide's Grave in *The
     Confessions of a Justified Sinner*', 10.

182 *more attractive metal*: compare *Hamlet*, III. ii. 114 (referring to Ophelia).
     Presumably the Editor means Sir Walter Scott, resident at Abbotsford,
     20 miles (30 km) north-east of Altrive.
     Mr. L——t of C——d: John Gibson Lockhart of Chiefswood
     (1794–1854), prominent Scottish man of letters, friend of Hogg, and
     son-in-law of Scott. A graduate of the universities of Glasgow and
     Oxford, Lockhart divided his residence in the early 1820s between
     Edinburgh and (in the summer months) Chiefswood, a cottage on the
     Abbotsford estate.

183 *as ingenious lies . . . ere now*: Lockhart himself, as one of the magazine's
     chief contributors, was responsible for many of the hoaxes, lampoons,
     and libels which made *Blackwood's* scandalous in its early years. 'Ingenious
     lies' involving Hogg ranged from the 'Manuscript translated from the
     Chaldee', a satire of the Edinburgh literary scene co-written in a pastiche
     biblical style by Hogg, Lockhart, and John Wilson (October 1817), to
     Hogg's appearances as 'the Ettrick Shepherd' in the comic symposium
     series 'Noctes Ambrosianae', composed by Wilson, Lockhart, and others
     (from 1822). See Introduction.
     classical country: because associated with the poetry of Scott, especially
     Minstrelsy of the Scottish Border (1802–3) and *The Lay of the Last Minstrel*
     (1805).
     Mr. L——w: William Laidlaw (1780–1845), Scott's estate manager and
     amanuensis, an old friend of Hogg's and a relation of his on the maternal
     side. Laidlaw introduced Scott to Hogg in 1802.

sheep fair at Thirlestane: September fair for the sale of ewes at the foot of Thirlestane Hill, near Ettrick; about 2 miles (3 km) south of Fall Law and Cowan's Croft, as the crow flies.

a romantic village: Ettrickbridge, about 7 miles (11.5 km) south-west of Selkirk along Ettrick Water.

184 *W——m B——e*: most likely William Beattie, a local name. Ettrick kirkyard has the grave of a William Beattie who died in 1827, aged 65 (Garside). Carey and Garside point out that shepherds named William Beattie feature in Hogg's tales 'A Shepherd's Wedding' (*Contributions to Blackwood's*, 22) and 'Renowned Adventures of Basil Lee' (*Winter Evening Tales*, ed. Ian Duncan (Edinburgh, 2002), 9).

Mr. S——t: Scott, another common local name; almost certainly not Sir Walter Scott, although his shadow falls across this closing episode. Garside suggests a 'sly' reference to Hogg's friend and neighbour Lord Napier, proprietor of Thirlestane, whose family name was Scott.

Faw-Law: Fall Law, 1,828 feet (558 m), 0.5 mile (0.8 km) north-north-west of Cowan's Croft.

customary in the south of Scotland: tradition forbade the burial of suicides in consecrated ground. The ancient practice of burial at a crossroads was legally abolished in England in 1823, according to Garside, who cites the case of a suicide buried 'at the junction of three lairds' lands' near Hawick, *c*.1790. A woman suspected of drowning herself is buried on a 'height . . . in the march, or boundary, between the lands of two different proprietors' in Hogg's tale 'The Wife of Lochmaben' (*Winter Evening Tales*, 427). Law as well as custom prescribed the burial of suicides at night.

185 *Robert Laidlaw*: no particular individual has been identified. Laidlaw was Hogg's mother's family name.

grey stone: 'A 2 ft. × 1 ft. slab, rather like a gravestone, still stands on top of a cairn on Fall Law', according to Carey in 1969. Garside reports a 1999 excursion that confirmed the presence of the cairn, consisting of 'a pile of small stones', but no gravestone-like slab: 'Hogg, Eltrive and Confessions', 17.

above the vent of the ear: phrenology, the science of determining character by the conformation of the skull, was fashionable and controversial in the early nineteenth century, especially in Edinburgh, where George Combe founded the Phrenological Society in 1820. The *Blackwood's* authors, including Hogg and Lockhart, ridiculed phrenology but also used it for satirical purposes. Its German pioneers, Franz Josef Gall and Johann Spurzheim, diagnosed this particular cranial protuberance as the sign of an 'organ of destructiveness', the seat of a 'carnivorous instinct': 'the sphere of activity of this faculty extends from mere indifference to the pain which another man, or a brute, may suffer, to the pleasure of seeing them killed, or even to the most irresistible desire to kill': Sir George

Steuart Mackenzie, *Illustrations of Phrenology* (Edinburgh, 1820), 108 (cited in Starr, 'The Bump Above Robert Wringhim's Ear').

187 *Mr. R——n of W—n. L—e*: Carey suggests [James] Anderson of Wilton Lodge, near Hawick (about 18 miles (30 km) east of the burial site), with a conjecture that the compositor misread Hogg's 'A' for 'R'.

188 *FIDELI CERTA MERCES*: the reward is assured for the faithful.

bound in with the volume: the facsimile (which is not in Hogg's hand) is reproduced in the current edition.

GLOSSARY

Compiled by Graham Tulloch, with additions by Ian Duncan

THIS glossary predominantly consists of Scots words and phrases used in the novel; it also includes obsolete or unusual English words or usages. Items in the long list of Scots legal terms in the charter on p. 135 are glossed in an explanatory note. Sources consulted include the *Scottish National Dictionary*, *Concise Scots Dictionary*, and *Oxford English Dictionary*, and, occasionally, *Jamieson's Etymological Dictionary of the Scottish Language*.

a' all
ado to do
ae one
aff off
afore before, in front of
aften often
ain own
aince once
aith oath
amang among
amuses, plural of **awmous** alms-giving
an if
an' and
ane one
aneath beneath
anent concerning
anither another
art and part accessory or accomplice to (Scots law)
atween between
auld old
auld ane, the the Devil
aw all
aw I
awthegither altogether
aye continually, always
ayont beyond, beside

back friend supporter
back green grassy ground at the back of the house

bagnio brothel
baillie town councillor
bairn child
baith both
bane bone
bannet flat cap worn by males
beadle minor church official who attends on the minister and serves as sexton and bell-ringer
bedstrae bedstraw
behoof behalf
belang belong
bicker wooden drinking vessel
bigging building
binna is not
bit small
blue bonnet see **bannet**
boardly burly
bodle two pence Scots, one sixth of an English penny
body person
bogle fearsome ghost, bugbear
bonnet see **bannet**
bourock cottage
bouzy fat
bowkail cabbage
brae hillside
braird first sprouts of grain
braw splendid
break break into (a house)
brikk break
brunstane brimstone

bum buzz, drone
burd offspring
burgh, royal borough with charter direct from the crown
burn stream

ca' call
caddy errand boy
callant young man
calm qualm, feeling of sickness
canna cannot
canny bringing good luck; with negative: not unnatural or supernatural (see **uncanny**)
canonical terms scriptural terms
carl man, fellow
cast n. chance, opportunity; toss (of the head)
cast v. dig out, cut (peats)
cast of grace religious conversion
cast up turn up, appear
cauler fresh, newly caught
cause, the hour of the appointed time for a trial
chafts cheeks
chiel man
circumfauld surround
clachan small village
claes clothes
claithing clothing
clapperclaw possibly 'to strike a blow as a spider at a fly' (Jamieson)
claymore large Highland sword
cloot hoof
close narrow alleyway, especially one leading to the entrance to a **land**
cock raise
collegian university student
commissioner see **lord-commissioner**
contrair contrary
corant a dance
corbie raven
corby-craw raven
crap crept
craw crow

creeshy fat
croon bellow, roar
crouping croaking
cuif fool

daft crazy
dangler someone who hangs around a woman
day, the today
dee do
dee die
deil devil
deil a bit not a bit, absolutely not
depone testify
deray disturbance, damage
didna did not
dike low wall
ding beat
dinna do not
disna does not
ditit foolish
div do
divot turf, peat
doesnae does not
doit stumble
doitrified dazed
dominie schoolmaster
donnart stupid
doubt fear
dree suffer
dung struck

easter eastern
een eyes
ell about four-fifths of the English measure
entry an alley-way leading to an entrance
ern iron
evite avoid
extraordinar extraordinary

fa who
fand found
fat what
fawn fallen

feele fool
fer far
flannen flannel
flaring flattery
flinders shreds, fragments
flitters shreds
flummery flattery
fock folk
foot lower end (of a street, piece of
  ground)
foreby let alone
fore-door front door
frae from
fra-yont from the other side of
fraze palaver

gae go
gae gave
gaed went
gang go
gar make
gate way
gaun going
gayan very
ghaist ghost
gie give
gin if
gizened withered
glaring ostentatious
Glasco Glasgow
glen valley
gloaming twilight
goodman a term of address
goodwife mistress of a house
  or farm
gowk cuckoo, fool
grit great
grumphing grumbling
gude good; God
gudewife mistress of a house;
  wife (used as a term
  of address)
guerdon reward
guidit treated
gull fool, dupe

ha' house, home
hae have
haena have not
haill whole
hale whole
halesale wholesale
halfpenny, Scots equivalent to
  one-twelfth of the English coin
hame home
hand-fast make a contract by
  joining hands
havers gossip
head of the passage point
  where an alley enters the
  main street
heartless disheartened
heritor landed proprietor
het hot
hench haunk
hind farm-worker, ploughman
hoad-road state of chaos
Hollin lawn fine linen fabric
hope small valley in midst of hills
horse-laid horse-load
houk dig
hout na definitely no
howk poke one's nose in
howlet owl
hunder hundred

ideal imaginary
in-by, in by further in
Indians Indies
indictment written statement of
  a criminal charge
ir are
ither other

jaud worthless woman
juggs pillory

keek peep
ken know
ketch toss
keust cast
kimmer gossip

kirk church
kist chest

lady title formerly given to a laird's wife, as in *Lady Dalchastel*
laird landed proprietor, owner of an estate held directly from the crown; the laird's male heir is known as the *young laird* and the laird himself, if he has a male heir, is known as the *old laird*
land building, of several storeys or more, divided into flats
lang long
lave remainder
lay silence (a voice)
lead produce (proof, evidence)
learn teach
leasing-making telling lies
leear liar
like likely
linn ravine, gorge
lint-swingling flax-beating
loaden laden
loun fellow
lounder thrash
loup leap
luckpenny a sum returned to the buyer by the seller as a discount
lucky landlady of a tavern; also used before the surname of an older woman

ma my
mae more
mair more
maister master
mak make
mall a mallet used for striking the ball in the game pall-mall
march boundary
margin explanatory note
maugre in spite of
maun must
meeting-house place of worship
mell thrash

mense credit
merk mark, two-thirds of a pound, the Scots money being valued at one-twelfth of the English
mind remember
momently instantly
mony many
muckil large
muckle much
mysel myself

na no
nae no
ne'er, the the Devil
neist next
no not

o' of
od God (in oaths and exclamations)
o'er too
ony any
outfield poorer, outlying parts of a farm
overhie overtake
ower over; too

pack-laid pack-load
packman pedlar, travelling merchant
pat put
paulie undersized, sickly lamb
peats pieces of peat cut for burning
peeous pious
pennyworths of, tak take revenge on
pink finest example
pirn spool
pit put
plack small coin; not a plack, nothing at all
plea go to law
pose interrogate
postern gate side- or back-entrance
pouk preen
precognition preliminary investigation of a case
professor someone making public profession of religious faith

put down kill, put to death
put off pass (time)

rack stretch
raip rope
reard roar
rede advise
reid red
reist bring to a stop, prevent from
   moving
rigging of it, ride on the be totally
   preoccupied with it, make a parade
   of it
rin run
rip worthless fellow
rowth abundance
run foul of collide with, become
   entangled with

sae so
saluted kissed
sanna shall not
sauchless foolish
sauf save
saur smell
scouder scorch
scragged covered with stunted bushes
   or undergrowth
shakel wrist
shan make a wry face
sib related
sic such
siccan, sickan such
side an' wide long and large,
   extending in every direction
sidie for sidie side by side
siller silver
sin' since
skair illuminate
skimmer glide easily, skim
slack slacken
slump, by the taken all together
snork snort
speeder spider
spleuchan tobacco pouch
spoke wooden bar used in carrying a
   coffin

staff's end, at the at a distance, away
   from close quarters or familiarity
stair staircase
stamack stomach
stane stone
stint stop
stool, black seat in a church on which
   offenders sat while being publicly
   rebuked, a 'stool of repentance'
stott bullock
strathspey a Scottish dance
strick strict
strodge stride, strut
swee sway
swire level place near the top of a hill

tak take
tane one
tap top
tartans full Highland dress
tauld told
tawpie scatterbrained young woman
tent notice
thae those
thief, the auld the Devil
thief's hole cell in a prison; Hell
thrang throng
thretty thirty
throng busy
tither other
tolbooth town prison
toom empty
trams legs
trow believe
twa two
tweel twill

uncanny linked with dangerous
   supernatural powers
unco very
unco-like peculiar, extraordinary

vapouring boastful
vera very

wa' wall
wab web

wad would
wadna would not
war were
waratch wretch
wark work
warlock male witch
wasna was not
wauken waken
waur worse
wee little
weel well
weird fate
wha who
whaever whoever
whan when
whaten what sort of
whiles sometimes
wife woman
windlestrae dried stalk of grass; figuratively, a weapon

winna will not
woodriff woodruff
wool-stapler merchant who buys wool from the farmer and sells it to the manufacturer
wore moved cautiously
wrang wrong
writer solicitor, lawyer
Writer to the Signet solicitor with special functions and privileges
wynd narrow alley

yelloch shriek
yerk sudden throb of pain
ye's you shall
yestreen yesterday
yon that
yooll howl, bawl, wail
yowe ewe

The Oxford World's Classics Website

www.worldsclassics.co.uk

- Browse the full range of Oxford World's Classics online

- Sign up for our monthly e-alert to receive information on new titles

- Read extracts from the Introductions

- Listen to our editors and translators talk about the world's greatest literature with our Oxford World's Classics audio guides

- Join the conversation, follow us on Twitter at OWC_Oxford

- Teachers and lecturers can order inspection copies quickly and simply via our website

www.worldsclassics.co.uk

American Literature

British and Irish Literature

Children's Literature

Classics and Ancient Literature

Colonial Literature

Eastern Literature

European Literature

Gothic Literature

History

Medieval Literature

Oxford English Drama

Poetry

Philosophy

Politics

Religion

The Oxford Shakespeare

A complete list of Oxford World's Classics, including Authors in Context, Oxford English Drama, and the Oxford Shakespeare, is available in the UK from the Marketing Services Department, Oxford University Press, Great Clarendon Street, Oxford OX2 6DP, or visit the website at www.oup.com/uk/worldsclassics.

In the USA, visit www.oup.com/us/owc for a complete title list.

Oxford World's Classics are available from all good bookshops. In case of difficulty, customers in the UK should contact Oxford University Press Bookshop, 116 High Street, Oxford OX1 4BR.

Late Victorian Gothic Tales

JANE AUSTEN   Emma
                           Mansfield Park
                           Persuasion
                           Pride and Prejudice
                           Selected Letters
                           Sense and Sensibility

MRS BEETON   Book of Household Management

MARY ELIZABETH   Lady Audley's Secret
BRADDON

ANNE BRONTË   The Tenant of Wildfell Hall

CHARLOTTE BRONTË   Jane Eyre
                           Shirley
                           Villette

EMILY BRONTË   Wuthering Heights

ROBERT BROWNING   The Major Works

JOHN CLARE   The Major Works

SAMUEL TAYLOR   The Major Works
COLERIDGE

WILKIE COLLINS   The Moonstone
                           No Name
                           The Woman in White

CHARLES DARWIN   The Origin of Species

THOMAS DE QUINCEY   The Confessions of an English
                              Opium-Eater
                           On Murder

CHARLES DICKENS   The Adventures of Oliver Twist
                           Barnaby Rudge
                           Bleak House
                           David Copperfield
                           Great Expectations
                           Nicholas Nickleby
                           The Old Curiosity Shop
                           Our Mutual Friend
                           The Pickwick Papers